PRAISE FOR THE BOOKS OF
UNEXPECTED ENLIGHTENMENT

The action is non-stop, with child's play, schoolwork, and danger all churned together. Lamplighter introduces many imaginative elements in her world that will delight....
—*VOYA*

The British boarding school mystery meets the best imagined of fantasies at breakneck speed and with fully realized characters.
—Sarah A. Hoyt, author of *Darkship Thieves*

L. Jagi Lamplighter, a fantastic new voice and a fabulous new world in the YA market! Rachel Griffin is a hero who never gives up! I cheered her all the way!
—Faith Hunter, author of the *Skinwalker* series

The Unexpected Enlightenment of Rachel Griffin, a plucky band of children join forces to fight evil, despite the best efforts of incompetent adults, at a school for wizards. YA fiction really doesn't get better than that.
—Jonathan Moeller, author of *The Ghosts* series

Rachel Griffin is curious, eager and smart, and ready to begin her new life at Roanoke Academy for the Sorcerous Arts, but she didn't expect to be faced with a mystery as soon as she got there. Fortunately she's up to the task. Take all the best of the classic girl detective, throw in a good dose of magic and surround it all with entertaining, likeable friends and an intriguing conundrum, and you'll have *The Unexpected Enlightenment of Rachel Griffin*, a thrilling adventure tailor-made for the folks who've been missing Harry Potter. Exciting, fantastical events draw readers into Rachel's world and solid storytelling keeps them there.
—Misty Massey, author of *Mad Kestrel*

Other Books By

L. Jagi Lamplighter

The Books of Unexpected Enlightenment

The Unexpected Enlightenment of Rachel Griffin
The Raven, The Elf, and Rachel
Rachel and the Many-Splendored Dreamland
The Awful Truth about Forgetting
The Unbearable Heaviness of Remembering (*forthcoming*)
Guardians of the Twilight Lands (*forthcoming*)
… and more to come.

The Prospero's Children Trilogy

Prospero Lost
Prospero In Hell
Prospero Regained

A BOOK OF UNEXPECTED ENLIGHTENMENT

RACHEL
AND THE
MANY-SPLENDORED DREAMLAND

L. JAGI LAMPLIGHTER

BASED ON THE WORKS OF MARK A. WHIPPLE

ILLUSTRATIONS BY JOHN C. WRIGHT

Wisecraft Publishing
A publishing company of the Wise

Published by Wisecraft Publishing
A publishing company of the Wise

This is a work of fiction. All of the characters and events portrayed in this book
are fictional, and any resemblance to real people or events is purely coincidental
or an Act of God.

ISBN: 978-0-9976460-1-6 (print)
ASIN: B01ILF5Q18
First edition
Revision 2.0.1 2017-12-06

Edited by Jim Frenkel

Cover art by Dan Lawlis
https://danlawlis.wordpress.com

Interior illustrations by John C. Wright

Typeset by Joel C. Salomon

Cover design by Danielle McPhail
Sidhe na Daire Multimedia
http://sidhenadaire.com

Chapter headings are set in RM Ginger, © 2009 Ray Meadows, licensed under CC
BY-ND 3.0; see https://fontstruct.com/fontstructions/show/258661 for details.

CONTENTS

DEDICATION

To John C. Wright,
the best husband,
the best father,
the best writer,
and the best Sigfried Smith,
in the universe.

AUTHOR'S NOTE:

This volume follows the revised edition of the first two books.
There are some differences.
Most notably, Valerie Foxx is now Valerie Hunt.

ONCE THERE WAS A WORLD

THAT SEEMED AT FIRST GLANCE MUCH LIKE OTHER WORLDS

YOU *MAY HAVE LIVED IN* OR READ ABOUT,

BUT IT *WASN'T*. . . .

CHAPTER ONE:

FALLING OUT OF DREAMS

"OH!" RACHEL GRIFFIN TUMBLED OUT OF DREAMLAND AND LANDED on her derriere. "Ouch!"

With thumps and loud cries Joy, Valerie, and the princess rained down on the grass around her. Rachel could see her friends in the brilliant moonlight. Newly-fallen leaves crinkled as the girls moved, filling the air with their autumn scent.

The starry sky overhead was mirrored on the reflecting lake, a hundred yards to her left. Also shimmering on its surface were the spires and belfries of the castle-like Roanoke Hall. Along the water's edge, college students, in their long dark robes, kept watch. Presumably—though, from where she sat wincing, it was too far away for Rachel to see—the glass cases suspended above the lake's silvery bottom were filled with conjurations and alchemical talismans undergoing degossamerization under the light of the full moon. The rowboats that normally floated on the reflecting lake had been pulled up onto the grass; their painted eyes glinted brightly.

The blow to her backside did not sting as sharply as her disappointment. Rachel had been longing to visit the dreamlands again, ever since her first trip a month ago, during the second week of the school year. It was quite a let-down to be back in the world of the waking so soon. Today had been so disturbing. She had faced both a rogue jumbo jet that nearly crashed into Roanoke Hall and a demon bent on destroying the world. When she had finally returned to the safety and comfort of her dorm room, she had felt so very weary, but sleep had eluded her. Instead, she had lain awake, reliving in her perfect memory the most upsetting parts of her day.

When the opportunity presented itself for this nocturnal adventure, she had jumped at the chance. A trip into the land of dreams promised to be a distraction from reliving the day's terrors. With high hopes, she had set off with the others. Then, someone had disregarded Zoë's instructions to hold hands at all times, resulting in more than half of their party tumbling into the waking world again.

"Ooooff!" exclaimed Nastasia Romanov, the Princess of Magical Australia. In her proper, Magical Australian accent she softly murmured, "That was... disturbing."

"Ow! I landed on my camera! Ow!" Valerie Hunt's voice rang out. "Boy, that hurt! I hope I didn't break anything!"

"You mean like a rib?" Joy O'Keefe gasped breathlessly, as if the wind had been knocked out of her. "Ow! Oh!"

"No, ribs heal. I mean a lens," Valerie replied, followed by some rustling. "I think it's okay. My father gave me this camera only a week before he disapp...." Her voice wobbled only the tiniest bit. "I wouldn't want anything to happen to it."

"Glad it's okay," Rachel said softly, rubbing the part of her that ached the most.

"Princess, are you okay?" Joy crawled rapidly to Nastasia, who still lay supine, and hovered over her. "Is anything broken? Shall I fetch the nurse?"

"I am whole," the princess replied, embarrassed as always by Joy's ebullient fawning. "The only thing bruised is my dignity."

"Shhhh!" Rachel peered around in the darkness, searching for movement. "We should keep our voices down. The proctors'll hear us and send us back to bed." She bit her lip against a wave of pain. Her eyes watered. "Oh. My tailbone smarts!"

Valerie rose to her feet, still fiddling with her camera. "You're so British, Rachel. And I don't just mean your accent! Who says 'tailbone'? Why don't you just say...."

Lamps lit up along the west side of the Commons.

The motion of Valerie coming to her feet had caused the will-o-wisps to swarm out of their nighthoods and flit around inside the glass globe of the tall lamps. The soft wisp-light illuminated a hooded figure who had previously been hidden by the darkness.

A frisson of terror shot through Rachel. Was this another Veltdammerung follower come to abduct her and her friends again?

She whistled sharply.

Magical energy rushed through her body, tickling her lips as tiny blue sparks left her mouth. Accompanied by the scent of evergreens, the sparkles flew through the air to swirl around the hooded figure. The figure stopped moving, paralyzed.

"Who's that?" cried Joy, frightened.

"Possibly one of the cultists who kidnapped us earlier today," exclaimed the princess. "They wore hoods."

Valerie raised her camera and snapped a picture. In the brighter light of the flash, Rachel found an instant match in her memory for the feminine nose and mouth visible beneath the hood. The last time she had seen this particular hooded figure, there had been a little paper soda jerk's cap perched atop her head. The paper hat was not currently in evidence.

Also, this hooded figure carried an oboe.

"*Obé!*" Chagrined at having frozen a fellow student, Rachel performed the Word of Ending cantrip by extending her index finger upward and moving it horizontally. "Ever so sorry, Miss Black! I mistook you for an evil Mortimer Egg follower."

The young woman in the hood rolled her shoulders, as if to confirm that she was no longer paralyzed.

"Understandable, Griffin. You had a hard day." Xandra Black's normally dry sardonic tone had a touch of compassion. "Being kidnapped, nearly sacrificed, and all that."

"You are one who warned me about touching Joshua March, are you not?" Nastasia stood up, brushing off the long black academic robes she wore over her pajamas, the legs of which stuck out at the very bottom. Her long flowing curls glinted golden in the wisp-light. Even having tumbled from dreamland, Rachel's friend appeared as incomparably lovely as a magical princess should. "The one who works in the Storm King Café?"

"That's me.   Flops-Over-Dead-Chick." Xandra Black nodded with wry moroseness. "Or perhaps, Constantly-Possessed-By-Annoying-Voices-Chick would be appropriate. Take your pick." She paused. "Or you could be truly non-conventional and call me by my actual name."

"What are you doing standing here... in the darkness... in the middle of the night?" Rachel asked, curiosity bubbling out of her.

Xandra gave an apologetic shrug. "Waiting for you."

Before Rachel could express surprise, Xandra's head snapped backward. Her lips opened, and a new, deeper voice came from her mouth. This new voice did not need to move Xandra's jaw to speak. *"In one minute and twenty seconds, the proctors will arrive. In thirty-two seconds, Zoë Forrest will reappear in the center of the commons. Run."*

Rachel ran. Valerie and Joy followed.

The princess called after them stiffly, "Why should we be afraid of the proctors?"

"It's the middle of the night," Rachel replied over her shoulder, holding up the skirts of her black academic robes as she sprinted, "and we're not in bed!"

Behind her, she could hear the other girls, feet pelting and breath panting—except for the princess, who glided calmly. To their left, two dark-clad proctors left the doorway of Roanoke Hall to head their way: a slight figure with light-colored hair and a very tall figure wearing a cowboy hat. Neither one was her friend, Mr. Fuentes, who might possibly have turned a blind eye to their midnight activities.

Rachel ran faster—not that it helped. She pumped her legs as quickly as she could, her breath coming in short spurts, but Joy, Valerie, and Xandra all dashed past her. She was just too small to keep up with the longer legs of her friends.

A puff of mist appeared in the center of the commons. Zoë Forrest stepped out of it, holding the hand of Sigfried Smith. Wrapped around the orphan boy was the long, furry, serpentine length of his familiar and best friend, Lucky the Dragon.

"What part of 'you must hold on' did I not make clear?" Regarding the other girls with a mixture of annoyance and amusement, Zoë spoke in a voice that held faint traces of a New Zealand accent. She twirled her right forelock, which was long and braided, A dappled feather had been stuck into it. The rest of her hair was cut pixie-short. Tonight, her locks were pale pink and the feather was magenta with maroon spots.

Unlike the other girls, Zoë wore her street clothes, blue jeans and a sweater. On her feet were a pair of marvelous silver sandals. These allowed her to move in and out of the realm of dreams. They had been made for her by a relative who was a Maori shaman.

"In our defense," Nastasia spoke graciously, as she joined them, "I do not believe any of us intended to let go. I tried to maneuver to lead us down the Way. But, as I was in the middle of the group, this proved impossible."

"That was wicked awesome!" Sigfried shouted, his voice carrying through the night. He was tall and brawny for a fourteen-year-old, with short curly golden hair and handsome boyish features. He spoke with a British accent, gesturing expansively. "We walked in dreams! Did you see that, Lucky? Did you see that, cute girl members of the Dreadfully Violent Adventuring Club? We're pioneers! Like astronauts going into space, only dreamier. We're dream astronauts. What's the Greek word for dream? *Oneiros,* or something, right? We're *oneironauts!*" He jumped up and flashed his girlfriend a brilliant smile. "I hope you took lots of pictures, Goldilocks! We want to record this for posterity!"

"Oh, I've been taking pictures!" Valerie Hunt, Fearless Reporter Girl, held up her camera and flashed another picture. Rachel could not see her clearly, but she knew that the other girl had short flaxen hair, a squarish jawline, and an intelligent sparkle in her eyes. She had been in bed when Zoë brought the others out of dreamland into Dee Hall to pick her up, so she was still dressed in her bright yellow Hello Kitty pajamas. "But whether the photos will come out? That's a different question."

"Freaky, spooky-strange place!" Lucky the Dragon spoke in his gravelly dragon voice, as he unwrapped himself and flew upward. His long sinuous body stretched between ten and twenty feet, depending on his mood. Rachel could not see the colors in the darkness but knew that the fur covering his body and his four legs was golden, and his long whiskers, his back ridges, and the puff at the tip of his tail were a fiery red. His short curling horns were of a tawny ivory. "Let's go back! I want to eat that dream chicken!"

"I... don't think you should eat up there," Joy O'Keefe said nervously, brushing her mousy brown hair from her heart-shaped face.

A bulky, hand-knitted sweater covered the top of her baby blue pajamas. As a seventh daughter, Joy's clothes consisted mainly of hand-me-downs. The sweater had been carefully darned in several places. "It might be like eating conjured food. The cramps, after it vanishes from your body twenty-four hours later, are terrible. Not that I would know, of course. But if you ever have a parcel of older sisters, and they dare you to eat the conjured sugar cubes and cupcakes at a children's tea party, say 'No!'"

Rachel glanced around. The tall figures of the proctors were halfway across the commons, moving purposefully in their direction. The shorter one broke into a jog. Her heart rate doubled. She so wanted something nice to happen to balance her horrid day. Getting caught for breaking curfew was not what she had in mind.

"Quick, the proctors are coming!" she spoke rapidly. "If we all hold hands, with Zoë on one side and the princess on the other, Zoë can lead us in. Then we can turn and follow the princess—without the huge rumpus caused by having the princess in the middle."

"But I need a hand free," objected Valerie, "or I can't use my camera."

"That is what caused the trouble last time," said the princess.

"Maybe the people beside her can hold Valerie's elbow," offered Rachel, "Or Lucky could wrap around her and then hold onto two other people."

Zoë shrugged. "That might work, Griffin. Let's try it."

• • •

The group grasped hands and ran, ignoring the proctors' shouts. Mist rose around them, obscuring the campus and the running adults behind them. Rachel moved through the thick pearl-gray fog, unable to see anything except her friends. She held onto the princess with one hand and Xandra with the other. Xandra held Joy's hand, who held Siggy's. Lucky's head and front claws rested on Sigfried's shoulders. His long, sinewy body wrapped once around Sigfried and twice around Valerie, and the claws of his back feet held firmly to Zoë's waist. His slender tail with its red-tasseled tip waved about freely.

Rachel breathed in the now-familiar dream-scent of lilacs and plaster-of-Paris. She gazed about alertly. Something about adventure, about learning new things, made her feel alive. She loved seeing previously unseen sights. It was as if her mind needed to drink in new knowledge for her mental gears to fully engage. She looked around eagerly, making certain that her eyes passed over everything. If she failed to notice something now, it would be preserved in her memory so that she could examine it later. Of course, surrounded by thick mist as they were, there was not much to see.

"Where... are we?" Xandra's jaw, the only part of her visible beneath her hood, gaped. Beneath her school robes, she wore a navy blue nightgown and pink bunny slippers. Rachel had no idea what had become of her oboe. "Where did the school go? What is all this mist? I've been swallowed by a mist whale, haven't I? Tell me the truth. I can bear it!"

"We're in dreamland," Zoë replied casually, as if people stepped into dreams every day, "where people go at night when they sleep."

"That's a... place?" The normally unflappable Xandra's voice squeaked in astonishment.

The mist parted around them, and Joy screamed.

Ahead of them, two bodies dangled in the air. Each hung from a hangman's noose. Black cloth bags covered their heads. From the neck down, they wore black trousers, black vests, and fresh clean white shirts with enormous sleeves pleated like the bellows of an accordion. These traditional Hungarian garments might have been humorous had their surroundings not been so grisly.

Their feet swung back and forth, the rope creaking. Somewhere, crows cawed.

At least, Rachel thought it was crows.

"That's just... a dream, right?" gasped Joy, her face pale. Rachel swallowed and grasped the princess's hand more tightly. Nastasia gave her fingers a reassuring squeeze.

"Someone's been watching too many horror flicks," Zoë smirked. "Don't get your panties in a bunch, girls."

"I'm not a girl," objected Siggy.

Joy elbowed him, giggling.

"Do you wear panties?" asked Zoë. "Hmm? I thought not. The point is: here in dreams, we see weird and horrible stuff all the time. Get used to it."

"Like naked people." Rachel shuddered, recalling her first visit to dreamland.

She tried not to stare at the dangling bodies, but there was something hypnotizing about their motion, as they swung back and forth from their scaffolding. Was some poor student at the school really dreaming about this? She felt sorry for whomever was having this nightmare. With a second shudder, she wondered if she, too, would now dream about this.

Turning away from the execution dream, she looked around. Long curtains of mist, much taller than the students, undulated around them. Each curve held a different living diorama, which Rachel knew, from her previous excursion to dreamland, was the dream of a single individual. Behind them, in a different curve of the mist curtain, a boy ran endlessly uphill. Around the next bend, Rachel glimpsed a red-headed girl and her father building a go-cart.

Valerie lifted her camera. The blinding flash lit the gallows and its unlucky burden.

The scene of the hanging in the town square changed to a rocky peak in bright sunlight. Mountain goats leapt from rock to rock. Across the way, the boy now ran uphill under a glaring sun. The girl's father held a camera. He took pictures of the go-cart using a bright flash.

"Look, Goldilocks," Siggy grinned enthusiastically at his girl-friend, "you changed people's dreams."

"So, I did," mused Valerie, her reporter-girl instincts intrigued.

"If you can get everyone to dream about going to Mars, the space program will become popular again," crowed Siggy. "Then, all we need is to turn invisible and sneak aboard the Mars ship. If we turn the crewmen into ferrets, it will compensate for the change in mass."

Lucky said hopefully, "Could we turn the astronauts into chickens? That would be tastier!"

"Okay, enough of this." Zoë glared at Lucky. "Now it's your turn, Princess. Lead on, Fearless Leader! We follow."

"Very well." Nastasia cleared her throat. "We shall now depart for Magical Australia."

"We're going to *Magical Australia*?" The words burst from Rachel in an explosion of pure joy.

"Ace!" shouted Siggy, punching the air with his free hand. Lucky's head bounced up and down on his shoulder, but the length of his body was wrapped around Sigfried, so he did not let go. His great jade eyes glinted with eagerness, too.

"We're... going to Magical Australia *tonight*? We're leaving school grounds?" murmured Xandra. "Oh. Just great."

Rachel gave Xandra's hand an encouraging squeeze. The older girl had not signed up for this, the way the rest of them had. She had been sent by her Voices. Xandra gave a very quick squeeze back. The upperclassman towered above Rachel, which was not difficult, as Rachel was particularly short. She shared her diminutive size with her part-Korean mother. She had also inherited her mother's Asian eyes and her power of perfect recall.

Unfortunately, she had not inherited her mother's beautiful, thick locks. Strands of Rachel's fine, black hair had escaped her hair clip and now tickled her face. Unable to use her hands to brush it away, she had to settle for twitching her nose and blowing.

"Zoë and I went two days ago," Nastasia continued. "We visited a dream version of the castle where I live when I am not at school. Zoë says she could take us down into the real castle—the waking world version—but it might be hard to explain to my parents how we came to be there." She paused. "Hard to explain to Mother. Father... would, no doubt, understand. Though by the time he was done, the explanation would invariably include wombats and emu." The princess sighed.

The others laughed, but a sharp pain stabbed through Rachel.

Nastasia and Zoë had gone to Magical Australia *without her*? They had experimented with Nastasia's secret gift *without her*? Zoë was supposed to be *her* friend. Rachel was the one who had insisted on including her in their group, and the princess was Rachel's best friend.

How could they have gone *without her*?

"We were at a castle earlier today," Sigfried volunteered. "An evil creature called a D-bone tried to sacrifice us to destroy the world. Glad we avoided that. It would have been messy, not to mention inconvenient. If the world were destroyed, where would Lucky and I keep all our gold? Not to mention that being sacrificed might have ruined our entire day! Fortunately, we were saved by some bloke named Finn. Probably a big fish or a shark or something."

Rachel's body tensed, but she managed not to blurt out: *No, you were saved by me!*

"That was *demon*, not *debone*," stated the princess. "Our rescuer was our math tutor's husband, Finn MacDannan."

"Finn MacDannan? You mean the rock star, Red Ryder?" Zoë sounded truly impressed for the first time since Rachel had met the laid-back girl.

Xandra mused, "He's thought to be the best enchanter alive today."

"He was amazing," Rachel admitted.

The MacDannans were family friends, and it was right to give credit where credit was due. Still, she could not help adding sadly to herself: *even if he wasn't the one who saved the world. I did that, and my uncle, Myrddin the Ghost Boy.*

Suddenly, her lips curved upward. She always felt uncomfortable when she ended up in the limelight or people made too much of her. She should be grateful no one knew of her part in the previous evening's activities.

"What castle was that," Valerie asked, snapping another picture. "The one where the demon nearly sacrificed you?" She sounded as if she did not quite believe Sigfried.

"Beaumont," said Rachel. "It's in Transylvania."

"Oooh, scary," laughed Joy.

The dreamscape changed. A huge gray castle draped in ivy rose above them.

"That's Beaumont!" Rachel craned her head to look up at the vast basalt walls.

A violent longing seized her.

All her life, she had wanted to visit this castle. Her hero, librarian-adventurer Darius Northwest had disappeared there in 1868, presumably slain by some monster he had been investigating. It was so frustrating to have been so close and not have had the opportunity to go inside. She wanted to explore it now but wisely restrained the impulse to pull her friends headlong toward the vast edifice.

If any clues to Northwest's final fate remained, they would not be in this dream Beaumont.

Siggy gawked up at the towering basalt walls. "Where'd this castle come from?"

Zoë peered downward, one hand resting on Lucky's sinuous tail where it slipped under her arm and around her waist. "Harder for me to look out of dreams than to look in. Still. Pretty sure we're in the dream of a Starkadder prince."

"Those are the princes of Magical Bavaria, right?" asked Sigfried.

Joy elbowed the handsome boy again, blushing and loudly giggling. "No, silly, that's Vladimir Von Dread. And besides, it's just Bavaria. Not Magical Bavaria. The Unwary know about it, too."

"Stop jabbing me, Joy," scowled Sigfried.

Joy wilted like a plucked flower. Rachel's heart went out to her. She knew from books that girls who fancied boys they were not dating often poked and hit them. Joy had a huge crush on Sigfried, but her love was unrequited. He was completely devoted to Valerie.

"Okay, people!" Zoë addressed the group. "This trip off into the wop-wops requires us to walk along some kooky rail that the princess creates. It's not very wide. But so far, we haven't fallen off."

A silvery beam like liquid moonlight, about as wide as a train rail, appeared before Nastasia. She stepped gingerly forward onto the narrow moonlight track.

"Wow!" Rachel breathed. She leaned toward the princess and whispered very softly, "Is *this* what our Elf taught you?" Nastasia nodded and squeezed her hand.

Rachel took a step forward. The silver track gave slightly beneath her foot. Her excitement swelled. Pushing aside the faint ache left by the knowledge that Nastasia had done this two days ago without her—nothing should interfere with the joy of the coming adventure—she stepped forward.

Sternly, she also tamped down her tremendous desire to possess this traveling talent of the princess's. It was not seemly to envy a friend's gift.

They were going to travel!

Rachel Griffin wanted to travel more than she could say—literally, for words could not express the depth of her wanderlust nor the breadth of her longing to see faraway places. Perhaps it was because she had spent so much of her life at so few places: Gryphon Park and its attached town of Gryphon-on-Dart, Hot Springs Beach at Thulehavn, occasionally London, and now here in New York State at Roanoke Academy. Perhaps it was because she had spent so many hours curled up in the library at the top of Grandfather's tower, reading fanciful tales; perhaps because she had spent so much time immersed in Daring Northwest's works of discovery and adventure.

She wanted to stand upon high peaks and catch glimpses of distant sapphire seas. She wanted to drink from "yet untasted wells." She wanted to meet fairy creatures that she had read about in books. She wanted to kick sand on the beaches of Neverland, to pick a ripe volume from the book trees of Oz, to drink the Mad Hatter's tea in Wonderland.

At the very least, she wanted to feel the hot desert winds of Magical Australia!

Rachel Griffin wanted to know *everything.*

But everything was a big subject, and even she had to occasionally admit that some things were more interesting than others. What she wanted, most of all, was to know *secrets*, things *unseen by eyes other than hers.*

Besides, a little voice whispered very quietly in the back of her mind, *if she did not discover more, if she did not learn about the greater world and the threats it represented, how could she protect her loved ones from coming dangers?*

Behind her, the others had stepped onto the silvery beam. Rachel gave the impressive edifice of Dream Beaumont one last wistful glance. As she turned her head, she caught a glimpse of the same wanderlust that burned within her reflected in the face of Sigfried Smith.

Their gazes met, and they grinned at each other.

"The Starkadders are the princes of Transylvania," she kindly answered Sigfried's previous question. "One of them must have heard us say the name of the castle, the way the dreamers saw Valerie's flash."

"Transylvania, Bavaria," Sigfried shrugged, "what's the difference? They're both made-up places, right?"

"No, you goofball! They're real!" Joy snickered, poking him again with her elbow.

"Don't do that!" Sigfried jerked away from Joy.

He jerked too hard.

Siggy and Joy lost their balance and tumbled off the silvery Way, dragging the others after them. Rachel fell knees-first onto the soft cloudy stuff of dreamland. Despite the wrenching to her shoulders, she managed to keep hold on the princess and Xandra.

Joy was not so lucky. Her hand slipped out of Sigfried's.

"Oops!" Joy cried, grabbing for Siggy again, but it was too late.

CHAPTER TWO:

TRAPPED IN TRANSYLVANIA

WITH A SHOUT, RACHEL, JOY, XANDRA, AND THE PRINCESS PLUM-meted out of dreamland. Determined not to bruise her already-tender tailbone, Rachel tucked her body and flipped. As she came out of the flip, spreading her arms and pointing her toes, she gave thanks for all the vaulting classes she had taken as a child. Years of learning to land lightly on the back of her pony had finally paid off.

Or would have if. . . .

Bang!

Just as she was about to execute a perfect gymnast's landing, Xandra and Joy knocked into her. Rachel spun wildly, arms wind-milling. She tried to right herself, but it was too late. She struck the ground cheek-first and slid.

Ouch.

Upside down, her rear in the air, her weight pressing her face into the sharp gravel, Rachel noted ironically that she had been granted her wish: she had not landed on her tailbone.

The other three rushed over, crowding around her.

"Rachel! Are you all right?" Joy had a long scratch down her arm and was holding her bleeding elbow. However, she lost her struggle to keep a straight face. Amidst peels of helpless laughter, she burst out, "You just hit the ground. . . with your face!"

Rachel ducked her head. The heat of embarrassment did not help her bleeding cheek. It ached. Her lip hurt, too. She tasted blood. When she breathed in, the chill of the air stung her lungs.

Somewhere inside her, a whimper began. That and the sympa-thetic yet amused faces of her friends threatened to undo her. The horrific events of the last twelve hours—discovering the truth about the horrific murder of her grandfather's first family; facing death to save the school from the rogue jumbo jet; seeing her friends get kidnapped; being asked to kill her family so a demon could destroy the world—pressed upon her. Unshed tears stung her eyes. Her ripped lip quivered dangerously.

She would not cry.

A young woman of quality does not cry in the presence of others. Her august Victorian grandmother's voice echoed in her memory. Gritting her teeth, Rachel called upon the dissembling techniques she had learned from her mother to hide her expression. Her face became as calm as a mask.

A jumble of pain and fear remained inside.

She felt lost.

Xandra pulled her oboe from a small bag at her hip. Obviously, it was a kenomanced bag, with extra room added, because there was no other way that the long black and silver instrument could have fit in such a tiny space. Lifting the instrument, Xandra played a lilting tune.

The music swelled. Tiny green sparkles swirled from the mouth of the instrument and danced over Rachel's face and Joy's arm. A delicious scent of fresh baked muffins wafted from the green glints of healing magic. The pain in her face eased, and her cheek stopped smarting. The flesh of her torn lip re-knit. Soon, the ache had become a tingle.

She sighed with delight and rubbed her face, finding no wound.

"Wait," Joy's voice squeaked. "Where are we?"

They stood in the middle of a gravel walk lined by stately elms. Something about the walkway struck her as familiar. Her brows drew together. Wasn't it the middle of the night? How could she see so clearly?

She spun around.

Behind her loomed a familiar gray castle. Much of its vast bulk was obscured behind dark green ivy that covered the flat walls and the six, rounded towers that served in lieu of corners. The only opening in this imposing structure was the gatehouse, the arched doorway of which stood open with no sign of a portcullis. Carvings on its rounded walls showed vultures defiling corpses and serpents swallowing children. These had been gouged into the wall recently, over the top of older, more pleasant bas-reliefs.

"Beaumont!" Rachel cried yet again. "We're at Beaumont!"

"Just my luck," Xandra mused resignedly as she lowered her instrument. "My first sojourn into dreamland, and I fall out next to a castle where people feed children to snakes. Are there vampires? This is Transylvania, right? With my luck, there'll be vampires… or maybe werewolves? Aren't the Starkadder princes actually werewolves?"

Zoë stepped out of a puff of mist, her free hand on her hip. Lucky's golden tail was wrapped around her waist, its red tip fluttering. The rest of him trailed off into the mist.

"Did you fall out again, you goofy kids? What am I to do with you?" She halted, blinking in the daylight and chafing her arms at the cold. "Um, Toto, I don't think we're in Kansas anymore."

"Beaumont," Rachel repeated with a laugh, rubbing her freshly-healed cheek, which tingled slightly. "We're in Transylvania. It's seven hours ahead of New York. It's daytime here."

Valerie and Siggy stepped out of the mist behind her, bringing the rest of Lucky with them. Their feet crunched on the gravel. The three newcomers examined the landscape, taking in the bulk of the castle, the mountains rising to the left, and, through the trees, the steep cliff falling away to the right, beyond which could be heard the *burble* of rushing water.

Zoë's expression became rather odd. She peered right and left, as if scouring the countryside. Her voice dropped. "Uh-oh. That's not good."

"What's wrong?" asked Valerie.

"There's no one dreaming here," replied Zoë flatly.

"Which means?" asked Xandra.

"That we're stuck till someone in the surrounding countryside goes to sleep." Zoë eyed the sun shining brightly overhead, "This might take a while."

• • •

The group moved briskly down the gravel path toward the castle, eager for some protection from the chilly wind coming off the mountain.

"What if one of us went to sleep?" the princess asked. "Would that be sufficient for you to regain the dreamlands?"

"The rest of us could leave," Zoë responded. "The sleeper would have to stay behind."

"Let's not leave anyone behind," Xandra murmured with glum resignation. "I already have a number of strikes against me. I can just imagine how *heedlessly abandoned underclassmen in Transylvania* would look on my record."

The elm-lined path led to the gatehouse, but the tall walls offered no protection from the wind, which blew alongside them. Sigfried and Lucky ran forward to examine the carvings. The girls, other than Rachel, huddled together, anxiously speculating about how long it might take for those back at Roanoke to notice they were missing—since there were no classes on Saturday morning. Rachel paid no attention.

Excitement bubbled up in her, pushing aside the fatigue that accompanied magical healing. The walls of the castle she had loathed and yet longed to see for so long drew her like a siren's call. Tumbling out here was like her birthday and Yule and the first day of school, all rolled up into one.

Nothing could stop them from exploring!

"Is this the same castle where we were earlier? The one that Egg was using as his secret base?" Siggy shouted over his shoulder. "Let's go inside! Maybe there are clues! Stuff to steal!"

"Certainly not," the princess called, alarmed. "This is private property."

"Private property owned by evil!" Sigfried volleyed back. "That rotter who blasted you with phantom fire owns this castle." He turned to Rachel. "Am I right? The guy I beaned with the apple core?"

Rachel nodded, gripped by a cold hatred for the despicable young man who hurt her friend. "Remus Starkadder made this castle available to Egg and his evil cohorts. In return, Egg promised to kill Remus's oldest brother, Romulus, Crown Prince of Transylvania."

"Did he?" Zoë raised one pink eyebrow. "How did you guys find this out?"

"Egg… who?" asked Xandra. "Scrambled egg? Or boiled egg?"

"He was boiled when Lucky was done with him!" quipped Siggy, ignoring Zoë's question. He and the dragon exchanged a high-five.

"Mortimer Egg," explained Rachel, "a Wisecraft employee who was possessed by a demon named Azrael. He led a coven of evil sorcerers, including Dr. Mordeau."

"You mean this Egg character was in league with our evil math tutor? The one who turned into a dragon and tried to kill us?" asked Xandra. "I had her freshman year. She gave me a D on a paper, because I turned it in late—due to having been shanghaied by spirits, so that I could give a message to the mother of a kid who died in a boating accident. An Unwary kid, to make it worse. The mother thought I was crazy—Anyway, Mordeau's the only tutor I've had who's refused to accept my 'shanghaied by spirits' excuse. I worked hard on that paper, too!"

"A paper? In math class?" Valerie Hunt lowered her camera. "The very concept is disturbing."

"We're going to have to write papers?" Sigfried looked so horrified that it was comical. "I thought this was a civilized school. Don't tell me we're actually going to have to… work?"

"Yes, the same tutor." Rachel nodded to Xandra, answering her original question. "Their coven performs a terrible spell, where they sacrificed people's entire families in front of one member, whom they keep alive."

Xandra made a low sound in her throat. Her normally-olive chin looked unusually pale. "That was real? Egg was with Veltdammerung, wasn't he? I… had hoped that was just another stupid vision. Boo. Sometimes I hate being a seer."

"Happened to Misty Lark," muttered Zoë. "Her family murdered before her eyes."

The others were silent, not certain what to say.

Valerie moved forward and snapped several pictures of the basalt and limestone edifice. A slight breeze and the click of her camera were the only sounds.

"Is it really called Beaumont?" Valerie asked, as she paused to advance her film. "Hardly sounds like a Hungarian word. They do speak Hungarian in Transylvania, right?"

"This is a Norman castle," replied Rachel. "But, I suppose you can all tell that."

The others stared at her.

Zoë twirled her braid. The feather made a *thwapping* noise. "Assuming, for one crazy moment, that a person didn't know what a Norman castle looked like," Zoë drawled, "what about this shouts 'Norman' to you?"

"Do you see the towers at the six corners?" Rachel gestured upward. "Before the Crusades, the Europeans built rectangular castles, because rectangular rooms are easy to live in. And they lived in their castles with their families. When the Normans got to Byzantium, where they were fighting the forces of the worshippers of Enki and Ereshkigal, who were trying to regain the Sacred Lands, they found round towers. Round towers were much easier to defend. They didn't have corners, which are hard to keep watch over but easy to sap. However, circular rooms were harder to live in. The Byzantines did not live in their castles. They just used them for defense.

"So the Normans compromised. They built castles in the shape of pentagons and hexagons and put round towers where the corners would have been—trying to get the best of both designs. This is such a castle, built after the first few Crusades and before gunpowder."

The girls looked less than thrilled, but Siggy listened intently.

He came over to Rachel and asked, "How did you sap a castle before gunpowder?"

"You dug under the wall… corners were particularly vulnerable to this," Rachel replied. "Then you set as hot a fire as you could make. Pig fat was good for this. During the siege of Rochester Castle, King John brought it down by setting the fat of forty pigs on fire beneath it."

"How does the fat of forty pigs defeat a tower?" Sigfried asked, fascinated.

He gazed up at the walls, as if plotting how quickly he could take the castle.

"It melts the mortar, I believe," Rachel replied.

"I could do that," Lucky said proudly. "I bet my fire burns a lot hotter than forty pigs. Come on, Boss. Let's start digging!"

"Pig fat burns at about two hundred and fifty degrees Fahrenheit," Rachel recited data from a memorized encyclopedia. "That's a hundred and twenty one degrees Centigrade."

"You know a lot of useless information," Zoë laughed. "You should go on a game show."

Rachel, who had kept her perfect recall a secret from everyone except the princess and Sigfried—and who had only the vaguest notion of what was meant by game show—just smiled.

"Let's go inside." Valerie snapped another picture. "It's freezing! Maybe there are clues as to Egg's other cohorts. If my dad were here, he'd dust for fingerprints and other cool detectivey stuff. But sadly, I didn't think to pack a fingerprint kit in my nightgown," she said sardonically, patting her yellow pajamas. "Of course, if my mom were here, she would have brought a camera crew and a make-up artist. I didn't think to pack any of those in my jammies either."

"I'm sure I could find a make-out artist," Siggy offered innocently, hands in his pockets.

Valerie elbowed him affectionately. Joy blushed darkly and looked away.

"She's right!" Rachel cried enthusiastically, ignoring Sigfried. "This opportunity's too good to miss! Let's explore!"

"Wait!" The princess stopped beside a stone pillar that stood next to a marble well. "We cannot enter. That would be trespassing."

"Would it?" Siggy turned to his girlfriend. "Goldilock, you are the repository of all things crime-related. What is the definition of trespassing?"

"*To enter the owner's land or property without permission*," Valerie replied, rapid fire.

"And what would the penalty be for trespassing here?" asked Sigfried. To the others, he said, "If it's not permanent dismemberment, we can just suck it up."

Valerie chuckled. "Even I, the repository of all things crime-related… in America, don't know the penalty for trespassing on royal property in Transylvania. Actually, I'm pretty sure that no one knows it—ahead of time. It's up to the whim of the king."

"The penalty is of no significance," the princess stated calmly. "Trespassing, as Miss Hunt ahs so kindly reminded us, is a crime."

"So," shrugged Zoë. "What? Do you think this is a D&D game, and you are playing Lawful Good? You don't have to always be goody-goody, you know."

"And it's crazy cold!" Joy jumped up and down, chafing her arms. "Let's go in. Please!"

"Trespassing is wrong," the princess drew herself up. "I shall not go in. And I forbid my knight to behave so basely."

Siggy called back. "You can't actually expect us to stand here in the cold until dark! There's exploring to be done! I can besiege and conquer it for you! Then it will be yours. I can start by sapping. Lucky, find pigs to burn!" Drawing his gem-tipped fulgurator's wand and waving it over his head, as if it were a sword, he charged through the gatehouse, followed by the gold and red streak that was Lucky. "FOR THE PRINCESS!!"

Valerie, Zoë, and Xandra ran after him. Joy paused in the archway, torn between the handsome Sigfried and her idol, Nastasia, who was not the least bit amused by Siggy's antics.

"Um. I'll check on the others and come back," called Joy, blushing as she rushed inside.

The princess sighed and pulled a chair, a winter parka, and a book out of her purse. She placed the chair beside the trunk of a venerable elm.

Rachel hesitated, torn. She never knew what to do when Siggy and Nastasia did not see eye to eye. She had secretly vowed to support Siggy. She hated the idea that the orphan boy was alone in the world, with no one on his side but Lucky.

The princess, on the other hand, was her dearest girlfriend. She hated to desert her, too.

"Come on, Nastasia!" Rachel called, hoping if she did not confront the matter directly, the princess might change her mind. "We could use you inside. You're a better sorceress than everyone here, except for Sigfried. What if we need help?"

Nastasia opened her book in her lap without looking up. It was a book Rachel had read. "You will not need my help inside, if you do not go inside."

Rachel swallowed.

She wanted so much to be a good friend, but she never seemed to do the right thing. She had such little experience with friendship. When she had read about it in books, it had sounded easy. You met the right friend, and you were instantly bosom buddies. She had not realized that friendship was a thing that one had to practice to be good at, like vaulting, or broom flying, or playing the flute.

She hated playing the flute.

A little nagging voice in the back of her head wondered: *To what lengths should she be required to go?* Her desire to explore Beaumont burned her like an acetylene torch. The basalt walls, vast and gray, mocked her with their hidden secrets. Must she deny years of longing, because of Nastasia's qualms?

Must she sit beside the princess, while the others explored, just as she sat beside the princess at every meal, secretly wishing she could sit next to Gaius Valiant?

She had wanted to invite her boyfriend on their outing tonight, too. After all, Siggy brought his girlfriend. Gaius's insight and clever wit—not to mention his talent as a duelist, should they get into trouble—might have come in useful. But Nastasia refused. Rachel understood that the princess did not want Gaius to know about her dreamfaring talent. Nastasia was afraid he might tell his boss, the Prince of Bavaria, whom the princess did not trust.

Still, Rachel missed him.

Nastasia might have qualms about entering the castle, but Rachel herself had none. During the first week of school, when the adults had given her instructions that would have led to the death of people she loved, she had lost her ability to blindly obey rules. She was not rebellious. In fact, she felt quite humble. But she would not let pointless rules stand in the way of keeping those she loved alive.

If rebellion was like turning a crank against the gears, Rachel's crank now spun without engaging any gears at all.

But for Nastasia, if the adults told her something, then it was written in stone. Still, if Rachel wanted to be a good friend, she could not just rush off and leave the princess as the others had done. She would have to make some effort to explain.

She walked over and knelt on one knee beside the chair. "I want to tell you why I am so keen to go in." She spoke very seriously, which, oddly, made her feel younger and more vulnerable. "I realize to you, this is some random castle we just happened to drop out of the sky next to. But this is *Beaumont*! I've wanted to come here my whole life... to see if there are any clues left. I... can't let this opportunity get away. I may never have a chance to come again."

"Clues as to what?" asked the princess.

"What became of Daring Northwest."

"He's the librarian adventurer who wrote *The Not-so-Long-Ago Dream Time: A Comprehensive Study of the Bunyip*, right?" The princess pinched the top of her nose as she thought. "You once mentioned that he died here."

Rachel nodded. "He went in and never came out. His body was never found."

"But that was over a hundred and fifty years ago, wasn't it? If there were clues, would not they have been found by now?"

"Found by whom? The Starkadders? I'm not sure they ever looked properly," Rachel gave a dramatic sigh and stood up. "You are probably right. But one cannot help wishing to try."

"I commend your desire to learn the fate of your hero," Nastasia said, smiling gently.

"Mortimer Egg and his cohorts may have left clues as well. To their activities. Or other members of their cabal."

"Shouldn't we leave that to the Agents of the Wisecraft? Aren't we interfering with an investigation, if we go within?"

Rachel rolled her eyes. "Do you think King Adolphus of Transylvania will let the Agents poke around?"

"The Wisecraft is an international organization."

"True, but not all countries are equally cooperative. Transylvania has not thrown out the Wisecraft, the way King Ludwig IV of Bavaria has, but they usually handle their own matters. I would lay good money that King Adolphus will come up with some excuse as to why the Agents are not welcome."

"Even though they saved the world here last night?" asked the princess. "Assuming that that Azrael fellow actually had the power to destroy the world... which I, for one, doubt."

Rachel stared at her, her teeth sinking slowly into her lip.

She thought of the *tenebrous mundi*—giant shadow-beings in the shape of great dragons—looming above her, as they waited for Rachel to kill her father and sister and Sigfried and Nastasia herself, to fuel the spell that would allow them to obey the instructions of Azrael to dismantle the Wall that protected the Earth from the forces of chaos Outside. She recalled gazing into the horrible eyes of the demon, as she spoke the masterword that caused the spell her grandfather had cast over a hundred years before to bind Azrael back into the body of the poor hapless clerk, Mortimer Egg.

But Nastasia remembered none of this. The princess merely recalled that she had been taken captive, geased, and then rescued.

Had the princess been the kind of friend Rachel could trust with secrets, she would have told her the whole story right then. She was dying to tell someone, anyone. She hated secrets. In fact, telling secrets was her greatest joy in life.

But the dean was a friend of the princess's family, and the princess had made it painfully clear that her loyalty to the dean was greater than her loyalty to Rachel. Chances were, if Rachel told Nastasia, the dean would know the next day. The dean would then tell the Wisecraft, which was not a chance Rachel was willing to take.

What was the point of having friends, if you could not share secrets with them?

"I wish I could go inside. It sounds as if it might be a valuable experience." Nastasia sighed. "But... I cannot."

Rachel's head snapped around. "Why not?"

"You are a private citizen, Rachel," Nastasia said slowly, "even if you are nobility. If you and the others are caught trespassing in Transylvania, nothing will come of it. It will be considered a harmless childhood prank. But I am a princess of Magical Australia. If I am caught on the grounds of a royal Transylvania residence, it will create an international incident."

"Oh," whispered Rachel.

The princess was right.

"The others don't understand this," continued Nastasia. "But you are a duke's daughter. You know what duty and responsibility mean."

Grimly, Rachel nodded her head. "It would be terrible, if you were caught here. Your kingdom would be put in a very difficult position."

"I might be thought to be a spy. Some nations still execute spies." Nastasia lay a hand on Rachel's arm. "You go inside. I will be fine out here."

Rachel's heart lifted. Nastasia did understand.

"Call us on our calling cards if you need us." Rachel squeezed the princess's hand, where it lay on her arm. "May I have my broom?"

Without a word, Nastasia pulled Rachel's bristleless from her bag and handed it to her. Rachel leapt onto the leather seat and zoomed toward the door.

Chapter Three:

A Day in the Life

of an Ordinary Girl

RACHEL FLEW HER STEEPLECHASER THROUGH THE GATEHOUSE, shivering with relief.

The arched tunnel that ran through the twenty feet of the outer curtain wall was cool, but the cold mountain breeze did not blow here. She chafed her still-cold arms and urged her broom forward. Emerging into the light again, she found herself in the bailey. It was warmer here, though still chilly. The sunlight was bright, and the outer walls provided protection against the bite of the wind.

Within the bailey were the formal gardens she remembered from the previous day. Or had it been only a few hours ago? In the bright glare of the sun, it was hard to remember that it was still the middle of the night back in New York.

With a second shiver, she realized she was flying over the very spot where the ghost of her Uncle Myrddin—or Thunderfrost's Boy, as she thought of him—had stood earlier in the evening. By this very wall, he had watched her speak his name, activating the spell his father had cast decades before—the spell to bind up the demon who had murdered him, turning him into a ghost.

Toward the middle of the gardens, Rachel halted and hovered Vroomie. Beneath her was the stone altar where Azrael had laid her family and her two friends, while he had tried to compel Rachel to kill them. Beside the altar were the remains of the great bonfire the demon had used to call the *tenebrous mundi*. Her escape had been so close last night. One false step and she—and maybe the whole world—would have been destroyed.

Despite the lack of chill, Rachel shivered again.

With a last glance at the site of her earlier adventures, she flew onwards. Other than the presence of the altar and the burnt-out bonfire, the gardens were unexceptional: a pleasant vista with sprawling fig trees. Statues, half covered in ivy, stood next to yews that had been clipped into fanciful chess pieces. To either side, fountains gurgled.

Beyond the gardens loomed the gray, ivy-covered keep. This rectangular structure also had rounded towers at its four corners. Narrow, double-arched windows and t-shaped arrow slits breached its otherwise solid basalt walls. The structure reminded her of home. It was similar to the Old Castle — the oldest section of the massive, sprawling mansion that was her family's home. At Gryphon Park, however, one of the towers—the one that held her grandfather's library—was significantly taller than the rest. Here the corner towers were of a matching height.

Rachel arrived as the others entered into the inner keep. She darted after them, the wake of her broom rustling the branches of a nearby shrub. The sides of the keep were not as thick as the outer curtain wall, meant to protect the entire fortress, but the passage inside still went through a good twelve feet of stone.

Once within, she shot through a mottled yellow room into the great hall, where the others stood *ooing* and *ahing*, their voices echoing in the emptiness. It was a handsome chamber with rugged ceiling beams. Diamond-shaped medallions of burgundy and gold covered the walls. Stone benches lined the east and west side. The place was rather dim. Little sunlight made it down the four-yard long arched tunnels through the thick castle walls that served as windows.

Valerie snapped pictures, her camera *whizzing*. Her flash illuminated heraldic crests and the occasional poleaxe. Joy and Xandra stood together in the middle of the chamber, gesturing up at the odd, triangular chandeliers dotted with small globes for will-o-wisps that provided the main lighting for the dim hall. Nearby, Zoë leaned against a wall with her arms crossed and a bored expression on her face.

Toward the far end, Siggy poked around the giant hearth, urging Lucky to breathe fire into the grate. The dragon did, causing the whole chamber to smell of ozone and soot. But Rachel noticed that Sigfried's eyes were unfocused, his attention elsewhere. She guessed he was busily examining the rest of the keep with his magical, all-seeing amulet.

Skirting the edges of the walls, Rachel peered through the side doors. Like the Old Castle back home, this keep had been built before the invention of hallways. Rooms spilled directly into other rooms, with no central walkway to separate them. The other chambers on the first floor were much smaller. Most were empty, except for the occasional open cabinet or stone bench. One had a huge bas-relief across the wall, showing a battle between knights on horseback and fulgurators with their conical helmets and their lightning-throwing staffs. Another contained nothing except a standing candelabra and a music stand.

The rooms at the north and south end of the hall were square. In the corners, where the towers stood, the chambers were hexagonal. Three of these hexagonal spaces contained spiral staircases. The last had stairs leading downward to a pool surrounded by white tile. Reflected in the blue-green water, Rachel could see the three stories of hexagonal, roofless tower above it.

"The evil castle has a swimming pool?" Joy came up beside her.

"No, that's a well." Rachel pointed upward. "See how the tower is open to the sky. That's so rainwater will fall in—to add to the water supply. No castle could survive a siege without a good water supply."

"And if I were going to build a house, I would definitely want it to withstand a siege," giggled Joy. "Unless it was Siggy besieging... then, I would throw open the doors." Then she bit her lip, recalling who Rachel had previously described as being fortress-like. "I wish the princess would come in. I hate thinking of her out there in the cold, all by herself. What if we find something, and we need her advice? It doesn't seem right that our leader is all the way outside."

Rachel nodded, but as she floated her broom back toward where the others were congregated, she frowned in annoyance. *Leader? When was the last time Nastasia made a leadership decision about anything?* That was unfair. The princess had made a decision: that they should stay outside. But no one had listened to her. *Which,* whispered a little voice in her mind, *was the same as not leading.*

Rachel wondered if she should explain to Zoë and Xandra that, Joy and Sigfried's fawning aside, their nameless group was not run by the princess. It was a collection of like-minded individuals, eager to find adventure and save the world.

With a sigh, she decided not to trouble them.

It did occur to her that the group was not going to remain nameless for long. If Siggy kept inventing crazy titles, one of them was bound to stick—most likely, the worst one. They needed to pick an official name before that happened.

"What were these for?" Valerie lowered her camera and pointed up at some deep slots appearing at regular intervals in the stone of the walls. "Rachel?"

Rachel flew over and hovered beside her, examining the wall. She recognized them. The Old Castle at Gryphon Park had the same grooves. "For lighting. They held cressets—fire baskets mounted on poles, which would have been stuck into these grooves. This keep was built before the domestication of will-o-wisps. Wild will-o-wisps are unreliable and very hard to catch—and thus very expensive."

Valerie snapped a picture of the grooves. "When did the World of the Wise start using will-o-wisps?"

Rachel searched her memory, calling up an encyclopedia and a number of magazine articles she had read. "The Chinese domesticated the *kitsunibi*—Japanese will-o-wisps that burn a fox red color —sometime during the fourth or fifth century. Marco Polo brought a sack of them back from his travels to the Far East. These were bred with our European variety to produce the soft buttery glow we know today."

"Learn something every day," Xandra murmured.

"I lived in a castle once," Zoë drawled, her silver sandals leaving prints on the dusty floor. "But it was not nice like this. It was outside of Cannes. You could see the Mediterranean from my window."

"You were living in a castle on the Riviera, and you are complaining," cried Joy. "I live in a room the size of some people's closets, which I share with my sister Charity. In Ohio. Did you know Ohio got voted 'Most Boring Place in the World?'"

Zoë shrugged. "Sure the weather was gorgeous, and the food was to die for. But it's creepy to live in a structure that might fall on you. There were whole sections we could not enter because they might collapse at any time. They were cordoned off by red velvet ropes—like we lived in a museum or something. Luckily, my father was only away a few weeks that time, and I got to go home before the cold weather came. That place was drafty! There was a crack in my room so big that one night I woke up staring into the face of a rat the size of a small dog."

Xandra had bent over to examine a bench. She straightened. "Why were you there?"

"My mother died some years ago. Her mother was a Moth. So I have...."

"A lot of relatives. Got it." Xandra gave a curt nod of her hooded head. "I hear the Moths are the largest family in the world." She paused. "So... forgive me if I am behind here, but... the lawns are well-kept—someone's trimmed the giant yew chess pieces—yet nobody lives here?"

"Not at the moment," Rachel frowned thoughtfully, "though Egg's cohort, Serene O'Malley, is still out there. She jumped away last night."

"Wait, you mean, she might come back here?" Joy looked around nervously. "Um...."

"Don't worry," Siggy slashed at the air with his poleaxe. "She wouldn't dare come back while Lucky and I are here. Right, Lucky?"

"Right, Boss," the dragon replied, "else her hair will be fiery red for real!"

A thought struck Rachel. She floated up beside the hooded upperclassman. "Xandra, why were you standing in the darkness after midnight, waiting for us?"

"The Voices told me to." Xandra shrugged. "Cruel taskmasters that they are. They show no concern for unimportant things like sleep or flouting rules. On the good side, at least this time, they didn't tell me I had to go naked. Or with a duck on my head."

"I could have helped you with the duck," promised Lucky.

"You mean the voices that come out of your mouth?" Siggy thrust at an invisible enemy with the top point of his poleaxe.

Xandra nodded.

"When they speak through you, do you hear them?" asked Valerie, her flash illuminating the chamber.

"No," said Xandra, "but they also speak to me. Usually in the middle of class, right when the tutor calls my name, and all my fellow students are staring at me. They're helpful that way."

"Should we be worried?" asked Valerie. "I mean, that these Voices asked you to come with us? Does that suggest that we're going to be in danger?"

"I like to think that if a catastrophe were in the offing, the Voices would have instructed me to tell you *not* to go," Xandra said dryly. "Usually, they are quick to tell me when I am doomed. They're helpful, that way, too."

"That's comforting," said Valerie. "They wouldn't send you into dire danger, right?"

"I'd like to think…" Xandra murmured again.

• • •

They stomped up the spiral staircase to the next floor, their feet clacking against the stone steps, except for Rachel, who was still flying. The tower was cool and damp and smelled of wet rock. It was dark as well, but Xandra had used the *lux* cantrip to create a ball of dancing lights that hovered above their heads. Rachel floated on her broom, just to the side of the rail-less staircase, angling upward. At one point, she shot ahead too quickly and ended up with her head stuck in the midst of the dancing ball of light.

"Why do you wear a hood over your face?" Siggy asked Xandra. "Were you burned by acid?"

Xandra chuckled. "No, it's just that hoods are terribly comfortable. I think everyone will be wearing them in the future."

"Really? Are they comfortable?" Rachel peered at Xandra's hood, blinking. Her eyes were still dazzled from the ball's brightness. "Don't they get hot?"

Zoë snorted with derisive amusement. Rachel's face remained calm, but inside she cringed, uncertain what she had done to warrant mockery.

Xandra gave Rachel a compassionate smile. "Wise-born, are you? Me, too. Those of us who are raised entirely in the World of the Wise sometimes miss out on some pretty cool stuff. You should ask your parents to let you watch more movies."

"Gaius likes movies," Rachel murmured dreamily.

"Gaius Valiant?" Beneath the hem of her hood, Xandra lips twitched with amusement. "Are you two really dating, then? He's in my class. We're upper school seniors. Isn't he a bit old for you?"

Rachel blushed. "He came a year early, so he's only sixteen."

"Sixteen to fourteen," shrugged Xandra. "That's not so bad."

Rachel stared straight up the stairs. She did not explain that she herself had also come a year early and was, therefore, only thirteen. Still, it was a pleasure to talk about Gaius without the princess's constant glare of disapproval.

"No… I was not burned by acid." Xandra turned back to Sigfried. "When I get possessed, sometimes, I make really stupid faces. Remember what I said about them talking to me right when everyone's looking? It's not that I mind being made a fool of occasionally, mind you. But, after a while, it can get dull."

"Why do we all wear robes?" Siggy asked suddenly, as he stopped upward. "At school, I mean? Are we constantly in a state of graduating?"

Zoë snorted.

"Because that is the way all scholars dressed back in 1624, when the school first opened," Xandra replied simply. "Originally, that was the only uniform students could wear, but when Oxford allowed subfusc for formal occasions, Roanoke decided to allow it, too."

"Is there a school of sorcery at Oxford?" Siggy asked in surprise.

"Of course," replied Xandra. "Isn't there a school for everything at Oxford?"

"Returning to your hood… you're not even ugly?" pressed Siggy, who apparently had forgotten that he and Rachel had once seen Xandra's face.

"You'll never know," Xandra quipped back.

• • •

The second floor, high above the first, was a collection of musty rooms. Tapestries covered the walls of the central room. A side

room held an office. Valerie looked through the drawers of the file
cabinet. She found papers written in Hungarian, but they were old
and yellow. Rachel glanced at each one, in case she wanted to have
them translated later; however, she suspected that they were laundry lists and the bills for gardeners rather than clues as to lost ad-
venturers or demon cabals.

She flew over to where Siggy and Lucky were guessing how
quickly the tapestries would burn.

"Have you looked around the whole place?" she murmured.
"No one's here, right?"

"Um... nope," Siggy whispered back, absentmindedly tapping
the spot on his robe under which hung his all-seeing amulet. "Not
yet. I was searching the dungeons downstairs for gold and loot. I
found some cool torture implements, but they're rusty. You don't
need torture, if you have magic, I'm guessing. I'll look upstairs soon,
but first cover for me. I'm going to take advantage of the fact that
the others have wandered off, to sneak into the office and smooch
my G.F."

Sigfried snuck into the office and closed the door. From inside
came a squeal, and then a sound like *mmmmm*. Rachel rolled her
eyes. She hovered before the door for a time, on guard, but as the
others seemed caught up in their own activities—and Rachel didn't
think they would care anyway—she abandoned Siggy and Valerie to
their fate and continued examining the room.

She could not help feeling a bit envious.

She wished her boyfriend were here, too.

A cloud covered the sun, casting a gloom over the chamber. So
long as she kept her attention trained on absorbing details, she felt
fine. The moment she let up, however, her eyelids began to sink.
Fatigue was catching up with her. Back home, it was the middle of
the night of one of the most difficult days of her life. Not to mention
that even a simple healing enchantment could be exhausting.

No wonder she was tired.

But her friends still seemed chipper; she would have to find a
way to soldier on.

Of course, her friends' last two days had been nothing like Rachel's. She had undergone a tremendous amount in the last thirty

six hours—from offering her life to the Raven, if it would help him save the world; to learning of the death of Mrs. Egg; to knocking herself out in Art class; to discovering that Azrael had killed her beloved grandfather's unknown first family; to figuring out that one of the bad guys was the mother of her classmate Juma; to flying at the rogue plane Juma's mother tried to direct into the school; to running into danger to save Siggy and Nastasia; to facing down the demon Azrael, as he tried to force her to kill her family.

Now that it was over, it felt if the fires had sputtered out in the furnace of her soul. It was only a matter of time before her limbs stopped moving. Once, she slipped sideways and nearly fell off the broom.

At least the horror was over.

A shiver ran up Rachel's spine. She gripped her steeplechaser tightly. The castle, which had seemed cheerfully mundane, suddenly seemed ominous. She could not put her finger on why. Was it the disappearance of the sunlight? The question of Darius Northwest's unresolved fate?

She flew closer to the tapestries with their fanciful unicorns and hippogriffs. They reminded her of some of her favorite of Northwest's books. She remembered the first time she heard of "Daring" Northwest. She had been curled up in her grandfather's lap, half asleep, while he read in one of the great winged armchairs in his tower library. Smoke from his pipe, far more pleasant than the odor of cigarettes, formed lopsided rings or fanciful castles and dragons. She had not known what he was reading at the time, but examining her memory now, she could see that the book was Polybius's *History of the Punic Wars*.

Half asleep in his lap, her gaze had fallen upon *A Field Guide to Gryphons and their Southern Cousins*. Pointing a stubby finger, she had cried, "Look! Gryphons! Like us!"

"Right you are, my child." Her grandfather's majestic eyebrows had risen in amusement.

Opening the book, he had read her the section about Abaras, the Arimaspian priest of Apollo from whom the Griffin family was descended. Then he read her Daring Northwest's tale of his own experience stalking gryphons in Hyperborea, north of the Rhipaean Mountains. How he had ventured, complete with the pale eye patch and hooded lantern of an Arimaspian, into a gryphon's lair and emerged with a handful of its treasure. There was even a drawing of two pieces of the treasure, a coin with a Roman eagle and an ancient medallion shaped like a plus-sign, perhaps a family heirloom or the symbol of some forgotten god.

In later years, when Rachel read the book herself, she had discovered that her grandfather's recitation had been the "good parts" version, spiced up with dramatic comments and wry observations. Nonetheless, the book remained a favorite. Her grandfather had gone on that day to speak of Daring Northwest, his cleverness and his courage—how bravely he had gone places no one else dared to go. Rachel, her imagination afire with images of smoke-castles and gryphon caves, had decided that this was the life she wanted when she grew up.

At the time, she had thought her grandfather was describing some ancient figure whom he had learned about through reading books—an author he had loved the way she had loved A. A. Milne, Beatrix Potter, Dr. Seuss, and Frances Hodgson Burnett. It was only now, after her recent conversation with her art tutor, Mrs. Heelis, that she realized the truth: *Blaise Griffin had been describing his own childhood friend.*

She recalled the photograph Mrs. Heelis had shown her: her grandfather as a young man—serious and handsome, already developing his impressive eyebrows—dressed in Victorian clothing and flanked by her grandmother and young Mrs. Heelis in their bustled gowns, with the dashing Darius Northwest next to Mrs. Heelis and the fierce Jasper Hawke on the far side.

They had looked so alive in the photo; but, oh, the terrible sorrows they had faced since.

Darius Northwest vanished over a hundred and fifty years ago. Jasper Hawke had been killed fighting Johan Faust the Sixth and the rest of Bismarck's black sorcerers. Her grandfather's entire first family, his wife and five children—aunts and uncles she had never met, unless one counted Myrddin, the Ghost Boy—had been murdered by the demon Azrael. Out of sorrow and sympathy, Amelia Abney-Hastings had broken her sacred vows and deserted the order of the Vestal Virgins to marry Blaise Griffin, becoming his second wife and Rachel's grandmother. To keep Azrael from doing even more damage, her grandfather had been forced to bind the demon into another friend, Aleister Crowley, turning Crowley into a fiend.

Her grandfather had not led an easy life.

Rachel looked around at her friends. Suddenly, they seemed inexpressibly dear. Sigfried, who had emerged again, looked so fierce and cheerful, as he fenced with the poleaxe he had taken from the downstairs wall. Lucky looped about happily in figure eights, egging him on. Joy bounced up and down with excitement, as she watched Siggy. Zoë tapped on Joy's shoulder and then, when Joy turned around, stood whistling, pretending that it had not been her. Xandra examined the tapestries curiously, one lavender eye peeking out from under her hood. Valerie, looking slightly pink-cheeked, held up her camera thoughtfully, contemplating how to use the last shot on her roll. In her mind's eye, Rachel added the princess, seated outside in her chair under the venerable elm, reading a book about an assistant pigkeeper.

Cold fingers of fear clutched at Rachel's heart. She suddenly felt so small and helpless. Her friends looked so vibrant, so alive. And yet, just yesterday—or had it been earlier today?—the earth had nearly been destroyed. Would these people she had come to care so much about, despite their short acquaintance, be allowed to live peacefully to adulthood?

Or would they, too, suffer fates as tragic as her beloved grandfather and his friends?

Taking a steadying breath, Rachel reminded herself that Azrael was bound up and in custody. She had seen the red and gold sparkles in the form of a gryphon, made by her grandfather's spell, sink into his body.

That meant everything would be fine now, right?

The world was safe again, and she could finally please her father by obeying his request. He had asked her to concentrate on learning sorcery and being a young lady.

He wanted her to be an ordinary girl.

What did ordinary girls do?

Rachel thought back over the last month and a half of school, pulling up memories and examining what others around her had done. Girls chatted together in small groups, occasionally bursting into laughter. Boys mocked each other good-naturedly. Couples walked arm-in-arm. She grinned at that. She would like to spend more time walking arm-in-arm with her boyfriend. Older students often sat alone reading books. That would be nice, too! She had done little else but fly and read before coming to school, other than occasionally riding her pony. Now she never seemed to have any free time. She almost envied the princess, sitting outside with her nose in one of the best books ever written.

Rachel sighed and smiled slightly. She could do this. She could be an ordinary girl. All it would take would be to stop rushing head-long toward ever possible adventure.

"Nice broom." Xandra had come up beside where Rachel was hovering, lost in thought. "What kind is it? It's too short to be a traveler and too long to be a racer. Besides, it has an awful lot of blades in the back." She counted the alternating slats of reddish and brownish wood. "... seven, eight, nine, ten! I've never seen a bristleless with ten blades! Most have four."

Rachel beamed with delight. Vroomie was her pride and joy.

She hopped off and let Xandra examine the bristleless. It had a shaft of polished dark walnut, a shiny black leather seat, and levers, handlebars, and footrests of black cast iron and shiny brass. The tail fan, where an ancient flying broom would have had bristles, consisted of ten blades, alternating mahogany and cherry wood. In the muted wisp-light, the three shades of reddish and dark wood gleamed like a living thing.

"It's a steeplechaser." Rachel patted the polished shaft proudly.

"Ooh!" Beneath her dark hood, Xandra's lips formed an O. "You mean like Sukie uses to beat the Good-Witch Mother, who was any-thing but, in the fairy tale? I didn't know they were real. I hear you're a really good flyer. They call you the Broom Goddess. Are you planning to go pro when you graduate? Join a flying polo team, or a broom dancing company?"

Rachel blushed, embarrassed by the praise. Flashbacks of the whole dining hall clapping for her when the Broom Goddess nickname was announced threatened to unravel her composure. She shook her head and quickly climbed back on Vroomie. "I want to be a librarian."

Nearby, Zoë snorted in derision, but Xandra's lips quirked with interest.

"A mundane librarian?" she asked, "Or an adventurer-librarian, like Darius Northwest?"

Rachel's whole face lit up. "Like 'Daring' Northwest. Exactly like Northwest!" Her smile faltered. She looked up at the castle around them. "Do you know he died here? In Beaumont? Or at least, he entered the castle, and no one ever saw him again."

"N-never?" stuttered Joy. She looked up at the strange triangular chandeliers as if they might suddenly come to life and drop on her. "I-I'm... going to check on the princess. She's probably lonely. She might need company."

Joy turned and ran back toward the spiral staircase.

"Hey!" Sigfried swung his poleaxe, jabbing wildly at the air. "There's a big room one floor up filled with colored mirrors. Like that belfry back at school. One of them has silver light coming out of it."

"Really?" Zoë's eyes narrowed as she looked left and right. "How could you know?"

"A glass hall!" Rachel engaged her broom, her eyes sparkling. "Let's go!"

As she flew toward the spiral staircase, a tiny self-amused quirk caught up the corners of her mouth. What was that resolution she had made, just moments before, about no longer rushing headlong toward adventure?

Maybe this ordinary girl thing was going to be difficult after all.

CHAPTER FOUR:

THE MYSTERY OF THE

MOONLIT MIRROR

MOONLIGHT SPILLED FROM A KEY HOLE IN A DOOR ON THE FOURTH landing. Crisp black shadows leapt up behind each young sorcerer as they approached the silvery light.

"*Libra!*" Xandra performed the Word of Opening cantrip. The door trembled, but it did not open. "It's warded. We can't get in."

"Oh please! Allow me." Valerie knelt in front of the door and examined the lock. "This is a very old fashioned lock. I should be able to open it if I only had...." She frowned at her camera, as if trying to decide which fastening from her red strap she wished to cannibalize.

"Would this help?" Rachel pulled from the pocket of her robes one of the bobby pins she kept to hold her hat on when she was flying, the hat she had lost today, while trying to stop the plane.

"Perfect!" Valerie exclaimed in delight. She rubbed her hands together. "Let's pop open this puppy." She wiggled the pin around in the lock.

Click. The door swung open.

"A girlfriend with criminal tendencies!" Sigfried grinned with fierce pride.

Valerie gave him a friendly punch and led the way into the Mirror Hall. Rachel and the others followed. Beyond the doorway was a chamber as large as the great hall below, though it was only two stories high, not three. Mirrors lined both walls. Some glittered with a bluish or greenish hue; others were hidden behind curtains. One mirror emitted a silvery light so bright that the chamber seemed to be lit with the brilliance of a full moon.

Rachel bent low over her handlebars and slipped through the door above the heads of her friends. Darting into the chamber, she flew up to the mirror from which the silvery light emanated. She had never seen anything like this before.

"What are we seeing, Griffin?" Siggy came up beside her. He peered at the silvery mirror with cautious interest. "Is this a weapon? Can we blind people with it? Cause them to jump at their own shadows?"

"That's a lame attack, boss," said Lucky the Dragon, sniffing the glass.

"Not if we could make their shadows come to life and strangle them!" crowed Sigfried. He tapped the mirror with the tip of the poleaxe. "That would be wicked cool!"

Rachel flew a quick circuit around the hall and returned. "Most of the others are green. That means they're talking glasses. There are some blue ones. Walking glasses."

"Any chance one of those would take us home?" asked Xandra.

Rachel rapidly reviewed her memory of the images she had just seen. "Most of the ones I could see, some were hidden behind curtains, looked as if they led to private dwellings, probably other places in Transylvania. Still, there might be one that leads to a public glass Hall. We can examine them more carefully."

"And the light?" pressed Siggy.

"No idea," admitted Rachel. She glanced at the upperclassman.

"Me, neither," murmured Xandra, shaking her hooded head.

Hovering beside the silvery mirror, Rachel peered into it, trying to catch a glimpse of the glass's hue. From the edges, it looked as if the glass itself was silver. But that made no sense. There was no known glass that shone like the moon. On the other hand, she had never seen a real looking glass before this year, either. So, maybe there was more to glasses than she knew.

"Hold on!" she cried suddenly. "Do you think this could be the moon glass?"

"The what?" Siggy jabbed invisible enemies with the tip of the poleaxe.

"Wait...." Valerie pressed her fingers against her temples, blinking several times. "Dr. Mordeau asked me about that. She wanted to know...." The blond girl screwed up her face, struggling to remember.

Rachel watched her uncomfortably. The difficulties that others had with their memories always unnerved her. Finally, she could not stand it.

"In your interview with the Agents, Valerie, you said that Dr. Mordeau asked, '*If Agent Griffin had told his daughter about the moon glass.*' I wonder if this could be it. The moon glass."

"There's a plaque." Valerie moved up next to the mirror and frowned at a brass rectangle set into the wall. "Oh. It's written in Hungarian. Of course. Duh!"

Rachel moved forward and glanced at the writing. A shiver ran through her from scalp to sole.

The plaque read:
Darius Northwest átment a hold tükrön, eltûnve mindörökre
She felt as if the breath had been sucked from her lungs.
He had been right here. In this spot.

She had hoped — she had so hoped — but she had not actually expected to find anything. Yet, this plaque next to the mysterious moon glass bore his name. Had he died here? Had he stepped through this glass to vistas beyond, never to return? Had the Transylvanians known his final fate all this time and never told the rest of the world?

Rachel peered at the sentence intently. *What did it say?* According to the dictionary from the main library at Gryphon Park, Hungarian was one of the few European languages that was not part of the Indo-European family of languages. It was, instead, from the Uralic family, related to Estonian, Finnish, and Thulese. Rachel knew some words of Thulese from summers spent at Hot Springs Beach, but none of them appeared on this plaque.

She could not puzzle it out, but she would remember the phrase forever.

"He must have gone through here," she whispered, her throat parched dry. "Where does it go? Did he... die on the other side? Or could he be trapped there. I...."

What was on the other side?

She peered and peered, her heart pounding, but she could not glimpse anything except silver light. Fingers trembling, she put her hand on the glass's surface, despite Xandra's and Zoë's warning cry. She concentrated, as one would to activate a walking or talking glass. Nothing happened. The glass did not seem to be working. Either that or something more was needed, the way a thinking glass needed an *ore* cantrip to activate it.

Wherever Daring Northwest had gone, Rachel could not follow.

"And that's the guy you want to be like when you grow up, right?" Valerie asked, trying to adjust her camera to take a picture in the unusual lighting. "The one who disappeared here?"

Rachel swallowed, nodding.

"I love his books," mused Xandra. "My favorite is: *Fifty-Nine Beneficent Fey and Where They Make Their Homes.* I've read my father's copy at least five times."

"Yeah, I love that one!" Rachel sighed, as she walked down the line of mirrors peering into the rest, looking for anything that might offer a way home. Over her shoulder, she called, "What about you, Xandra? What do you want to do when you grow up?"

Xandra snorted sadly, as she peeked behind one of the thick velvet curtains. "Be a hermit... and a nurse."

"Going out on a limb here...." Valerie snapped a picture of the glass with the silvery light, using her last shot. "But isn't it hard to be both? Don't nurses have to, um—you know—*talk* to patients?"

"It's a work in progress," muttered Xandra.

Rachel glanced at Valerie. "What about you, Ace Reporter?"

"I'm thinking of majoring in True History and Obscuration," Valerie paused to wind her film and change the cartridge. Under her breath, she murmured, "If I had known we were going to leave Roanoke grounds, I would have brought my digital camera."

"True History?" Siggy paused, mid-swing with the authentic Fifteenth century poleaxe, and gaped at his girlfriend. "You mean, True Snoring? The class of Utter Boredom? You know I admire you tremendously, Coochie-Pooh, but I think your rocking horse might have just flipped off its rockers."

"Sigfried," Valerie's voice was soft yet deadly, "don't ever call me Coochie-Pooh again."

"You're right," Siggy nodded sagely. "What was I thinking? I'll call you Pert Bosom."

"I'm going to slap him," murmured Valerie, turning red.

"Go for it!" Zoë cheered. She reached into in her backpack and pulled out what looked like a large solid paddle made of greenstone. "Or, if you prefer, I can whack him for you! What is the point of having a magic-infused war bat, if I never get to whack anything." She made a few practice swings.

"It's okay." Valerie watched her swing. "If Siggy needs whacking, I'm quite capable of providing said whack."

"True History." Xandra shuddered. "I'm with Sigfried... not about the Coochie-Bosom thing, but the rest. But you live with the scholars of Dee Hall, right? I guess that makes sense."

"Why?" quipped Zoë. "Are people in Dee all crazy and eager to subject themselves to unnatural intellectual torture?"

"Before I found out about magic, I wanted to be an investigative reporter. I wanted to know the truth. I wanted to get to the bottom of things." Valerie explained as she closed up her camera again. "But what's the point of investigating, if the Obscurers working for the Parliament of the Wise are altering the records—hypnotizing witnesses, mucking with historical documents? Anything I find out is probably wrong.

"If I want to find the truth, I am going to need to understand how records and memories are changed. What are the signs that the World of the Wise has meddled with something? How is Obscuration done? Can you make a person believe anything? Or just some things? If I understand the process, then maybe I can find the truth. The *real* truth."

"That's quite noble." Rachel nodded admiringly, wistfully recalling the photograph of Dee she had kept under her bed for years. She had wanted to live there, but, when she arrived at school, she had been automatically put in Dare Hall with her siblings. "And you, Zoë?"

Zoë was in the act of running her hands over her head. As she did, her hair changed from pink to the yellow damask pattern on the downstairs walls. The others gawked. Rachel had never seen hair with patterned design before.

Zoë shrugged. "Don't care, really. Whatever."

"Really?" Valerie stared at Zoë as if she had just grown a second head. "You don't have plans for the future?"

"The future is a long way away," Zoë replied. "I'll be lucky if I pass my classes today. I'm a sucky sorceress."

Sigfried and Lucky had stopped to make faces at each other in a broken mirror. Suddenly, Siggy shouted. "Upstairs! They're sacrificing a boy!"

The others all cried out at once.

"What—?"

"Who?"

Sigfried was already pelting across the hall toward the staircase. The poleaxe swung beside him as his legs pumped, his new sneakers pounding against the tile floor.

Mounting her broom, Rachel zipped up beside him. "Leap on!"

He vaulted onto the steeplechaser. The two of them zoomed to the staircase. Rachel was grateful that flying up spiral staircases was a particular specialty of hers. Banking hard, she flew straight upward through the middle of the spiral, just as she did when she flew from her room to her grandfather's library at the top of his tower.

As she flew, her awareness of distances and three-dimensional spaces became crisp and immediate. Unimportant things, such as emotions, were shunted to the background, to be sorted later.

As they shot toward an open trap door in the ceiling above them, Rachel shouted over her shoulder, "Siggy, do you have any charges in your wand?"

"Not sure," he shouted back. She could feel him shrug. "I haven't put in very many spells yet, and I used most of them in the battle against Egg's minions. I have my trumpet, though."

"Better use that." Rachel pursed her lips, preparing to whistle.

• • •

They burst through the open trap door into a hexagonal chamber at the top of the Southeast tower. Tall, narrow, arched windows opened onto the overcast sky. Carved into the chamber's floor was a circle inscribed with a summoning triangle and a seven-pointed star.

Above the summoning triangle, a churning darkness manifested, as if a cloud of soot had come to life and was attempting to coalesce into a solid shape. At the center of the seven-pointed star stood a large stone slab.

Five figures, garbed in the deep purple robes of the Veltdammerung, bent over the stone slab. Strapped to it was a young boy, maybe six years old. Between the boy and the slab was piled a layer of straw and dried pine boughs. The tallest robed figure stood at the boy's head. He held a knife high in the air. The other four stood two to either side, holding flaming torches.

As Rachel and Sigfried entered the chamber, the tall figure chanted: "*Come forth, Moloch, Devourer of Children. We pass this child through the fire to you. Come to us now, through the way we shall open for you! Great Moloch! Hear us!*"

He spoke English. His accent sounded like an American, from New York, where Mortimer Egg had been living. Rachel guessed this was one of Egg's cronies.

The little boy thrashed in his bindings. He had olive skin, dark hair, and very wide, dark eyes. His face was round, with large ears and a little cleft in his chin that reminded Rachel just a bit of Wulfgang Starkadder. Her heart went out to him. She had no idea how she and Sigfried could beat five adults, but she was determined that the two of them must prevail.

Behind her, Siggy blew his trumpet. Rachel whistled. Silver and blue sparkles swirled forward amidst an aroma of fresh rain and evergreens respectively.

The cultists spun in comical surprise. They had a moment to gape before the wind from Sigfried's instrument lifted the two closer robed figures and tossed them against the far wall. Their torches went flying out of their hands and dropped sputtering to the stone floor.

Rachel's attempt, on the other hand, failed. The blue sparks faded before they reached the stone slab. Ordinarily, she should have been able to reach a target at this distance. The warding circle carved into the floor was interfering with her enchantment. It was probably affecting Sigfried's, too, but his spells were so powerful that the difference was not as significant.

Siggy blew again. He had his trumpet in his right hand and the heavy poleaxe in his left, which he held one-handed with ease. He clung to the broom with his knees. A second swirling of silver sparks swept toward the darkness, just as the tallest figure threw the knife in his hand. Instead of flying toward them, his blade was caught by Siggy's wind and carried backwards. It struck the far wall and clattered to the floor.

The darkness in the air above the summoning triangle churned and swirled angrily. Rachel halted her broom at the edge of the circle carved into the floor, wary about crossing over the ward. It was designed to keep the creature they were summoning contained. If her passing over it dispersed it, the creature within might be released upon the unsuspecting world. She pointed at the darkness and shouted to Siggy.

"Get that! Blast it with wind!"

He blew a third trumpet flourish, this time toward the summoning triangle. His wind sparkles parted at the edge of the triangle. The coalescing darkness remained untouched.

Two torch-bearing cultists remained on the far side of the stone slab. The flame on the closer torch had blown out. The farther torch flared as the passing breeze fanned its flames. The fire spread, igniting the robes of the man holding it. Letting go of his torch, he shouted, dropped, and rolled around on the stone floor, trying to smother the flames.

Lucky darted beyond the stone slab to where the men Siggy had sent flying lay sprawled.

"The kid and the kindling are safely behind you now, Lucky," Siggy shouted. "Pull!"

Lucky breathed out a short plume of flame, just enough to keep the two men on the floor at bay. They shouted and scurried backward.

To Rachel's relief, none of the robed figures pulled out wands. Nor did they grab musical instruments or raise their hands to perform cantrips. Not being graduates of Roanoke Academy, they must only be practitioners of one or two of the Sorcerous Arts.

These men were obviously thaumaturges—as they were in the act of performing a thaumaturgic spell. Rachel guessed they were attempting to summon some particularly dreadful being, using the boy as their sacrifice. Four of them wore chains around their necks, from which hung *Kalesei Astari* or Summoning Stars—quartz crystals used as a covenant between a thaumaturge and some supernatural entity that has agreed to come at the sorcerer's bidding. Poorer thaumaturges, such as these men probably were, often could not afford the high-quality gems needed for a fulgurator's wand, but they could have as many *Kalesei Astari* as they had creatures to call.

The cultists also had two talismans among their accoutrements. Short rods, one of ebony and one of ivory, rested to either side of the boy. Each had a carved end piece. The head of the ebony rod was of ivory and looked like a fish head. The head piece of the ivory rod was of ebony and looked like a wind god, its black cheeks blowing. Alchemical talismans worked best if they resembled their function. Rachel guessed the ivory rod with the wind god top produced a wind much like Sigfried's. She was not sure about the other rod.

The inner ward — the summoning triangle — was powerful enough to bend Siggy's enchantment. Rachel decided to trust it to contain the dark manifestation. She rocketed closer, whistling again. Blue sparkles left her lips and struck the closest figure. He went utterly still, frozen in the act of bending over to reach for a rod.

Having spent her last battle unable to make a sound, it felt really good to finally accomplish something.

The tallest figure, standing by the boy's head, grabbed the ebony rod. He pointed the fish-head at Rachel. It glowed with an orangey light. Rachel's throat constricted. She grabbed her neck, unable to breathe. It was as if water filled her wind pipe, blocking it. Only there was no water there—nothing to cough away. Her chest rose and fell, trying to suck in air, but none reached her lungs.

Without air, she could neither breathe nor whistle.

Little dots danced before her eyes.

Siggy blew again, blasting the tall man from his feet. He tumbled, end over end. The fish rod went flying. The orangey glow died. He landed on his own knife, which scratched his cheek He now lay on the floor next to the first two whom Sigfried had bowled from their feet.

All three cringed away from Lucky's threatening flames.

Breath rushed into Rachel's chest. Wasting no time with frivolities, she whistled again.

The last of the Veltdammerung followers was rising, having extinguished the flame on his robes. Now he froze, paralyzed by Rachel's enchantment. Siggy blew his horn and knocked over both this man and the fellow who was caught leaning over with his behind in the air.

Vroomie hovered above the slab now. Out of the corner of her eye, Rachel noticed the tall man, who cowered behind Lucky, reaching behind him for his fallen blade. She tensed. Her precise three-dimensional mental picture of the room told her the man was out of her whistling range.

But not out of Canticle range! She pointed at the knife lying next to the tall man and performed the cantrip she had practiced at least a thousand times in her secret hallway, upstairs in Roanoke Hall.

"Tiathelu!"

The knife rose into the air. With a gesture, she drew it across the room into her hand. As she caught it, she silently vowed to get Gaius to teach her the Glepnir bonds. The constricting golden bands were the most effective attack of any cantrip she had seen. Considering how often she had found herself in fights, it would be useful to know.

Sigfried leaned over and sliced the ropes holding the boy with the poleaxe. With a second, massive swing, he also chopped the ivory rod in two. Rachel cringed, as breaking a talisman sometime produced a bad result. This one merely fell to the ground in two pieces. The little boy leapt up. He backed to the far edge of the stone slab, gazing in fear at the coalescing darkness. Pointing, he jabbered in a language Rachel did not understand.

"Here, you take him, Rachel." Siggy slipped off the broom and lifted the frightened child onto it. "Get him out of here. I'll hold them off. Okay, Lucky, let's get 'em. You burn 'em. I'll run 'em through. Not the paralyzed guys. That wouldn't be sporting. We'll get to them later. But the rest of these murderers of innocents are going down!"

"Uh… boss, I think I should get that shadowy… whatever it is. Before it manifests." Lucky the Dragon gestured with his cat-like head at the summoning triangle above which the darkness was forming into a huge, vaguely-humanoid shape with horns and wings. "It doesn't look good."

"Go for it, Lucky!" crowed Siggy. He ran toward the three robed men, brandishing the top point of the poleaxe like a spear. "Okay, you child murderers, do you understand what I am saying? You die. Today!"

Rachel helped the boy get his balance on the steeplechaser and began heading for the trap door. Behind her, a voice spoke from the darkness—a deep voice, steady and slow, as if the speaker were partially asleep.

"Who disturbs my slumber?"

A strange tingle of familiarity raced through Rachel. She felt as if she should recognize that voice, and yet a quick check of her memory assured her that she had never heard it before. The sound itself was not unpleasant to the ear, and yet something colder than terror gripped her.

They must do anything—pay any cost—to stop this monster from waking.

Lucky shot forward and breathed fire on the swirling darkness. It bellowed. A shadowy hand swiped at the flames. Then came an eerie wailing, followed by a loud *pop.*

The darkness vanished.

"Got 'im!" chortled Lucky.

BOOM!

A wave of immense force, set into motion by the dark figure's gesture, lifted Sigfried from his feet and catapulted him into one of the narrow, arched windows. The window was too small for Siggy to pass through. His body made a terrible cracking noise, as it slammed against the stone casement.

The ancient stone casement wobbled. With a horrible grinding sound, it tore free of the tower wall and fell backwards, plummeting toward the ground—and taking Sigfried with it.

CHAPTER FIVE:

FLOPS-OVER-DEAD CHICK

SAVES THE DAY-SORT OF

"GRAB ON!" RACHEL SHOUTED TO THE LITTLE BOY, EVEN THOUGH she knew he did not understand her. He grabbed her waist as the broom shot forward. Rachel darted through the newly-made hole where the window and Sigfried used to be and dived. Without the protection of the castle wall, the chill of the mountain wind cut through her garments. The little boy clung to her more tightly.

Siggy plummeted headfirst toward a duck pond on the south side of the keep, amidst a rain of rocks and debris. To her horror, Rachel's sense of speed and direction told her that the distance was too short for her to accelerate sufficiently to catch him before he struck the ground. Behind her, Lucky let out a horrible keening sound and dived out the window.

Rachel lifted her hands from handlebars, and, thus, the levers. This was not the wisest move. Due to her young passenger, she could not slip into the lying down position required to steer with her feet. As the steeplechaser pulled hard to the right, she again cast the *ti-athelu* cantrip.

Sigfried was too heavy and moving too fast for her cantrip to stop him. Leaning back, she pulled against his weight, slowing his rate of descent. She felt a strange *déjà vu* sensation. Hadn't she used this same cantrip to save her father at this same castle only a few hours before?

Did it count as *déjà vu* if it really had happened?

Lucky shot past her. Reaching Sigfried, he wrapped his body around the boy's. The slender dragon was not strong enough to carry his master, but between his efforts and Rachel's, they slowed his rate of descent.

Siggy splashed down into the shallow edge of the pool. Lucky remained wrapped around him, keeping the boy's head out of the water. Ducks swam away from him. A lone goose ran forward and honked at them raucously.

Rachel landed beside them and leapt off her broom. Siggy's eyes were open and unfocused. His chest rose and fell rapidly. A dark liquid, presumably blood, was spreading outward through the murky waters of the pond. Rachel wanted to pull him out of the chilly water, before it sapped the heat from his body, but she knew one was not supposed to move an injured person. Lucky slowly inched toward the shore, but he stopped when he hit solid mud. He would have had to jar his master to move him farther.

Pulling out her mirror, she called, "Zoë! Valerie! Siggy's hurt! We're downstairs! Er... outside. Outside, downstairs! Nastasia, come quick! They were trying to hurt a little boy, and I can't speak his language!"

Zoë's voice came back. "We're on our way!"

Rachel walked into the water and leaned over Sigfried. Gently she touched his shoulder. He did not respond. Rachel's heart began to pound so hard her ribcage shook.

No. Not now.

Not when she finally thought all would be well.

Staring at his motionless body, she felt as if the most important thing in the world was slipping away from her. Panic rose inside her; scattering her thoughts like startled birds. As clear as if he stood beside her, her grandfather's voice rang out from her memory: *Think now, Child. Feel later. There will be time enough to mourn when you bury the dead. If you think first and mourn later, you might not have as many dead to bury.*

Rachel straightened. Rallying, she called upon the dissembling techniques she ordinarily used to keep her features calm, concentrating on that false calmness until it pushed aside her fear. Her mind became focused and alert. In the back of her thoughts, she was aware that her terror was still there, but she did not care. It would come back and hit her harder later on, but later would be after the emergency.

She reviewed her options, searching rapidly for any useful action. She wished she knew some healing songs, but she did not. But there must be something. . . .

Xandra!

Rachel lifted the little boy from her broom, giving him a quick, encouraging smile. Gazing at her warily, he muttered something, turned, and ran toward the gatehouse. Rachel leapt on the steeplechaser and headed for the door of the keep. Over her shoulder, she saw the princess and Joy running through the archway of the gatehouse, coming toward her. The princess had the Gift of Moira and could speak any language. She would be able to help the little boy.

Rachel flew into the keep. The other three had left the spiral staircase and were pelting across the great hall. Zooming by them, she banked and came around beside Xandra.

"Quick, get on!" she cried. "Get your oboe ready!"

The two of them rocketed out of the keep with Zoë and a very worried Valerie sprinting behind them.

• • •

"Not sure I can fix this. He broke his back." Xandra lowered her oboe. The last of the green sparkles from her recent song of healing danced over Sigfried's prone form. "I have done what I can to keep him more comfortable and possibly help heal internal bleeding, but I'm only an Upper School student. I don't know how to repair nerve damage or. . . I don't know a heap of stuff."

Sigfried rested on the edge of the pond, still surrounded by water. Valerie had insisted they not move him due to the severity of his injuries. Lucky the Dragon was still wrapped around him, peering tenderly into his face. Sigfried's skin had turned an ashen gray. His chest rose and fell in rapid, shallow breaths. Valerie knelt beside him on the shore, holding his hand. Rachel and Zoë stood together, watching helplessly. In the distance, she saw Nastasia speaking with the child.

"Can't anyone help? Come on, you have magic! You should be able to do something!" Valerie whispered, her face white. She shooed away the goose that kept honking at her.

"There is no physical damage the World of the Wise can't heal," Xandra assured her. "It's magical damage—from spells gone awry— we have trouble with. Because it is different every time. The problem here is that we are miles from help and illegally in a foreign country. By the time we figure out how to get him to a healing hall, it might be too late."

"Don't say that!" Valerie's voice was low, almost menacing. "He can't die. He won't."

Rachel stood by helplessly, reviewing their options over and over in her head, without coming to any new conclusions. She could feel a sense of panic rising inside her, but she clamped down on it, refusing it access to the surface. Her mind kept trying to show her Siggy, as he had been just moments before: grinning maniacally and charging at the bad guys with the stolen poleaxe, followed by the almost comical look on his face, as he went flying over the side of the tower.

How could this have happened?

"Is there anything we should do?" she whispered. "Offer a rooster to Asclepius?"

"Does sacrificing an animal help?" Valerie asked hurriedly, grabbing at the goose. "We Unwary don't do things like that. My family has only ever given money or food to the temples."

Rachel shook her head sadly. "Not that I have heard."

"I could...." Xandra's voice trailed off.

"What? You could... what?" Valerie seized Xandra's arm, her nostrils flaring. "Look, Flops-Over-Dead Chick, three months ago, I didn't even know about magic. Now the world's gone crazy. My dad went missing this spring. It had something to do with that stupid Egg-bozo. Since coming to school I've been geased, raped, and someone tried to kill me! I'm not going to lose my boyfriend, too! Get away!" She kicked at the goose pecking her leg. "I'm sorry we're on your nest or whatever, but chill! Or I will sacrifice you to... whomever!" She turned back. "Xandra! If you can do something, *you do it!*"

"You gotta! You gotta!" Lucky begged frantically. The dragon's jade eyes were as large and weepy as a sick kitten's.

"I'm… not supposed to," murmured Xandra. She turned her hooded head to the right and left, as if checking to confirm that no one was watching. Rachel automatically glanced up toward the tower, but did not see any of the robed figures they had left behind.

"You're not supposed to do something that could help Sigfried?" Rachel could feel her eyes growing wide as saucers. "Why?"

"Okay. Okay." Xandra sounded annoyed yet resigned. "I'll…" she tilted her head upward, as if talking to the gods, spreading her hands. "He's alive, right? You all see that he's alive. Hopefully, this'll… be okay. Painful, but okay."

"Just do it!" cried Valerie.

Xandra knelt and touched Siggy's cheek. Her hood covered her face, but from the set of her shoulders, Rachel guessed she was concentrating hard. She stood. Her body went rigid.

"Can't feel my body below the neck.… Weird. Disturbing even," murmured Xandra. "Still, it's better than if he'd lost a limb or something."

Sigfried sat up. He looked fine. The color had come back into his face.

"Hey," he gave them all a blinding smile, "what happened?"

"Sigfried!" Valerie launched herself at him.

"Boss!" Lucky extended like furry elastic, wrapping around his master even more times.

Xandra was trying to look down at Sigfried, too, but she was doing it without moving anything except her head, which made it difficult. Also, her face was rapidly turning an ashen gray, and her chest was starting to rise and fall rapidly.

Rachel stepped forward. "Xandra, are you okay?"

"Hey," beneath the hem of her hood, the other young woman wet her lips, "wanna know why they call me Flops-Over-Dead Chick?"

"Sure," Zoë was standing by with her hands in her pockets, "I'll bite. Why?"

"Here goes," sighed Xandra.

Her body sagged. She flopped over bonelessly, her head snapping backwards. Her hood fell back from her face. She was a pretty girl with Levantine features, an olive complexion—which was currently grayish—shaggy chestnut hair, and lavender eyes, eyes that currently stared vacantly at the sky.

"I think… she's dead." Zoë took a step backward.

Valerie ran around to Xandra and put two fingers against her wrist. "Quick, Rachel, hold a mirror over her mouth. See if she's breathing."

"How?" Rachel pulled out her mirror and held it over Xandra's face.

"If she's breathing, the heat in her breath will mist up the glass," Valerie instructed. "Yet another advantage of having a police detective for a father. You learn useful stuff like this."

Rachel peeked at the mirror, which remained clear. "Not breathing."

"No pulse," Valerie said. "Okay, clear her airways, and we'll start CPR."

Siggy frowned. "Wait. What happened to her? She was fine a moment ago. Hey… she's not burned by acid. She's a hottie! Er… sorry, Goldilocks!"

"She took your wounds, I think. Then she flopped over dead." Rachel's brow narrowed. She cried hopefully, "Wait! If that's what her nickname's based on, doesn't that imply she's done this before? That she's going to get better?"

"Maybe, but we still need to start CPR!" Valerie insisted. "Just in case. I'll do the chest. You do the mouth."

"Woohoo! This I've gotta see," grinned Siggy, staring eagerly at the young women.

"CPR?" Rachel frowned. "What's that?"

"Griffin, you're hopeless. I'll do it." Zoë pushed Rachel to one side and knelt by Xandra's head. She stuck her fingers into the other girl's mouth and made sure her tongue was lying flat. Then, she leaned over the prone young woman.

With a loud gasp, Xandra sucked in air. She sat up and nearly bumped heads with Zoë, who jumped backwards shouting, "Whoa!"

"Ouch. Ouch. Lake of flame. Hate that! Ouch!" Xandra's whole body shuddered. She yanked her hood back over her face. "Was I dreaming? Or did someone try to kiss me?"

"Not kissing. CPR," Valerie said. "Um. What just happened?"

"CPR?" Xandra echoed, holding her head and rocking slightly. "What's that?"

"Um... an Unwary medical thingy."

Zoë murmured, "She can quote *Princess Bride*, but she doesn't know what CPR is. Boy, sometimes our World of the Wise ain't so wise after all."

Caw. Caw.

A giant black Raven as big as an eagle with blood red eyes swooped at Xandra. She screamed and threw up her arms to shield her face.

"I'm sorry! I'm sorry!" she shouted.

It cawed one last time and vanished.

Rachel immediately remembered back a quarter-second, until she could see the Raven flying away in her memory. The illusion that hid the black bird from her senses popped. Rachel could now see the real Raven, as it flew away. It turned its head and looked at her.

Time froze.

Her friends stopped moving. Siggy's arm was frozen mid-gesture. Lucky stood motionless, a statue of a dragon. Even the goose was frozen, mid-peck on Valerie's leg. Only the Rachel and the Raven moved.

It flew back and circled Rachel's head. This was the first time she had seen him since she had offered him her life in order to save the world, and he had given it back to her. Gratitude flooded her heart merely at the sight of him. She longed to find some way to be of service to him, to repay him for his extraordinary gift and trust in her, but she could think of nothing.

The Raven cawed, "She breached my walls, in direct defiance of my instructions."

"But she saved Sigfried!" cried Rachel.

"Sigfried Smith is important." The Raven's rough caw seemed kinder, yet sad. "And yet, now I cannot block what comes, Rachel Griffin. I go to repair the hole in my Wall."

Time restarted. This time the Raven was truly gone, even thinking back did not reveal his presence. Her friends were moving again. Valerie cried out in frustration and kicked at the goose.

"Why won't this thing leave me alone?" she cried. "Let's move. We must be on its nest."

"I can take care of it for you!" Siggy grinned hugely and brandished his fulgurator's wand, a length of oak and gold with a ruby tip. "Sigfried the Dragonslayer to the rescue! Too bad I don't have any fireballs." He paused. "Lucky?"

"I'm on it." The dragon darted forward.

Xandra's head snapped back. A loud voice boomed from her mouth. "Lucky the Dragon! Do not slay Kenneth Hunt!"

Lucky paused, staring googly-eyed at Xandra. Then he did a dragon shrugy thing with his whole body and turned back toward the honking bird, opening his mouth.

"Wait!" Rachel dived between Lucky and the goose. She threw her arms around the goose, catching it to her. Only this required that she lunge out at a rather severe angle. Nor could she windmill her arms to keep her balance.

The two of them crashed into the pond. Frigid water splashed into her face. Her chest seized up from the cold. The smell of pond scum mixed with blood filled her nostrils.

A burst of red and orange dragon flame shot right over her shoulder, before Lucky caught himself. Rachel could feel the extreme heat. The acrid odor of dragon fire scorched the air.

"Geesh, Boss! I nearly roasted the short brainy one!" Lucky darted forward and stuck his head in Rachel's face. "You should be more careful!"

Rachel sat up, dripping, still holding on tightly to the struggling goose. The cold wind blew through her wet garments, causing her teeth to chatter. "Didn't you h-hear the Voice? This is Valerie's d-dad!"

"Wha...?" Siggy blinked. Lucky blinked, simultaneously.

Valerie stared at the goose. "Are... you sure?"

"Isn't Kenneth Hunt your dad?" asked Rachel.

"Yes. Yes it is." She grabbed the goose away from Rachel, bringing her face close to its frenzied beak. "Dad! Can you hear me?

Dad!"

"They aren't intelligent in animal form," said Zoë.

"Though he does seem to recognize you," Rachel felt a slight pang of envy. Gaius had not recognized her when he was a sheep. Then, she scolded herself. Gaius had just met her. This was Valerie's *father*.

Rachel sat in the cold pond, dripping. Now that the emergency was over, her limbs were shaking. The stress of recent events combined with her extreme fatigue made her lightheaded. She caught herself wondering if she could lie down in the water and sleep. Shaking her head in hopes that it would rouse her, she forced herself up onto her trembling legs.

The princess came across the lawns toward them, a vision of loveliness with her long curls floating around her like a golden cloud. She was followed by a panting Joy. Nastasia glanced from one to another, her gaze taking in Rachel's dripping robes, as Rachel absentmindedly brushed pond weeds from her sleeve.

She *squelched* when she walked. Everything dripped.

"*Silu varenga. Taflu.*" She tried to copy the cantrip Gaius had used to remove the orange juice from her garments. Nothing happened. She sighed, shivering.

With a slight smile, Xandra performed the same cantrip. Water gathered from Rachel's robes and formed into a large ball in mid-air. With a gesture, Xandra sent it splashing back into the pond. The robes were still damp in spots—not toasty dry, like when her mother cast this cantrip—but she felt much more comfortable. She threw Xandra a grateful smile.

"Everyone is well, then?" asked the princess.

"I found my dad! My dad!" Valerie held up the goose. Tears ran down her cheeks.

"Indeed?" The princess blinked in surprise. "That is... unexpected." She eyed the bird warily. "What makes you believe this is your father?"

"Xandra's voice said so," Rachel said quickly.

"Perhaps, that is why Miss Black was sent to accompany us?" asked Nastasia.

"Will he be all right?" asked Sigfried, peering suspiciously at the goose.

"No worries. Everyone's relatives get turned into animals now and then," smirked Zoë. "Well, at least in my family."

Rachel looked at Sigfried. He was so vibrant, so alive. It was difficult to believe he had been otherwise, though she only had to rewind her memory a little while to recall how ashen and ill he had been.

Suddenly, adventure did not seem so appealing.

She wanted to go home.

"Uh, oh!" muttered Lucky, looking over his shoulder. "That doesn't look good!"

They all turned. In the spot where Xandra had been standing when she flopped over, a dark cloud coalesced.

CHAPTER SIX:

FEASTING UPON

THE FLESH OF INNOCENTS

THE GATHERING DARKNESS SWIRLED AND GREW THICKER. IT COAlesced into a ten-foot tall bull with huge horns and massive wings of smoke and flame. The fiendish creature had a human face. Its eyes burned like live coals.

The fiend moved its head from left to right. When its gaze fell over the young sorcerers, it gestured impatiently. An invisible force lifted Rachel and her friends and threw them.

"*Varenga*, Vroomie!" Rachel shouted, as she careened through the air. She reached out toward the broom, where it lay by the side of the duck pond. If she could catch it before she struck the ground, she could avoid more bruising.

The broom rose obediently and shot through the air toward her.

It did not reach her in time.

The ground rose rapidly and slapped her, knocking the air from her lungs. Only then did her broom arrive. Breathless, she grabbed at it and missed. The front of the polished haft thumped her in the forehead.

Rachel lay on her back, unable to breathe, the scope of the world reduced to the throbbing pain in her head. She blinked several times, fighting tears. Around her, the others stirred. Out of the corner of her eye, she saw Sigfried and Nastasia sit up, unharmed. Xandra and Joy were both moaning, and Zoë had grabbed her shoulder and was rocking back and forth. Valerie must have landed painfully, because Rachel could hear her whimpering.

Yet, somehow, she had kept her hold on the goose.

The fiend looked upward. It gestured with its horns. From the gaping hole in the tower, five figures in purple robes emerged. They floated though the air, coming to land on the ground before him. Three of them moved freely. Two were still frozen. Despite the throbbing in her head, Rachel could not help smiling.

The fiend snorted fire. The two paralyzed men began to move. Rachel sighed.

Caw!

The harsh cry of a raven sounded nearby. Or perhaps it was the Raven, for a cut appeared across the fiend's shoulder. Black ichor flowed from the wound. It bellowed. Rachel and the others grabbed their ears in pain. Snorting, the fiend pawed the ground with one foot. The earth shook. Sniffing the robed figures, it indicated one of them with its long horns. *"You! Come forward. I must clothe myself in living flesh, else my brother will evict me from his world."*

The man stepped forward nervously. The bull dissolved into darkness, which swarmed through the air and down the man's throat. The man in purple gasped and gargled, his eyes bulging. Then he straightened, looking suddenly larger. His eye sockets held burning coals.

"Great Moloch!" The tallest man knelt before his possessed comrade. "We thank you for answering our call. Our master, Azrael, has been captured. We ask that you come to our aid and free him. Or, if it should please you, help us to destroy this world!"

"Destroy the world?" The fiend regarded him with his burning eyes. *"It does no good for my kind to destroy a world. Calamities are but breeding grounds for martyrs. Opportunities for victims to turn to the Enemy in their last hour."*

"B-but...." The man faltered. "Are you not one of the demons who serv...," he cleared his throat quickly, "... who lead Veltdammerung?"

"I am not Moloch. He sleeps. I am his servant Morax. My lord hungers after the destruction of worlds—but those dwelling within must be the engines of their own downfall." Morax lifted the head of the man he now wore like a coat, scenting the air with breathy sniffs. *"Too much innocence and hope still clings to this place. But soon... soon, with our help, it will be ready for harvesting."* He looked left

and right. "*Where is the sacrifice prepared for my coming? The tender morsel?*"

"Lord Morax, we furnished the sacrifice as was due, but...," the tall man's voice shook, "these meddlesome children stole it from us. Eat them instead!"

Valerie's voice also trembled, but that did not keep her from quoting under her breath: "If it wasn't for those meddling kids and their dragon...."

Morax glanced toward the Roanoke students who lay sprawled across the ground. He dismissed them with scowl. "*They are too old. Too impure.*"

"We are not impure!" the princess murmured indignantly.

Xandra, her hood askew, so that it revealed one lavender eye, leaned over and lay a hand on Nastasia's shoulder, whispering, "Princess, this is one you just might want to let go."

"Come on, Lucky!" Siggy rolled onto the balls of his feet, crouching with his trumpet in hand. "I think we can take him."

"No!" Valerie rammed into him, bowling him over and falling on top of him, miraculously still holding tight to the goose. "Are you crazy! He's letting us live. Let's go!"

Siggy lay on the ground, his expression fraught with conflict, as if torn between his desire to attack the fiend and the assault on his senses from the sheer cuteness and feminine warmth of his girlfriend, who lay on top of him.

"Ub! Glab!" he cried, waving his arms and legs.

The goose honked raucously.

Rachel regarded the possessed man intently. She replayed the portion of her memory of when the Bull stood outside his fleshly vessel. *This was not the one.* This fiend was not the *thing* that had started to appear in the tower chamber. That *thing* must have been the master, Moloch. Rachel shivered at the memory.

"*I thirst. Bring me the blood of innocents to drink,*" called Morax. "*I hunger, bring me the flesh of suckling babes.*"

"Eew," murmured Zoë.

"Ditto," Xandra muttered. Rising to her feet, she pulled her hood down over her eyes. "What is that thing?"

"A demon," Rachel whispered back. "A creature of malice that desires to do as much harm as possible."

Xandra tugged her hood lower over her nose.

"Yes. Lord," cried the tall man in purple. "Of course, your wickedness. Immediately."

I go now to my place of power. There to prepare all that is necessary to wake my lord. We shall call him upon his name day. He shall rise again and wrap all the world in his ruthlessness. Men shall slay their wives for favors. Women shall sell their children for trinkets. Thus the whole world shall rush willingly to its destruction.

"Of course, Great One."

"Call me when my feast is prepared." The fiend gestured toward Rachel and her friends, without even bothering to glance their way. *"And kill them."*

The fiend started to fade. As an afterthought, before it vanished, it waved its other hand toward the nearly eight-hundred-year-old keep.

Grrrrrrrcckkkrruuuukkkk!

The keep imploded. Rocks tumbled. With a cacophony of grinding basalt, the entire structure collapsed inward. The earth shook. Dust rose in a huge cloud.

Joy screamed.

Rachel and her friends fled from the falling rocks. They ran until they were in the midst of a grove of fig trees, some two hundred feet away from the pond. Behind them, stray pieces of the tumbling tower slammed into the ground. The purple-clad men followed more slowly—ugly, eager expressions on their faces. The falling chunks of rock did not hit them.

The tallest one drew out the fish-headed rod. The other three remaining men held up their *Kalesei Astari* and began to chant. The quartz crystals glowed with an eerie blue light.

"Quick! We must retreat!" cried the princess. She glanced at the tumbling keep, the wide garden, and the high basalt wall encircling them. "Perhaps all but one of us should climb into my purse, and the last person could take Rachel's broom and fly us over the wall to safety!"

"Escape!" Siggy cried in outrage. "Let's attack!"

"If we leave," Rachel spoke urgently, "they're going feed a *baby* to that... thing! It'll take time for their fetches to manifest. We must stop them now... before the fetches come!"

"Attack how, Mr. Smith, Miss Griffin?" Nastasia asked severely. "With the three spells we have learned in the month since school started?"

"Yes! Exactly! And with our knives or fists or sticks. Bite through their kneecaps, if we can't do anything else!" cried Siggy, gnashing his teeth to show his willingness. "Besides, we have Lucky. He can light their heads on fire and then eat them from the feet upward, while they're burning alive, screaming. That'll teach them to kill babies! What an outrageously ridiculous idea—even for evil blokes!" He paused. "Oh, wait. You all are girls."

Siggy turned to Lucky. "Boys are yellow-bellied cowards when they turn tail and flee. Does that rule apply to girls?" Lucky shrugged. Sigfried turned back to the others. "On second thought, the princess is right. You girls should retreat."

"I'm not running anywhere." Zoë scrounged around in her backpack and drew out her greenstone Maori war bat. "I'm ready! Let's jump 'em!"

"Too late," murmured Rachel. "The fetches are here."

Creatures manifested before the robed men: a large black horse with glowing red eyes, a two-headed wyvern-like beast about five feet in length with fins for feet, and a dog made out of smoke and shadows. All three beasts turned and glared at the children. The horse pawed the ground. The dog growled. The two-headed dragon-thing spat a sharp glittering gemstone, which flew quite a distance to clatter at Joy's feet. It looked like a ruby.

Siggy picked the gem up eagerly. It burst into flame on his palm. Shouting, he dropped it into a flower bed, where it smoldered among the dry stalks of last summer's irises.

The earth beneath their feet shook again; more of the keep collapsed. The northeast tower, on the far side, crashed to the ground.

"Kill the Romani children," the shortest of the purple-clad men ordered the beasts.

"Master, beware!" The smoky dog spoke in a voice that barked and snapped. "They are more than they seem!"

"What did that guy just say we were?" Siggy cleaned out his ear with a finger and then leaned forward, his hand cupped around his ear as if to listen better.

"Gypsies," replied Rachel. Her eyes were fixed on the fetches. Her mind whirled, searching for options.

"Why do they think that?" Joy glanced from the men to the princess's blond ringlets.

"Because Siggy and I used enchantment against them," Rachel murmured back. "In this part of the world, those kinds of spells are secrets known only to Gypsies or Bavarians. Not a lot of Roanokeans here."

She eyed the men carefully. If the Veltdammerung followers understood that they were not facing mere enchanters would they be cowed? Might they listen to reason? Or even flee?

Between the students and the purple-robed men, the gardens were strewn with debris from the fallen keep. Rachel broke away from the others and ran toward the men. About fifty feet from them, she leapt onto a large chunk of masonry. The purple-robed figures watched her, curiosity warring with their sneers of disdain.

"Listen to your fetch!" Rachel's voice rang out. "We are not merely enchanters! We are students from Roanoke Academy for the Sorcerous Arts!"

"Roanokeans!" All four men took a step back.

Rachel crossed her arms and glared at them.

"We should flee," the master of the kelpie urged.

"We cannot," said the tallest. "Lord Morax has commanded us to kill them."

"But… they are Roanokeans," cried the shortest one, the master of the barghest. "They know spells we have never heard of."

"They are but children," the tallest one scoffed. "How much can they know?"

"A great deal," Rachel shouted fiercely. Her eyes blazed, her face shining with righteous fury. "Information loves us. It comes and finds us."

Both the robed men and her friends gazed at her oddly. Blushing, she hurried on. "Before you kill us… answer a question: Why? Why destroy the world? I mean, you live here, too!"

"Yeah," Sigfried chimed in, coming closer. "Where will you keep all your stuff?"

"This world has become poisoned and corrupt," said the tallest one. "It is polluted by the filth that lives here. Filth that abuses children; mistreats minorities; destroys the resources of the earth; cares only for selfish pleasures. This filth must be eradicated."

"So you are going to sacrifice an infant to keep people from abusing children?" Rachel rubbed her temples, his craziness threatened to make her head ache. "What about the innocents... the people they are abusing? Won't they die, too?"

"They are better off dead than living in such squalor and depredation," said the tall one. "We shall be doing them a favor."

He pointed the fish-headed rod at Sigfried, whom, after the fight in the tower, he perhaps deemed most dangerous. Siggy grabbed his throat, choking. This did not stop the orphan boy from using his other hand to point his wand at his attacker. Apparently, he had a spell left after all. A wintry blast of silvery sparkles swept up the tall man and threw him head over heels.

As the tall man tumbled, the fish-headed rod went flying. The master of the kelpie scuttled after it. Rachel leapt onto her broom, whistling as she shot forward. Blue sparkles danced through the air toward the scuttling man. The spell caught him, half leaning over, as he reached for the rod. It froze him there. Unable to steady himself, he toppled to the ground.

Rachel pointed at the rod. "*Tiathelu!*"

The fish-headed rod rose into the air. The two purple-robed men still standing leapt after it, but it soared up, over their heads, and into Rachel's hand.

Rachel grinned and waved. "Sure you want to fight Roanoke-ans?"

The owner of the barghest, the shortest man, threw off his robes. Underneath he wore a charm bracelet and intricate armor, each plate enameled with arcane symbols and leering faces. Unhooking a metal fan from his waist, he opened it, forming a circular buckler. A shimmer went out from the device, like the magical shield formed by the *bey-athe* cantrip.

"An alchemist," Xandra shouted. "Take him out first!"

Zoë ran forward, brandishing her *patu* and shouting obscenities.

The alchemist shook his bracelet. A charm dangling from his wrist glowed orange. Zoë shouted and grabbed her eyes. Her greenstone war club tumbled to the grass.

The three beasts stalked forward. The dog-thing growled and bared smoky fangs. The two-headed lizard spat an emerald. The horse snorted a foul-smelling mist from its nostrils.

"Lucky, get them!" gasped Sigfried, still rubbing his throat.

Leaping forward with great eagerness, Lucky engaged the two-headed serpent-creature. The two heads spat more gems. Lucky returned dragon fire, charring one head. The smell of roasted reptile rose into the air. The girls scrunched up their noses, but Siggy breathed in deeply.

"Keep some of that, Lucky!" he shouted, pointing his wand again. "We can eat it later."

"Right on, boss!"

The serpentine enemy darted forward, biting Lucky with its second head. Lucky bit it back. The two of them tumbled across the gardens like a giant snaky hoop, splashing through the pond and sending ducks quacking.

"What are those things?" cried Valerie, clinging to the honking goose. With her arms full, she could not perform cantrips. Having been a freshman for one month, she did not yet know any other magic. "Those beasts?"

Xandra had taken out a small device that looked like a pepper shaker. With it, she sprinkled black powder on the ground in a line in front of the other students. "A kelpie, a barghest, and... I don't know the other one."

As she flew back to the others, Rachel mentally riffled through reference books she had read in the past. She recalled a picture of a similar two-headed dragon creature with fins in Daring Northwest's, *Dragons, Drakes, and Other Fire-Breathing Foes.*

"It's a *balaur*," she called down to Valerie. "Local to the mountains of Eastern Europe." She gestured at the peaks rising to the north. "They are poisonous. Their saliva forms gems. They are not related to the dinosaur of the same name."

"Thanks," Valerie called back dubiously. "That tells me… nothing."

Rachel circled above the others, whistling again. Siggy's wand had finally run out of charges. He went back to blowing his trumpet. As their respective spells swept forward, the alchemist lifted his round shield. The blue sparkles of her spell and Siggy's silvery ones swerved from their targets and were sucked toward his alchemical buckler. They splashed harmlessly against it.

Below, the other girls had leapt into action, except for Zoë, who was still clutching her eyes and occasionally rubbing her injured shoulder. The princess had taken out her violin and played a wind blast. Silver sparkles swirled against the glistening coat of the black horse, but the wind was not strong enough to stop the creature. Frowning in annoyance, Nastasia ran her bow across her strings again.

Joy raised her hands and shouted. She was one of the best sorcerers among the freshman. She had not brought an instrument; however, and she knew only the few cantrips they had learned in class. Whatever she had attempted accomplished nothing. She tried a second time.

Xandra continued sprinkling the warding powder, tracing a circle around her fellow students. The smoky dog charged to the edge of her ward and then drew back snarling. The black horse slowed its forward trot.

"That's an Enochian ward!" cried the alchemist in dismay. "The power of my talismans will not reach them now!"

As Lucky fought the now-one-headed reptile, Rachel hefted the fish-headed rod. Some talismans needed a special key. Others could be used by anyone. Should she try it? It was one thing to paralyze a man. It was another thing to smother him to death, which was the purpose of this device. True, these men were trying to kill them—and to feed an innocent babe to a demon. But did that mean that Rachel should lower herself to their level?

Frowning, she slipped the rod into the pocket of her robe.

The alchemist shook his charm bracelet. With his other hand, he drew out of a bag at his hip an amulet carved with the head of a dog. He pointed it at the princess. The charm and the hound-head amulet glowed orange. Whatever he had hoped to accomplish must have been stopped by Xandra's ward, however, for nothing occurred.

Siggy blew his trumpet again. Again the sparkles swerved toward the alchemist's shield. He scowled. The master of the *balaur* picked up a sharp chunk of basalt and chucked it at Xandra's head, possibly hoping to keep her from finishing her ward.

"*Tiathelu!*" Rachel shouted again, gesturing. Her cantrip caught the rock and sent it flying off into the duck pond. It landed with a *plop* and a splash.

"Cantrips, Rupert!" cried the man who had thrown the rock. "They have enchanters, an Enochian, and a canticler, too! We cannot beat them! We should flee!"

Rachel glanced around to see who responded to the name Rupert. It was the tallest man, who was groaning and holding his head as he rolled to his feet. Glancing at his height and build, she referenced a thousand-thousand news glass images—pictures and names flashing through her memory.

"Rupert Lawson," she shouted, pointing, "head of security for Smiths, Smythe, and Smullyan, Fine Amulets and Talismans Shoppe on Fifth Avenue? You should be ashamed of yourself, Mr. Lawson!"

"She knows who you are," the alchemist shouted in alarm.

The tall man scowled and grabbed his own *Kalesei Astari*, which began to glow. "Kill her! Kill them all!"

Xandra completed her ward. The circle closed. Zoë stopped grabbing her eyes.

"That was disturbing. Everything had gone black." Zoë retrieved her fallen war club. "Okay, now they're in for it!"

Zoë stalked forward. Joy lifted a rock with the *ti* cantrip, which was a much weaker version of *tiathelu*. She bounced it off the side of one man's head. He cried out and grabbed his ear, his hand coming away with blood on it.

The kelpie broke into a canter, bearing down on the students. Foul-smelling mist steamed from its nostrils. Unlike the barghest, it did not stop at Xandra's ward but barreled over it, unhindered. Joy, Valerie, and Nastasia scrambled backward, skirting behind the fig trees. Zoë leapt forward swinging her *patu*. The Maori war club connected with the fey horse. There came a loud *pop*. The monstrous face carved into the green stone of the patu let out a piercing screech.

The girls, other than Zoë, all grabbed their ears. The horse reared up, neighing in pain and dismay. Across the lawn, the robed cultists also grabbed their ears. One yowled in pain.

A second blast of silver sparkles from the princess's violin struck the kelpie. Again, the black horse was unmoved, but the wind caught Zoë, who lost her footing. Her feet flew into the air, and she slid underneath the bulk of the steed's body. One of the heavy hooves trod on her, as the kelpie continued forward.

Zoë screamed.

Rachel, who remembered vividly what it felt like to have been stepped on by a sheep, winced in sympathy.

The goose began honking madly. Valerie knelt down behind Sigfried, using his body as a shield. She wrapped herself around the bird to protect it.

"No, Dad! Don't do that! It's okay!" She glared up at Xandra. "I am so going to kill you, if this turns out to just be a goose."

The alchemist shook his arm again. A glowing spear of golden light flew at Joy. Lucky, still crunching the remains of the *balaur*, bathed the spear in dragon-fire. It popped with a weird crackling noise Rachel had never heard before.

The paralyzed man remained prone. The master of the *balaur* wept over the remains of his fallen fetch. The alchemist examined his charms. He also called to his barghest, urging it forward, but the smoky dog could not cross Xandra's wards. It paced back and forth along the line of black powder, barking and growling. Rupert Lawson crowed in triumph as a fierce, evil looking creature with a man's head, a lion's body and a huge stinger tail appeared before him. The manticore immediately leapt forward, running directly at the girls.

"Back off, Ugly!" shouted Lucky, descending upon it with a burst of dragon fire. The manticore made a high-pitched sound of extreme pain, its stinger tail flailing wildly.

"*Argos!*" shouted Joy.

A Glepnir bond shimmered in mid-air, encircling the kelpie, but the glowing golden band constricted the black beast's body rather than its legs, accomplishing little. More mist poured from its nostrils, causing Joy, Sigfried, Xandra, Nastasia, Valerie and the goose to cough.

Rachel looked down from her broom in concern. She whistled. Silver sparkles came from her mouth, but the burst of breeze she summoned did little against the miasma. Another burst of silver sparks from the princess's violin; however, and a brisk breeze cleared away the foul fog. Behind the horse, Zoë climbed slowly to her feet, holding her stomach.

Rachel turned back to their attackers. She whistled, but her sparkles swerved to strike the alchemist's shield. This happened three times in a row.

"Siggy! We must stop the man with the shield!" she cried. "It's diverting our enchantments!"

"I'm on it!" Sigfried shouted.

Leaving the protection of Xandra's circle, he charged at the alchemist. In his hand was the Bowie knife that had been a gift from his girlfriend. Rachel followed him, diving. The alchemist's armor protected him from the boy's blow. The knife skidded sideways on the leering enameled faces, but the man was so distracted by Siggy's attack that he did not notice Rachel. Flying up beside them, she grabbed the enchanted fan that was his shield talisman and yanked it from his hand.

"Take that!" Sigfried shouted, punching the man in the face. Blood spurted from the alchemist's nose.

The shield stung her hand. Rachel yelped and dropped it.

Unfortunately, Sigfried's departure from the circle had scuffed Xandra's ward. The barghest leapt through the opening. Landing on Valerie and the goose, it bit Valerie's shoulder. She screamed.

Sigfried thrust the alchemist away and pelted back across the distance to his girlfriend. Throwing his weight against the insubstantial dog did nothing, but the more of Valerie's blood the creature lapped, the more substantial it became. Sigfried's knife began to leave long rents in its smoky substance.

Lucky landed on the barghest and breathed. A huge gout of fire barely missed Valerie and her goose-father. The shadow dog let out an ear-piercing shriek and ran, its back flaming and smoking.

Xandra blew five notes on her oboe. The sparkles were blue, like the paralysis spell, but they smelled of grapes. Rachel, who was trying to figure out how to pick up the shield without its defenses going off, recognized those notes. She had heard her parents play them while facing down a giant who had left his chair on the Dartmoor.

It was the *Spell of Bedazzlement*.

With the alchemist's shield no longer protecting them, the sparkles struck Rupert Lawson, as he was pulling out a second *Kalesei Astari*. He dropped the large red quartz and began walking in circles, muttering to himself.

"*Dreaming!*" Zoë shouted. "Whatever just hit that joker, he's dreaming! Quick, everyone! Grab my hand! Let's get out of here."

CHAPTER SEVEN:

THE VULTURES, THE WOLF, AND

MRS. MARCH

THE SEVEN OF THEM GRABBED ONE ANOTHER'S HANDS AND RAN. Lucky breathed fire on a second golden spear before wrapping around Sigfried. Zoë took three running steps forward. The others followed, cheering. Mist surrounded them. As it parted, their cheers died away.

Around them spread a thick forest of twisted evergreens. Ahead rose the largest tree Rachel had ever seen. She had thought the Roanoke Tree, where her friend the Elf lived, was enormous. That was nothing compared to this tree. Its trunk was so thick that it looked like a massive wall of rough bark. It went on, to the left and to the right, as far as the eye could see. But not up. After a few hundred feet, it ended in a jagged broken point that jutted toward the gray sky like the tip of a skyscraper. The rest of the tree had fallen and lay across the landscape, a rounded mountain range stretching beyond the horizon.

Beside the broken tree lay the corpse of an enormous deer—truly enormous, as massive as Roanoke Island. Crows and vultures, larger than horses, picked at its flesh. Beside the deer growled an equally large white-blue wolf. Next to this first beast lay the corpse of a black wolf. The throat of the second wolf had been torn out by what looked suspiciously like wolf-teeth.

In the way of dreams, Rachel understood that the white wolf had killed the black one, but that it regretted this. A sense of inevitability clung to the scene, as if fate had decreed these events, and they could not have been otherwise.

There was no odor of decay. The forest smelled of lilacs, and soft *shakuhachi* music played in the background. Both were entirely incongruous with the sights around them.

Rachel shivered.

Zoë limped slowly, one hand on her stomach. She winced as she rotated her injured shoulder. Behind her came the princess and Joy, both coughing. Xandra, who followed after Joy, held the arm of Valerie, who looked pale but resolved, the goose still clutched tightly in her arms. Blood dripped down her upper back, where the barghest had ripped her pajamas away and bitten her. Lucky was wrapped around both her and Sigfried. Rachel was at the back of the line, one hand holding Siggy's, the other clutching her broom.

"So, the *Spell of Bedazzlement* makes people dream?" murmured Xandra. "That's very useful to know, if you are planning to travel by dreamway."

"Very!" agreed Rachel.

She shivered, her clothing still damp.

Joy blinked twice. Her eyelids drooped, and her face was pale. "Um. Let's go home."

"Not that easy." Zoë held up her free hand in "halt" gesture. "I can only go to places people are actively dreaming about. No one here is dreaming of America, much less Roanoke. The only dreams I see are either meaningless baby-nap dreams, or they are not very pleasant."

"So... we can't go home unless someone in Transylvania dreams of New York?" Siggy scowled. "We'll be here forever."

"It's not all that bad." Zoë shrugged. "We just need someone to dream of a place closer to home, and then find another dream of a place even closer, et cetera. Until we get back. That's how I usually travel. Of course, I don't normally cross the Atlantic."

"Even easier than that," Rachel stated. "If we can find a dream of a place with a public glass house, we can go back down to the waking world and make our way from one travel glass to another back to school."

"What about you, Princess?" Joy asked. "Can you get us home? The way you were going to bring us to Magical Australia?"

Nastasia shook her head. Her pale locks shimmered, even in the dark forest of dream. "I can only go to the place a person is from. No one here is 'from' Roanoke. Rachel and Mr. Smith are from England. You are from Ohio. Zoë, Xandra, and Valerie are all from other worlds."

"I am?" Xandra murmured in surprise.

"That won't help, then," Zoë murmured. She looked around, taking a step away from the giant trunk. "But we... need to go!"

Atop the corpses, three vultures turned their wrinkled heads and stared at the students. The white wolf the size of an island rose and took a stiff-legged step toward them, growling.

"Okay, that's scary!" Joy swallowed, stepping back as far as she could without letting go of the hands of those beside her. "I think...." She began coughing and could not continue.

"Quick, this way!" Zoë limped quickly toward the only curling curtain of mist.

They went as fast as they could, all moving together. When they reached the eddies of the mist, there was only a single dream diorama. It showed a dark, spooky wood filled with the glint of staring eyes. Something deathly pale moved behind the trees.

"That's a nightmare. We don't want to go there!" Zoë glanced nervously over her shoulder at the carrion birds.

"We don't want to stay here, either," Xandra replied, equally nervously.

"I think we can take 'em, don't you Lucky?" Sigfried announced.

"Of course, Boss," the dragon answered loyally. "How tough can dreams be?"

Zoë asked sarcastically, "You're going to fight them *without letting go* of anyone?"

"Oh." Sigfried looked at his girlfriend and her goose-father and frowned. "Maybe the princess should take us to Magical Australia. I mean that would be better than this, right? How did you get back last time?"

"Valerie," Rachel said suddenly. "Snap your flash! Maybe the dreamer will dream of a sunny place."

"That is a splendid idea," cried Nastasia. After a fit of coughing, she added, "Did not you say that the poor dreamer was suffering a nightmare? We will be doing the person a favor!"

"I can't," Valerie objected. "I'm holding a goose!"

"I can!" Lucky declared. He reached around with his talons and picked up the camera resting on Valerie's hip. After a bit of awkwardness, the camera *clicked*. A brilliant flash of light illuminated the landscape.

The wolf and the vultures drew back. Then the birds let out raucous cries, and the wolf howled. The eerie sound of it made Rachel's blood freeze. The vultures launched into the air swooping forward, and the wolf stepped forward, toward the students. Ahead of them, however, the spooky forest nightmare had changed into a sunny beach.

"Quick!" Zoë cried. "That blue water is the Mediterranean! Maybe it's the Riviera! Come on! And—by all you hold dear—don't anyone let go!"

They ran.

Zoë dashed into the dream of sun and blue sparkling water as quickly as her limp would allow her to move. The others followed. She took three steps. Her silver sandals glowed like moonlight. The broken tree, the two gigantic corpses, the pursuing carrion birds, and the rushing white wolf vanished.

They stood on a grassy hillside, gazing down at islands that sparkled on a blue, blue sea. Nearby, a spring flowed from an opening in the hillside. The rushing waters danced merrily, chiming like music. In the distance stood an amphitheater. Ten women lounged on its marble steps. Nine of them were tall and bronzed and draped in white. One held a comedy mask; another a tragedy mask. A third balanced a bronze globe on her palm. A fourth strummed a golden lyre.

"The Muses," Rachel whispered hoarsely, gawking at the tall, elegant women, all of whom stared back at the Roanoke students with interest.

"Dream wardens. Not real goddesses," drawled Zoë, adding, "Not the Riviera, then. The Aegean. We're in Greece."

"Which one is the Muse of Snark?" quipped Joy, giddy with relief. "All you sarcastic girls should thank her. My sister Faith, too. Faith's the snarky O'Keefe."

"Thank her or curse her," Xandra snarked beneath her hood.

Over by the amphitheater, the tenth woman rose and padded toward them on bare feet. She moved with the grace of a panther. She was shorter than the muses and dressed in a black cat-suit that clung to her like a second skin, glistening over her curves as she moved. Siggy made a high-pitched sound and then studiously turned his head away.

Valerie's face was covered by a light sheen of sweat, but she muttered, "I could use some of that snark inspiration about now."

As the woman drew closer, the princess called out in surprise, "Mrs. March?"

"Wait," Zoë whispered as the woman crossed the hillside toward them, "you mean that's the Grand Inquisitor's wife. *The* Cassandra March?"

Rachel nodded wordlessly. They were right. It was the wife of Rachel's father's boss.

Valerie stopped glaring at Sigfried and gazed at the approaching newcomer with great interest. "Isn't she the only conjured person ever to become real?"

Rachel nodded again.

Joy giggled. "I heard she was a courtesan before her husband married her."

Rachel nodded wordlessly for a third time.

The princess stated stiffly, "Gossip is unbecoming. Mrs. March is a family friend."

The black clad figure moved toward them with cat-like grace. She came to a stop a few feet from where the eight of them stood.

"Hello, Nastasia." Cassandra March's gaze flickered over the others, resting for a moment on the goose. Her voice was so throaty, it almost purred. "Lady Rachel. Miss Black. I don't believe I have met the rest of you, though no one could mistake Sigfried the Dragonslayer and his valiant dragon, Lucky."

Siggy grinned and puffed himself up, looking very pleased. Valerie rolled her eyes.

Cassandra March's eyes, which were very dark and ever so slightly tilted, were filled with laughter. Rachel had always liked her, and she could not help smiling back now, even though her heart was beating quickly. Mrs. March would tell her husband that she had seen them. Her husband, Cain March, the Grand Inquisitor, the head of all law enforcement for the World of the Wise, the man famous for using the *Spell of True Recitation* on anything and everything that moved—the spell to which Rachel was immune.

It was hard enough to hide her immunity from the Agents. She had no illusions that she could hide it from their boss. If the Grand Inquisitor found out, he would find another method of compelling her to tell the truth. To someone such as Rachel, who knew secrets that might destroy the world—secrets she had vowed to tell to only one person—this was a terrifying prospect.

Mrs. March surveyed them with amusement, her eyes resting on the goose. "If I touch one of you, will I become stuck, too?"

Rachel, Nastasia, Xandra, and Joy all laughed.

The others looked puzzled.

"Mrs. March, what brings you here?" asked the princess, struggling not to cough.

"I am dreaming," Mrs. March smiled wryly. "My body's asleep in my house—on our estate outside of Athens. I think the more interesting question is: what brings you here?"

Before anyone else could answer—and perhaps say something that it might be better if Cain March did not hear—Rachel blurted out, "There are four men at Beaumont Castle in Transylvania, Rupert Lawson and three others. They plan to sacrifice a baby to appease a demon named...."

Cassandra March threw up her hands. "Don't say a demon's name aloud!"

"Oh!" Rachel blinked.

Mrs. March knew what a demon was? Rachel had only learned this herself a few weeks ago—from the Raven. The word did not appear in any dictionary or encyclopedia.

What else did Mrs. March know?

"Thank you for telling me," said Mrs. March. "I'll wake up and tell my hus—"

Xandra Black's head snapped backward. Though her lips did not move, a deep yet melodious voice spoke from her mouth.

"*Cassandra Galatine March! We apologize for failing you. We warned the Romanov princess, but she would not heed us.*"

Mrs. March's dark eyes seemed even larger and darker. Her voice became very quiet until it was almost too soft and hoarse to hear. "Warned her... o-of what."

"*Not to touch your son. She has not yet mastered her wayfaring powers. She was drawn into Joshua's past. He followed her back here. He* now knows the way."

"No," whispered Mrs. March. She took an involuntary step backward. "My... daughter?"

"*We can do no more.*" Xandra's head snapped forward again. She gasped and stumbled. Lucky's head shot out and grabbed her robe with his teeth, just as she lost her hold on Valerie.

Rachel bit her own lip painfully. She did not know what it meant, but Mrs. March's soft plea had cut through her heart like a razor. Rachel had been the one who urged Nastasia to disregard Xandra's warning and touched Joshua. Whatever had upset Mrs. March was her fault.

What had she done?

"Nastasia." Cassandra March stared at the princess, her face utterly devoid of color. "That creature that came into your dreams... what did he call himself?"

"The Lightbringer," replied the princess, frowning slightly, as if she was uncertain whether or not she should be upset.

"*No.*" Mrs. March breathed again, her hand pressed against her breast. She made an odd noise, as if the mere act of drawing in breath were painful. "Not now. She's not yet ready!"

"What is the trouble?" the princess asked with concern.

"This... Lightbringer. He once did my daughter a great harm. A terrible harm. Greater than you could possibly imagine." Mrs. March's gaze was distant, as if she were seeing events from long ago.

Rachel recalled Nastasia's description of her vision of Joshua March. The Lightbringer had been torturing the young man upon a field of ice. If that was "merely" what her son had suffered, how much worse must it have been for her daughter?

"H-he did not know we were here," Mrs. March continued. "He thought we were dead. Please, Nastasia, if you can possibly help it—

Do not do anything that might bring my daughter to his attention. I beg you!"

Nastasia nodded grimly, chagrined. "I promise. If it is within my power, I shall not."

"Very good. Thank you." Mrs. March's face suddenly looked entirely calm. She gave them a charming smile.

Rachel also appeared calm. Inside, she reeled with astonishment. In an instant, Mrs. March had changed from tremendously upset to cheerful. But Rachel's eyes had been drawn to the woman's fingers. For just a moment, before her body relaxed, her pinky had gone rigid.

A memory hardly twelve hours old leapt to the forefront of Rachel's thoughts: her sister Sandra, undercover as a member of Veltdammerung, receiving instructions from Mortimer Egg to kill Rachel and her friends. Sandra's face had been utterly calm—and her pinky entirely rigid.

Cassandra March was dissembling. She was not merely hiding her expression, as normal people sometimes did. She was using the exact same technique for hiding her emotions that Rachel and Sandra had learned from their mother. But, as her family's little saying went: *No Griffin Girl can fool a Griffin Girl.*

Mrs. March could not fool her either.

Rachel wet her lips, gazing at the Grand Inquisitor's wife. Mrs. March was beautiful. It was not hard to believe she had been a courtesan before her marriage. She had a perfect golden tan and those exotic, slightly-tilted eyes that had catapulted more than one model or actress to stardom—eyes just like Sandra's. If Mrs. March was an ordinary person, Rachel might wonder if their families were related.

But Cassandra March had been conjured.

What did that say about Rachel's mother's family?

"So, you hang out with the muses?" Valerie's reporter instincts came to the fore, despite her debilitated condition. "That's exciting. How did you come to meet them? Does it help you with speech writing? Who writes Mr. March's speeches?"

"I told you, they're not the real muses," Zoë replied, bored. "They're dream wardens."

"Dream wardens.   Of course," said Cassandra March.   Only with her perfect memory Rachel caught the amusement that flashed across Mrs. March's face before it disappeared behind her mask of calm. "They couldn't be real. No real gods or angels are allowed on this world."

Rachel's lips parted in wonder yet again. She murmured to herself. "Is that why the Raven was arguing with the Comfort Lion my first day of school?"

"*Lion?* What Lion?" Mrs. March's face had gone utterly still. Yet, to Rachel, her dark eyes betrayed a tremendous alertness and something else. *Not fear. Awe? Hope?* It was like looking into the eyes of a drowning person who had suddenly glimpsed a ship under full sail upon the horizon.

"My roommate Kitten's familiar," explained Rachel.

"Oh." Mrs. March deflated, as if the ship in her sights had resolved into clouds. She looked away, muttering, "Can't be the same one."

Rachel wanted to ask her to elaborate, but the princess spoke first.

"Mrs. March, we need to get home." Nastasia coughed. "Might you know if there is a glass hall nearby?"

"Wait, didn't you say you're asleep?" interrupted Zoë. "So, you're a lucid dreamer? Any chance you could dream about New York?"

"You mean like this?" Cassandra March tipped her head back and spread her arms.

Mist rose, and the landscape changed around them. The amphitheater remained in the distance, but now they stood on the docks of Roanoke Island. Before them rose the steps leading to Bannerman's Castle. Through the archway above lay the path that led to Roanoke Academy. To their right, the green and yellow ferry, the *Pollepel II*, was moored at the dock.

Zoë looked around, her grin slowly widening. "This is perfect! We're home! Let's go!"

She limped up the stairs. Mist rose around her silver sandals, which glowed like moonlight. The others followed. As Rachel was last in line, she had a moment to examine her surroundings. Unlike the other dreamscapes, this image of Roanoke was crisp and clear. Rachel glanced rapidly back and forth, gauging the spacing of the poles on the docks, the distance between the stairs, between boulders and trees. She compared the image with her memory.

It was perfect.

It was exactly accurate.

A stick lay next to the stairs that lead to the ruined castle, a short branch with a Y in it. Rachel remembered that branch. It had been next to the stairs, in this exact position, when she arrived on the first day of school. When she and Siggy flew down those stairs the next day, it had still been there. By the time they returned and found Mortimer Egg on the docks, however, it had moved. Perhaps the wake of her broom had shifted it.

Yet, in Cassandra March's dream, the branch lay exactly where it had been on the first day of school—which would have been when Mrs. March last visited Roanoke to drop off her children.

Only a person with perfect recall could reproduce such specific details.

Just before she stepped into the mist, Rachel turned and glanced back at the woman who had eyes like her sister and knew her mother's secret dissembling techniques. Cassandra March stood with her hands on her black-clad hips, watching them go.

Mrs. March winked.

Chapter Eight:

Awkward Homecomings

Stumbling out of the dreamland into the foyer of Dare Hall, they came out in front of the great oak doors that led to the theater. It was eerily disturbing to go from the silence of dreams to the loud clacking of soles striking the black and white marble floor.

"That was great!" crowed Sigfried. "When can we do it again?"

The others stared at him, weary and sore.

"What do I do with my father?" pleaded Valerie, who was looking very pale.

The goose had stopped struggling and was visibly trembling.

"Come on," Xandra sighed and put her hand on Valerie's shoulder. "The proctors will know what to do. I'll explain that the voices that torment me told us where to look for him."

"We better keep her company," Siggy told Lucky, "in case she needs a professional liar."

"Lying will serve no purpose," the princess announced pointedly, as the four of them opened the doors out into the cold night. "I plan to tell my friend Dean Moth everything."

"That'll go well," muttered Zoë.

Zoë and Rachel exchanged glances. Rachel sighed.

"Here, take this and give it to the proctors. Maybe it will help them locate the Veltdammerung cultists." Rachel handed the fish-headed rod to Sigfried and the alchemist's fan, who nodded and stuck them under his arm. He, Valerie, and Xandra departed.

Nastasia, Zoë, Joy and Rachel headed up the sweeping staircase toward the girl's rooms. When they reached the fourth floor, Rachel and Nastasia headed for the room on the right, which they shared their other two, presumably-sleeping roommates. Zoë limped toward the door on the left, supported by the coughing Joy. Neither of them looked well. Rachel and the princess waved goodbye and slipped into their room.

The chamber was dark, except for where the moonlight shone in through a crack in the curtains. Rachel could hear their sleeping roommates breathing and the clatter of Beauregard's nails against the floor as the Tasmanian Tiger rose to greet his mistress. The princess dropped to one knee and stroked her familiar. Mistletoe was nowhere to be seen, but with the special senses that bound sorceress and familiar, Rachel could feel her cat curled up under her bed.

Her cat, she finally admitted, would never be a proper familiar. She had been wrong when she disregarded the advice of her family and insisted on bringing him to school. Because of her bad judgment, she was doing horribly in art class. She had even passed out earlier today. She had attempted to conjure with no familiar to help her and failed. All this because she had not heeded her grandfather, years ago, when he told her that the bold, little black and white kitten that had so charmed her was not of familiar-grade.

Sighing, she pulled off her robe and found her sleepwear and towel. Heading to the bathroom, she showered, washing off the bloody swamp water from the duck pond. Fresh and clean, she slipped into her nightgown and returned to her room, striving not to wake Astrid or Kitten, who were asleep on the other set of bunks. Nastasia had climbed up into the upper bunk. Her cough did not seem as bad as earlier. Still, Rachel wondered if her friends should go to the Infirmary. She made a note to insist on it in the morning, if Joy and Nastasia had not improved.

Mistletoe emerged from his hiding place and rubbed against Rachel's leg, purring. She knelt and rubbed her cheek against his. He might not be able to help her in art class, but he was still a comforting presence.

Picking up the cat, she climbed into bed. She snuggled close to Mistletoe, basking in his warmth and the vibration of his purr. She was so exhausted she felt ill with fatigue, but it felt good to be curled up in her own bed. So much had happened, she could hardly comprehend it all. In the last twelve hours alone, she had been to Beaumont Castle twice! And if she thought back one more day, there was the even more momentous occurrence, involving Sakura and the Raven, which she had been told she could only share with only one person. She knew who she wanted that person to be. First thing in the morning, she would hunt him down and tell him.

"Rachel," the princess whispered urgently from the bunk above Rachel's. "It is very important that you do not tell Mr. Valiant about anything that happened tonight!"

"Wha...." Rachel shot up to a sitting position, disturbing her cat. "Why?"

"We must have no truck with evil. No matter how pretty a face it might show."

Rachel tried to swallow, but it did not quite work. She lay back down. She wanted to please her friend, but she felt she must defend her boyfriend. "Y-you hardly know Gaius! Why do you say such horrid things about him?"

The princess answered seriously. "It is because you insisted on sharing our information with him and Mr. Von Dread that Mrs. Egg is dead."

Agony pieced Rachel. "W-we don't know that! You told the Dean! She told the Agents. Valerie warned us that the Wisecraft might be compromised!"

"The Wisecraft de geased us, using the *Spell of True Recitation*." Nastasia's voice was stern. "Do you think that they did not also carry out similar protective measures on their own people? If there were a spy among them, they would have found it."

"But...."

"A woman is dead," Nastasia said severely. "Do you think the decision of who should live and who should die should rest in the hands of children our age? Let us leave these matters in the hands of the legitimate authorities: the Dean and the Wisecraft."

Rachel's heart fell. The princess was correct. She had no way of knowing who had betrayed Mrs. Egg, and the King of Bavaria did have a very unsavory reputation. The darkness seemed ominous, and the night filled with uncertainty. Mistletoe, who had been such a comforting presence, leapt off the bed and trotted away.

Despite this, Rachel had to admit that she no longer believed Gaius to be the wicked boy the princess made him to be. She was tired of hearing him bad-mouthed.

Screwing up her courage, she blurted out, "I... don't think you're right, Nastasia! I am certain Gaius can be trusted!"

The princess's voice was gentle with regret, as if she hated to hurt Rachel's feelings. "You were also certain that a house cat would make a good familiar."

The princess's breathing soon became regular with sleep, broken by an occasional cough. Rachel, however, lay awake, her body uncomfortably cold where the warmth of the cat had been.

• • •

The next morning, Rachel was awoken from a heavy sleep by someone coughing. Opening one eye, she saw the other bunk was empty. Kitten and Astrid had already departed for breakfast. The hour on the clock was absurdly late. Alarm gripped Rachel. Then, with a rush of relief, she realized it was Saturday morning. She had not slept through class.

The coughing came again. Joy leaned against the door, her eyes red, her nose swollen. She mumbled, "Zoë and I are going to the Infirmary. Do either of you want to come?"

"I will accompany you," said Nastasia, from somewhere above Rachel. "I seem to have acquired a persistent cough."

The princess climbed down from her bunk to greet her. Even when ill, Nastasia looked lovely, wan but ethereal, like a character out of a Victorian novel who was wasting away due to some mysterious ailment. Joy just looked thoroughly miserable.

"Probably from the kelpie." Rachel tried to convince her eyelids to stay open. "They spread disease."

"Why didn't you mention that last night?" Joy's voice squeaked from fear.

Rachel blinked in surprise and sat up. "I... thought everybody knew."

Sitting up turned out to be a mistake. Her body was sore in numerous places. Each stab of pain brought a vivid memory of its origins. The tenderness of her tailbone was from the original fall out of dreamland; the pain in her shoulders was from the wrenching they suffered when she tried to keep hold of Nastasia and Xandra when Joy and Sigfried first pulled them off the silvery Way; that twinge in her hip and the more persistent pain in her back and shoulder were from hitting the ground after the demon threw them. Xandra's oboe-playing, however, had entirely healed the results of her fall out of dreamland onto the gravel walk. When she rubbed her face, she felt no pain in her cheek and lip.

"In the future, don't assume! If we died because of—" Joy's voice cut off. She was gazing at Rachel. She covered her mouth, trying not to laugh, but giggles escaped from her the side of her mouth.

"What?" Rachel looked around, stifling a groan from the pain caused by the motion.

"Er... maybe you should look in the mirror."

Rachel rose gingerly and crossed to look in her mirror. A large black and blue spot had formed in the middle of her forehead, where her broom had struck her.

"You look like a bruise-icorn!" Joy guffawed, bending over and slapping her thigh.

Rachel sighed.

• • •

As the other three left for the Infirmary, Rachel leaned against the tall, arched window and stared out at the ferns and the paper birches with their curling, parchment-like bark, that grew behind Dare Hall. She had been wrong, in the castle, when she had thought that capturing Azrael would bring everything to a close. Azrael was no longer a threat, true, but this new demon had come to take his place, and he was trying to call up something worse—something much worse. *It must be stopped at all costs!* She did not know why she was so certain. She just *knew* that Moloch was worse than this Morax, worse, even, she suspected, than Azrael—who had killed whole families.

Currently, this new fiend was far away, in Europe, but she felt a strange certainty that she and her friends would encounter it again.

It was not over.

Nothing was over.

It was as if she were watching the ship of her previous life—the life where she had been an obedient, bookish girl—as it burned, smoke billowing from the slowly sinking craft. She wanted to rush to it, to rescue it, to extinguished the flames and prop the tiny foundering vessel upright, but she could not. Too much had happened.

She had learned too many secrets and had seen too many terrible sights. She had made too many decisions that others—parents, tutors, Agents—should, by right, have made. Staring out the window —the bruised spot on her forehead pressed against the soothing coolness of the glass—Rachel came face to face with the truth.

She was never again going to be an ordinary girl.

That ship had sunk.

Finally, she turned away, took a new mortar board cap from her trunk (she had lost her old one when trying to stop the plane) and pulled it low over her forehead. Then, she headed over to the boys side to see how Sigfried had fared. She wondered as she walked whether he might need to visit the nurse himself and how matters had gone with Valerie's goose-parent.

The door to his room was open. As she came down the hall, however, Sigfried came from the other direction wiping his wet hair with his towel.

"Hallo, Freaky Dwarf Genius!" He gestured toward the open door. "I need to get Lucky and my books. Then, I'm off to the infirmary to see Goldilocks. Wanna come?"

"I jolly well do." Rachel stuck her head in the door.

Inside the room, the window was open, but the crisp autumn breeze only partially-obscured the odor of dirty socks and half-spoiled food. Rachel made a mental note to pour a pitcher of milk into the bowl that stood in the hallway next to the door, so the cleaning *bwbach* would visit this room. She suspected Sigfried and his roommate Ian had neglected to do this for some time.

To the right, Lucky had wrapped his elastic body around the entire hoard of treasure that cascaded off of Sigfried's bed like a skirt of gold. The precious metal clinked as the dragon busily counted each coin, reciting its name. He looked up fondly at his master as Sigfried tossed the damp towel onto a rung of the ladder leading to the top bunk.

"Hey, it's my roommate, Mr. Not-Dead-After-All." Sigfried leaned toward his familiar and whispered, "what's the nerdy kid's name? The one they said was dead, but now isn't?"

"Is it Edwin? Eldridge? Eckblat the Destroyer?" Lucky looked up from where he was shining a silver chalice with his soft golden nose. "Wait, no, it's Enoch. I'm like almost, nearly, absolutely, sort of certain it's Enoch. It might be Earscratcher. I am seventy-three and three-eighths percent sure it starts with an E...."

Rachel stuck her head farther into the room. To the left, Enoch Smithwyck unpacked a small suitcase on his bed. He was a pale British boy who had been raised in Japan and spoke with a Japanese accent. He had sandy-colored hair and wore glasses.

"Enoch! You've returned!" Rachel exclaimed with secret delight.

Enoch smiled and bowed to each of them. "Hello, Griffin-san, Sigfried-kun, Lucky-sama. It's good to see you again."

Striding over to him, Siggy smacked Enoch on the back, almost knocking off his glasses. He grabbed the other boy's hand, shaking it enthusiastically. "Hey, Roomie! Good to see you!"

The sound of bells came jingling down the hall. Sakura Suzuki burst through the door; tiny bells were plaited into her two long black pigtails. Enoch looked very pleased to see her. His smile faded when he saw her angry glare.

"Shut up, Enoch!" she shouted. Rachel jumped backward, alarmed. The tall Japanese girl was normally so calm and somber.

Enoch blanched. "Sakura-chan! I didn't say anyth...."

Siggy stepped away from Enoch, mumbling, "Sorry, man, I don't fight girls. Good luck!"

He yanked Rachel out of his room, shutting the door as soon as Lucky snaked through it. Outside, he looked carefully up and down the hallway. Then, he pulled a green mirror the size of an old fashion calling card from his pocket. A gold chain had been clamped to it. Lifting it up, he murmured, "Rachel Griffin." Then, he put the chain around his neck and slipped the calling card under his robes, taking a moment to adjust it.

"Look what Valerie and I worked out," he whispered. "Check your card."

Rachel pulled her own calling card from her pocket and gaped. In the mirrored surface, she could see the scene on the far side of the door.

"I said shut up!" Sakura shouted. She stalked toward Enoch. Enoch backed away until his legs hit the bed behind him.

"Did you think about what you were doing when you threw yourself in front of that girl with the whip?" she exploded. "Did you stop to consider how dangerous what you did was?"

Enoch blanched again, shocked and bewildered. "No. I-I didn't."

"*Shut up!* And then you go and get yourself killed! Dead! They said you were dead! *And then you were too stupid to even do that right!*"

Enoch's expression changed from shocked to miserable. He pushed his glasses up from where they had slipped to after Siggy manhandled him. They were too big for his face, so they constantly needed adjusting. Sakura watched him make the motion as if she had seen him make it a thousand times before.

Her rage melted.

She lunged forward, wrapping her arms around him, and started to sob uncontrollably. Enoch looked relieved. He patted her back with concern, speaking softly to her in Japanese.

"Okay... I hate mushy stuff," said Siggy. The calling card returned to blank, green-tinted glass. "Girls! They are crazy...."

Lucky nodded in sympathy.

"Enoch died... er, I mean, was injured and thought to be dead... saving Sakura's life," Rachel explained softly. "He jumped in front of her to protect her from the crazy, possessed girl with the whip. He saved Mr. Fisher, too. That's why Sakura's so upset."

"That was brave." Sigfried nodded his approval.

Rachel continued, "She knew him in their other world—before the two of them were brought to Earth and turned into teenagers. So, she was particularly upset at his death."

"Huh. I guess that makes sense." Sigfried shrugged. "Except, he wasn't actually dead."

Rachel bit her lip. Only she knew that Enoch had been dead. Something the demon Azrael had done had created enough uncertainty to make it possible for the Raven to undo his death. What this meant, exactly, Rachel did not understand, but she grasped enough to know that this was an extraordinarily rare occurrence—not likely to happen again in her lifetime.

Eager to change the subject, she asked, "How did you do that? Make what was happening on the other side of the door appear in my card?"

Siggy grinned. "The girlfriend worked that out. She used the cantrip that attunes a person to a glass to attune my wailing card—or whatever it's called—to my All-Seeing Amulet. So, whatever I see with it, I can make appear in the cards. Nice trick, eh?"

The ramifications of this were so astonishingly glorious Rachel trembled from sheer delight. All the secrets he might be able to show her, all the information she could learn.

She grinned. "Best. Trick. Ever!"

• • •

Outside, rain poured from a gray sky. Rows of ten-foot wide umbrellas bobbed along the pathways in long lines. Their J-shaped handles all pointed the same direction, forming two-way paths as students passed to one side or the other. Balls of will-o-wisps glowed beneath each dome, lighting the otherwise dreary morning. As Rachel and Siggy headed along the Commons toward the Infirmary, she saw Gaius and a few of his classmates leaving Roanoke Hall, where breakfast was held. He did not see her.

Or he pretended not to.

Rachel stared at the gravel beneath her feet. She wanted to run over to him, to let the many things she urgently wanted to tell him come spilling from her lips. She had seen so little of him lately, since he had been spending all his free time for the last month filling his new wand—a task she desperately wished she could help with, especially as the old one had been broken because he had dueled his friend and boss on her behalf. But she remembered Nastasia's comments from the night before. Nastasia was right about one thing: If she did not have enough judgment to pick a decent familiar, what made her think she had the discernment to distinguish good boys from bad ones?

The worst thing was, if she told Gaius what Nastasia had said, he would probably just turn around and blame the leak on the dean and the Agents. She loathed the thought of living her life as the ping-pong ball, volleyed back and forth by her groups of friends.

Lowering her head, she continued to the infirmary with Sigfried and Lucky.

They reached the brick building with its tall white marble columns, a rather odd architectural choice to Rachel's way of thinking. As they opened the door and stepped inside, the smell of fresh baking and cinnamon filled their nostrils. Green sparkles, beautiful to behold, swirled through the air from a flute in the hands of Nurse Moth. The emerald twinkles danced around Zoë, Joy, and Nastasia, who stood before her. Some of the tiny lights swept toward the door, swirling around Rachel, who breathed an audible sigh of relief as the soreness in her hip and back eased. Running toward the others, she pulled off her cap, so that the healing magic could reach her forehead.

As green sparks played over her body, Rachel passed the burbling fountain at the center of the room and came to stand beside her friends. She glanced around the infirmary with its periwinkle blue walls with their silver tracery, and its black-veined green marble floor. Flame-orange curtains separated the various beds from one another. Many curtains were pulled back showing empty mattresses. Two were pulled semi-closed around Valerie. Overhead, a clockwork orrery hung beneath a ceiling painted like a cloudy sky. According to an almanac Rachel had once read, Mars, Jupiter, and Venus were all in their correct positions for the date of the festival of the healing goddess Eir—thought to be the most propitious day for healing.

The pain in Rachel's body eased and lifted. Beside her, Zoë sighed with relief and stopped holding her stomach, where she had been stepped on by the kelpie. Her bruises faded. She waved goodbye to the others and ran off to grab a bite before breakfast closed. Joy, Nastasia, and Valerie were not as lucky. As Xandra had explained, physical damage was easy to heal. Magic-induced damage was not as obliging. Nurse Moth led Joy and Nastasia to cots. Then, she went to look up the songs for kelpie contagion and barghest bites.

Valerie, still in her pajamas, sat on the same bed she had been in last time Rachel visited her here, a few weeks ago. She was drinking some kind of hot pink liquid and had a book open in her lap. Her camera sat on the windowsill. Her Norwegian Elkhound, Payback, sat on the bed with her, the dog's muzzle resting on her mistress's lap. Valerie gave Rachel and Sigfried a big smile as they approached.

"Hey, feeling better?" Siggy asked, leaning over and kissing her cheek.

"Much." Valerie gave him a satisfied nod. "Though the nurse says I have to stay here until the ruby on the scrutiny sticks stops lighting up, whatever that means."

"Has to do with blood levels, most likely," Rachel said, after consulting her memorized copy of a medical encyclopedia her mother kept in the main library at Gryphon Park. "You probably lost too much blood."

"How about you?" Valerie brushed her short flaxen hair out of her face and smiled up at her boyfriend solicitously. "How are you feeling after breaking your spine yesterday?"

"I didn't break my spine," Siggy scoffed.

Rachel grabbed Sigfried's arm and looked up at his face in concern. She turned to Valerie. "He was unconscious! No one told him!"

"Told me what?" Siggy looked back and forth between the two girls.

Valerie leaned forward and said earnestly, "How Xandra Black saved your life… or at least, your back." Between them, the two girls told Sigfried what had happened after he had been tossed out of the tower by the coalescing Moloch.

"So… this girl Xanwhatshername. She took my wounds. And then she was paralyzed?" Siggy asked. The other two nodded. "And then she died and came back? And this ripped open time and space and let the big ugly in?"

"That's right." Rachel nodded.

"Ace!" Siggy cried. "That's wicked cool! How often can she do that?"

"Sigfried Smith," Valerie grabbed her head and shook it, chuckling, "sometimes you are sooo predictable."

Rachel added severely. "The Raven came and told her never to do it again."

Siggy's eyes narrowed. "I think Lucky and I can take that Raven."

Valerie rolled her eyes and went back to her book.

"What's that?" Rachel, always curious about what other people were reading, tilted her head to catch a glimpse of the cover.

"I found it on the shelf on the back of my door." Valerie held up the book. To Siggy, who had never been in her dorm, she said, "Everything has a book shelf on it in Dee Hall. Doors, walls, the area between steps on the staircase. There is even a shower that has a bookshelf in it, all full of waterproof books."

"*Sword at Sunset* by Rosemary Sutcliff," exclaimed Rachel. "Oh, I loved that one! My favorite part was the blood brother ceremony." She absently touched the outside of her wrist.

Valerie made a face. "Mingling blood. Ew! So unsanitary!"

Rachel, who loved the notion of blood brothers, opened her mouth to object but was interrupted by the ringing of the bell above the Infirmary door. A man in gray sweats came hesitantly inside. He was short and balding but fit, with an easygoing manner and an engaging smile that looked somehow familiar. But Rachel had never seen him before, which meant that she was recognizing a family resemblance.

"Hello? May I come in? I'm looking for...."

"Daddy!" Valerie launched herself from her bed and threw herself at the newcomer. Payback leapt from the bed and bounded with her, barking furiously. "You're not a goose!"

"Not any more. Thanks to my intrepid daughter!" He hugged Valerie tightly, swaying back and forth, looking so pleased and proud.

"Don't thank me." Valerie's voice was muffled by his sweatshirt. "Thank Xandra Black. Or rather Xandra's Voices, and Rachel Griffin here, for figuring out what they meant."

"Well then...." Kenneth Hunt let go of his daughter. He turned toward Rachel and bowed slightly. "Thank you."

Rachel blushed and looked down shyly, curtseying. "You're welcome, Sir."

The elkhound continued barking and running in circles. Detective Hunt squatted down and petted the eager dog. "Hey, Payback. Yes. I see you. I love you, too."

Straightening, he glanced around at the others. Spotting Sigfried, he grinned and pointed a finger. "I know you! Most famous boy in the World of the Wise. Sigfried the Dragonslayer. And this must be Lucky!" He bowed toward Lucky, who was wrapped around the fountain, drinking the healing waters. "It's an honor, gentlemen."

Joy had struggled to her feet, perhaps curious as to what the former goose looked like. "So you're okay with your daughter dating the most famous boy in the world?"

Kenneth Hunt friendly expression froze as rigidly as if Rachel had paralyzed him. "Dating? Who said anything about dating?"

Chapter Nine:

The Goose

and His Intrepid Daughter

Police Detective Kenneth Hunt crossed his arms and looked Sigfried Smith up and down. "Valerie, you can't be dating this guy! Look at him!" He gestured at where Siggy stood in his brand-new robe with his still damp golden curls sticking out under his square mortar board cap with its tassel. "Hair that's neither too long nor too short? Decent clothing that aren't ripped? No visible tattoos? Why, this guy's not even a bad boy!"

"Am so a bad boy!" Sigfried cried, offended. "I even wear a knife. Wanna see?"

"He's not a member of the criminal element," continued Detective Hunt.

"I nick food and murder dragons! That's vermicide!"

"He probably doesn't even have a record!"

"Only because I'm too clever to get caught!"

Valerie watched the two of them, her expression walzing between mortification and amusement. "Dad, please. You are embarrassing me. What will these people think?"

"That my daughter is attracted to all the wrong kind of boys?" Detective Hunt smirked at her. "You should have seen the characters she used to hang out with. All current perps or future perps in the making. And now this dashing young man. I don't know if I should be annoyed or pleased. Annoyed my only daughter is dating at fourteen? Or pleased that, for once, she's picked a boy I might not be ashamed to be seen talking to."

"I'm sure if you knew me better, you'd find a reason to be

ashamed," promised Siggy.

"Really? You wanna date my daughter?" Kenneth Hunt turned suddenly and jabbed a finger against the young man's chest. "See that I never do!"

"Okay. Okay. Nothing to see here." Valerie's face was bright red.

She dropped to one knee and hid her face in Payback's silvery fur.

"Anyway, as you can imagine, I am rather disoriented, and I can't wait to get home and see your mother," Detective Hunt turned back to Valerie. "But first, I have an appointment to talk to the dean and some Agents. They have some questions for me about the case I was working on when I... got transformed. When I come back—"

"You remember the details of a case you were working on before you got turned into a duck?" asked Sigfried, impressed.

Kenneth Hunt tapped his balding head. "I keep it all right up here. In the old noggin."

"The case involving Sakura Suzuki and Misty Lark," Rachel asked earnestly, "and the murder of whole families?"

Detective Hunt's expression became calm. "Who are you, again?"

"Agent Griffin's daughter," giggled Joy.

"Ah. Yes. That makes sense. Sorry, I can't talk about a case in progress."

Valerie gawked. "You know who Agent Griffin is? And Sigfried the Dragonslayer? How much about the World of the Wise did you know? Why didn't you tell me?"

"It's okay," Rachel replied solemnly, "fathers never can."

Detective Hunt gave Rachel a curious look and then turned back to his daughter. "Like I was saying, when I come back, I am going to take you home with me for a few days. I think your mother would appreciate some time with both of us."

Valerie looked up, her dark eyes shiny with tears. "I... can't believe you're back! You've been gone so long! Months and months! Were you a goose all that time? And how did you find out about the World of the Wise?"

"I guess so. I really don't know. I don't remember much.... I was leaving for the airport to check out a lead on the case... then I was in the Halls of Healing, listening to some tiny red-haired broad play the bagpipes."

The students all laughed, except for the princess, who frowned slightly. Apparently, she did not appreciate their diminutive Math tutor being called a broad—which Rachel knew from her extensive reading was considered on the derogative side nowadays, but was originally a stage term, meaning a beauty so astonishing that she was worthy of the broadest spotlight.

"As to how I know about magic? I found out a while back from Kyle Iscariot. He had to fill me in to get my help on a couple of cases," said Kenneth Hunt. "What is mind-blowing to me is that now—not only does my daughter know, but she's a student at Hogwarts."

"It's called Roanoke Academy, Daddy," Valerie smirked. "Much as I wish it were not, the other one is imaginary."

"Are you sure? Lots of stuff I thought was pretend turned out to be true. Like people being transformed into animals." Detective Hunt raised his right hand like a man before the bar. "A year ago, I would have sworn in front of a court of law that was imaginary."

"He has a point," muttered Sigfried.

"Yeah... You. Kid. Come here." Kenneth Hunt gestured with his head, indicating that Sigfried should follow him. He did. Lucky slunk along as well—which was too bad, because otherwise, Rachel could have asked the dragon what the other two were saying.

"Awk-ward," Valerie murmured in a sing song voice.

Joy's voice squeaked with excitement. "How many bad boys have you previously dated?"

"He wasn't talking about ex-boyfriends!" Valerie snorted. She took a sip of her pink goo, made a face, and then shrugged, as if it did not taste too bad. "He was talking about some boys I interviewed for the school paper. We did a piece on 'Outside the Box.' You know, kids who don't go with the flow? The artistic weirdoes, the animal activists? My assignment was to interview the kids who snuck outside to smoke. He and Mom later took advantage of this to have me do some undercover work for them among this same criminal element. So, it's hardly my fault I was hanging out with them. Oh... and I have a few friends with less-than-parent-friendly fashion sense."

Detective Hunt stopped near the fountain and spoke seriously to Sigfried. For once, Siggy did not look either wild-eyed or casual. He stood attentively and answered Valerie's father very seriously. Rachel could not hear their conversation, but she was impressed by her friend's demeanor. The two spoke for about a minute. Then, Detective Hunt came back and gave his daughter a last hug and Payback a last pat.

"So," Valerie asked Sigfried sweetly, the moment the door sung closed behind her father, "how did it go?"

Sigfried shrugged. "Well enough."

"What did he say?"

"Man stuff. Nothing for you to worry about."

"I'm worried," muttered Valerie. "Believe me, I'm worried."

Siggy paused. "What does *capeesh* mean?"

"It's short for *tu capisci*, which means: *you understand?* My grandmother was Italian."

"I *capeesh*," was all Sigfried would say on the subject.

Valerie turned and glared at where Joy lay on her cot, her face flushed, her eyes feverish.

"What?" Joy cried. "How was I to know you hadn't told your father about a boy you had been dating for *a whole month!*"

Valerie narrowed her eyes. "I did mention that Siggy was my boyfriend to *the goose*."

"Oh...." Joy looked mortified. "Right. Sorry."

"How long was he missing?" Nastasia asked. She had drawn back the flame-orange curtains and was resting comfortably on a pile of pillows.

"Over nine months."

"How propitious that he was found!" said the princess sincerely.

"Do you think that's why the Voices sent Xandra along?" mused Rachel.

"Could the Voices have known we were going to fall into Transylvania?" asked Joy.

"Who knows?" Rachel shrugged.

The door jangled again, and Zoë Forrest returned with a tray upon which rested breakfast food. Behind her, carrying a second tray, swayed Valerie's best friend, Salome Iscariot.

"Val! I just saw your dad! They found him!" Salome's cheeks were pink with delight. Her huge luminous eyes shone with joy.

Salome placed the tray on Valerie's bed and sat down, crossing one fishnet-stockinged leg over the other, so that her shorter-than-regulation skirt revealed more thigh than school uniforms were meant to allow. Siggy studiously looked away. Salome smirked.

Valerie dove into her breakfast. Rachel happily picked a scrambled egg wrap from the tray Zoë offered. Nastasia also accepted an egg wrap, but Joy, who felt queasy, settled for toast.

"Yep," Valerie spoke despite a mouth full of hash browns. She swallowed, wiped her mouth with a napkin, and continued. "We found him last night, on this huge adventure. I'll tell you about it later. These guys already know."

"How exciting!" Salome leaned forward, straining the buttons of her too-tight blouse. "Though really, you should have taken me with you."

Sigfried's eyes gravitated toward her chest as if magnetized. Then he made an outrageous face, coughed, and averted his eyes, placing his hand beside his face like blinders.

Salome leaned close to Valerie. "Your father... does he know?"

"About... Strega?" Valerie's cheeks lost what color they had. She shook her head mutely.

Meanwhile, Siggy was addressing Nastasia. "Princess? What next?"

Joy bounced on her bed, and then winced as this caused an ache in her head. "Yes, our fearless leader! What do we do next?"

Everyone turned toward the Princess of Magical Australia, whose brow was furrowed with a thoughtful frown that only bordered the slightest bit on poutiness. Maybe the others thought she was pondering, deciding their next course of action, but Rachel knew better. Nastasia had no idea what to say.

How could anyone consider the princess a leader?

Didn't they notice that Nastasia not only had no plans, but that she had not the slightest idea what was going on? She looked so lost, floundering before their hopeful gazes.

Rachel sighed.

Taking a deep breath, she sprang to Nastasia's aid.

"We should do more dream tests," She said. "Quickly, in case the authorities decide we must stop."

"What would we test?" The princess continued to frown.

Rachel struggled not to grind her teeth. "We just discovered two important things. One, the *Spell of Bedazzlement* makes a person dream. Two, a lucid dreamer can deliberately dream places Zoë can go. This is fantastic news for us!"

"Because now we can have a dreamer any time we like, can't we?" Zoë grinned with delight. She sat on the floor, leaning against the bed next to Valerie's, running her hands over her hair. The top part was an electric teal blue. The rest was still the yellow pattern from the walls of Beaumont. "That could make such a difference! Now we can go exploring during the middle of the day, instead of having to wait for people to sleep. Though it still would not have helped us get out of Transylvania."

Rachel nodded. "We should zap one of us with *Bedazzlement*. Then, Zoë steps into that person's dream and sees if she can wake that person up in dreamland."

"Sweet as!" Zoë grinned. "Absolutely sure I can."

Valerie sat cross-legged on her bed, with Payback on one side and Lucky on the other. Siggy pulled up a chair and sat beside her.

Valerie said, "Right! And we should test to see if you can put the dreaming person in a bag, like the princess's purse, and take them with us. That would make traveling much easier. We'd never again be stuck, like we were at the castle!"

"Great idea!" Siggy said. "I volunteer to be knocked out and bedazzled, so long as Valerie is there to make sure that no girls take advantage of me in any way she objects to."

"What if she doesn't object?" purred Salome, looking at her long nails, which were currently painted like strawberries, green at the base and then red with white spots.

Siggy shrugged. "Then, why would I?"

Valerie and Salome both giggled. Joy looked on, her expression torn between jealousy and eagerness. Perhaps she was hoping she would be invited to join in on the Siggy defiling.

"There are so many destinations I want to visit!" Wanderlust made Rachel's voice thick. "We could go to Zoë's world, or Valerie's, or...."

She thought but did not say, *Gaius's.*

She let her imagination free, picturing the distant places, the marvelous vistas, that might now be open to them. The desire to see these places burned in her and shone through her eyes.

"That would be *wicked cool!*" Siggy's face had taken on a similarly rapt expression. "We could go to the Moon! To Mars! We could visit other solar systems! Maybe even other galaxies! We could meet Metaplutons in their native environment! We could go beyond Pluto and become Metaplutons ourselves! Loot their technology! Steal their warp drives! Drive their steel warps! Warp their drive steels! Where are all these worlds the princess keeps visiting? Are they circling Alpha Century? In the Andromeda Galaxy! Lucky, we could visit your world!"

"I am from here," Lucky frowned. "You hatched me from an egg."

"But... before that!" Siggy insisted. "That Japanese place the princess saw with the river and the cherry blossoms and the floating masks."

"I don't care about the before-you." Lucky shrugged.

"Who're we inviting?" Valerie leaned toward her friend. "Can Salome come?"

"She is welcome." The princess inclined her head toward the other girl. "Anyone who wishes can join us."

"Can I bring Gaius?" Rachel blurted before she could stop herself.

"Certainly not," replied the princess sternly. "We cannot trust him. Or, at the very least, we know Dread is untrustworthy. Remember, the prince forced me to disobey my father, after I had explicitly instructed him not to." She paused and then added with a thoughtful frown. "Does your family approve of you dating a commoner?"

Rachel pressed her lips together and did not reply. Her family did not approve of her dating, though *commoner* was possibly lower on their list than such issues as *older* or *thaumaturge.* Father had married a commoner, so it was unlikely that he would make a fuss about Gaius's lack of nobility.

Ironically, it irked her slightly that her family was not more concerned about her boyfriend being a commoner. Not because she wanted them to give her more grief over dating Gaius, but because she knew how disappointed her grandparents would be by their lack of concern for propriety. Rachel sighed.

Life. Never as simple as one might like.

"Who is coming aside, these experiments sound like they might be interesting," Zoë mumbled around her bite of egg burrito. "I wouldn't mind knowing more about what I can do with my sandals."

"I can't wait!" Joy's feverish cheeks glowed with a rosy hue. "This will be so much fun!"

"These are some good ideas," the princess acknowledged. "I would like to find out about other worlds, too. I think we should tell people about them. I would like to open trade."

"We can't do that," Rachel said wistfully. "It would damage the Wall."

"I hardly think a Wall that keeps us from other worlds could be a good thing," said Nastasia. "We should endeavor to take it down."

"But...." Rachel was so alarmed, she jumped forward. "The Raven told us...."

She thought of the great shadow dragons who would have done just that the previous night—had she not stopped Azrael.

"I do not trust that creature." The princess drew herself up and settled her blanket over her shoulders. "I believe it may be evil. Remember, the Raven let the Lightbringer come into our world and pester me. And we know he is wicked. We cannot trust anything it says."

Thanks to her mother's dissembling techniques, Rachel was somehow able to nod calmly. Inside, anguish wracked her heart. She could not tell the others that merely hinting to Sakura Suzuki had been enough to cause her to remember her past and instantly grow into an adult. Or that this alone might have been enough to spark other people's memories and upset the delicate balance that kept the Wall in place. Or that the Raven had been forced to take from Sakura the power that had allowed her to disrupt the appearance of her being a teen. Or that the Raven had wished to remove Rachel's memory of the incident, as he removed Sakura's, Joy's, and Zoë's, but that this would have damaged Rachel, turning her into someone else—basically killing the person she was now, so he had spared her.

She felt strongly, as well, that she should not let on that Enoch had actually been dead.

So how to convince Nastasia of how horribly wrong she was about the Raven? Because what she had just said was so unfair.

Rachel blinked.

When had the Raven become so tremendously dear to her?

"That is what we will do," Nastasia stated quietly. "As soon as we are well, we will do some experiments with Zoë regarding dreamland."

"Great ideas, Princess!" Joy's eyelids were starting to flutter close, but she gazed at Nastasia's face fondly. "I knew you would know what to do. You're the best leader ever."

"Three cheers for the princess!" shouted Sigfried.

Rachel rubbed her temples and sighed.

• • •

The nurse returned with a music stand. On it, she placed sheet music that read: *A Curative for Those Who Have Inhaled the Kelpie's Miasma*. Rachel, who had been up in the air on her broom—and thus away from the foul fog—took leave of her friends. As she turned to go, Sigfried fell in step beside her.

"Not going to hang with your girlfriend?" she asked, as they walked toward the door.

"Nah, she's got Salome to pal around with," Siggy splashed his hand through the fountain, disturbing its rushing beat. Cold water splattered across Rachel's face. She licked some of it off. It tasted cool against her tongue with the slightest touch of sweetness.

He said, "Besides, I need to be about my secret mission."

"A secret mission?" Rachel asked, curious.

Siggy looked right and left. He leaned toward her and whispered, "The Lf-ea... Elf-lay? How do you say *elf* in Pig-Latin? Anyway, the... you know who I'm talking about... came into my dream last night and asked me to do a task for her."

"Truly?" Rachel's jaw gaped, envious that Sigfried had received secret communications from their elf friend. "What did she want?"

"She wants me to make an elixir for Zoë's friend, Misty Lark—the one who saw her family get killed? She says it will help her with her grief."

"What a lovely idea," marveled Rachel.

"If you trust her," said Sigfried, holding the door. Rachel ran down the stairs and waited for him at the bottom. "Otherwise, I could be about to poison the poor girl. Do you trust her?"

"Who, the Elf?" Rachel thought about this. "Yes. I do. She had ample opportunity to hurt us, if she wished to. Instead, she risked a great deal on our behalf."

"She said I need a couple of herbs I don't have yet: yarrow and goatweed, which she first called St. John's wort. I remember yarrow from detention. How do I get a wart off St. John?"

Rachel giggled. "It's a plant. Well, goatweed is. It's also called rosin rose—which I've always found rather hard to say. Not sure about St. John's wort. Saint is one of those orphan words. I think they might have something to do with Outside."

"The wort or the word has something to do with Outside?" asked Siggy. "Never mind. Do you know where I can find some?"

"Certainly." Rachel gestured to the east. "The alchemy herb gardens are along the path that leads from the infirmary to Staff Village."

"Staff Village?"

"It's a little community down by the creek," explained Rachel. "The tutors and proctors live there. There's a dorm for the single folk and thatched-roof cottages for the married couples. I see it when I fly down that way."

They walked along the wood-chip covered path through the feathery hemlocks. The gymnasium and the track stretched to their right. The eastern dorms—Dee, Raleigh, Drake, and De Vere—were to their left. Fog lay low over the campus, its touch damp against their cheeks and clammy down the back of their necks. Tree trunks more than ten feet away loomed ominously, blurry and indistinct.

To either side, herbs grew: mint, basil, and anise, rosemary, and thyme. In the autumn drizzle, the freshly-washed plants smelled heavenly. Rachel spotted the herb Siggy wanted, with its long slender leaves with translucent white dots, growing beneath a cinnamon tree. As they squatted down to pick some, a familiar voice rang out through the trees.

"Rachel!"

She glanced up, startled. An older boy ran through the fog toward her—a very cute older boy, his face a mix of concern and delight. His robes were old and worn and bore several patches. His wand, which hung from a lanyard, clattered against his hip. His short chestnut ponytail flew out behind him.

"Gaius!" Rachel leapt to her feet.

He reached her and pulled her to him. His arms closed around her. As she wrapped her arms back around him, a slow, joyous smile crept across her face.

After over a month of dating, her boyfriend had finally hugged her.

CHAPTER TEN:

"DON'T EVER GIVE IN!"

RACHEL SANK INTO GAIUS'S ARMS, HER EYES HALF-CLOSING, HER cheek resting on one of the patches on his robe. She leaned against his chest, luxuriating in the warmth and strength of his body, breathing in the scent of him. Gaius gently rocked her back and forth. He kissed her on the top of her head.

"Lucky and I are off to the alchemy lab," Siggy called over his shoulder. "See ya."

Rachel waved without moving anything but her hand. The rest of her stayed pressed tightly against her boyfriend. With the fog so close around them, it was as if they were in their own private world.

"Are you okay?" Gaius murmured into her hair, squeezing her tightly. "I heard you were kidnapped by crazy cultists!"

"Wha...? Oh!" Rachel brushed a stray lock of hair out of her face and straightened her cap. "Oh, was that only yesterday? Yeah. I'm okay."

Gaius drew back and peered into her face, searching it. "Has something else happened?"

"Yes, last night..." Rachel began eagerly. Then, her voice went flat. "The princess doesn't want me to tell you."

Gaius's whole face fell. He looked utterly crestfallen. "I rather don't blame her. Of course, she's angry with us. After you trusted us, and then Mrs. Egg died? Vlad is really upset about this. He and his father are working to find the leak. He wants you to know that when they find the culprit, the person will be suitably punished."

Rachel stared at Gaius, who looked much more sincere than his normal casual demeanor. He had not turned the accusation on her. The heat of embarrassment moved slowly through her cheeks. How could she have thought so badly of him?

Wait!

She did have proof!

"Gaius!" Rachel grabbed his shoulder. "It's not Vlad's fault!"

His whole face became alert. "Why do you say that?"

"You weren't the only person we told," explained Rachel. "The princess told the dean. The dean told the Agents."

"You think the Wisecraft is compromised?"

Rachel took a deep breath, sorting her thoughts. She spoke rapidly. "Do you remember what a short time it was between when you and I told Vlad about Juma O'Malley's mom, and when that plane nearly hit the school?"

"Do I remember? I was standing dead center, in the dean's office, watching the Giant Silvery Jumbo Jet of Winged Death come right for me! Vlad said he could see you and Sigfried. That you saved us."

Rachel blushed deeply. She had hoped no one would find out about her part. She had not thought about the fact that some people could see through chameleon elixir. Lucky had even warned them that Von Dread could see through the dragon's invisibility.

"That's neither here nor there." She hurried on. "The point is: you showed me the picture. You and I told Vlad. We all went to meet Juma and escorted him to the dean's. The dean called the Agents. The Agents took him off campus. And the plane showed up just afterwards."

"Right. I remember. Is there a connection?"

"That plane went haywire because Juma's mother made it do that. Serena O'Malley's a technomancer."

"Serena O'Malley?" asked Gaius. "The same woman who murdered Mrs. Egg, right?"

"Yes. Exactly." Rachel pressed. "And she had to be on campus, to control the plane."

"So... you're wondering why she showed up right then?" Gaius's mind leapt rapidly. "Right after the Agents were called to talk to her son?"

"Exactly!" Rachel nodded. "Even if no one at the Wisecraft offices is voluntarily working for Veltdammerung, someone could be geased."

"Vlad certainly didn't have time to tell his father about Juma!" Gaius continued, excitedly. "You can't call people off campus except in the Glass Room downstairs. So, that leak couldn't have been from his father's people! So, the first time probably wasn't them either —considering that it was the same person, Serena O'Malley, who received the secret information!"

"Exactly!" Rachel repeated, smiling.

Gaius let go of her and grabbed her shoulders. "I've got to tell him! Right now."

"Oh. Okay." Rachel's voice sounded thin and tinny.

"Afterwards, I want to hear all about last night! Oh, and I need your help!"

Four more glorious words had never been spoken.

"You need my help?" breathed Rachel.

"Definitely! If you're willing. Meet me in our hallway in about twenty minutes!"

• • •

Rachel ran eagerly through the fog toward Roanoke Hall and her favorite abandoned hallway on the fifth floor. *Our* hallway, he had called it. The thought glowed like a warm coal inside her. She spun around for joy in the midst of the fog-covered commons.

Too late, she realized she was not alone. The first person she saw, Agravaine Stormhenge, looked entirely charmed by her fey behavior. The college senior, who was the Dare Hall Senior Resident for the boys' side—and whom Rachel secretly thought of as "Sigfried grown-up and calm"—was walking across the lawn with his fencing helmet atop his sandy curls, and his gear bag thrown over one shoulder. The whiteness of the bag glowed against the dimness of the fog. He winked at her.

Her elation was short lived. Agravaine was not the only one on the commons. A group of older Dare upper school students were making their way to the gym. They regarded her with mocking grins. Rachel recognized Claus Andrews, Arun Malik, Katie Thebes, Lena Ilium, and John Darling. They chatted loudly as they headed across the grass, their voices carrying through the fog.

"Did you know that little girl is actually like eleven?" asked Lena, a slim young woman with auburn hair and a model's symmetry to her features. Rachel happened to know that Lena was her brother Peter's secret crush.

"They shouldn't have let her come to the upper school so young," scoffed the super-athletic Katie Thebes, the girls' champion for the upper school at Track and Broom. She wore her arm in a sling, the result of her latest daring stunt. Rumor had it she had been injured so many times that the nurse was reluctant to further enchant her. "She should be in the lower school with other children her age."

"Peter and Laurel are idiots for letting their little sister date that idiot Valiant," said Arun, a tall Arabian boy with jet-black hair wearing dark glasses, who spoke with an Egyptian accent.

"I know!" cried Lena. "What are they thinking?"

"Peter and Laurel?" smirked John Darling, running a hand across his short, unruly, black hair. "What's Valiant thinking? I realize he's a first-class jackass, but who'd want to date such a short scrawny thing? It's disgusting! She doesn't even have breasts."

"Yeah," Claus Andrews's mop of white-blond hair shook as he laughed. "When he cops a feel, what's there to feel up?"

Their mocking laughter rang in Rachel's ears. She ducked her head and ran. Her face remained calm, until the fog had closed in around her like a protective cloak. Then, she stopped holding the pain at bay.

It struck her like a stallion at full gallop.

Darling was such an eejit! The others did not bother her so much. Lena had sounded concerned for her, and Claus Andrews was his class's clown—hardly even worthy of her contempt. John Darling's words, however, reverberated in her thoughts over and over.

This was the boy she had adored for three years? This was the boy over whom she had hesitated to accept Gaius's offer to be her boyfriend? Her cheeks burned so hot they ached.

One thought cheered her up. John Darling was not a girl. That meant Siggy would have no compunction about taking him on. The hair-on-fire look might suit Mr. Darling. Or maybe Siggy could conjure another skunk. The soaked-with-flaming-skunk-spray-and-stinks-to-high-heaven style might suit him, too.

• • •

Rachel sat on the table in the abandoned upper hallway that was her private study place. Beside her was the rock she used for spell practice. Across from her was the suit of armor that stood beneath the high round window. Through this window, she could barely make out, in the thick fog, one of the many towers rising above Roanoke Hall. Normally, a whole forest of spires and belfries were visible. The only other object in the hallway was a trash can she had brought up so that she would have a large object to manipulate with her spells.

The air was stuffy, but not as dusty as it had been a month ago. Her numerous wind blasts had put an end to that. Still, she wished she could open the window.

As she sat waiting, Rachel contemplated: *what might Gaius want her to do?*

Her initial jubilation at being asked to help slowly drained to a more reasonable curiosity. When he first asked her, she assumed he meant help filling his wand—the project he had been working on non-stop for the last three weeks. But it probably wasn't that. He probably had some simple question, or wanted her take on what to wear to a party, which was a question boys asked girls in books. Frankly, if she were to be brutally honest, whatever happened next was likely to be a disappointment.

She wanted so much to tell Gaius everything that had occurred recently; to wow him; to dazzle him; to watch his eyes fill with wonder as she revealed her marvelous secrets. But something would surely interrupt them. Something always did. Either he would have to go. Or she would have to go. Or, worst of all, he would listen but not care.

She doubted it would be that. Still, it was wise to be philosophical. So very little had gone right for her of late. It would hurt less if she kept her expectations low.

It was not that her life had been so bad. Wonderful things had happened. But most of them she could not share with anyone. Like meeting an Elf. Or discovering she was immune to the *Spell of True Recitation* and geases. Or choosing to sacrifice her life to save the world and then being spared.

Things nobody else knew.

Except, of course, the Raven.

Rachel slipped from the table and began to pace. She stalked out into the main hall and leaned against one of the windows overlooking the reflecting lake. The glass was cool against her forehead and nose, especially on the spot where the bruise had been, though now only a faint tingle remained. Normally, the whole campus would have lain before her, but all she could see now was mist.

Standing there, Rachel again stared into the fog. She thought of her friends: the princess who could not see obvious connections; Sigfried who lived in the present, unconcerned with even the largest threats; Joy and Zoë, who looked to Nastasia, as if she were the font of all wisdom. Even Valerie, who was so clever about practical things, seemed lost when it came to tracking and comprehending the significance of magical events. Rachel recalled again what had happened in the infirmary, how she and Valerie had carefully laid out the next steps for their nameless group to take, and everyone had praised the princess.

Was she truly too young to be at Roanoke? Should she have stayed home until next year and come with students her own age? Was she really just the freaky dwarf genius Sigfried had so humorously named her?

Staring into the fog, she was reminded of another misty day. As with all her memories, her recollection of it was as crisp and clear as if it had only just occurred. She had stood on the balcony of her room at Gryphon Park. Behind her had been her enormous dark wood-paneled bedroom with its walk-in fireplace and its pink canopy bed with lacy curtains and collection of favorite plush animals. To her right, as she looked off the balcony, had risen the Old Castle. Before her, over the moat and across the lawns, had stretched the fanciful shapes of the topiary gardens, beyond which lay the boxwood maze, the lake, the forest, and, high above, about half a mile away, the ruins on Gryphon Tor. That day, however, she could see none of this. The fog lay so thick over moors that she could hardly see as far as the yew figures of elephants and winged horse on the other side of the moat or the stone statue of a giant carrying a child that was directly below her.

Beside her had stood her grandmother, The Duchess of Devon. She was a tall, severe woman who wore her steel gray hair in a tight bun and still dressed in the Victorian gowns that had been popular in her youth. They had been talking of inconsequential matters, and Rachel had innocently corrected her grandmother on some point that the older woman had forgotten.

"You are far too clever for your own good," her grandmother had snapped.

Rachel, who had only ever been praised for her cleverness by her parents and grandfather, had gazed at her grandmother in puzzlement.

The Duchess had frowned down at her diminutive granddaughter. Her voice had barked like a drill sergeant. "Cleverness is the curse of women, grandchild. Nobody wants a woman to demonstrate intelligence. You will learn this when you are grown. They will not thank you for your insights. They will not cherish your achievements. They will not praise you, as His Grace and your father do. This gift that blooms like a precious flower—" Her clenched hand lifted, unfolding, and then shot forward as if snatching something from the air. "One day you will wish you could pluck it from you and trample it underfoot."

Rachel had not known what to say. The two of them had stared into the mist. The skin of her grandmother's hands had been a bloodless white. Rachel had been too young to realize this was because she held her fists so tightly that her nails were biting into her palms, but she recognized it now.

Armed with this realization, she saw the entire incident with new eyes. It had never occurred to her six-year-old self that her grandmother could have been talking about her own life. That the life of an intelligent and talented sorceress—who had lived through the Victorian Age, through the Depression, through both World Wars—might have been fraught with difficulty. Rachel had not known at the time that Amelia Griffin had abandoned her vows as a Vestal Virgin, weakening the Sacred Flame over which she had stood guard, out of love for Rachel's grandfather—after Blaise Griffin's first family had been slaughtered. She had not even understood that the death of her father's younger brother Emrys, who had died right here at Roanoke, fighting the Terrible Five at the age of seventeen, meant that her grandmother had lost one of her two children. Little Rachel had only understood that, once again, her exacting and prickly grandparent disapproved of her for reasons that she could not understand.

There on the balcony in the fog, her ordinarily-standoffish grandmother had dropped to one knee. She had seized Rachel by both shoulders, her normally-distant eyes blazing. "But don't you ever give in, Lady Rachel Jade Griffin! Intelligence is a gift, no matter how often life tries to teach you otherwise. Don't you ever give in and let the forces of ignorance win!"

"*I won't, Grandmother*," whispered thirteen-year-old Rachel hoarsely, her forehead still pressed against the cold glass. "*I won't give in.*"

Out there before her now, invisible behind the fog, lay the memorial garden with its many shrines, where offerings could be made to numerous gods. Rachel wished, not for the first time since she came to school, that her family had chosen a household god—someone she could pray to for guidance, for strength. She wished recklessly that some deity would manifest, as in the tales of old, and offer her comfort in return for loyalty.

No figure appeared amidst thunder and lightning. The only moving thing visible on the lawn below was Kitten Fabian's familiar, padding its way across the damp grass. The little Comfort Lion, a golden-maned feline the size of a house cat, stopped and turned its head. Its golden eyes seemed to stare straight up at Rachel. It was probably a coincidence, but an eerie horripilation ran across Rachel's body.

She thought back three seconds.

In her memory, the Lion was gigantic—bigger than elephants, bigger than houses, bigger than trees. It looked down from the sky, its expression reminding Rachel of Mistletoe, when he sat watching a hole from which he expected a mouse to emerge.

There was no mistaking it.

Its great golden eyes were focused directly upon Rachel.

Chapter Eleven:

Uncommon Commoners and Kings

FOOTSTEPS ECHOED IN THE MAIN HALLWAY. RACHEL TURNED HER head. When she looked back, the Lion in the sky was gone. Below, the tiny feline vanished into the fog.

Gaius came running around the corner, slightly out of breath. He looked utterly adorable. He seemed more like his normal self than he had outside. He had regained his air of nonchalance and his wry grin. Slowing to a walk, he gave her a warm smile. Rachel wanted to rush forward and hug him, but she felt too shy. Then, something in her rebelled. She had waited all this time for him to hug her. She was not returning to hugless limbo.

Dashing forward, she threw her arms around his waist. He returned her embrace, looking quite pleased.

Rachel lowering her lashes demurely to hide her eagerness. "What can I help you with?"

Gaius spoke with his customary British drawl. "You remember that enchantment I helped you learn, the paralysis hex?"

"Of course."

"I can't help notice that you're rather good at it."

Rachel beamed shyly.

"I was wondering if you might consider casting it, so I could store a few in my wand."

He did want help with his wand.

"I would be honored," she replied simply. "When would be convenient?"

"It's Saturday morning. I have no plans." He grinned. Leaning toward her, he added mischievously, "Except to spend time with my girlfriend."

Rachel lit up like a lantern. "Now would be fine!"

They walked back to their hallway, hand-in-hand. As she came to the table, Rachel paused, frowning. "I am rather good with the spell, but I don't succeed every time. What if I mess up? Won't it go awry when you fire it?"

"Ah! That's what this little brilliant device is for." Gaius pulled out a small object and put it on the table. A small brass base supported five folded petals of golden foil. Below them, a little bar stuck out from the stand, ending in a feathery gold tip.

"A *cinqfoil!*"

"You know it?" Gaius made an expansive gesture. "Good!"

"Only sort of," she admitted. "My father uses one when he refills his staff. I don't know what they do, but I must admit to being ever so curious."

"Then, we must satisfy your curiosity. After all, the desire to know is the origin of all scientific pursuit. Behold!" Gaius placed the device on the table top. "See this little feathery bit here? It's sensitive to sorcery. The stronger the spell, the more it reacts, causing these gold foil petals to open. If the *cinqfoil* starts looking like a flower— opens beyond half way—the spell is good. Shall we try it?"

Rachel gazed at the curious little device in wonder. Then, she took a deep breath and whistled. A rush of magical energy rushed through her body and out of her mouth. Blue sparkles danced through the air perfuming the hallway with the scent of evergreen. The gold-foil petals opened to about two-thirds of their full extent. The device formed a delicate gold blossom.

With a deft gesture—the same fingertips pressed together into a beak that was used for the Word of Bridging and conjurations— Gaius directed the spell into the sapphire at the tip of his fulgurator's wand. Swirling like a tiny whirlwind, the cobalt sparkles sank into the gem.

• • •

They worked in concert, concentrating upon the task. Neither of them paused to chat. Rachel whistled. The *cinqfoil* bloomed. Gaius caught the spell. They repeated this again and then over and over again. Underneath her extreme focus, Rachel was aware of how close he stood; of how cute he looked as he bent in concentration;

of the fierce, pure joy that thrilled through her, caused by working together so harmoniously.

She could not imagine any place she would rather be.

• • •

Forty-five minutes later, the petals of the *cinqfoil* would no longer unfold far enough to make catching the spell worthwhile. Rachel's lips had gone numb from the sheer amount of raw sorcerous power. Her head spun. She feared she might swoon. Noticing her distress, Gaius insisted she squat down and put her head between her knees. He knelt beside her with one hand on her shoulder, a comforting presence.

Rachel felt unpleasantly lightheaded.   She wanted to lean against him, but an image rose from her memory of Vladimir Von Dread, his black-gloved fist resting on the table at the Knights meeting, his voice icy with disdain as he denounced weakness. Gaius admired Vlad tremendously. He might distain weakness, too. She dare not let him know how weak she was.

Forcing her chest to rise and fall normally, she insisted upon standing. Gaius helped her rise, his hand on her elbow, smiling kindly.

"That was amazing!" Gaius gazed at Rachel, his dark eyes filled with appreciation. "If my count is right, you did that four hundred and two times! And they were rather good spells, too! I'm going to be unbeatable!" He assumed a dueling stance, flicking the teak and brass length of his wand. "Beware my paralysis! Blue Sparkle's light!"

Rachel giggled with sheer delight. "My pleasure!"

Still grinning triumphantly, Gaius grabbed her and hugged her tightly. Rachel melted against him and sighed contently.

"Do you know any other enchantments?" he asked, letting her go. His hand shot up. "Not today, of course."

"A wind blast, but it's truly pathetic. I plan to work on the *Spell of Bedazzlement*. It is a hex in the Aeolian mode, same as the paralysis spell. Maybe I'll turn out to have a proper talent for hexes."

"If you master it, I'd love to be the first to know." Gaius grinned fiercely. "Do you…" he looked around, as if only now noticing that something was missing, "… ever use an instrument?"

Rachel's eyes flickered downward, suddenly embarrassed.

"Because, you know," he drawled, gesturing airily, "all the other Enchanters I know can't perform spells by just whistling. They are stuck playing a tuba or a nose flute or something."

"Yeah." Rachel chewed on her lip again. "I have a flute. I just don't like playing it."

"Oh. That's...."

"Inconvenient? Bizarre?" Rachel sighed.

"Rather cool?" Gaius said. "No one else I know can do that!"

"I learned it from my mother. She can do it, too," said Rachel, not explaining that it was a side effect of their secret dissembling technique. She wondered obscurely if Cassandra March could whistle enchantments, too. "As to the instrument.... I told you I didn't want to be in Dare."

"I didn't realize the matter was so serious! Why don't you move?" he asked. Then, he answered his own question. "Of course. Your brother and sister. I'm sure Laurel and Peter want their little sister near them." His grin grew wider. "Especially if you're dating some awful older boy, who is a thaumaturge to boot! And now, apparently, the princess doesn't like me either. Good grief!"

"I'm not sure she doesn't like you. She doesn't trust Vlad, so she doesn't trust his people. Also, she doesn't think I should be dating a commoner."

"A commoner?" He blinked a few times. "Didn't expect to hear that at school. People here don't usually stand on ceremony. Not the decent ones, anyhow. But enough about that. Thank you! You have no idea what this means to me." He clutched his wand to his chest. "I filled my old wand over a period of three years. Two years ago, we had two Enchanters working with us. One..." he peered at her carefully, "... graduated last year. The other lost his memory in an industrial accident."

There could not have been two such students.

"You mean Blackie Moth?" Rachel asked.

"You know him?"

"He's my second cousin." Rachel paused. "That nearly happened to me two days ago."

"You nearly lost your memory in an industrial accident?" Gaius asked, amused but puzzled.   "Or you almost became a second cousin?"

"Not an accident," Rachel said seriously, "but I nearly had my memory taken away. I wonder if I would have ended up like Blackie."

"What do you mean?"

Rachel leaned out in the main hallway, but no one was around. Coming back, she said in a low voice, "I was told I might tell only one person. I would like that person to be you. But you have to promise not to tell anyone. Not even Vlad."

"Rachel, I haven't repeated anything you asked me to keep private! I swear!" Gaius insisted. "But only one person? Are you certain it should be me?"

"If I picked Siggy or Nastasia, I would have to choose between them."

"I wasn't thinking of them," said Gaius. "Shouldn't you tell your father?"

Rachel blanched. "I... can't."

"Why not? They say he's a famous Agent. He's one of the best, right?"

"Of course!" Rachel cried loyally. "But...."

"Don't the Wisecraft need to know what you found out?"

"Gaius, you trust me, don't you?"

"Yes."

"And if I say: 'I can only tell you this much and no more'?"

"I trust you have a good reason."

"There are parts I cannot tell—not even to you. When I say this, you believe me." Rachel struggled to explain. "My father would not trust that I knew enough to decide what to tell him and what to leave out. He would expect me to make him my first loyalty."

"Shouldn't you?" frowned Gaius.

"What if he didn't believe me when I said I couldn't tell him— or that he should not tell anyone else—until it was too late?"

He searched her face. "Too late how...?"

"Until," she swallowed, "someone had died."

"Oh. Okay." He tipped back on his heels, thinking. "Don't get me wrong! I really, really want to know!" Gaius put his hand over his heart. "I give you my word, I will tell no one."

Rachel regarded him earnestly. She understood Nastasia's point, that her judgment might be suspect. It was true she had been entirely wrong about her cat. But she could not believe this boy was evil. Would an evil boy try to talk her out of choosing him as her confidant?

"Thank you!" she said sincerely. "Let's go somewhere else. I'd like to sit down."

• • •

Rachel fetched her broom, and they found an out-of-the-way place inside a belfry tower on the roof of Roanoke Hall. They sat on a cold marble spiral staircase. Tall windows surrounded them, so that they seemed to be alone on an island enveloped in fog. When the wind blew, they could occasionally make out other nearby spires, looming like ghostly towers.

Rachel leaned against the misty glass and gazed out into the fog. She could barely make out a flying buttress and a bell tower. The belfry smelled of autumn dankness. The marble stair was hard, but she felt no desire to move. Rumbles of thunder came from the north, where the storm goblin, the Heer of Dunderberg, was imprisoned in Stony Tor.

She was tremendously eager to tell her boyfriend of her adventures and to see his reaction—whether awe, admiration, or dismay, but the sheer volume of what had occurred since they last spoke daunted her.

Finally, she admitted, "I don't know where to begin."

"How about at the beginning?" Gaius squeezed her hand. Stretching, he slid his arm around her shoulder. Rachel snuggled against him. His body was so warm compared to the cold of the dreary day.

"I don't know where the beginning is," she sighed.

"Start with the plane."

"Oh, right." Rachel traced the folds of her robe with her finger. "So, Vlad saw me from the dean's office?"

"Vlad saw you from the plane."

Rachel's head snapped up. "What?"

"Vlad jumped to the plane to see if he could stop it."

"He was *on* the plane. On purpose?" Rachel's jaw dropped. "He's... very brave!"

Gaius struggled not to laugh. "Says the girl who was flying *at* the plane."

Rachel told him how she and Sigfried had disenchanted the rogue airplane, freeing it from the control of the technomancer Serena O'Malley and the pilots from the obscuration that had hidden Roanoke Hall from their sight. Gaius listened avidly, his gaze never wandering. Delighted, she grew more animated as she explained her backup plan of flying as high as she could and diving at the tail, hoping to strike the plane hard enough to cause it to swerve.

"Wait!" Gaius cut her off. "Move a jumbo jet with the weight of your bodies? How would that work?"

"I tried to *turlu* it first, to stop it the way I was stopped on my broom, but that didn't work. So this was my next idea." Rachel held out her broom and imitated striking the tip with her fingers. The back swung down. The front tip swung up. "I thought it would work like this. If we struck it at the very back, hard enough, it would tip the front up. Right? At least that's how brooms work."

"Planes don't work that way."

"How could they not?"

"Jumbo jets have stabilizers. Pushing the back down on ninety-nine percent of modern aircraft tips the horizontal wing on the tail. This pushes the tail back up, causing the jet to level out almost immediately." Gaius took the broom and held it. He pushed one end down and then moved the hand holding the shaft so that the end he pushed down popped up again.

"But if we pushed the back down for even a second, that would have been enough to make it miss the school, right?"

"Um.... Rachel, force equals mass times acceleration. The gross weight of your quintessential jumbo jet is, oh, probably about... 975,000 pounds, with cruising speed of 570 miles per hour. Let's be generous and assume you and Siggy together weigh 200 pounds." Gaius glanced at Rachel's petite form. "Which I doubt. We'll go with 150, though that might be a tad on the light side. An object of that weight would have to be going," he tipped his head back as he calculated, "370,500 miles per hour to be noticeable to the jet. That's four hundred eighty three times the speed of sound. The space shuttle traveled at twenty-two times the speed of sound on reentry—You would have had to be flying twenty-one times faster than the shuttle.

"Even if we assumed that the plane's unloaded and unfueled, weighing only 800,000 pounds, and it's going slower than normal —say, two hundred miles per hour—you would still have had to be going about 24,500 miles per hour. That was the speed of the Apollo spacecraft on its trip to the moon. At that speed, you would have burned up from the air friction way before you hit. Ouch." Gaius took the broom and pushed his finger against it, making a smashing sound effect.

"Oh." Rachel was quiet for a bit. "So... I nearly killed us both for nothing?"

"You would have splatted like a bug."

Something large blocked her throat. She swallowed, but it did not budge. "I knew we'd die. I just thought everyone else would live."

Gaius leaned forward and brushed a stray lock of hair from her face. "I'm still very proud of you. I'm not sure I could have done something so brave."

His touch sent tingles through her cheek and neck. Her breath caught; her eyes half closed. He was so chivalrous, so respectful and kind. She felt so cherished and safe.

Claus Andrew's voice rang in her ears: *When he cops a feel, what's there to feel up?* Rachel shivered, suddenly aware of the chill. She had been so pleased that Gaius had not tried any of the bad things people had warned her an older boy might try. Now, she felt uncertain. Why was he not pressing her harder?

She looked up at him, her eyes pleading. Smiling with shy amusement, Gaius leaned forward and kissed her, sending tingles all the way down her spine to her toes. His lips were warm and sweet. Delighted, Rachel kissed him back, even though her lips were sore from whistling and the motion hurt.

They kissed twice. Gaius was more at ease with the intimacy between them than she, but his cheeks did grow a little red. He then pulled her closer, so that her head rested on his shoulder. They stayed there for a time. He stroked her hair with one hand, the other gently caressing her back. Rachel rested her hand on his robed chest and sighed.

A thought came to her. She smirked, glancing up at him sideways. "If you'd rather not be a commoner, you could prevail upon Vlad to knight you."

She watched his expression carefully. Did he mind being a commoner? They had been so busy since they started dating. This was the first time she had had the luxury of speaking with him at any length. She was extremely curious as to what he thought—about this or everything.

"Possibly." Gaius made an airy gesture with the hand that had been stroking her hair. "But then I would be a Bavarian knight rather than an Englishman. Not sure how I would feel about that. Besides, I would have to apply myself rather diligently if I wished to receive such an honor." He tapped her on her nose. "I had better not make a habit of getting into duels with him over pretty girls."

Rachel blushed with pleasure. Then she looked down shyly. Moving away from him, she ran three fingers along the window beside her, leaving parallel lines in the condensation. "Nastasia said y-you only dueled Vlad because he insulted your pride. That it had nothing to do with your liking me."

Gaius laughed out loud. He pulled her back against him. "If it were about my pride, it never would have happened. I have too much respect for Vlad. I was mad at him for claiming that my feelings for you were inappropriate. They are *not*. It's how I treat you that decides whether or not I am an upstanding gentleman."

Her cheeks grew rosy. His words made her feel all glowy inside. He had just admitted to having feelings for her! That was very different from merely not wanting to dump her, which had been her assumption.

He had never said anything like that before.

As for Claus Andrew's claim, if Gaius wished to prove to Vladimir that his behavior toward her was chivalrous, no wonder he was treating her so courteously!

"I told her you would not have fought Vlad for a frivolous reason!" As if a weight had been lifted from her shoulders, Rachel's whole outlook lightened.

"As to my being a commoner," Gaius drawled, gesturing with his free hand. "Being a farmer isn't glamorous, true. But my grandfather was knighted, and we can trace our family all the way back to Arthur's court. I am a direct descendant of King Bors, who was king of *Gaunnes*—which I believe is another name for Gaul... or, in other words, France. He's Lancelot's uncle."

"King Bors!" Rachel cried. "Wasn't he the father of Sir Bors? Sir Bors was one of Arthur's truest knights! He saw the Questing Beast. Only the most *valiant* knights did that!"

She giggled at the pun.

"The very same. We're descended through Sir Bors, too." His eyes danced merrily. "It's too bad our family lost its kingdom. I could have been a prince."

"I knew you were knightly!" Rachel replied with delight. "Sigfried would be jealous! He's a huge King Arthur fan. My brother Peter, too. He lives and breathes Arthurian tales. Does he know, about your connection to Sir Bors, I mean? Maybe that's why he dislikes you so."

"I doubt it's that," Gaius murmured, covering his mouth—and perhaps his smirk—with his hand, "but you never know."

"Most commoners don't worry about acting like a gentleman," Rachel said admiringly. She added with impish cheer, "It's for the best that you no longer have a kingdom. I thought about it, last time a prince spoke to me of marriage, and decided I'm not cut out to be a queen."

Only after she had spoken did Rachel realize what had come out of her mouth. She had as much as said that if he had had a kingdom, she would have wanted to be his queen. Her cheeks grew uncomfortably hot. Marriage was not a subject girls were supposed to introduce. Ever. Especially when speaking to a boy who had not yet said or done anything to indicate that he might want her for his wife.

He had not even spoken of love.

Eager to distract him, she blurted out, "If I were Salome Iscariot, whose goal in life is to irk her mother, you would be the perfect boy to date. You have four strikes against you: older, thaumaturge, interested in mundane things, and commoner. Unfortunately, I'm not Salome, and I don't have any desire to irk my family." She paused, "Though being descended from King Bors might negate being a commoner."

"Is the issue of my being a commoner important?" asked Gaius. "To you, I mean?"

"To me? No! To my family?" Rachel sighed. "Old families only get to be old families by jealously guarding their prerogatives. They are ever so sensitive about these things. Though, of course, I'm a girl, so it doesn't matter as much."

"Why is that?"

"I won't inherit Gryphon Park or the dukedom," explained Rachel. "It's Peter who must carry the weight of the Griffin Family legacy on his shoulders. He has to marry the right type of girl. That kind of thing. It's Mum's fault, of course, for not producing the required Heir and Spare." Rachel giggled at the foolishness of this notion. "But instead, only one boy and three useless girls. Not that Father would ever voice a word of complaint. But my grandparents cared enormously about such things."

"The heir and the spare." Gaius chuckled. "That's a term I haven't heard outside of old literature and True Hiss class."

Rachel chuckled at his abbreviation for True History. "The life of a duke's daughter is fraught with all sorts of matters that are out of fashion for everyone else."

"Fair enough." Gaius gestured airily. "We commoners know little of such things. My father had no idea we were descended from royalty."

"How did you find out?"

"When I came to school here, I found a painting of my family's farm. I did some investigating and discovered it had been painted during my grandfather's youth. He was a sorcerer but chose not to practice. He ended up staying a farmer."

"Hang on. Your grandfather had the gift of sorcery, but he chose to remain mundane?"

"Can you believe it?" he asked. "I guess the world was much different then. The idea of being apart from his family was too much for him. Anyway, it didn't take me very long, once I knew where to start, to find out the history of the painting, and, from there, the history of my family." Gaius grinned suddenly. "My father is completely unimpressed by this news. Our being related to knights and kings. He just wants to know if magic can milk cows without getting him lynched by our neighbors."

Rachel giggled gleefully. "Magic can help with cows. But whether he would get lynched by his neighbors—that's a stickier question. Can you show me the painting of your farm?"

"Sure, when we go downstairs," he promised. "What happened next? After the airplane?"

"Oh! Right. Um… the Comfort Lion told me my friends were in trouble. Serena O'Malley was taking Sigfried and Nastasia off campus. I went after them."

"You… went running off into danger?" He frowned seriously. "Without calling me?"

"I-I tried to call for help. There wasn't time. I asked Zoë and Joy to tell the proctors," said Rachel, wishing fervently that she could have called on Gaius and Vlad for help. She made a mental note to discuss the matter with Sigfried.

"I must admit, that's rather brave." Gaius placed his hand over hers. He paused and then asked, "What's the Comfort Lion?"

"Kitten Fabian's familiar."

"Ah. *That* Lion." Gaius looked thoughtful for a moment. Rachel recalled how he had remembered, under the influence of the *Spell of True Recitation*, having seen the Lion as larger than the universe. He shook his head slightly and ran a hand over his brow. "Um… why did they want Smith and the princess?"

"According to Azrael, Sigfried and Nastasia are two of seven prophesied Keybearers."

"Keybearers?" asked Gaius. "For what?"

"No idea."

"I'll ask Vlad. Maybe he's heard of this prophecy." Gaius pulled a notepad from the pocket of his robe and jotted something down. "What happened then?"

Without precisely lying, Rachel worded her description to suggest that Serena O'Malley's geas had not affected her because it had not been cast on her properly—as if her arriving after the others had protected her. She had not yet told Gaius about her perfect memory. She was not certain this was the right time.

She described the battle between the Agents and the followers of Veltdammerung. Gaius listened attentively and asked many questions, especially about Sandra's part. He seemed very interested in how a student who had graduated from Roanoke only last year had come to be an undercover Agent. Rachel began to wonder if maybe she should not have mentioned her sister.

"Please don't tell anyone about Sandra's part," Rachel pleaded. "I'm not sure she wants anyone to know. Especially if she plans to go undercover on another project."

An odd look flashed across Gaius's face, but he nodded. "Of course. I would never tell."

"Then, we went to Transylvania. Azrael had a bonfire set up as an Obscuration Lantern. With it, he called up *tenebrous mundi*— dragon-like shadows that are apparently responsible for maintaining the Wall around the world."

"Good grief!" Gaius's head jerked up. "You mean this Wall you've been telling us about is *an obscuration*?"

Rachel's jaw actually dropped. "Of course! How could I not have seen it?"

"It certainly would explain why the beliefs of the people living on our world matter to the integrity of the Wall," he spoke intently. "I mean, a wall made out of metal or brick wouldn't fall apart because someone discovered I was from another planet, right? But an obscuration... they work that way, don't they? I've heard of mundane people seeing through obscurations—when enough people learned the truth about what was being hidden. Isn't that what happened at Findhorn? That came up in True Hiss."

"Yes!" Rachel nodded eagerly. "The owners shared their giant vegetables with so many Unwary visitors that the obscuration around the garden failed. Now everyone can see it. The Obscurers who work for the Parliament of the Wise had a proper time of it, trying to convince the Unwary that all those folks babbling about fairies being responsible for such a lovely garden flourishing in the cold of Scotland were daft."

"But it is fairies, right?"

"Of course." Rachel nodded. "Back to last night. To get the *tenebrous mundi* to tear down the Wall...." She paused and waved her hands in exasperation. "The Wall that the princess thinks is evil and wants to tear down! *Hallo*! If it were *good* to tear it down, would *the demon* have been trying to do it?" Rachel took three deep breaths and then continued calmly. "Azrael needed a sacrifice. He wanted to sacrifice my father, my sister, Nastasia, and Sigfried. He thought I was geased, so he had Serena O'Malley hand me a wand and ordered me to kill them."

"Good *grief*!" Gaius's pupils had grown gratifyingly large. "What did you do?"

"Do you remember that we found out that Azrael was originally summoned by some Germans who sicced him on an English sorcerer. And that this sorcerer had outwitted him and bound him into a human body?"

"Of course."

"That sorcerer was my grandfather."

"Your grandfather, the great cryptomancer?"

Rachel nodded.

"So, there was a masterword!" Gaius exclaimed with the glee of someone who has been proven right. "Vlad and William and I debated that."

"You did?" gawked Rachel.

"We knew Blaise Griffin was one of a small number of sorcerers who were intimates of Crowley in his youth. And after you told us about your ancestor—the one who bound brollachan into human hosts to capture them—we realized your grandfather had both the knowledge and the opportunity to cast the spell that bound the demon into Crowley."

"I had no idea you figured out so much!" Rachel exclaimed, impressed.

She did not add that it stung to learn they had figured out so much and not shared it with her. Of course, she had not shared her suspicions with them either. But then, the matter had not concerned either Gaius's or Dread's grandfather.

"What happened?" Gaius urged.

"I pointed the wand at my family, looked the demon in the eyes, and pronounced the masterword." Rachel could not help feeling rather smug.

"Good for you!"

"Grandfather's binding spell then activated," said Rachel. She continued describing, to Gaius amazement, the appearance of the ghost of her young uncle and the phantom horse, Thunderfrost. Finally, she finished, "The demon Azrael is now bound tight inside the clerk Mortimer Egg again."

"Excellent!" Gaius laughed out loud.

"Then, Finn MacDannan arrived and captured him. Everyone thinks I was geased, and Finn saved us all."

"Wait! You knew the masterword?" Gaius gawked. "Did you have it the whole time?"

"I figured it out yesterday, from a clue given me by my Art tutor, Mrs. Heelis."

"You *figured out* the masterword?"

She nodded.

"You are truly amazing, Lady Rachel Griffin." Gaius gazed at her raptly.

Ah. This was what she had been longing for. *This.*

Right now.

His admiration went to her head like wine.

It was like being drunk on secrets.

CHAPTER TWELVE:

ANCIENT ECHOES OF

SARDONIC LAUGHTER

"YOU DO REALIZE HOW AMAZING YOUR GROUP IS?" GAIUS LEANED forward, smiling at her very nicely. "By now? One month in? Most freshman can't pull off a single spell. Sigfried Smith and the Princess of Magical Australia are the most powerful sorcerers—other than Vlad—anyone's seen in a generation. Possibly two. Even the big names of the previous generation—Scarlett Mallory MacDannan, Finn MacDannan, James Darling—weren't like them.

"And Joy O'Keefe and Wulfgang Starkadder aren't far behind. They are both the seventh child of a seventh child. Traditionally, that makes a child powerful or lucky."

"Then there's me." Rachel looked sheepish, tracing a spiral on the misty window.

"You should not put yourself down. Look what you just did for my wand! And your family is very powerful. Your sister Sandra achieved five rings of mastery! There's no way they would have let her become an undercover Agent so quickly, if she weren't supremely talented."

"I'm not like Sandra," explained Rachel, chagrined. "She's good at everything. That paralysis spell is practically the only thing I can do properly. Apart from the wind blast and the lifting spell you taught me. But to do the little that I can with those, I had to practice for days. Literally. I've added up the hours I've spent practicing. It comes to over forty-eight, gaining on seventy-two, in fact." Recalling a comment made by her boss, the P.E. instructor, Rachel added, "Though, apparently, I'm unusually good at flying."

"I say!" Gaius grinned at her. "Have you considered going out for Track and Broom?"

Rachel hated sports. Gazing off into the fog, she blew out of the side of her mouth, sending a stray lock of hair soaring.

"Okay. Never mind that." Gaius's voice held an odd note of tension.

Rachel's eyes darted to his face. His hand rested casually in front of his mouth, blocking his expression; however, the corners of his eyes crinkled with humor. When he saw her looking, he murmured something. Rachel could not quite make out his words. After recalling the memory three or four times, she thought he might have said: *Sorry. Too cute.*

Three loud peals of thunder came from the north. The two of them moved closer together. They sat quietly side by side, watching the swirling mist, occasionally glimpsing graceful spires and domed belfries. Gaius drew a cylindrical mundane device, like a cigar with fins, in the condensation on the window.

"You know, your grandfather was an extremely clever man." Gaius turned toward her, brushing a hair from her cheek. "I hope if a demon ever comes to kill me, I can outwit it."

"He did outwit it. But at a terrible cost." Unexpectedly, Rachel's eyes filled with tears. She jerked her head to one side to hide them. "Oh, Gaius! He lost his entire first family—a baby boy, three girls and a young heir. Aunts and uncles I had never heard of! And his wife! All slaughtered by the demon Azrael!"

"Rachel, I'm so sorry. I didn't know."

"Neither did I."

Gaius pulled her close, hugging her again. She rested against him, drinking in his warmth. She wanted to break down and weep for the relatives she had lost, but she desperately did not want her boyfriend to think poorly of her. If she cried, he would know she was weak. He had not been exactly comforting the time she had wailed in front of him in the infirmary, after she found Valerie Hunt bleeding in the girl's bathroom. Instead of crying, she shoved her grief and sorrow behind a mask of calm.

This gift comes with a price.

Her mother's voice rang in her memory, warning her that the emotions she chose not to experience using the dissembling technique did not disappear. They remained inside, becoming stronger. On the surface, Rachel felt calm and collected. Underneath, the jumble of rejected emotions was growing wilder. What if they grew so strong that she could no longer control them? Would they all come tumbling out?

If she did not find a way to deal with them, something bad was going to happen.

But not today.

Not now.

Right now, she had this chance to spend long awaited time with Gaius. She did not want to mess it up by crying like a ninny. She lifted her head and smiled at her boyfriend. Leaning forward, he brushed his nose against hers. A sense of peace settled over her.

"We've been trying to figure out where you get your information," Gaius said, breaking the silence. He ran two fingers up and down her back. "Vlad has concluded from what you shared with us that you have a contact in the Wisecraft, but we can't figure out who. You could be getting info from your father. But from what we know of him, we figure probably not."

Rachel shook her head, smiling mysteriously. "I'll never tell."

Of course, she did not actually have a Wisecraft connection. It was Siggy's all-seeing amulet that had allowed her to learn the secrets that Gaius and his friends thought came from the Agents. Rachel did not mind keeping Sigfried's secret. She understood intrinsically that the more Gaius knew about her sources, the less amazed he would be by her information. She would rather he not know how she figured things out. Otherwise, her reports might become predictable, dull.

This led to a problem.

She could not tell Gaius about the Raven—and why he had spared her—without also explaining about her perfect memory. But to do so would reveal one of her main sources of info. Gaius clearly liked the fact that she regularly wowed him with her revelations. If she failed to continue to impress him, might he lose interest in a too young girlfriend who did not yet even have a figure?

Moistening her suddenly dry, sore lips, Rachel considered what she could tell him without revealing her secret. She was dying to tell him about meeting the otherworldly Illondria, but she dare not do that, as it would endanger the Elf's life. The Raven had said clearly that the more people knew about the Elf, the less likely that she would survive. She also wanted very much to tell him about the previous night's occurrences and their trip to Beaumont. True, Nastasia had asked her not to tell, but Rachel had not agreed to keep the secret.

After all, didn't Nastasia plan to tell the dean? Also, the events were no longer an Inner Circle secret. Other people knew as well: Xandra Black, Mrs. March, and, by now, probably Detective Hunt. Plus, there was the fact that Bavaria was relatively close to Transylvania and might be harboring members of Veltdammerung—who might be serving that demon.

"Never mind the princess, I shall tell you about last night. In fact, I really should tell you!" she declared. "It might turn out to be terribly important to Vladimir's father."

She repeated the entire adventure, from their trip into the dreamlands to arriving back at Dare Hall with the goose. The only thing she left out was their original plan to go to Magical Australia. Nastasia had requested that they not tell anyone about her travel power. Remembering Mrs. March's warning, she wrote down the demon's name on a piece of paper from her pocket, rather than pronounce it aloud.

"Wow. That's...." Gaius sat quietly for a few seconds. "Wow. Was the goose really Valerie's father?"

"Rather!"

"That's both creepy and very good. I'm pleased for her." Gaius tapped his fingernails against the marble stair. "This demon—when he said his brother would evict him—did he mean the Raven?"

"I..." she paused, "don't know. Maybe. I think so. I heard a caw."

"Does that mean that the Raven is a demon, too?"

"I think he's... something else."

Rachel could not explain that the Elf had said that the Raven was the brother of her mother—who was the guardian of the World

Tree—or that the Elf had called him a god. So she said nothing at all. Rachel also had her own opinion about the Raven. They involved a statue that had once had wings and a page in a book that had been hidden from her memory, an entry in an old bestiary for something called an *angel*.

"Um.... I hate to ask. It sounds so callous," said Gaius, "but I think you'd rather I do: If Azrael sacrificed your grandfather's family, was he casting his spell? The one that kills a family in front of one surviving member and sucks something from another world."

Rachel sat up straight. "Possibly."

"Did the spell summon someone?"

"Who do you think it could have brought?"

"The other four members of the Terrible Five, didn't they...." Gaius paused as if searching for the right word. "Couldn't they do things no one else has ever done?"

"I say!" cried Rachel. "You jolly well may be onto something!"

"Maybe they were... what is it your group calls them, Metacrutons?"

Rachel's lips twitched. "Metaplutonian."

"As in Beyond Pluto? Got it." Gaius nodded. "Are the other four Metaplutonians?"

"Are you thinking some of the people Azrael's spell brought were so wickedly evil that the Raven turned them to stone and made us all think it had happened long ago?"

"Could be." Gaius nodded. "The demon those guys were trying to summon the first time—I keep thinking I've heard his name before. I could swear it came up in class. Either in True Hiss or in Thaumaturgical Rites."

"We should go to the library and see what else we can find."

Gaius leaned toward her, smiling. "It's a date."

She nodded with a sweet, calm smile, but inside, she had lit up like a bonfire. She wanted so much to tell him that she loved him, but he was the boy. He had to speak such words first. Her grandmother had regaled her again and again with the unhappy fate of girls who were too forward.

"Let's go to the library right now." Gaius rose to his feet. "I can show you the painting of my family's farm on the way."

• • •

They flew down from the roof, Gaius seated behind Rachel, his arms tight about her waist, and landed by the west entrance of Roanoke Hall. Walking down the hallway toward the dining hall, they stopped in front of a painting. Rachel recognized it immediately. It was the one Gaius and Tess Dauntless had been looking at the time she had run by covered in orange juice.

The landscape showed a picturesque Cornish farmhouse with old-fashioned windmills in the distance. There was a crest above the barn doors, but it was too small to make out clearly. Rachel stood on her tiptoes scrutinizing it and memorizing the whole picture.

"When you graduate, do you intend to go back to your farm to live?" She kept her eyes on the house and spoke lightly, as if she were not asking about something that might affect the rest of her life.

"No, I am a sorcerer," Gaius said firmly. "Unlike my distant grandparent, I am not going to hide on my farm, away from this world. Before I came here, I was thinking I would be a scientist. Now I think I will be something else. Plenty of places to do research on magic and magical creatures and the like, right? That's where I'll be. Perhaps I will go work for Locke's company. They have both sorcerers and mundane folk working for them."

Rachel, who loved farms and knew a good deal about them, hid her disappointment.

"William worked on a really interesting project this summer. It's based on what could be salvaged of your second cousin's research, from before his accident. It's still secret, so I can't tell you much about it, but if they can get it to work, it might turn out to be very useful in times to come. Could have been useful to you last night. I would love to work on a project like that."

"Interesting," Rachel smiled. "I must admit to being curious now. So you could join him. Or I suppose you could go to Bavaria and work for Vlad. I bet he's going to want sorcerers doing research, too."

"Considering that, too."

Rachel gazed at the painting and imagined the two of them as a married couple, standing in front of that farmhouse as they told their children about this day.

What a wonderful life they would have together.

• • •

The library took up three stories in the eastern leg of the hollow square that was Roanoke Hall. It was a place of enormous stacks and narrow spiral staircases. Rachel and Gaius breathed in the pleasantly musty smell of books and exchanged smiles. If there was anything more wonderful than an enormous collection of wisdom, it was someone with whom to share it.

They spread out, gathered books, and met at a table hidden between two semi-circular stacks. Together, they pored over the various volumes they had discovered. Gaius muttered under his breath about the inefficiency of not using mundane computing devices.

"Found it!" Gaius cried suddenly, poking a spot on the page of the huge thaumaturgical volume he was skimming. "I haven't found your human-headed bull guy. But that first name? His boss?" He wrote *Moloch* on a scrap of paper. "It's an alternate name for Kronos."

"The Titan?" She tipped her head back, thinking. A reference came to her from an encyclopedia she had once read. "The Titans were worshipped by the Phoenicians, right?"

"Phoenicians, as in Carthage and Hannibal?" Gaius asked as he searched for a page number referred to in his book's index.

"Exactly."

"Do you think he rides elephants?"

"The demon or Hannibal?"

"The demon," drawled Gaius. "I already know about Hannibal's thing for elephants."

Rachel ducked her head but could not quite restrain her giggling. She clapped her hand over her mouth, so as not to disturb her fellow patrons.

"The Romans rather hated the Carthaginians," Gaius continued. "They hated them so much that they completely destroyed the city, ploughed the entire country under, and salted the lands."

"That's where the phrase *delenda est* comes from," said Rachel, "as in '*Cathago delenda est.*' 'Carthage must be destroyed.'"

"Found something. This is from Alexander the Great's historian, Cleitarchus." Gaius peered at the text and made a noise of dismay. "'*There stood in their midst a bronze statue of Kronos. Its* hands were extended over a copper brazier. The flames from the bra-zier surrounded the child. When the flames burnt the body, the limbs seized up and the mouth opened, so that, until the body was engulfed in flames, it almost seemed to be laughing. This "grin" is known as "sardonic laughter," as they died "laughing.""

The two of them sat quietly, wordlessly staring at each other. Gaius reached out and squeezed her hand. He gazed at her face, his dark eyes filled with concern.

"I'm really sorry, Rachel, that you have to face all this. Attacks. People killing children. Murdering whole families. What happened to Valerie. I wish I could protect you from them."

Rachel looked down, absently rearranging her reading mater-ial. "I want to know everything, Gaius. But some things are hard to know." She looked up, as if pleading, "I would rather know painful things than be ignorant. I just wish they were not there to know. That nothing so painful existed."

"I wish that, too. Unfortunately, the real world is not like that."

Rachel nodded wordlessly.

They read a bit longer. There was a horrible picture of the statue of Kronos, like a giant, bull-headed furnace with its arms extended over a blazing fire. And another picture of the Tophet of Carthage, a graveyard filled with urns containing the charred remains of burnt children, along with a few animals. After seeing those, Rachel began merely glancing at the pages, to read them later. While she could recall the words by glancing at them, she still had to read them to know the information. Otherwise, it was like recalling a picture formed from letters but without meaning. While her memorization speed was nigh instant, her reading speed was no faster than any other good reader.

"Gaius," Rachel looked up suddenly. "Um.... I hope this ques-tion doesn't offend you."

"Go ahead. You can ask anything. I might not answer, but I won't be offended."

"How does what this monster does differ from what you do?"

"What *I* do?" He looked puzzled.

"As a thaumaturge."

"Oh!" Gaius tipped back his chair and blew out his cheeks. "First of all, I don't sacrifice human beings. At all. Ever. That's black magic. I don't do black magic. Second, I'm more of a duelist. The only sacrifices I have been involved in personally have been things like feeding rabbits to chimera we've summoned. Not that different from feeding one's pet tiger. But you mean thaumaturgy in general." He considered, absently running his thumb across his lip. "Well, how does, say, sacrificing a goat to some chthonic entity to convince it to give you ten charges of, say, the power to see in the dark, differ from what priests do? They perform sacrifices, right?"

"Father says thaumaturgy is bad because the sacrifice is not done for a sacred reason."

"Frankly, I can't see what the difference is between the gods and the creatures we thaumaturges call up. I mean, look at this stuff...." He gestured at the books on the table. "The Carthaginians were sacrificing to their god, right?"

"But if their god is the same creature I met..."Rachel shuddered. "Then he's not a god at all. He's a demon."

"So?" Gaius gestured as if to indicate a gallery of deities. "What is to say that all these other gods are not demons, too? Maybe all these deities are the same. Some of them are nice enough. But many of them... well, I've read the stories. Girls turned into trees? Men torn apart by their own dogs? I wouldn't want to be at their mercy."

"I don't think they're the same things at all," Rachel objected fiercely. "The nuns of Asclepius are so very kind. They're wonderful healers who selflessly devote themselves to the sick. And the librarian here is a monk of Athena. Don't these people strike you as good?"

"They do good works. True. As do many of the other orders. The monks of Hephaestus run the best foundries and make the best mechanics of anyone," countered Gaius, "but we still sacrifice cocks to Asclepius. And nobody says that's evil. Though, I've never heard of anyone sacrificing anything alive to Athena. I grant you that."

"Supplicants usually leave offerings of honey cakes or scrolls with essays written on them. Things like that. Even her major temples stopped doing live sacrifices after Athena's famous visit to the temple at Constantinople during the reign of Diocletian."

"True." Gaius flipped his pen in the air and caught it. "And no one sacrifices humans to the gods anymore. At least not the gods the Unwary worship—the Greek, the Norse, the Egyptian, the Hindu, et cetera. But then we thaumaturges don't sacrifice human beings either. We sacrifice rabbits and chickens and goats. Things people eat. I can't see how this is so bad. Don't gods and monsters have to eat, too?"

"Maybe." Rachel stared off into the swirling fog. She felt there was a difference between priests and thaumaturges but could not put her feelings into words. "You know... Mrs. March said, 'No real gods or angels are allowed on this world.' Why is that?"

"Allowed by... whom?" Gaius straightened up, alert.

"The guardian, maybe? The Raven tried to make Kitten's familiar leave, too."

"Interesting." He cocked his head, thinking. "So, you think some gods are gods, while others are demons in disguise?"

"I think so." Rachel nodded. Then she shuddered. "That creature... the first demon. He was only there for an instant, but there was something...." Her voice faltered. Gaius drew her closer. "S-something horrid about him. He must be stopped. *At any cost.*"

"You sound like Vlad."

"Is that a bad thing?"

"No. Not at all. I like Vlad."

Rachel pursed her lips, and then stopped quickly, as they were still sore. Getting to know a boy was like trying to solve a puzzle. She wanted to know all about him. The princess thought he was evil, but was he?

She blurted out, "Why did you choose Thaumaturgy?"

If he truly were evil—if he had chosen Thaumaturgy from a desire to pursue black magic—might he not answer with a lie? No. He had shivered in the midst of the *Spell of True Recitation.* If he were a boy who lied, the spell-sparkles would have burnt him. She leaned forward, very curious to hear his reply.

"I guess because I wanted to study the nature of magic itself. Thaumaturgy's the closest thing to science here at Roanoke."

"I would have thought you would have chosen Alchemy. We even call it Science class."

"Alchemy is applied magic, like chemistry. I wanted to study pure magical theory. Like physics. That left either Gnosis or Thaumaturgy... which is why I considered Dee and Drake. I went with Thaumaturgy because dueling sounded like more fun than omen-reading."

Rachel giggled. She chewed on her sore lip and considered his answer. It put the Thaumaturgical Art in quite a different light from the way her family saw it.

"Being a thaumaturge," she asked suddenly, "does it give you any insight? Any clue we can use to stop this beastly monster before he starts sacrificing modern children?"

Gaius tipped his chair back farther, thinking. Then, his chair slammed into an upright position with a *bang*.

"Yes!"

"Really?"

"These greater entities that thaumaturges call up—daemons, deva, djin, furies, *gui*, rakasha, *yokai*—they have certain qualities in common. One is that they are all obsessed with calendar dates. That's why there are so many holy festivals: Equus-October, Samhain, Agonalia, Yule, Lupercalia, Liberalia, the Dragon Boat Festival, Saturnalia, Zagmuk. The list goes on and on.

"Every deity has sacred days," he continued. "Each one is jealous of how they are observed. Though one does not hear as many horror stories about revenge for forgotten sacred honors carried out during the last few centuries. In fact, everything's been rather quiet the last few centuries god-wise." He looked thoughtful. "But that's another conversation. Point is, this creature may have a date when it would expect major sacrifices to be carried out."

"Of course!" Rachel clapped her hands. "They are going to summon him on his name day! That's what the other demon said. What date is sacred to Kronos?... do we have a *Calendar of Feast Rites*?"

Gaius retrieved the slender volume that contained the days in the current year set aside to honoring various gods. He flipped through it.

"They said his name day?" he said. "I don't see Moloch or Krono... Saturn!"

"Of course, Kronos's other name is Saturn! The Titan of Time who ruled during the Golden Age and was overthrown because he had the bad habit of eating his children," said Rachel. "So his name day would be...."

"Saturnalia!" they both cried simultaneously.

They stared at each other incredulously. Saturnalia was a major holiday among both the Wise and the Unwary.

"That gives us until December 17th," Rachel's eyes widened until they were huge. "That's the *demon's* name day? Saturnalia? It's one of the biggest holidays of the year, after..." she paused for a moment, mentally sorting the really big holidays from the medium ones. "Yule, Lupercalia, Vernal Equinox. May Day, Midsummer's Night, Lammas, and Halloween."

"We always treated it as the official beginning of the Yule Season," Gaius said. "Here at school, don rags are done and we're always out and home by Saturnalia. At home, back when I was an Unwary, we used to have a five day celebration, eat a lot of pork, drink Doom Bar, and smash a pig-shaped piñata."

Rachel blinked slightly at the notion of a boy guzzling Cornish beer, but what she said was, "A piñata? You're lucky. In the World of the Wise, we still do it the old way. My father, as duke, always had to be the one to make the first ceremonial cut on the pig's throat, before the priests sacrificed it."

Now it was Gaius's turn to blink. "You used a live pig?"

She nodded solemnly. "Actually, we use a boar. For Freyr. That's not so bad. It's hearing the horses die, during Equus-October festival, that I hate most. I always try to get out of going."

"And you guys don't like us thaumaturges? I can't see the difference."

Rachel bit her lip, which was still sore from all the whistling, uncertain what to say.

"But back to Saturnalia," he continued, "So, this Titan, whose day is celebrated by the whole Western world and even portions of the Far East—both Wise and Unwary—is a *demon*?"

"Disturbing." Rachel shuddered.

Gaius tipped his chair back again, tapping his pencil against his temple. "Okay, what else would the demon need? Oh, I know!"

He jumped up and ran off into the stacks, coming back with a book. "This is by Diodorus Siculus, a Greek historian who lived in Sicily in the First Century. He records the particulars of the ceremonies needed to invoke various gods and Titans. I think he is quoting from an older work. This volume did not survive in the mundane world. The World of the Wise must have thought it too dangerous."

Gaius flipped quickly through pages. "Here! Rituals to consecrate a temple to Kronos! There are... let's see... ah!... three things that must be done before a temple is complete: consecration of priests; consecration of the ground; consecration of the sacred statue—the one used to hold the victims. According to this, each step needs sacrifices. And each step has to be performed during the dark of the moon. Between now and December seventeenth, that leaves us...."

"October fourteenth, November thirteenth, and December twelfth," Rachel recalled the schedule of the moon she had seen in an almanac. Gaius's eyebrows shot up. Rachel continued speaking before he could ask her how she knew. "Do you think the temple might have been built already?"

Gaius considered and then shook his head. "Azrael was supposed to be the head honcho, right? They only lost him yesterday. So, they haven't had time to prepare for this new demon, whom they called to take his place. My guess is they are only just starting."

"You know, you're brilliant." Rachel beamed at him.

"I'm brilliant? It's rather amazing, everything you've found out," Gaius declared. "Vlad would be impressed with you. And that is high praise indeed!"

A shiver ran from the crown of her head to the soles of her feet. That was high praise.

He continued sincerely, "You're the second most impressive woman I've ever heard of."

Rachel blushed and lowered her lashes—as much to hide the sting of discovering someone else impressed her boyfriend even more than she did as out of humility. She smiled slightly, amused at her own expense.

Ah well. Such was the fleeting nature of praise.

"I'd better tell Vlad," Gaius continued, before Rachel could ask him whom the first most impressive woman was. "He would definitely want to know about this."

Rachel nodded. "I should share this information with my father —about Saturnalia."

Gaius rubbed his temples. Then, he asked, chagrined, "Look, really sorry, but... which part of what you told me was so secret someone would die if I repeated it?"

"Oh! I... didn't get to that part. I...."

Zoë's voice spoke from her pocket. "Rachel!"

Rachel pulled out her calling card. "Hello?"

"The nurse has released Joy and Nastasia." Zoë held the card too close to her face. Only one eye and her nose were visible. "We're going to go carry out the princess's plan."

"The *princess's* plan?" Rachel sighed in exasperation. "Um... can you wait a bit?"

"Nope. The princess has an appointment with the dean in two hours. We want to learn more before we all get expelled or they confiscate my shoes or something. If you want, you can join us."

The card went green. Rachel sighed. She desperately did not want her friends to go into the dreamland without her. She very much wanted to participate in the experiments. And besides, someone needed to be present who would remember the results.

"I'm sorry." She looked up regretfully. "I have to go. I need to be there for this. We're about to do something important."

"Oh."

Gaius's obvious disappointment made her heart soar. He wanted to be with her. She gave him a very sweet smile. He reached out and squeezed her hand.

"My big secret will have to wait." Rachel rose to her feet.

"I await the revelation," Gaius drawled dryly, amused. "Seems like you're not too happy with the 'princess's plan'? Is her noble highness up to something of which you disapprove?"

"It's not the *princess's* plan," Rachel rolled her eyes, "it's *my* plan."

"Your princess took the credit?"

"No, she's as much of a victim as I," laughed Rachel. Even as she said it, she realized it was the truth. "Other people attribute my ideas to her."

"Ah. I'll leave you to sort that out then."

He rose and walked around the table to where she was. Leaning over with a twinkle in his eye, he kissed her goodbye.

Chapter Thirteen:

The Die Horribly Debate Club

"I'm here! I made it! We can...." Rachel burst in the door of the abandoned classroom Zoë had described as their meeting place and halted.

No one was there.

"Where is...?" She looked around the room, which was empty except for the large, polished, central table and its twenty-odd straight-backed chairs. Then she glanced up again at the number above the door. "Hang on. Am I in the wrong...?"

"Oh, it's you, Freaky-Genius-Dwarf-Girl." Lucky stuck his head over the edge of the table, his yard-long red whiskers twitching curiously. "The boss told me to tell you that you took too long. They'll get you for the next experiment."

A *scratching* from the corner, and Beauregard, the princess's Tasmanian tiger, scrambled to his feet. He trotted forward and nosed Rachel's hand, before returning to his previous spot and curling up to sleep. Turning her head, Rachel noticed that that Valerie's Norwegian Elkhound was also in the room. Payback sat alertly, watching Rachel's every move, but, being an excellently trained dog, she did not rise from the position her mistress had commanded her to take.

"Oh...." Rachel blinked several times, until she no longer felt the treacherous, tell-tale sting of tears. For this, she had had abandoned Gaius? "What are they about?"

"Experiments. The boss went there. I stayed here. To see if we can talk to each other."

"Oh, really?" Rachel perked up at the word *experiment*. "Did it work?"

"Can't really tell." The dragon cocked his head. "I... think so.

But he's talking so fast. I can't quite make out what he's saying. I should have gone and he could have stayed here. There isn't even a single chicken in this room—dream or otherwise. Of course...." The dragon turned and gave a speculative glance out the window in the direction of Drake Hall and the collection of sacrificial animals kept in cages behind the dorm.

Rachel put her hands on her hips. "Lucky!"

"What?" the dragon asked innocently. "They're just going to feed 'em to supernatural beings, right? I'm a supernatural being? Why shouldn't I get my fair share?"

"If you're hungry, you should visit the menagerie. That's where they feed the big animals and the ones that eat live food." Rachel pointed across the campus toward the menagerie, which could not be seen through the fog.

Lucky gaped in astonishment. His jaw unhinged like a snake's. His mouth was now so big that he could have swallowed a chicken or even a young lamb. "You mean this school comes with free, live take-out? This place is the best!"

Rachel giggled fondly at the dragon.

"Wait. Boss is trying again. I'll try to tell him you're here." The dragon closed his great eyes. Then they popped open again, like huge jade lamps.

"Did it work?" Rachel peered at him curiously.

"Think so."

A puff of mist appeared in the middle of the room. Zoë, Nastasia, Joy, Valerie, and Sigfried stepped out of it, apparently in the midst of an argument. Beauregard immediately rose to his feet and trotted to Nastasia's side. The elkhound remained seated until Valerie gestured to him. Then the dog ran forward, nails clipping against the wood, and happily bumped against her mistress.

"But I like that one," Joy objected.

"Nobody cares, O'Keefe," drawled Zoë. Her bright-eyed, tiger-spotted quoll sat on her shoulder, observing the room curiously.

"Too childish," quipped Valerie, letting go of Siggy's hand and advancing her camera. "People would mistake us for a club for preschoolers, and dorky preschoolers at that."

The princess said, "Society for the Promotion of a Beneficial Future has a nice ring to it."

"Too old fashioned," replied Valerie, kneeling to pet her dog. The dog licked her cheek. Valerie made a face. "Everyone would think we were frilly Victorians... or communists. And both of those options are frightening in my book."

"Annoy Zoë Club," suggested Zoë, "or maybe the Nearly-Decapitated Regularly Club?"

"Too personal and doesn't scan well," replied Valerie.

"Hallo," Rachel interrupted. "What are we all discussing?"

"Ah, Griffin did make it." Sigfried nodded at Lucky with sagely satisfaction. "Good."

"We've decided we want a clubhouse," Joy chattered. "So we need an official name."

"What O'Keefe is trying to say," Zoë explained lazily, as she fed her quoll a treat, "is that to be issued a room on the north leg of Roanoke Hall—where clubs meet—we need to register with the Assistant Dean's office. For that, for some dumb reason, we need an official name."

"What names have you come up with so far?" asked Rachel, eager to join the discussion.

"You've just heard most of them." Valerie snapped a picture of Lucky sitting on the classroom table. "The ones you haven't heard were even worse."

Rachel giggled again. She looked around. "I thought Salome was coming?"

Valerie shrugged. "She had a thing."

"How about: Sigfried Smith and His World-Saving, Monster-Mugging, All-Girl Jazz Band?" announced Siggy grandly. "Or, for something less jazz band-like: The Ancient and Honorable Military Order of the Knights of King Arthur, Junior Auxiliary Branch? Or: The After-School Vigilante and Vengeance Squad? The Underpaid Lunatics? Or, maybe, the Cosmic Danger Ignoring While We Squabble Brigade? That one has a surprising percentage of truth for something coming out of my mouth."

"I do not find these to be appropriate"—the princess's brow creased in patient thoughtfulness—"though Underpaid Brigade would have a bit of a poetic ring. Still, hardly the right appellation for a gathering of school children."

Valerie snorted derisively. "I am a fearless reporter girl who fought a demon's servants, and my boyfriend here has fought Velt-dammerung. The word *children* really doesn't cover it."

"Maybe for Griffin," Zoë gestured at Rachel. "She's only thirteen."

"Nevertheless," the princess spoke primly, "children we are, and we would do well to remember it. A time will come when it is our turn, but that time is not yet. If we wish to live long enough to reach it, we should heed our elders and not put on airs regarding our age and abilities."

Nastasia's words made Rachel's skin crawl. She wanted to shout: *Where were these adults when I was facing Azrael? Where were they when Dr. Mordeau nearly killed Mr. Chanson? Where were they when Serena O'Malley kidnapped you and Sigfried?* But she did not wish to quarrel with her best friend, especially not in front of the others. Zoë, Valerie, and Joy were sure to pile on against one side or the other.

Instead, she said, "As far as a name, Sigfried has already called us the Fire-Breathing-Tutor-Hunting and Vigilante-Retaliation Club and the Dreadfully Violent Adventuring Club."

"Only you would remember that!" declared Joy, her hazel eyes dancing with playful amusement. "I know: The Die Horribly Club! Sigfried and the princess and Rachel are all super important, I'm sure. They probably have a great destiny awaiting them. But Zoë and I are going to die horribly. I can feel it!"

"Thanks a lot for the vote of confidence," grumbled Zoë.

"What am I?" murmured Valerie. "Already dead?"

Zoë said, "How about the: Going To Die Horribly Defending The Princess And Joy Club?"

"Hey!" cried Joy.

"That is *not* the official name of the club," objected Siggy sternly. "The club is officially called the Giving Up All Chance For A Comfortable And Normal Life Club In Order To Die Horribly And In Lingering Pain Defending The Princess And Joy. You left out the 'and in lingering pain' part. That is what makes our club different from the Vampire Hunting Club and Von Dread's clique. Their enemies will wipe them out instantly, without paralysis, killing family members, dismemberment, and torture."

Valerie rolled her eyes.

"I've been thinking," Siggy continued, "that the Giving Up All Chance For A Comfortable And Normal Life Club In Order To Die Horribly And In Lingering Pain Defending The Princess And Joy takes too long to say. We need something short and snappy: What about the Skunk Tossers? Or the Egg Beaters? What about Zoë and the Pussycats?"

"Zoë and the Pussycats it is," quipped Valerie. "Everyone will have to wear cat suits and furry ears berets."

"I still vote for Die Horribly Club," pouted Joy.

"We do spend a great deal of our time arguing," the princess said thoughtfully. "Perhaps the Dream Debate Society?"

"Oh, I know!" Joy bounced with excitement, nearly knocking over a chair. "The Die Horribly Debate Club!"

"That's great!" Sigfried declared, "The Die Horribly Debate Club!"

"No!" Rachel exclaimed. "Please let's call it...."

But it was too late.

The name had stuck.

The others began repeating Die Horribly Debate Club and laughing—everyone except the princess, who looked pained. Rachel completely sympathized.

"Enough about this," Valerie interrupted finally. She turned to the dragon. "Let's get down to the proverbial tacks of brass. Lucky, did the experiment work?"

"Yep, only the boss was talking super-duper fast. Faster than a singing chipmunk."

Siggy said, "You were really slow. Every word you said, Lucky, took an entire ice age."

"You really can talk to your dragon in your head?" Zoë blinked. "Creepy!"

"You talk to your dragon in your head, too," Siggy countered. "The only difference is my dragon is real, and yours is imaginary."

"How did you know I have an imaginary dragon?" quipped Zoë.

"You have an imaginary dragon?" asked Joy, wide-eyed.

Zoë rolled her eyes. "O'Keefe, you are so naïve."

Valerie snickered, while Joy pouted.

"We have successfully performed experiment one: the communication of Mr. Smith and his familiar," said the princess. "Before we move onto our next step, I would like to speak privately with Miss Griffin."

"Certainly." Rachel stepped aside with Nastasia. They stood in a corner next to a painting of some ancient tutor in green and black robes.

"Rachel," Nastasia lowered her voice and whispered seriously, "I have a matter that I wish to discuss with you. It is on the subject of the boon Mr. Von Dread offered to us in return for our having saved him and his friends from death at Dr. Mordeau's hands. I have thought of something I desire, but… I do not want to impose on you, to tread on your toes, so to speak."

"My toes." Rachel wiggled hers. "Um… how would it affect me?"

"I was thinking I might ask him for membership in the Knights of Walpurgis, but I did not wish to do this if you felt the Knights were your special project."

"I would love to have you in the Knights with me!" cried Rachel, absolutely delighted. Then she would no longer have to worry about getting in trouble with the intimidating Dread because she repeated something she learned there to her friend.

"I am relieved to hear you say that." Nastasia looked shyly pleased. "I am certain we shall enjoy attending together."

"Yes, we shall!" Rachel declared. The two girls smiled at each other in delight as they walked back to join the others.

"Shall what?" Joy asked eagerly.

"I shall be cashing in my boon with Mr. Von Dread to join the Knights of Walpurgis."

"Oh! Me, too! Me, too!" Sigfried raised his hand. "I adore Dread. He's totally boss. I want to be a Knight! I even have a wand." He lifted the length of cherry wood and gold with a ruby tip and waved it back and forth over his head. "He owes me a boon, too!"

"Certainly, Mr. Smith," the princess smiled happily. "We would love to have you join us, wouldn't we, Miss Griffin?"

"Indeed," Rachel nodded, eyes sparkling.

"Then, it's decided," decreed Nastasia. "Back to current matters: what's our next step?"

"Let's experiment with *The Spell of Bedazzlement*," replied Rachel.

"Let's dazzle O'Keefe," quipped Zoë. "She said she was expendable."

"Told you this was the Die Horribly Debate Club!" groaned Joy.

"Yeah," murmured Valerie, "and now we get to debate who is going to die horribly. Aptly named club."

"I'll do it." Joy heaved a sigh. Spreading her arms, she squeezed her eyes shut. "Zap me."

"None of us know *The Spell of Bedazzlement*," the princess reminded her. "Miss Black performed it. She is an upperclassman."

"Maybe I can do it," Rachel said slowly. "I seem to be good at defensive enchantment, as hexes are officially called, I believe. Actually, it's the only thing I'm good at."

"Other than flying," smirked Joy.

The corners of Rachel's lip quirked upward. She nodded shyly. "I meant sorcery-wise."

Rachel recalled the moment when Xandra performed the hex on her oboe. She listened to the notes. Then, she whistled them. Magical energies rushed through her lips, tickling terribly. Her cheeks and mouth ached painfully, sore from her recent efforts on Gaius's behalf.

Nothing happened. She tried again.

After three tries, the princess said, "Apparently not. Why don't we adjourn until after...."

"What do you mean, apparently not?" Rachel interrupted, taken aback. "I've hardly begun! Give me a moment."

It took her thirteen tries before her sore lips could maintain the five notes long enough to produce blue sparkles. Remembering what Gaius had told her about the paralysis hex, she concentrated. Blue sparks flew from her mouth and danced around Joy.

Joy's eyes glazed over. She began to weave around the class-room, bumping into chairs and giggling uncontrollably. The elk-hound barked excitedly.

"Ooo. Siggy. You're so cute. I love your golden curls. Kiss me again."

Zoë and Valerie burst into laughter. Siggy frowned and ran a hand through his hair as if he had not previously noticed that he had thick golden curls. Then he saw Valerie watching and put his hands behind his back, trying to look nonchalant.

Valerie stomped on his foot.

"What? It's not my fault," he scowled. "I'm not Zoë. I didn't pick my hair color."

Joy's performance was terribly embarrassing. Rachel felt weak at the thought that she might someday make such a spectacle of herself. She whistled again, the paralysis hex. Her sore lips and cheeks hurt, but more blue glints of light played over Joy's body. Joy froze.

"In the future," Rachel stated, her cheeks afire, "let's paralyze the person first."

"The victim, you mean," Valerie stated cheerfully. "Paralyze the victim! Rule noted."

They lay Joy on the table and left Lucky to watch her. Valerie sat her elkhound down and told her to "guard." Beauregard retreated back into the corner. The rest of them followed Zoë into the mist. When they emerged, they found themselves in a dream version of Joy's bedroom.

Joy was bouncing on her bed while chatting animatedly into a round talking glass. The walls were covered with posters. Among the K-pop bands, which Rachel recognized because her sister Lau-rel's room had similar pictures, was a poster of the rock star Red Ry-der, grinning in his skin-tight red and blue glittering garments with gold safety pins piercing his ears. The poster was only visible for an instant, and then was replaced with something else. The other posters, too, seemed to flow from one to another as Joy dreamed. The room got fuzzier as it moved father from where Joy sat. The far side was just a brownish blur.

Joy's bed was covered with a collection of bobble-headed, pastel Witch Babies and a big, white, cat plushy that was the spitting image of Joy's familiar—a big, long-furred, white cat she had creatively named Fluffy. Her sister Charity's bed was neater, but scattered with issues of *Original Tongue Today* and *Wise Wear* magazines, along with an issue of the comic, *James Darling, Agent*. The posters on her side of the room featured popular broom jockeys.

At first, Joy's gaze did not track them, as if she did not see them. Zoë leaned over and shook her shoulder. Joy gave a little cry. The talking glass in her hand vanished, but the rest of the room became slightly sharper. It was a small room, cramped. With two desks and chairs taking nearly all the available space. It could have fit in Rachel's bedroom at least three times.

"Is this your room?" Siggy gawked, staring around him.

"Yeah, it's not much." Joy blushed and looked like she wished she could hide the room.

"It's huge!" Siggy's eyes bugged out. "And you share it with less than four people? Wow. At the orphanage, fourteen of us lived in the same dorm room. And the new guy always had to sleep on the floor. This is wicked cool!"

Rachel thought Sigfried was kidding, but his eyes were so wide, his expression of admiration so sincere that he must have been serious. Her heart went out to him. She wished she could give him one of the hundreds of rooms in her family's huge, drafty, nearly empty mansion—any of which were bigger than this one, including the closets.

"I share it with Charity, the youngest of my six older sisters," explained Joy.

"You have a sister," Siggy sighed dreamily. "I'd like to have a sister."

Valerie snapped a picture, illuminating Joy's dream room with her flash. The whole room grew lighter, a pleasant view of the sky replacing one wall. "Okay. That worked. What now?"

"We now know we can find our way into dreamland at any time, so long as one of us is willing to be bedazzled," replied Nastasia.

Rachel said thoughtfully. "Right now, if we were in Transylvania, at least one of us would still be stuck. Let's try Valerie's idea:

bedazzle one of us inside your house, in your purse, Nastasia. Then, you can try to carry the bag into the dreamlands. If this works, we can leave anywhere, at any time."

"That's a brilliant idea!" Siggy grinned. "Then, we'd never be stuck. Good thinking, Griffin!"

"It was Valerie's idea."

Siggy gave his girlfriend a huge grin. "Good thinking, Goldi-locks! I knew you were the smartest girl in the girl-pack! Or do you call it a herd? Gaggle? Huddle? What's the term for a gathering of girls?"

Zoë shook her head and took them back to the waking world. Lucky nudged Joy's sleeping body. She sat up on the table.

"Ow." Joy rubbed her elbow and her side. "Why do I hurt?"

"Sorry," Rachel murmured. "You walked into a chair after we bedazzled you."

"What else did I do?" Joy's face went from pink to bright red. She looked so embarrassed, Rachel suddenly found that she liked the other girl more than she had before. Recalling Joy's earlier comment, *Only you would remember that*, Rachel made a decision.

"Use me," she said aloud. "I want to show you all something."

Nastasia said, "But you're the one casting the enchantment. You can't bespell yourself."

Sigfried grinned and pulled out his battered trumpet. It was a school loaner and had streaks in the brass where it had once been bent and hammered back into shape. He played the notes Rachel had whistled. Blue sparkles swirled around the mouth of his instrument on his very first try. Rachel smiled and sighed and froze that way.

"You know you're an amazing child prodigy, right?" mused Valerie. "It takes the average student a month to three months to learn a simple enchantment. There are records of students graduating with less magic under their belt than you have already."

Sigfried spun the trumpet on his finger. "Did I explain that I can do magic tricks? I have an empty mind, which gives lots of spare room to stow this stuff."

"Then, why can't you learn True History?" she asked.

"That name sounds familiar. Is that one of the classes we have here? I think I use that class for naptime. Because, how does knowing the date when something boring happened help you smash bad guys and set them on fire?"

Valerie sighed.

It took him three tries to get the *Spell of Bedazzlement*. Rachel waited patiently, unable to scratch her nose. She was reminded of standing for inspection before her Victorian grandmother.

Then....

Dreams danced through her head, or maybe she danced through dreams. The field around her sparkled with flowers under a dark starry sky. Or maybe those were stars in the meadow. A unicorn munched nearby, whinnying slightly as it swallowed a star-flower. When Zoë touched her shoulder and Rachel woke to herself, she found she was stroking the unicorn's silky coat.

Zoë's hand held that of Sigfried, who was stepping from the mist. Siggy's arm trailed off to where the others were beginning to appear behind him.

"Nice unicorn," began Zoë, smirking.

Then her eyes went wide and she uttered a strangled, *ack*. She and those behind her were jerked backwards, as if pulled by a collapsing rubber band. Then, they were gone. Rachel stood alone under the starry sky. The unicorn nuzzled her ear.

"Hey, cutie, want a ride?"

Gaius leaned down from the unicorn's back, his hand extended. Or at least, the dream figment looked a lot like Gaius, though Rachel instantly knew it was not really him. For one thing, Dream Gaius was taller than real Gaius. Dream Gaius gave her a huge grin, bigger and more showy than his waking counterpart.

"Why, yes, thank you!" Rachel reached out and took his hand.

Dream Gaius lifted her up and placed her on the unicorn in front of him.

The beast raced across the meadow, sending tiny multi-colored stars flying in its wake. Rachel laughed with joy. Dream Gaius's arms tightened around her waist.

They ran across fields and through a forest that was thick and deep and filled with mystery. Dark limbs of evergreens hung low over their heads like deep green feathers. In the strange way of dreams, they were accompanied by the noise of drums and the smell of lavender. Through the trunks, Rachel caught a glimpse of the giant Lenni Lenape woman, whom she had seen the first time she had come to the dreamlands. The old lady patiently cut lopsided, five-pointed stars from yesterday's moon and stuck them to the black velvet sky. A waterfall ran beside her. A pale face with a nimbus of dark hair peeked out from behind the rushing water. Then that scene was gone, and the forest was everywhere. From the high branches, funny little faces peered down at her, leathery, wrinkled faces that were neither animal nor human. Rachel waved.

Then they galloped again across the star-studded meadow. Her dream steed raced on. It was glorious, and at the same time, peculiar. It was not like riding any real horse. The motion of its stride was all wrong. Horses did not move like rocking chairs. Also, no wind pressed against her face or tugged at her hair.

"Whoa!" Zoë stepped from a puff of mist. "Enough horseplay, Griffin. Get down here."

The unicorn halted. With a tiny giggle, Rachel slipped down from its back and waved goodbye to Dream Gaius.

"You should be careful about interacting with dream figments," Zoë warned her as the others appeared behind her. "Aperahama Whetu said it's best not to pay attention to them."

"Oh...." Rachel frowned and glanced to her right.

The unicorn was munching grass again. Standing beside it, his hand resting on its mane, Dream Gaius stared apprehensively up at the night sky where a fleet of many-masted clipper ships sailed among the stars. In the way of dreams, Rachel understood that, as he watched the star ships, he was worried about the vision the princess had seen regarding his past.

Was real Gaius worried about his past, too?

"Which reminds me," Zoë continued, flipping her braid in a circle. "Remember how your father told you about a dream expert coming to Roanoke? Turns out, that was Whetu. He says he won't be able to come for months, maybe not until next year. I'm not sure if he's really busy, or if he made up a reason to put them off for my sake. Either way, for the best."

"Who is not coming?" asked Nastasia, appearing out of the mist behind Zoë.

After her came Joy and then Sigfried with Valerie taking up the rear. Joy looked smug. Rachel recalled that Siggy had been between Zoë and Valerie the last time they had appeared. Apparently, Joy had maneuvered things to her advantage, as now she, rather than Zoë, held the hand of the handsome boy.

"Aperahama Whetu." Zoë pointed at the silver sandals on her feet. "The Maori shaman who made my dream-walking shoes. He's supposed to come examine the wards around Roanoke, to protect us from stuff like what happened to you, Princess, when that hot guy with the smoky wings... what was his name... snuck into your dream."

"Lightflinger," stated Sigfried.

"Lightflinger, whatever." Zoë shrugged. "Rachel was afraid that any precautions Whetu put in against dream attacks might stop us from coming up here."

"None of which will matter if the dean confiscates your sandals." Valerie gave an exaggerated sigh. "It's bad business, turning ourselves in, but I had to tell them something so that they'd restore my father. Couldn't keep him as a goose forever. It didn't suit him. Sorry."

Zoë shrugged again. "Losing my sandals would suck."

"I don't think they'll take them," Joy said cheerily, swinging both Nastasia's and Siggy's hands as she spoke. "My sisters told me some crazy stories about things that happen here. School policy seems to be pretty hands off when it comes to private talismans and such. And with experimentation. Hope's freshman year, two boys in her class blew up the forest behind Roanoke Hall. Sorcery still doesn't work properly there—to this day, it's all scrubby, and they can't use even the most basic cantrips to get the trees to grow. Forget expelling them. The school didn't even forbid those boys from performing more experiments."

"They probably wanted to know how to repeat the effect that stops sorcery," said Sigfried. "I would want to know that."

Rachel said slowly, "I wonder if it's because of the Terrible Years."

"When those villains took over the school?" asked Valerie.

"And nearly the world," quipped Zoë.

Valerie continued, "How exactly would that apply?"

Rachel blinked. Calling the Terrible Five *those villains* struck her as strange. It was like hearing someone refer to Hitler as *some dictator*.

She replied, "What saved the day and allowed the YSL to overthrow the Terrible Five was things like personal talismans and unusual sorcery they learned by experimenting—James Darling and the others. I bet the school decided it was better to let the students take risks than to lose an entire generation to evil."

"That's... so weird." Valerie shivered. "No mundane school would ever allow stuff like this. In my hometown, you can't even bring chapstick to school. In elementary school, I got suspended twice for pretending I had a gun."

"They outlawed pretend weapons?" Siggy gawked at her as if she had sprouted hot-pink beans from her ears. "We were not allowed television, and we had to eat bread and water nearly every other day. But even the orphanage wasn't that cruel!"

"That's modern America for you," muttered Valerie.

"Maybe they were afraid you'd conjure guns." Joy's expression was sweet and sincere. "Weapons like that don't work here, but if they did, I bet our tutors would worry about that, too."

Valerie stared at Joy.

"What?"

"Mundanes don't have conjuring. That's why we're mundanes."

"Oh." Joy's face grew pink. "Right."

"What happened just now?" Rachel asked eagerly. "When you all disappeared?"

"Experiment Three was a failure," drawled Zoë. "When the bag with your sleeping body in it came into dreamland, we all fell out. O'Keefe's fat butt landed on my hand. Still hurts."

"Hey!" Joy objected. "Look who's talking!" The two girls glared at each other good-naturedly. Joy stuck out her tongue.

"Oh, that's too bad!" exclaimed Rachel, "I had so hoped that plan would work."

"Yeah," Valerie sighed. "It would have been really convenient. Then all we would have needed was a bedazzle spell and a kenomanced bag, and we could have gone anywhere."

"We left Lucky guarding my purse, with your body asleep inside," explained Nastasia.

Valerie paused and looked around. "You know, everything looks...."

"Woodsy? Chartreuse?" Zoë offered, urging her to continue. "Zebra-polka dotted?"

"Crisp," Valerie said. "Like it's in focus. Joy's room was blurry and constantly in motion. Nothing has changed since we got here."

Nastasia looked left and right. "You are right."

Zoë was also looking around and frowning. "This is your dream, Rachel, the meadow. The unicorn. The flying boats."

"Those are star ships," Rachel corrected her.

"What?" Zoë looked up, puzzled.

"They're ships that fly among the stars." Rachel's voice faltered. "Isn't that what a star ship looks like?"

The others started chuckling, except for Nastasia.

"Good grief, Griffin," drawled Zoë. "Only you would mistake a galleon for a rocket."

Valerie glanced at the sailing ships in the sky and then at the crisp, clear surrounding landscape. "But what is making everything look so different this time?"

Rachel's lips quirked into a mischievous smile. "That's what I wanted to show you all."

Chapter Fourteen:

Memories in Dreamland

"I want to show you the one thing I can do that very few other people can do, but first," Rachel looked at her friends very seriously, "I need you to promise me that you won't tell anyone. I hate it when people know. They... get funny."

Actually, Rachel herself had never had any trouble with people learning about her memory. She didn't know enough people outside her family and close friends for it to matter. However, her mother had emphasized so emphatically how important it was to keep her memory secret—telling her dozens of stories of occasions where she had been put upon or embarrassed by others due to her gift—that Rachel felt great reluctance to tell anyone.

Zoë held up her hand. "Girl Scouts honor. Wait, you don't know what that is probably. Yes, I will keep it a secret."

Rachel rolled her eyes. "I know what the Girl Guides are. We have Scouts in England."

"Magical Scouts?" asked Sigfried.

Rachel nodded solemnly.

Joy and Valerie also promised to keep her secret, though Joy grumbled about the number of things she could not tell her sisters. Nastasia, Sigfried and Lucky already knew.

"Look." Rachel tipped her head back and remembered.

The landscape around them changed. They stood on the windy top of Gryphon Tor, with moors stretched out beneath them. To the left, far below, lay Gryphon Park mansion. To the right, in the distance, rose the giant's chair upon Dartmoor. Behind them were the ruins of the original castle built in 878.

Rachel recalled again. The scene changed. They stood at the foot of the Roanoke Tree, the enormous, skyscraper-tall trunk, with its seven different types of branches, that grew on the northern-most part of the island. Since the scene came from Rachel's memory, the tree was as her memory had recorded it, with golden light curling like flame around the branches. The mouths of the other girls opened in awe. Even Sigfried made a noise of wonder. Gazing up, even Rachel herself was struck anew by the sense of sacred glory.

"I remember this tree, but where did all that fiery gold-stuff come from?" asked Sigfried. "Did it get hit by lightning? That's wicked cool!"

"That's what the tree looks like in my memory," Rachel explained. "Sometimes, I can see things when I remember back that I can't see with my normal eyes."

"Wait. I remember when we were here, you asked that El...." Joy cut off what she was about to say. Nastasia was glancing at her sharply. Joy blinked for a moment and then continued. "You asked about your memory, and you freaked out when you accidentally crossed the wall. So, what's so special about your memory anyway?"

Valerie flashed a photo of the marvelous tree left-handed. She paused for a moment. Then, her eyes widened. "This is the first time I've taken a photo in dreamland, and it hasn't washed everything out. Everything is so crisp. I can make out individual leaves and grass blades. A policeman could gather evidence from this scene. In fact...." She pressed her lips together. Then, she turned to stare at Rachel. "You have photographic memory, don't you?"

Rachel nodded, her lips curled into a tiny half smile.

"Really?" squealed Joy. "You mean you remember everything perfectly? Show us... us."

"If you like." Rachel thought back.

The landscape changed again. They stood in the center of the commons in the semi-darkness. A huge silvery moon shone overhead. Fallen leaves swirled beneath their feet. In front of them, was the scene as Rachel remembered it from the previous night: Zoë stepping from the mist with Siggy and Lucky behind her. Valerie, Joy, and Nastasia running toward her, panting.

The others gawked, pulling this way and that in order to move the group toward the dream version of themselves, as they each examined their dream-selves.

"I could not possibly be that fat!"

"I'm a lot thinner than I expected."

"Did you have to make me look so goofy?"

"Hey! Look at me! I'm one good-looking bloke!"

Only Nastasia had made no comment. She stood composed between the others, glancing around the dreamscape.

Finally, she said, "It does look as I remember it. Well done, Miss Griffin."

"Where are you?" Joy looked around. "I only see us."

"I cannot see myself," Rachel explained. "So I have no memory of what I look like, except when I happen to glance down at my hands or something like that."

"Ah, that makes sense," Valerie agreed. She snapped a picture, her flash momentarily blinding everyone. "It will be interesting to see if these pictures come out differently from the ones taken in other people's dreams."

"Why didn't everything change when you used your flash?" Joy asked.

"Flashing a light at me right now doesn't change my memory," Rachel replied.

"Does anyone else find this whole thing truly creepy?" Valerie gestured with her camera at the landscape around them. "I for one have dreams—nightmares, many of them—that I would not want anyone to see. Ever."

"Dreams are weird," Zoë agreed. "But you get used to it. I don't judge anybody by what they dream. Who knows why it is there? And, besides, it doesn't really mean anything. A guy can dream about one naked girl, and that's not even the girl he likes. You can't make anything of them." She paused and then added, "What creeps me out is Griffin's memory. So, you remember everything? Every stupid comment we make? Every mistake we hope nobody will ever see?"

Rachel nodded.

"What a bummer," muttered Zoë.

"Oh, I get it," cried Joy, "That's why you know crazy things like the number of pigs to burn a castle or the ridiculous names Siggy called us all!"

"Yes," said Rachel.

"Hey, everything I say is worth remembering," replied Siggy, who was still admiring the dream-statue of himself.

Valerie's eyes lit up. "Can you imagine how useful a trait that would be in witnesses? If they could tell the police every detail they observed. If there are any crimes committed, Griffin, I want you to be there and be our eyes."

"I'll see what I can do," replied Rachel.

"And homework! Oh my gods! You must be great with homework!" Joy gasped. "You remember everything the teacher says! Will you help me with mine? I took the worst notes in true history class yesterday!"

Rachel sighed. There it was, exactly what her mother had warned her about—people trying to avoid doing their own work by relying on her memory. She wondered if she had made a mistake in revealing her secret.

They wandered around examining themselves a bit longer. Rachel felt grateful that she had chosen to be the one they bedazzled. She didn't have to stand still and hold hands. She was free to wander, since it was her dream, and she didn't need to stay near Zoë.

"What are those guys doing?" Valerie pointed off into the distance. Following her finger, Rachel realized that her memory had recreated the whole scene from the previous night, including the upperclassmen standing watch at the edge of the reflecting lake.

"Guarding the materials undergoing degossamerization, I assume," Rachel replied.

"Oh, you assume it's de-gopherization?" Sigfried nodded sagely. "And why is that? Why not assume de-badgerization? De-hedge-hogization? Or de-weaselization?"

All the girls started giggling.

"Degossamerization, you silly!" cried Joy. She moved closer to Siggy, gazing up at him with such a blatant simper that Rachel had to glance away in embarrassment.

Valerie gave Joy a steady look. "Please don't elbow my boyfriend, even if he exasperates you. I don't want to fall out of dreamland yet again."

"Oh. Right." Joy's cheeks turned pink.

"Degossamerization," Rachel repeated. "It's the process for making conjurations and alchemical talismans permanent."

"They're not permanent?" Sigfried asked.

Rachel blinked. How could he have been in art and science classes for over a month now and not have picked up on that?

Patiently, she explained, "Conjurations vanish after twenty-four hours and alchemical talismans only last a month... unless they are put out under the light of the full moon for a certain amount of time. They need moonlight on all sides, so the normal practice is to put them in glass cases over a mirror or a silvery surface, such as the bottom of the reflecting lake. The water is supposed to help amplify the effect. We have a little reflecting pool on the roof at home.

"Anyway, once a month, when the moon is full, all the conjurers make stuff they'd like to keep, and the alchemists bring out the talismans they want to make permanent—and they put them in the moonlight."

"Then by morning, they're real?" asked Sigfried.

The Wiseborn, Rachel, Joy, Zoë, and Nastasia, all shook their heads simultaneously.

"Takes thirteen months," said Zoë.

"That's thirteen full moons in a row," clarified the princess. "Thirteen full moons—a year from the moon's point of view—makes them permanent. It takes a great year to make something truly real —so that a conjured object is indistinguishable from the original."

"In a row?" asked Valerie, "What happens if they miss a month?"

"Then all the work is for naught," replied Nastasia. "The conjuration vanishes. The talisman loses its power."

"That sucks," said Valerie. "What happens if it's overcast?"

"That's what enchanters are for," replied Rachel.

When Valerie and Siggy looked puzzled, she added. "Remember how we are learning to make a wind in music class? Eventually, we'll learn how to clear clouds from the sky."

"What's a great year?" asked Siggy. "A year when everything goes right for you?"

Joy giggled. "No. Silly. That's a fantastic year. A great year is something else entirely."

"Eight years," Rachel replied. "The amount of time it takes the moon to come back to the same point in the Zodiac."

"That's a long time!" Siggy scowled. "Hasn't anyone found a way to speed this up?"

"Nope," replied Zoë. "You just have to live with it."

"Actually," Rachel began. The others looked at her. "Analysis of Ouroboros Industries, of how quickly they retool their products, such as Flycycles or Thundersticks or slendering rings, shows that O.I. can respond to market changes much faster than the eight years it should take, considering the quality of their workmanship."

"Um… you know this how?" Zoë asked dubiously.

"My father's an Agent with the Wisecraft. They investigate such things."

"Oh! Agent Griffin. Right. The guy Merlin Thunderhawk is based on."

"Merlin Thunderhawk!" boomed Sigfried. "What a great name!"

"He's a character from *James Darling, Agent*. Kind of like Batman, only with magic," said Zoë.

"I confess to knowing very little about comics," said the princess, "But he did look rather impressive when he came in the window last night, with his cloak flying around him."

"Neat! He looked wicked cool!" cried Sigfried. "And he saved our as… bacon, too!"

Rachel did not say anything, but she beamed. She loved her father so much. She was glad that she had been able to save him, twice. She could not wait for him to come see her, so she could tell him what really happened.

Siggy turned to her. "Show them!"

Rachel recalled the moment. Stone walls leapt up around them. Above, the glass of a high window shattered. Through it leapt Agent Griffin. His Inverness cape billowed about him like the dark wings of a falcon. He aimed his long fulgurator's staff at the heart of the robed Mortimer Egg. Crackling white-gold flame leapt from the fist-sized gem at the tip of Ambrose Griffin's staff and struck Egg's chest.

Rachel froze the scene.

"Wow!"

"Ace!"

"He's... really cool!"

"Okay," Zoë drawled after a moment. "Maybe Merlin Thunder-hawk isn't an exaggeration. Griffin, your dad's hot!"

Rachel blushed but she beamed with pride.

"What's that?" asked Valerie, pointing.

Rachel turned her head. The scene around them stretched to the edge of her vision. Then there was darkness. Her memory did not fill in what she had not seen. Right at the edge of the scene hung something she did not recall from the first time around.

A gigantic wing hung in the air, cut off, because it left the edges of Rachel's vision, before it reached the shoulder of whatever kind of being to which it might have been attached. The wing reached eight or nine feet into the air and was made of curling smoke. The smoky feathers were composed of shades of gray—pearl gray, dove gray, steely gray, charcoal gray. Those shades formed an eye pattern, as if someone had plucked the tail of a giant peacock formed of cloud and soot and formed them into the shape of a giant wing.

It was eerily beautiful. Rachel gazed at it, spellbound.

"I have... no idea."

"The being who accosted me in my dreams had wings much like this," stated Nastasia. Her perfect brow creased. "But they were more like eagle's wings. Not peacock feathers."

"Azrael had wings of smoke, too," Rachel said, "but they did not look like these."

"Let's see the rest of it." Siggy stepped closer to the wing, drag-ging Joy and Valerie along. "What were they attached to?"

"I... don't know. I didn't see it. Hold on." Rachel reviewed her memory to see if it had caught any more glimpses of the unexpected wings, but she found nothing. "Sorry. Whatever those wings are attached to... it was never in front of me."

"Creepy!" sang Valerie, drawing out both syllables.

Sigfried frowned at the smoky wing. He thrust his head for-ward, sticking it into the wing and shaking it back and forth. The dream stuff dispersed, the pearl and coal gray smoke drifting away. The moment he straightened up, it sprang back to the way Rachel remembered it.

"Reminds me of that thing that threw me out of the tower. It was made of smoke." His expression grew more serious. "Or maybe it just hadn't finished forming. Is that what things look like when you summon them? We'll have to ask a thaumaturge. Dread's a thaumaturge. Let's ask him. I'd love to see him summon something big. Could he summon Godzilla? It would be wicked to watch it stomp on the school. But, anyway, that demon thing that threw me out of the tower was bad news. We've got to stop them from summoning that thing again."

"At any cost!" Rachel and Sigfried spoke together.

Their eyes met and they nodded at each other.

"It was...." Rachel shivered. "There was something truly horrid about it. Oh, do you know what Gaius and I discovered?" The dreamland shifted to the school library. Gaius sat at a table covered with books. "That being, whose name we've been told not to say," She imagined the word MOLOCH written on a piece of paper on the table. It appeared. She grinned, pleased. "It is the same being as Kronos... Saturn. So the feast day that the other demon mentioned is probably Saturnalia." She filled them in on everything that she and Gaius had discovered.

"That gives us a little over two months. I'll tell my dad, in case the mundane police can help," said Valerie. She picked up one of the books on the table and flipped through it. The pages were blank or covered with random squiggly letters. "So this is not a real library."

Rachel grinned and pointed at one of the tomes on the table that read *Roget's Calendar of Feast Days*. "Try that one."

"It will be like that." Zoë lounged against one of the stacks. "You can't read in dreamland. Not dream books, I mean."

Valerie opened the large volume and flipped through it. "Hey! I can read it! Everything is here." She read aloud, "'*Lupercalia – February 15: sacred to Lupercus and Faunus. Cakes made by the Vestal Virgins from corn of the previous year are offered to the gods along with goats and one dog. Two teams of young men dress in goat skins and run around whipping onlookers with* februa, *goatskin strips, that purify those struck. Women hoping to produce male heirs attempt to be struck by the Wolf's Strap.*' Oh, that's ridiculous!" Valerie giggled, but she stopped when she saw the serious faces of the Wise-born.

"How are you doing that?" Zoë flipped rapidly through the book, stopping at first one page and then another. "I can read this! I've never read any dream book before! Not the same words more than once, anyway."

"I've seen every page." Rachel shrugged. "I remember it."

"That's... scary, Griffin." Zoë blinked.

"But back to the matter of any cost," the princess frowned stubbornly. "Sigfried, if you are to be my knight, we must be clear on this issue."

"But it doesn't—" Sigfried began hotly.

Zoë cut him off. "You two argue on your own time, okay? Not while I have to stand by holding your hand... literally." She paused and then chuckled. "Griffin, I can't believe you didn't know what a rocket ship was."

"I know what a rocket ship is," Rachel defended herself. "I just did not know that a star ship was a rocket ship. In my defense, we have lots of flying ships in the World of the Wise. The Starkadders came to school in one."

"What a great idea," Siggy cried enthusiastically. "A star-faring clipper ship! Maybe that's how the Metaplutonians get about! Can we use magic to outfit one to be space-worthy? We could be Metaplutonian-raiding pirates! I want a coat like Captain Harlock's!"

"I saw it!" Valerie said enthusiastically. "The Transylvanian flying ship. When it came by to pick up some of the royal family the second week of school." Valerie paused. "What I don't understand is: Why does the World of the Wise avoid modern things... movies, cars, toasters, rocket ships? I understand why the Unwary," she rolled her eyes, "don't use magic. We don't have any. I mean, even if we knew about magic, most Unwary are unable to use magic. But, why keep the children of the Wise from using technology? Why live like mechanical Unwary?"

"No reason," Zoë snorted. "A lot of the American Wise use both. Look at my family."

Joy spoke up. "Oh, I know! Because people who grow up using both aren't as good sorcerers as those raised only in the World of the Wise."

"Thanks a lot, O'Keefe," quipped Zoë.

"But... it's true," Joy objected. "I didn't make this up, Zoë. My father told me. When people grow up believing that technology solves their problems, they tend to make poor sorcerers. Their magic is not as potent."

Zoë glared at her.

"No, Really!"

Valerie smirked "You gotta give it to her, Zoë. She's *much* better at magic than you or I."

"True," Zoë shrugged. "But then nearly everyone is a better sorceress than I am. I suck."

"But what about Mr. Smith?" asked the princess. "He was raised among the Unwary, and he's one of the best natural sorcerers that Roanoke has ever seen."

"Sigfried is an enigma wrapped in a mystery," quipped Valerie.

"That's me," Sigfried shot back, "an egg-McMuffin wrapped in tortilla."

Rachel said slowly, "I think that actually makes sense... what Joy's father told her."

"How?" Zoë stuck her free fist on her hip.

"It's like what the Raven told us," Rachel struggled to make her thought clear. "He said that the laws of nature changed slowly, as people's subconscious ideas of the world changed—that's how he fits in the powers of the new people, as Azrael and his cabal brought them here. He said that that if people found out too much too quickly, the Walls that protect the world would fail, and the world would be destroyed.

"So... if the laws of nature can change, and if they are affected by what people believe, what would happen if everyone in the World of the Wise started subconsciously believing in the laws of physics as the mundane world teaches them? Could magic stop working?"

The others thought about this.

"What makes magic and technology not work together?" asked Valerie. "Is it because people can't believe in both at once? And, if so, why can't they?"

Rachel shook her head. "I don't know. But I do know that O.I. is working on this very question. They are trying to learn to combine the two. That's what Gaius is interested in doing."

"If they could, that would be wicked awesome!" Siggy crowed. "I want to be first in line for a rocket-powered flying broom. Or maybe a magical bazooka!"

"You and blowing things up!" Joy rolled her eyes.

"But it would explain why people raised in the World of the Wise would be better sorcerers," said Rachel, "And Joy is correct. I've heard that, too."

"So have I." The princess nodded primly.

"Great," Zoë scowled. "Television ruined my magical potential."

"Sorry about that," Rachel said sadly.

Zoë shrugged. "Television is good for a few things. At least I know what a starship is." She suddenly snorted. "And I have things to be grateful for. For instance, I'm not dating a ewe."

There was a momentary pause.

"Ram!" objected Rachel hotly.

"Oh, I don't know," Valerie joined in, her eyes crinkling with wicked amusement. "Salome described the duel to me in great detail. I even wrote a piece on it for the Roanoke Glass. She didn't mention anything about horns."

"I didn't see horns, either," giggled Joy.

Rachel, who was quite familiar with sheep, as many of the Gryphon Park tenant-farmers kept flocks, steadfastly refused to recall Gaius in sheep form. She was pretty sure she would be able to tell a ewe from a ram at a glance, even without horns, and she resolved to take a stand for her boyfriend's masculinity, regardless of what the real facts of the matter might have revealed.

"Of course, not," she exclaimed indignantly. "People don't leave horns on rams. They cut them short."

"Face it, Griffin," drawled Zoë, "you're dating a ewe."

"You mean an *eeeew*!" Joy burst into giggles.

Rachel sighed.

There was the noise of a chair being pushed back. The dream image of Gaius stood up from where he had been sitting at the table.

Valerie squawked, jumping back, and Joy screamed. Sigfried pulled Valerie closer.

"I think it's nonsense," Dream Gaius said with a casual gesture of his hand. "The science and magic issue, I mean. Not whether I was a boy-sheep or a girl-sheep. Though I am grateful that my girlfriend stands up for me so loyally." He flashed Rachel a wide grin. "Science is the study of how things work. We will figure out how this magic stuff works, too."

"Where did he come from?" Nastasia sniffed, dismayed. "I thought we distinctly agreed that he was not to be invited."

Rachel looked up at the Gaius before her, comparing him with the Gaius in her memory. He was definitely about two and a half inches taller. His grin was also wider, more relaxed.

"This is Dream Gaius. He's a figment of my dreaming imagination, according to Zoë." Rachel gestured toward Valerie. "Dream Gaius, meet my friends. Friends, Dream Gaius."

"How do you do?" Dream Gaius gave her another huge grin. He extended his hand.

"Pleased to meet you." Valerie let go of Sigfried and shook his outstretched hand. With an inarticulate scream, she fell through the library floor and out of dreamland.

CHAPTER FIFTEEN:

THE LIBRARY OF ALL WORLDS

"WHOOPS!" MURMURED ZOË, LOOKING DOWN. "SHE HIT HER HEAD on the table. There's blood."

Siggy bent his legs, bracing for impact. Then, he let go of Joy. He, too, fell through the floor, vanishing.

"I wish people would stop forgetting not to let go. Ah well, we'd better go back and help." Zoë waved with her free hand. "Ciao, Griffin."

The others tromped off into the mist, leaving Rachel alone in the dream library with Dream Gaius. He smiled down at her.

"Looks like it's just us."

"We should make the most of that," Rachel replied, her eyes sparkling with mischief.

He looked so cute. He was her dream boyfriend, right? Impulsively, she stepped forward much more boldly that she would have in the waking world and lifted her face to be kissed.

"Well! Can't say no to that!" Dream Gaius's grin widened.

Stepping forward with a huge smile, he spread his arms and encompassed her in a sweeping embrace. He leaned down and kissed her—a real kiss.

Rachel panicked.

This was not the way her gentlemanly, chivalrous boyfriend acted!

With a squeak of fear, she ducked out of his arms and stood a few feet away, her arms wrapped defensively around her body.

"Be gone, sweet figment. Frighten not my little one," said a familiar voice that rang like the sound of bells.

Rachel spun around. "Illondria!"

The elf-woman towered over Rachel. She stood seven feet tall, more glamorous and voluptuous than any mortal. Her skin had the luminous gray of beech bark. Her eyes, warm as polished wood, had starshine where mortals had pupils. Her features were upswept, high cheek bones, slanted eyes. Her brows and her long flowing hair were fern-green.

The Elf knelt down and opened her arms. Rachel ran forward and squeezed her tightly, resting her head on the tall elf woman's motherly shoulder. The Elf hugged her in return.

The tall woman leaned back and touched Rachel's head fondly, her fingers brushing over the spot where the Rune of Memory was hidden beneath Rachel's hair.

"You have so much resting on your shoulders, little one. But fear not. I see wonderful things ahead for you."

"What sort of things?" Rachel asked curiously.

The Elf stood and glanced around the dream facsimile of the school library. "I am not surprised to find you here. I see you, years from now, in a place of great knowledge. A library such as no other that has ever existed. And happy, with these things far behind you. Do not falter, I think your victory is assured. Though achieving it will be great work."

"A library such as no other that has ever existed?" breathed Rachel.

The elf woman smiled down at her fondly. "The Library of All Worlds."

Rachel repeated the name silently.

It was so wonderful that she almost feared to speak it aloud. Her imagination ignited with visions of faraway places and vast halls of learning.

"That's what I want to do," she vowed. "To create the Library of All Worlds!"

"If you wish to, you shall."

Rachel was quiet for a bit, caught by the wonder of it. She and Illondria sat close together for a bit. Towering palaces grown from trees atop trees rose around them. Roses bloomed everywhere, their fragrance heady and sweet.

In the way of dreams, Rachel realized that much time had passed. She sighed audibly. "I think they forgot to wake me up."

The Elf looked down, as if peering through the library floor. "Yes. Your body is in a house inside a bag in the dean's office. Dean Moth is berating the Romanov princess for having departed from the school grounds."

"We fell out of dreamland," Rachel said sorrowfully. "I'm not sure how to not do that."

The lovely elf-lady tilted her head to the side and tapped her cheek thoughtfully with her long, tapered finger. "Maybe I can help. Perhaps, I. . . ."

Rachel awoke on a bed inside the princess's purse house.

"Wake up, sleepy-head," Joy leaned over her, shaking her arm. "The assistant dean wants to see us."

• • •

"I can't believe we got saddled with detention every Saturday for a month and a half!" Joy moaned as the group who had spent the previous night in Transylvania tromped out of the assistant dean's office, out of Roanoke Hall, and over the bridge that spanned the reflecting lake. After standing so nervously while the ordinarily cool and witty Mr. Gideon lectured them at length—his fingers tapping rhythmically against the high collar of the turtleneck sweater he wore under his robes, his handsome, dark face fearsome in his disapproval—it was nice to move again. Rachel felt chagrined but relieved that it had not been worse.

"I'm just glad they didn't take my sandals." Zoë ran a hand over her head, changing her hair to a vibrant, electric blue. "I hid them just in case. Gave them to Seth and told him not to tell me where they were. I was going to pretend I couldn't find them, but... Mr. Gideon never even brought them up."

"Told you," said Joy smugly.

Thunder shook the heavens, echoing from Stony Tor to the north. The answer from the tor seemed even louder than the original. It seemed to Rachel that the ground shook.

The fog still lay thick across the campus, but the rain had reduced to a drizzle. The large umbrellas still hung above the walkways. The soft glow of will-o-wisps shone out from beneath each brim, eerily beautiful as they illuminated the mist. The umbrellas were ten feet wide and black, except for one hovering over the path that led from the Commons to Marlowe Hall, which was silver. Rachel wondered how that one had come to be there.

"I am surprised that the punishment was not more severe." Nastasia glided along in her lavender sou'wester with its matching galoshes and wide-brimmed rain hat. Her familiar walked in step with her. "Though, perhaps, not something as strange as Father's punishment. We once had a theft problem in the palace. Finally, Father caught someone red-handed. He had the man covered in peanut butter, rolled in bird food, and sentenced to stand in the garden with his arms spread like a scarecrow until the birds had eaten him clean. Or the opposite of a scare crow. Beckon crow? Come hither crow? Either way, it was a ridiculous punishment, if truth be told. After that, however, not a single object went missing, even though that man was not the only culprit. I guess the risk of being made a mockery and spending an afternoon as a feeding trough for birds is more to be feared than time in jail."

"It's because they're embarrassed," said Xandra, walking beside the rest of them, her hood nearly covering her nose. "The school, I mean, not your father's servants. Three students got snatched yesterday, on campus grounds. And not just any students: a royal princess, the daughter of an Agent of the Wisecraft, and the most famous boy in the World of the Wise. Roanoke's supposed to be safe. But this year: first Dr. Mordeau, then the airplane and this? They don't want the kidnapping getting out, so they aren't going to make a big deal about this either."

Walking beside her, kicking the freshly fallen leaves into the air and watching them float back to the ground through the drizzly mist, Rachel thought that it was a very good thing for her future career as a student that nobody but she and Gaius knew that only two of those students had been kidnapped. The third one had left school grounds of her own volition.

"But they did limit us to staying on school grounds, which means no more midnight trips to Magical Australia." Valerie threw a stick for her elkhound. "Rachel, why did you cut me off just now, when I was speaking to Mr. Gideon?"

"And let you ask what constituted school grounds?" Rachel arched her eyebrows and kicked the next batch of leaves extra hard. "Are you bonkers? Right now, we can still follow the rules, so long as we don't leave the island in dreamland. But what if they had said, just the physical campus? We would be forbidden to enter dreamland!"

There was also the question of whether "school grounds" constituted the whole island, which technically belonged to the school, or the area within the school's wards. Rachel preferred to use her own interpretation.

She also was the only one in the group who had not given her word. Once again, she had merely stood looking very attentive, and Mr. Gideon had taken that as assent. He had not made her repeat his words, the way he had done for Sigfried.

Disobeying adults no longer troubled Rachel, so long as she acted in a good cause. She knew so many secrets that she could not share with the grown-ups around her, that she could not rely on their judgment as to what was important and what was not. However, she did not wish to give her word and then break it.

"Ah. Got it." Valerie nodded once.

All the girls gave a shout of surprise as Lucky swooped in and set fire to the latest batch of red and gold leaves Rachel had kicked into the air. The colorful foliage blazed and crisped. The fire glowed brightly against the mist, smoke curling upward. Only a few embers were left by the time the ashes floated to the ground. The smell of burning leaves filled the air along with the ozone-like odor of Lucky's flame.

"Lucky," exclaimed the princess, "you could set the whole commons on fire!"

"Sorry," growled Lucky. "Couldn't resist. I mean they were just flying there… like tiny chickens. Who could be expected not to want to annihilate them utterly with super-hot flame?"

Siggy merely nodded sagely.

"As to the matter of what constitutes school grounds, we should err on the side of caution." Nastasia recovered her aplomb, though she gave the dragon a stern look. "When we are in dreamland, there is a chance we could fall out elsewhere. We must avoid this danger."

"I may have found a solution to that," Rachel said, recalling the Elf's parting words. "I'll let you know as soon as I find out."

• • •

At dinner that night Rachel noticed the proctor Mr. Fuentes on duty in the cafeteria. She had not spoken to him since the day he had ordered her dragged to the Watch Tower, after she turned in the whip that had killed… er, injured… Enoch Smithwyck. As her lingering sense of disappointment resolved itself into particular objections, she marched up to him.

"Mr. Fuentes," she stood before him, her expression sad and a little resentful, "next time a thirteen-year-old approaches you and says, 'Hey, here's something I found in my pocket that I didn't know might be important,' you might consider just believing her—rather than dragging her off to undergo *the Spell of True Recitation*."

Carlos Fuentes was a handsome young man of Spanish descent with thick, curly hair and a ready smile. Now, however, he gave her a thoughtful look. "Where, in how I acted, was I mistaken, Miss Griffin? Was it because I was concerned that a murder weapon, 'found' right after the murder, had not been turned in until days later? Or was it because a young woman, whom I felt was extremely trustworthy and intelligent, seemed baffled by why I was wondering how she could 'forget' she was carrying it? If you wish, I will go out of my way to not forget that you are thirteen in the future."

Rachel blushed, caught by her own stratagem. She bit her lip. "I-I don't understand why there was anything suspicious about it. I wasn't concealing a murder weapon. I just hadn't thought about the whip. After the battle against Dr. Mordeau, my boyfriend got turned into a sheep, and then I had a huge row with my brother— whom I greatly admire, and now we're not speaking to each other. So, the whip was not the thing in the forefront of my mind. Besides, if I were under a spell, would I have turned it in?"

"Miss Griffin," he replied seriously, "I have been told that you have an intellect far, far beyond your years. Yet, you seemed confused. I thought you might be turning the whip in, even though geased not to. This would have made you act strangely. That's why I wanted you checked. I didn't mean to harass you or, er, make you fight with your brother?"

"Oh!" Rachel exclaimed softly. Only now did it occur to her that Mr. Fuentes, who had been ensorcelled himself and nearly killed a student while in that state, might be extra nervous about geases. She admitted truthfully, "I was scared when you brought me to the Watch Tower. I didn't know why I was there. But if you were looking out for me, that's all right."

"Honestly, sweetie, I was trying not to say anything that might trigger the spell… that might force you to act even more against your will. The geas on me was quite complex. We still don't fully understand it."

All this made sense, yet she still felt slightly betrayed. "If something like this should happen again, couldn't you stay with me? Send some other proctor to get the Agents?"

"Last time, I was ambushed and geased. This time, I wanted to make sure the message got delivered." He leaned closer, a kind smile creasing his face. "If something like this happens again, sweetie, I'll stay with you, and send someone else."

"Thank you," Rachel murmured, her feelings of having been ill-used evaporating. She gave him a smile as she sought for something else to discuss, so she could depart on a happier note. "Do you like it here, working as a proctor?"

He grinned sheepishly. "Like most of us, I'm what we in the business call an embryo-Agent. Working as a proctor at Roanoke is one of the best ways to get into the Wisecraft. It gives us a chance to learn the ropes, strut our stuff. That kind of thing."

"Can't you just join the Wisecraft right out of school? Sandra did."

Mr. Fuentes threw back his head when he laughed. "Sandra Griffin is one classy lady. She gradated with five Rings of Mastery. I, alas, only achieved three." He held up his hands, upon which he wore three black rings etched with arcane runes. One bore an amethyst, one an emerald, and one a polished chip of jet. Rachel knew these represented mastery in enchantment, canticle, and Enochian magic—warding and obscurations. She also knew that, Sandra aside, three rings of mastery was no mean feat. "Also, her father's a duke and an Agent. Mine works as a canticler for a company that makes talismans. Not a lot of strings to pull there."

They grinned at each other. Out of gratitude, Rachel shared with him the last of the sweets from home that her father had brought her during the first week of school, after her fight with the wraith. He gave her a big smile as he finished off her Smarties.

They chatted a while longer, mainly about his favorite Flying Polo team, the Windcolts. Rachel knew very little about sports. As they were speaking, however, she noticed out of the corner of her eye that, over at the central table near the fountain, Gaius, Locke and Dread were watching her closely.

A plan had formed in her mind.

She knew from Gaius that Von Dread was curious about where she was getting her information. He believed she had a contact among the Wisecraft. Most students knew that many of the proctors were Agents-in-training. If she seemed on friendly terms with a proctor, maybe Dread would think that was where her secret information came from, and he would not look farther. She did not want him to discover Siggy's amulet.

Rachel decided to make a show of her friendship with the handsome young proctor, talking to him in the dining hall and the like. However, she made a promise to herself as well. The idea of pretending to be someone's friend appalled her. If she was going to use her friendship with the proctor for her own benefit, she was going to do her best to actually be a good friend!

When she left the dining hall, she went down to the mail room and sent off a subscription to a popular news glass. The glass used for viewing the issues was in her mailbox the next day. She began the practice of memorizing the sports page. Sports turned out to be surprisingly boring. She could not actually get herself to read what the page said regularly, but if she looked at it once, she could pull it up in her memory while she was speaking to Mr. Fuentes. This allowed her to sympathize with his joys and agonies as his team faced victory and defeat.

It was the least a friend could do.

• • •

The dreary weather continued Sunday. Rachel and her friends spent the day in Dare Hall, reading and doing homework, except for Valerie, who went home for a few days to celebrate her father's return with her mother. Rachel wondered why Peter and Laurel did not come by to make much over her, as they had after the battle with Mordeau. Then, she realized that neither of them had been informed that she had been missing.

Not that Peter would have come anyway. She sighed.

Monday dawned bright and clear, with a brilliant display of fall reds, oranges, and yellows. The smell of autumn greeted her during her morning flight. The foliage was even more brilliant than at home in Devon. The sugar maples glowed apple red. Some trees had two-tone leaves, yellow-orange toward the outside, orange-red towards the center, so that they appeared to be aflame. Rachel flew over a tree like this in the midst of dark green hemlocks. The maple rose like a burning torch amidst a sea of green.

Back on campus, fresh leaves covered the brick paths between the buildings, so that everyone's footsteps made a *swooshing* noise as they walked.

The week went quickly. Thursday evening, Nastasia and Sigfried accompanied her to their first Knights of Walpurgis meeting. They swung by the mailroom after dinner, before heading for the gym. Rachel found a padded envelope from home addressed in her mother's looping script. She frowned for a moment, wondering when she was finally going to hear from her father. Wasn't he going to come and find out how she was after her—he believed— kidnapping? She could not wait to tell him what had really occurred.

She took the package with her, running to keep up with the others, who had already started up the long spiral staircase that led from the basement of Roanoke Hall to the main level. The sky was already dark as they headed across the leaf-strewn Commons. Arriving at the gym, they entered the open door leading into the large room used by the Knights, with the long table on one side and dueling strips on the other. As they approached the table, Rachel realized that she had a problem.

With whom was she going to sit?

It was one thing to forgo sitting with Gaius in the dining hall, much as she really wanted to join him each day. It was another thing entirely to not join him during the Knights meeting. Gaius was her sponsor. This was their activity, which they did together. Did she go up to the head of the table and sit with Gaius and Dread's crew? Or did she sit with Sigfried and Nastasia, who were currently heading for a spot beside the cheerfully-waving Salome Iscariot?

She was rescued from this horrendous dilemma by Gaius himself. He rose from beside William Locke and crossed the room to bow before her, offering his arm. Rachel accepted, delighted. He then accompanied her and the others to sit next to Salome, Carl, and Devon Iscariot.

The other two immediately launched into a conversation with the Iscariot siblings. Rachel turned to her boyfriend, smiling gratefully.

"What do you have there?" he asked, seeing the envelope.

"No idea," Rachel held it up and shook it. "Shall we open it?"

"Most definitely," Gaius replied with a gallant smile.

Rachel tore open the envelope and held it upside down. A narrow cedar box with rounded edges slid onto the table. Rachel gasped, her heart humming with joy.

She knew that box.

"What is it?" Gaius asked curiously.

"Look!" she cried.

She pried it open and held it toward him. On the pale peach velvet lining within lay a slender length of silver about the size and shape of a chopstick. It was ornately inlaid with mother-of-pearl and tipped with a glittering diamond. There was a note, written in her father's hand, that read merely: *We thought you might need this.*

"Grandmother's wand!" she breathed.

Gaius's brows shot up. He grinned in delight. "A wand! Now you can be a real duelist! But I thought your parents turned down your request for a wand?"

"That was before I ended up in a spell-flinging fight with Veltdammerung," Rachel replied, her eyes sparkling. "Perhaps, they have finally faced the inevitable and accepted the truth... that, whatever this is that is happening in our world, I am on the front lines."

"You certainly seem to be. First tangling with Egg, and now this other demon. I wonder why?" Gaius asked slowly. "I mean, no offense! I think you're amazing. But that doesn't explain why you seem to be at the epicenter of so many of these disturbances."

Rachel glanced at her friends, who were deep in conversation, and then moved her head closer to her boyfriend, lowering her voice. "I think it's Sigfried and Nastasia. Whatever this Keybearer business is, it makes them important. So important things happen around them."

Gaius was watching her face carefully. He lowered his voice as well. "And was it some magic Keybearer destiny that was responsible for you being involved in the battle against Mordeau?"

Rachel blushed slightly. "No, I did that myself."

"What about facing Veltdammerung?"

"They were there because of the Keybearer prophecy."

"True. But you?"

Rachel smiled like a pixie. "You mean, I am only in the midst of trouble because I stick my nose into dangerous places?"

"And a very pretty nose it is, too," Gaius leaned closer and briefly rubbed his nose against hers. "But that wasn't what I meant. I mean, yes. You were only there because you chose to be there, but you seem to have an uncanny talent for finding trouble. Believe me, Vlad and William and I would be in the thick of things every time, if we knew where the thick of things was. We have all of the resources of Vlad's entire group at our disposal. And yet you were there, and we were not. Impressive, Griffin."

Rachel giggled.

Von Dread opened the meeting in his usual crisp, business-like manner, the fingers of his black leather, dueling gloves steepled before him. He described the incident of the plane nearly striking the school and led a discussion on what could be done to defend Roanoke from such dangers in the future. As he covered this and other topics, he spoke with such confidence about protection and law that Rachel felt that she had no doubt he would someday be a great king. But he spoke so fiercely, especially on the subject of duty and loyalty, she could not help wondering whether his intensity would result in his becoming a just man or a merciless one?

She recalled her thought that Dread was like a fortress in need of besieging. If someone could touch his heart, teach him the meaning of love, of mercy, he might become a great man indeed! But who could do such a thing? Out of the corner of her eye, she examined Nastasia as she sat upright listening intently. Her blond ringlets fell around her shoulders, making her look like a girl from an earlier century. Her robes were perfectly creased, her hands calmly folded in her lap. The more familiar Rachel became with both of them, the more the idea that had initially amused her and her friends—of a future match between Nastasia and Vladimir Von Dread—seemed like a bad call.

A tiny voice whispered to her, *you could reach him*. That voice came from a part of her mind that felt she understood Dread the way she had understood her grandfather. Rachel ignored this as impractical. How would someone like her befriend such an intimidating boy? And why would he pay any attention to her?

Maybe Dread's future as an evil tyrant was inescapable.

As he continued with matters of business, Rachel turned her attention to her cute boyfriend. She noticed that other girls were watching him as well, especially Tess Dauntless and Colleen Mac-Dannan, the cousin of Ian and Oonagh. At the beginning of the school year, both girls had watched him with active interest. Now that a month had gone by, and he was showing no sign of breaking up with her, the expressions of the other two girls had changed to lovelorn wistfulness, and, in the case of Tess, petulant envy.

Von Dread closed the meeting section of the evening with a reminder of the upcoming election for the position of his assistant during the next year. Currently, the nominees were Gaius and Freka Starkadder. When no other names were volunteered, Dread pronounced the nominations closed and reminded them that elections would be held during the winter.

Rachel wondered how she could help Gaius win the election. She was eager to meet the other members of the Knights. She pictured herself chatting with various members and casually mentioning some aspect of the Knights that Freka hoped to change, and thoughtfully exclaiming over how she felt that particular aspect of the club was perfectly good the way it was. The longer she thought about it, the more she felt certain this approach would work. Especially, if she could mention the matter in passing, without even mentioning Freka or Gaius or the election, before Freka had a chance to talk to the person about her plans. All she needed now was to discover Freka's platform for her candidacy.

The meeting broke up, and the dueling portion began. Gaius took Sigfried and Nastasia aside to teach them the basics of dueling. Rachel squared off with Wanda Zukov and then with Salome. She lost her first duel and won her second one.

As she was waiting for her next opponent, Rachel paused to watch the March siblings, Evelyn March and her younger brother Joshua, square off against each other. She recalled Nastasia's description of her vision of Joshua being vivisected by the being with the smoky wings. Rachel felt a sharp jab of guilt as she remembered how she had urged Nastasia to ignore Xandra's warning not to touch young Mr. March. Mrs. March had looked so frightened when she heard that this being had visited Nastasia's dreams. Rachel bit her lip and turned her face away.

She glanced over at Michael Cameron. She still had not had a chance to thank him for stepping up as Cydney Graves's second during their duel. She wanted to do so, but he was busy dueling another junior. Nearby, Topher Evans stood by himself, rocking from foot to foot as he watched the other duelists. Rachel had become quite curious about him, ever since Von Dread mentioned that Topher had perfect recall. Did his ability work like hers? Could he recall things that he had not seen the first time?

She walked over to him. He pushed his glasses up on his nose and gave her a smile that was half-cheerful and half-goofy and swallowed, causing his Adam's apple to bob.

"Hi, there," Rachel began.

"Hi, yourself," he replied amiably, looking amused at his own wit.

Rachel said casually, "So I hear you have perfect recall."

"You heard right. I hear that your mother also has perfect recall. Is that true?"

"It is." Rachel nodded. She opened her mouth to say "me, too" but she thought it would be disloyal to tell Gaius's friend before she told him.

"My mother, too," confessed Topher.

"Really? Do you think it is inherited?" asked Rachel. She wondered for the first time if any of her mother's relatives shared their gift.

"Possibly." He grinned. "We might be related."

"That's possible, I suppose," Rachel said thoughtfully, "though wouldn't you be related to my father's side? It's my mother who has the gift."

"Actually, I'm one-eighth Korean," said Topher.

Rachel started to laugh, but he was serious. "Truly?"

"I realize I don't look it, being a 'big-nose', but I had a Korean great-grandmother."

She looked him up and down, his Occidental features, his five o'clock shadow, his wavy medium brown hair. "*You* are as Korean as *I* am? I'm one-eighth Korean, too!"

"One-quarter," corrected Topher.

"Wait?" Rachel frowned, confused. "You're a quarter? Or an eighth?"

"No, you." He pointed from her to himself. "You're one-quarter. I'm one-eighth."

"I am one-eighth Korean," said Rachel. The conversation had taken a surrealistic turn.

"But...." He rubbed his forehead, running a finger from his glasses to his hair line. "Your brother Peter said he was one-quarter Korean."

"He... must have made a mistake."

"Peter...." Topher tipped his head back as he called upon his memory, just as Rachel might have done. "Yes. He said 'a quarter', twice. Once when I first met him. Once on the occasion that ended in his duel with Gaius. The one where...."

Topher tried very hard not to smirk at his memory of Rachel's brother's humiliation at the hands of Gaius, but he did not entirely succeed. Rachel felt her cheeks growing warm on Peter's behalf. Topher noticed and looked miserable. Embarrassed though she was, Rachel felt sorry for the likable yet awkward boy

"Peter said he was one-quarter Korean?"

"Quite distinctly."

"How bizarre." Rachel blinked, thinking of the portrait over the fireplace in the Rose Sitting Room of Grandpa Kim's parents. The woman in the picture was clearly British, a large woman with blond hair. "Once could have been an accident. Twice... that's very strange."

They paused for a moment, watching the duels. Jenny Dare and Freka Starkadder had somehow hexed each other simultaneously and both stood frozen. Sigfried, who had squared off with sophomore Ethan Warhol, was hanging upside-down by one foot. Nastasia, who was facing Salome, was frowning at the vines wrapped around her waist. Gaius stood by them, trying to hide how amused he was.

"Well, nice talking to you." Rachel started to walk away.

Topher's hand caught her shoulder. He looked straight at her.

"You, too... don't you?" He blushed at his awkwardness. "I mean... you're like me and your mom, aren't you?"

Rachel bit her lip but nodded.

"Knew it." Topher gave her a lopsided grin. "Figured it out weeks ago."

CHAPTER SIXTEEN:

IN PURSUIT OF TELL-TALE GLINTS

"HEY THERE, CUTIE." GAIUS CAME UP BESIDE RACHEL, WHO STOOD panting after losing to Salome's snarky boyfriend, Ethan Warhol, an embarrassing three times in a row. Her opponent had used a cantrip that increased his speed, so he won each match before she could so much as move. "How's tricks?"

"Smashing." Rachel stepped closer to him with a mischievous smile. "And, speaking of tricks I know, they'd be even better, if you taught me the Glepnir cantrip."

"That's a difficult cantrip."

"It seems very effective." She gestured toward where the braggart Seymour Almeida had caught Bernie Mulford, the son of her parents' friends, in one of the glowing golden bands. Bernie was struggling, but the Glepnir bond constricted him about his wrists and thighs, clamping his arms to his side, so there was little he could do to fight back. "During our fight in Transylvania, I rather wished I knew how to cast them."

"Your wish is my command." Gaius bowed with a flourish. "Come."

He spent the next fifteen minutes instructing her privately. The cantrip itself was *argos*. In the Original Tongue, *ar* meant "belt" or "cloak" and *gos* meant "to gather". Rachel and Gaius stood very close together as he showed her the accompanying hand gestures and how to focus the attack so as to make sure that the band would catch your target where you wanted it to. A constricting band around the waist, for instance, was not nearly as useful as one that also captured the arms or encircled the ankles. Rachel practiced diligently, doing everything he said. Her progress was slow, but she refused to give up. By the end of the quarter hour, she had produced her first, faint, pathetic golden circle.

"Excellent!" Gaius declared, giving her a nod of approval that made her tingle all the way to her toes. "I thought there was at least a thirty-seven percent chance you wouldn't be able to master this. It's not an easy cantrip. Many students don't master it until their sophomore year or beyond. I should have rather known better! From here, it's just a matter of making it your own. I know you're good at that." He grinned at her. "I expect to see golden rings all up and down the suit of armor next time I come by our hallway."

Rachel beamed. She loved it when he called it *our* hallway.

"Can I see your new wand?" he asked curiously.

"Sure." She drew the box out of her robe pocket and handed it to him.

Gaius opened the box and withdrew the slender length of silver, running his fingers across it. The embedded mother-of-pearl formed a rose pattern.

Gaius peered closer. "This is a vestal wand!"

"A vestal wand? Is that a proper wand?"

"Oh, definitely. It's just that most wands are designed for fulgurators—soldiers who shoot deadly lightning in war. This wand was designed for the Vestal Virgins who guard the Eternal Flame—that white and gold fire that harms the guilty but spares the innocent that Vlad likes to throw about." He looked up from the box. "Dr. Mordeau said your grandmother was a Vestal Virgin, didn't she?"

Rachel nodded.

"Huh. I wonder how vestal wands differ from regular ones. Would you mind if I did some investigating?"

"Do you need my wand for that?"

Gaius looked down at the delicate silver length. He shook his head, closed the box, and handed it back to her. "Not yet, anyway. I'll let you know what I find out."

Rachel stuck it back in her pocket. "How did my friends do?"

"I think they've grasped the basics. As much as Mr. Smith will ever grasp anything, that is." Gaius shook his head ruefully. "He kept trying to direct his trumpet at the floor, on the theory that a sufficiently strong blast of wind would blow him upward, into the air. Unfortunately—or possibly fortunately—magic doesn't work that way."

Rachel giggled. "The two of them are very good at magic. They are going to be great duelists." She sighed.

"Maybe," shrugged Gaius.

"Hang on. What do you mean?"

"There's more to dueling that being a strong sorcerer. Oh, it helps! Don't get me wrong. But it only helps with putting the spells into your wand… or with throwing them naturally, as the princess is doing right now. But a sorcerer with a fulgurator's wand or a dueling ring will always beat one casting naturally, given enough time. You can fire spells much more quickly from a gem. Also, with thaumaturgy, you can do tricks, such as make it so your conjuration can't be instantly undone during the first ten minutes of their existence."

"That's useful."

"Yes. It is. But my point is, there's more to dueling than the spells you have on hand." Gaius's eyes lit up, and his face became animated when he spoke about dueling.

"Like what?" Rachel leaned forward slightly, caught up in his enthusiasm. He looked totally adorable.

"Dueling consists of three parts. The first is the spells. But anyone can have good spells if they have someone else to cast them, like you did for me. The next part is speed and reflexes."

Rachel's face fell.

Gaius gave her an encouraging grin. "But even that isn't enough. A trained monkey with a wand might have quick reflexes and a stack of good spells. But no performing ape, however fast, is going out-duel me."

"What's the third part?"

"Ah. This is where people like you and me excel. The last part of dueling is what you know." He tapped his temple. "The better you understand what each spell does—how to recognize it, and how to counter it—that is what really makes a duelist. Knowing his craft.

"Oh and a good memory helps, too. You need to keep track of how many of each spell you have left in your wand. There are gadgets and gismos to help with that—or you can even just keep a good, old-fashioned list." He pulled a card out of his pocket with a series of words and hatch marks on it and waved it back and forth. "But only between duels. During the duel, you have to be able to keep track in your head of what you have on hand at any given moment."

Rachel grinned. That would not be a problem for her. "How did you learn all this?"

"Ah," Gaius's eyes twinkled. "I learned from a master. The best duelist at Roanoke." He flashed her a cocky grin. "At least before *I* arrived."

"Vlad?"

"No, though Vlad is very, very good." He glanced over at where Von Dread had just slammed Seymour Almeida into the padded far wall with a blast of silver sparkles. "This guy was even better. At least back when Vlad was younger. But, he's not here anymore." Gaius's face fell, a sadder expression that could be accounted for by mere graduation.

"Blackie Moth?" Rachel asked.

"He was fantastic, Rach. Quick as lightning and sharp as a laser. Never lost his cool." Gaius looked crushed. "Blackie used to be so much fun. Cool and dry but with a fond twinkle. Now... nothing. He doesn't know who I am, and he doesn't care."

"I'm sorry," she said softly, remembering her second cousin and that fond twinkle.

"And you know the worst thing? I think there's at least a sixty-seven percent chance that I could beat him now. But he's not here for me to try my skill against... not the Blackie I knew, in any case." Gaius grinned suddenly and leaned toward her, lowering his voice. "I'll teach you a secret he taught me. All the best duelists know it, but a lot of people here don't. Look over there." He pointed at where red-haired Naomi Coils stood facing Rachel's second cousin, Blackie's sister Beryl. Both college girls stood on the balls of their feet, alert. "Watch the tips of the wands when they begin. Now. See anything?"

Rachel watched the glittering gem-tips. There came a glint of light. Or was that her imagination? Carefully, she compared her memory of now with the moment before. No, it definitely glinted. She watched a bit longer.

"The gem shines... a very small spark of light inside... right before it fires."

"Exactly," Gaius looked extremely pleased with her. "Many people can't see that. You're rather sharp-eyed, Rachel Griffin. You're going to make a very good duelist. And speaking of duelists, I will not remain the foremost one in my class if I don't keep my hand in the game. I had better—"

Rachel grabbed his shoulder. "Before you go, can you introduce me to Freka Starkadder?"

"It would be my pleasure." He offered her his arm.

Freka was practicing with her younger brother Beowulf. When she saw Rachel and Gaius, she held up her hand. Beowulf grunted his assent. Freka turned and smiled at Rachel.

Gaius bowed graciously. "Your highness, may I introduce to you our fellow Knight, Lady Rachel Griffin? Rachel, Princess Freka Starkadder of Transylvania."

Leaning over, Gaius gave Rachel the lightest of kisses on her cheek. "And now, I'm off to duel. Tally-ho!" He saluted with his wand and strolled away to challenge Topher Evans.

Freka watched all this with amusement. When Gaius departed, she held out her hand to Rachel, who shook it. Across the room, Rachel noticed Prince Romulus frown in annoyance. Apparently, the crown prince of Transylvania did not approve of his sister shaking hands with mere freshmen—or maybe he did not approve of her shaking hands altogether.

Freka Starkadder had an almost feral beauty that recalled to Rachel's mind the memory of her brother Fenris turning back into a man from being a wolf. She had intense brown eyes and oak-colored straight hair with long bangs that came almost to her eyes.

She gave Rachel an impish smile. "Gaius the Cutie-Pie aside, when I'm at school, I really prefer it if people don't use my title. Please just call me Freka. Do you mind if I call you Rachel, or should I use Miss Griffin? Lady Rachel?"

"Rachel is fine, thank you." Rachel curtsied. "Should I wait until your match is over? I don't wish to intrude."

"Nope. We're done. Go ahead." Freka mopped her brow with a small towel she wore around her neck.

"I just wanted to meet you," Rachel explained. "I'm trying to meet everyone. You seemed like a good place to start."

"That's very nice. Welcome to the Knights. You've acquitted yourself quite well, so far. Makes the rest of us Knights look good."

"Thank you." Rachel curtsied a second time. "That's very kind."

"Do you have any particular questions?"

"I suppose I am curious how you are planning to run the Knights, if you win the election," Rachel said casually. "Which you probably will, because my boyfriend hasn't expressed the slightest interest in actually running. At least, not to me. Will you keep things the same? Or make changes?" Rachel kept her expression calm and attentive, but inside she felt as tightly wound as a watch spring.

"So he... never mind." Freka shook her head. "I am not planning on changing things at all. Vladimir has done a fine job with the Knights. I hope I can lead as well as he."

Oh.

So much for clever ideas.

Rachel sighed.

"I think he has, as well," she agreed. "Especially compared to the YSL, which does nothing at all. Or so I hear."

"Oh, the Young Sorcerer's League isn't so bad." Freka tossed her head, sending her long brown hair flying about her. "It's not as intense as the Knights. Maybe because it's open to anyone. Of course, I only attended a few of their meetings. Years ago, before I joined the Knights. I don't have time for both, alas. Not if I want to pass my classes. Or even breathe. And breathing is important, or so they tell me. I seldom have time to do it regularly, nowadays." She paused and pantomimed attempting to take two or three huge breaths. Rachel grinned.

Freka continued, "But if I did have more time—if the magic time fairy came and waved her timey-wimey wand and granted me the power to do to hours what kenomancy does to space—I might join both. I wouldn't mind a chance to duel some new people. The intimacy of the Knights is great. It leads to strong friendships— the kind that are useful throughout your life. But always winning or losing to the same people gets a bit repetitive."

"I can see that," Rachel said thoughtfully, a seed of an idea beginning to sprout in the back of her mind.

"Yeah." Freka gestured so as to encompass the room. "Beowulf and I used to keep a betting sheet—as a joke—trying to predict who would win against whom. We gave it up because it became utterly predictable. We couldn't invent odds great enough to get either of us to risk betting on the expected loser."

"Did Romulus bet, too?" Rachel asked, glancing over at the somber and distant crown prince, where he stood with his cronies, talking quietly.

"Oh, no! Rom would never do something so pedestrian!" Freka laughed gaily. "We let Remus try a few times, but he would bet on the underdog and then play tricks on the favorite to skew the outcome of the match. We asked Fenris, too, but he just sneered at us." A look of intense sadness crossed her features and then, as quickly as it had come, was gone again. "Luperca's too cool to belong to a club, even a prestigious one like the Knights, and Wulfgang is too young. Too new. Though," she frowned very slightly, "not as young as you, I suppose."

Rachel paused, not certain what to say next. She wanted much to ask for a translation of the plaque beside the mirror with the silvery light that might have been the moon glass. Perhaps, she could pretend she read the phrase in a book. But she did not know if Freka would instantly know that this was a lie. After all, Rachel had read all about Beaumont castle in the past and about Darius Northwest. She had never seen reference to such a plaque. What if it were a family secret? Perhaps she could ask Freka about her home and find a way to work up to it.

"What is your home like?   I hear Transylvania's beautiful?" asked Rachel.

Of course, she knew it was beautiful, but it seemed unwise to admit that she had recently invaded the country.

Freka tilted her head to one side, very wolf-like. "Take mountains, mix in dark forests, sprinkle with vampires, werewolves, giant spiders, and the occasional dragon. Bake for at least a few generations with insane people who kill their siblings so often that it could be declared the national sport, and that will give you a nice recipe for my home country. Oh, but we do have some of the deepest, richest mines in the world."

"Sounds utterly lovely!" Rachel said. "Except for the killing your family bit, of course. That's rather sad. Isn't there some way to encourage everyone to get along?"

Freka's smile took on a brittle quality. "If you think of one, please let me know."

"I'll work on it," Rachel said thoughtfully. "Though to solve the problem, one might have to study the inheritance rules for your kingdom. You probably know that England put in the rule of primogeniture particularly to stop that very kind of behavior. Not that it works as well as one might have liked."

As she spoke, another thought came to her. Nastasia had touched Freka's younger brother Wulfgang and had seen a vision of a frozen landscape—so they were definitely originally Metaplutonians. If Nastasia touched one of the other Starkadders, was there a chance that she might have a vision that would reveal some clue about their family curse?

"I… don't think my father would approve of that. He likes to hold the throne up as a prize to encourage us to compete. He says it brings out the best in us." Freka scowled. "Which is ridiculous, because we all know it's going to be Romulus." Then, she sighed. "Please, let's discuss things that do not have to do with my family."

"Certainly," Rachel said quickly. "I didn't mean to upset you. What do princesses do when they graduate? I've asked Nastasia, but she just says, 'go wherever I'm needed', which isn't much of a basis for a study plan."

"Nastasia is correct," Freka sighed again. "We go where our father tells us. I haven't been given an assignment yet. My father or whomever has the Kadder Star." She gestured in the direction of her eldest brother and the purple stone he wore in a ring. "Traditionally, in Transylvania, my uncles would also hold positions of power, but all of my father's siblings are dead. Our line bottlenecked with him. That's why he's had so many children. You probably know we have two siblings who are not at school yet, right? Wulfgar and Ulrika. Wulfgar's very goofy and sweet. Ulrika's a bit of a tomboy. I worry about them left at home, though maybe not so much now.…"

"Yes, I know. I look forward to meeting them. I'm sure if they're your brother and sister, they'll be delightful," Rachel said politely.

She felt rather charmed by the older girl's spunk and cheer.

Tears began streaming down Freka's cheeks. She blinked and wiped at them in an impatient manner that reminded Rachel very much of what her own reaction would have been under the circumstance.

"Excuse me. I... need to take a break. It was nice speaking to you, Rachel. I hope you're not planning to poison me, so Gaius can win. If the election's that important, please tell me and I'll withdraw instead, okay?" Freka gave Rachel one last smile and rushed out of the room.

"No. It isn't that important," murmured Rachel. She watched sadly as the other girl departed. Her own eyes felt a little teary.

So much for asking for a translation of the plaque.

What had she said?

What was going on? Was Freka really so upset? Or was it some kind of trick? A stratagem by a Machiavellian princess? And where was she going?

Rachel ran across the room and grabbed Sigfried by the arm, dragging him away from where he was about to duel upper school sophomore Carl Iscariot. "Sorry! Emergency. I'll bring him back!"

"What's up? Do you need somebody eviscerated? Burnt? Skunked?"

"Actually, I do need somebody skunked, but not right now. Right now, I need somebody spied on."

"Ah, I can do that, too," replied Sigfried, but he looked less enthused. "Who."

"Freka Starkadder."

"Who?"

"That girl who just went into the hallway."

"Can't see her. My amulet can't see through the walls of the magic rooms in the gym."

"Oh... well...." She grabbed him and dragged him into the hall. "Can you see her now?"

He was quiet a moment. "Straight hair? Smart-looking and pretty?"

"Yes. That's her."

"Yeah, she's... oh no!" Sigfried threw up his hands, as if to block his view of something. Then he grabbed his head and staggered in a circle, shouting, "Kryptonite! She went into the PLACE THAT IS NOT!!!"

Rachel gawked at him. "Crypto night? What place is not?"

"The place I can't look! Oh, my eyes!"

"Oh. Good gracious, Sigfried! Can't you just say, 'She went to the loo?'"

"I could, but I won't. What is the point of life without drama? What fun would that be?"

"Yeah," Lucky swooped through the air, circling his master. "Don't cramp the boss's style."

"Er... sorry." Rachel blinked. "Could you make an exception this once? Not if she's in a stall, of course, but if she's just standing at the sink, or talking on a calling card or something?"

"How do I make sure she's not... doing something unmentionable? If I saw so much as a glimpse of her underwear, even by mistake, I would be a cad, a caitiff, for as long as I lived! And no caitiff ever sat at the Table Round!"

"Just look by the sink. Please! Double please?"

"Look, Racks—may I call you Racks?—"

"Racks?" Rachel interrupted. She resisted the temptation to look down at her lack of anything impressive—or existent—in the way of a chest.

"As in short for Rachel."

"Ooooo."

"What did you think it meant? Anyway, I am willing to help out the Inner Circle of Way Cool Demon Prattkickers and Flaming Skunklaunchers, as I like to call our little group, but it has to be something related to a threat. Or Metaplutonians. What crimes do you think Freka's committed? Is she planning on poisoning someone? Is she withholding information about the greater world beyond our solar system?"

"This isn't about threats, Siggy, though she did ask if I planned to poison her...."

"Do you?"

"No!"

"Look, Grif—may I call you Grif?—I am not going to use my vast yet privacy-invading powers for politics or soap opera. If you like, I will give you a supply of chameleon potion, and you can follow your victims around unseen and eavesdrop on them, but I cannot help you look into the girls' loo. If you want me to look through the teacher's desks to find the answers for test and such, so we can cheat, that I can do. Especially for true-hissy-fit class. But anything else? No way."

"Please, Sigfried? I can't figure out what just happened. I want to know if she's serious? Angry? Playing me? What is she doing?"

"I'll make you an offer," Sigfried said. "I will help you out—if you say the word *Sheepsmoocher!*"

"That's *ram*smoocher," Rachel shot back. She sighed. "Isn't there something I could do for you to make it worth your while?"

"Yeah, write my True-Hisss-story essay. Try to impersonate my handwriting."

She hesitated for only a moment. "Okay. Done." She paused and then added fiercely, "But don't you tell *anybody* that I'm doing this for you! Ever!"

"Great." He held his hand out to Lucky, who did a fly-by high-five. "Look at your calling card, Griffin-Rack."

Rachel pulled out her card. In it, she could see an unoccupied area of floor with a counter, three sinks, and a mirror. After a moment, a stall door opened in the reflection, and then Freka walked up to the sink and washed her hands. She wiped the tears from her eyes and stuck out her tongue at her reflection. She said out loud to her reflection, "'The slings and arrows of outrageous fortune' are not worth your tears. Remember, Romulus says, they aren't worth it! Keep your chin up!"

Tears threatened to well up in Freka's eyes again. She wet a paper towel and pressed the cool damp surface against her face. Then, she shook her arms, checked her hair, and put on a small amount of lip gloss. Returning to the meeting, she passed Siggy and Rachel, who were facing the other way, their shoulders hunched over their mirrors. Rachel kept her expression calm, but inside, there was a sharp pain brought on by the thought that she had accidentally said something that hurt this spunky girl, so much so that the young woman had felt it necessary to declare Rachel not "worth it."

As soon as Freka passed, Rachel and Sigfried surreptitiously moved back into the Knight's room, still watching the mirror, as Siggy's amulet viewpoint followed the Transylvanian princess. In the image on the calling card, Freka crossed the room and asked her brother Beowulf if he'd like to continue their duel.

Beowulf was taciturn and sardonic. Rachel might have thought of him as dark and broody, if she did not have his younger brother Wulfgang in her core group. Wulfgang took the gold in dark and brooding, leaving his older brother a distant bronze.

"What was that all about?" grunted Beowulf.

"Gaius's, um, girlfriend... was scoping me out about what I wanted to do with the Knights, if I beat Valiant for the assistant position. She seems nice."

"If you truly want to win, get the cat familiars to spy on their masters for you."

A mischievous pixy-grin danced across Freka's features. She scolded, "You know I hate doing that."

"You going to make a show of it, or not? You know Romulus thinks all this participation in the democratic process is beneath you."

"I'll talk to people." Freka shrugged her shoulders prettily. "I dunno, if it were someone I didn't like so much, I'd be much more interested in winning. But it's cutie-pie Valiant. He might be a better choice. Some people seem intimidated when they talk to me. Don't know if it is the title thing or the wolf thing. Everyone gets along with him. The girls adore him—or they did, before he started dating a kindergartener—and the guys respect him for his dueling skills. I'm just one princess among many, and I'm not all Goth like Luperca, or super-beautiful like that little Romanov girl."

Beowulf actually smiled. Rachel had never seen him do that before. "You're the best of them. I know that, even if no one else does."

His sister smiled, mollified.

He leaned forward, his voice gruff. "Think Rom's having the nightmares, too."

The smile fled from her face. She glanced over at her oldest brother, her lips bloodless.

"I just wish Father hadn't made us come home to watch," she whispered.

Beowulf squeezed her arm gently. "The nightmares'll pass... eventually. Or... we'll learn to live with them."

She nodded grimly. Without a word, they started practicing again.

"Aw!" murmured Rachel, over by the doorway of the Knight's chamber. She now felt very fond of Freka, ever since she had heard the older girl say "she seems nice." It made her feel slightly less bad about having been so upsetting as to be not "worth it." Laying her hand on Sigfried's arm, she said, "I know enough. You can go now."

"I wonder what their nightmares are like?" Siggy's eyes glinted with maniacal interest.

Rachel frowned at him. "We know exactly what their nightmares are like. We were standing in them."

"Wha... oooh! You mean the guys who were swinging by their neck!"

"Their father must have made them watch a hanging." Rachel shuddered.

"I'd have nightmares, too," Siggy nodded stoutly. "I've had nightmares just from seeing their nightmares."

Rachel nodded and patted his arm. "Thanks again. You can go back to dueling now."

"Woohoo!" Sigfried ran off whooping. "Get ready, Lucky, we're gonna fry us some sophomores!"

• • •

Rachel stood a moment watching the duelists and their glinting gems. Then she went off into an empty corner and recalled her duels with the sneering, sarcastic Ethan Warhol. She played the events of the duels over and over, noting each glint of his wand. Each time, at the split second that she recalled the spark of light, she performed the Word of Ending. This was extremely difficult, because the moment his cantrip triggered, young Mr. Warhol moved so quickly, she could hardly see him.

Rachel slowed down her memory, calling it back to her millisecond by millisecond. When she saw the flash of the gem, she performed the cantrip. She did this ten times. Then, she increased the memory's speed. She continued for over an hour, until she could do it in real time.

Then, she went looking for the scornful Mr. Warhol.

Ethan leaned casually against one of the separating posts, leering down at his curvaceous girlfriend who was giving him smoldering looks through her overly-long lashes. The son of a flamboyant American Senator, Ethan was an indecently-handsome bad boy with sandy blond hair. Unlike most of the young men here, who were in robes, he wore perfectly-tailored subfusc—black slacks, white shirt, black jacket, white bowtie, black thigh-length half-cape.

When Rachel walked up to him, he flashed her a crooked smile, giving her a look that made her feel uncomfortable, as if she were too skimpily attired—this despite that she was garbed in full-academic robes.

"Come back for more punishment, Shrimp?" Ethan smirked.

Rachel bowed, as duelists were supposed to do before a match.

"Okay. If you're a glutton for punishment, no skin off my knee." He tossed his half-cape over the post and came out onto the dueling strip in his shirt sleeves. "It's your life."

Rachel and Ethan squared off. Salome cheered them both on with the same enthusiasm that she did everything that did not bore her to tears. This drew the attention of some others. Next thing Rachel knew, they had an audience—including Sigfried, Nastasia, Gaius, and Vladimir Von Dread, who observed them with his arms crossed and his expression inscrutable.

"Speedy Gonzales coming at ya! Prepare to be boarded," leered the arrogant sophomore.

Rachel turned sideways like a fencer, as Gaius had taught her, and held her right hand out, ready to perform the cantrip.

"Go!" shouted Salome, clapping her hands with their overly-long strawberry nails.

Ethan bounced on the balls of his feet. Rachel kept her eyes trained on the tip of his wand. It was an emerald, apparently Mr. Warhol favored cantrips.

Nothing happened, and then....

"*Obé!*" Rachel shouted, moving the index finger of her right hand horizontally.

The blur that was Ethan Warhol lost its supernatural speed. With a loud cry, he windmilled his arms before tripping and falling face first on the mat.

Rachel shrieked with joy and jumped up and down. She was still jumping when a stream of blue sparks came from Ethan's wand and struck her, paralyzing her limbs. She, too, would have fallen on her face, if Gaius had not called the match in Ethan's favor and freed her before she hit the mat.

"Never rest on your laurels," Gaius told her seriously. "The match isn't over until one person cannot continue to cast."

Rachel acknowledged the wisdom of his words and filed them away for later reference. But her loss of the match did not dim her enthusiasm. She had stopped the arrogant git, and he would not be able to baffle her with his extra speed again. And he knew it.

As she turned away, she noticed Vladimir Von Dread watching her, a hint of approval in his gaze. Rachel risked shooting him a shy smile.

This time, he definitely winked at her.

Chapter Seventeen:

Beautiful Children of the

Immortals

Over the next couple of weeks, the weather grew colder, and students buckled down to their studies in earnest. Rachel and her friends spent more time studying and less time in frivolous pursuits, except for Sigfried, who aced every practical exam but seldom handed in homework assignments. As promised, Rachel wrote out his paper on Shaman of the World, carefully inventing errors she thought Sigfried might make to help it look authentic. She did a passable job, but it made her feel tremendously uncomfortable. She swore that she would never again agree to do this.

Next time she wanted a favor from Sigfried, she would find something less dishonest to offer him.

As the days progressed in to weeks, Rachel did not get to spend as much time with Gaius as she might have liked. He was studying hard to make up for the time he had lost while he was working on restoring his wand, and she had to spend her Saturdays in detention —cleaning and polishing equipment for Mr. Chanson. However, Gaius did come by their hallway and help her put some paralyzing hexes, tiathelu cantrips, and wind blasts into her wand. He even cast a few Glepnir bonds for her and put those in as well. He also took her down to the Roanoke Alchemical Shoppe, underneath Raleigh Hall, and helped her pick out her own *cinqfoil*. Eventually, he asked to borrow her wand so he and William could examine it and let her know more about what it could do. Rachel agreed.

She searched the news glass she had subscribed to for anything that might be a hint of the actions of the demon Morax but could find nothing. Did that mean that the demon had been caught and stopped? Or that it was still at large? It was at times like this that she wished that she actually had the Wisecraft contacts that Von Dread believed her to have. Of course, Von Dread did have such contacts, and Gaius insisted that they had not heard anything either.

She longed for the time when her father would arrive. He might not be willing to share sensitive information, but surely he would at least let her know if the problem had been resolved. Meantime, Gaius assured her that Dread had shared the information they had discovered in the library with the appropriate authorities, and the princess had as well. Hopefully, no news meant that all was well. Yet, whenever she thought about the demon—about the dark, shadowy shape of Moloch coalescing in the tower—an odd pain formed in her chest and refused to go away.

Thinking of her father often sparked the number one conflict troubling her. She knew secrets no one should know and secrets she had promised not to tell. The question of whom she should share this knowledge with weighed on her thoughts constantly.

To whom did she owe the greatest loyalty?

During the crisis that struck her during the first week of school, Rachel had picked Gaius as the person to be loyal to, first and foremost. But that decision alone was not enough to sort out her troubles. What did she do with issues of conflict between her various friends and loved ones? Did she put Siggy before Sandra? Her father before the princess?

After some thought, she came to the decision that she had to weigh her loyalty to each person around her and form a strict hierarchy. She spent hours contemplating her loyalty chart and moving names up and down the rungs of its ladder. Gaius was always at the top. Currently, he was followed by Sigfried and Nastasia, both on the second rung. Then, the Raven. Then, her father, then everyone else.

Classes progressed apace. In Music, they finished reviewing the song for dispersing a low-hanging fog and moved on to the basic principles of songs of protection. Rachel had no trouble memorizing the notes. Convincing her fingers, however, to move in the right order against the holes of the flute was another matter entirely. She played so badly on one song that she made a desultory attempt at practicing her flute that night.

But her heart was not in it.

In Science, they read Aristotle's *On Magic*. On Thursday, Mr. Fisher taught them the spider-cling elixir, which granted the drinker the power to climb walls like a spider. Rachel and Nastasia worked quietly and produced a decent elixir, while Zoë and Siggy kept snickering and addressing each other as "Parker." Sigfried called the tutor over and asked him why alchemists with elixirs did not rule the world. Mr. Fisher demonstrated by having Siggy cling to a wall, just a foot up, and then using the Word of Ending. Sigfried instantly fell to the floor.

"As you see." Fisher smiled and bowed to a scattering of applause.

In Geometry, they were still studying the first book of Euclid, working through Propositions 20 through 28. Mrs. MacDannan also covered the anti-magical properties of running water and its usefulness as a ward to stop ghosts, vampires, and other undead—along with the usefulness of a twig of a broom and salt. There were, however, some spirits so strong that even running water did not stop them. One of these, the tutor warned, was the Headless Horseman, who led the Wild Hunt up the Hudson from Sleepy Hollow at midnight every Halloween on his way to the Dead Men's Ball—a gathering of the unquiet dead that took place that night at Bannerman's Mansion, on Roanoke Island, just north of the school. Mrs. MacDannan warned them to stay safely inside the wards of the school on Halloween night.

The other issue that arose in math class was, as the year progressed and the terrors of the first week drew further away, the Thaumaturgy students from Drake Hall, who had all been geased by Dr. Mordeau, began to recover from the shell-shocked state in which they had spent the month of September. They began talking loudly again and returning to their previous arrogant behavior. Rachel had not yet come to their attention again. She felt certain that it was only a matter of time, however, before Cydney Graves would remember her grievances, and Rachel would again become the target of her malice.

Language was mainly grammar and reading Shakespeare—including the three plays lost to the Unwary, *A Midwinter Day's Folly*, *The Wylde Hunt*, and *Emrys Myrddin*—Shakespeare's take on King Arthur. They also learned two new cantrips: *bey-athe*, the basic shield Gaius had taught her, and *muria*—which technically meant "bringing into being"—the cantrip used by conjurers to manifest their creations.

In True History, they were still studying early humans and their relationship to the magical world. This included the origins of certain ancient ceremonies, and how Demeter, while she was mourning the loss of Persephone, taught agriculture to tribal hunter-gatherers. In art, the students continued their efforts to conjure a hoop. Mrs. Heelis excused Rachel from this project and let her spend the class delving into the books on drawing. She read book after book, learning the rudimentary steps and discovering which parts of the process her perfect recall aided and which it could not.

Drawing turned out to be exactly what she had been looking for—an activity she could do in class, while tutors reviewed material they had previously covered. Unless the tutors walked around the large central table and looked over her shoulder, they could not tell whether she was drawing or taking notes. This meant she had something she could do, other than listen to them recite again and again the same material she had already memorized, and still not appear rude.

As she drew, she imagined being a librarian for the Library of All Worlds. Just the name filled her with awe. What would such a library be like? To what strange and magical places might she travel in pursuit of it—far vistas, distant worlds, the gateway to an undiscovered country in which yet unknown secrets lurked? Inspired by this thought, she drew a sketch of a hand pushing aside the branches of a weeping willow to glimpse beyond a magnificent rushing waterfall. The completed picture looked nothing like what she imagined. It was all ink blots and wiggly lines, but now she had a goal, something she wished to portray with her new skill. She also drew a picture of the vision she had seen in the Elf's garden, a forest growing atop the canopy of a second forest. That also looked nothing as it should.

She also drew pictures of the Raven, though she burned them

afterwards. She did not want anyone to see them, even though her skill was still not so good that he was likely to be recognized—in either of his guises. As she drew, she daydreamed about a day when she might do something to repay him for his faith in her. Of course, she thought, with a tiny smile, he might be rather pleased with her for stopping Mortimer Egg from commanding the *tenebrous mundi* to tear down his Wall. Still, she wished she could do more for him, that he would ask something of her, some task she could perform, preferably something difficult and great.

The quiet activity of drawing had a disadvantage. With no disasters to occupy her, the shock, fear, and horror she had so cleverly cast aside in order to remain clear-headed during the emergencies came crashing back.

They struck with the force of a run-away wrecking ball.

She would be sitting in class drawing, or in the library with her friends, and suddenly she would discover that she was trembling, as she vividly relived the moment Moloch threw Sigfried through the wall of the keep tower; or Sigfried lying in the duck pond; or watching her father fly toward a head-on collision with the side of the same keep; or seeing Agent Carlson crash down atop the standing candelabra, its iron tip protruding from his chest; or the looks on the faces of the pilots of the runaway plane as it flew directly toward Roanoke Hall; or the sight of Mr. Fuentes lying on the gravel, bleeding after falling because she had paralyzed him to keep him from killing Valerie; or seeing Mr. Fisher, bloody and unconscious on the floor, his glasses splattered with his blood; or the vision Nastasia had showed them in the thinking glass where Gaius and Locke lay dead while Dr. Mordeau killed the defiant Von Dread; or Nastasia's description of Juma O'Malley's mother snapping the neck of Mrs. Egg.

These memories would crowd in on her until she felt as if there were a constant buzzing of voices at the edge of her consciousness, all clamoring to be heard. If she did not resist, the buzzing grew louder, and she felt as if she were falling.

Rachel never let herself find out what would have happened next.

Each time it started, she resisted. She would throw herself into actively studying or practicing. She was finding it harder and harder to concentrate, but if she kept herself supremely focused, she could keep what felt like the growing madness at bay. Practicing in the hallway was by far the most effective method. Or flying. She spent a great deal of her free time on her steeplechaser. So long as she kept her attention on something practical spells, the past terrors left her alone.

Yet she knew this was only postponing the issue, not solving it.

She recognized this buzzing, this feeling of falling, and the encroaching darkness that sometimes accompanied it. She had experienced it after her grandfather died. She tried drowning out the buzzing by socializing with her friends, but this was as likely to backfire as to help. When they were open and inclusive, she could become swept up in their activities and good cheer. But every so often, they snipped at one another, or the girls chose her as the person to gang up against and tease that day. Their teasing was humorous, but it still made her feel excluded, which caused a gap, and into the gap rushed everything she was striving to avoid.

The trouble she had being among her friends did not extend to Sigfried. He did not ask anything of her. Spending time with him and Lucky was always immediate and fun. But spending time with Sigfried usually meant spending time with the others, and she was finding it harder and harder to get along with Nastasia.

Rachel wanted so much to please her friend the princess, but she also wanted to spend time with Gaius. She wished she could be getting to know his group of friends. Yet, even during the brief time she spent with him at the Knight's meeting or after classes, she could feel disapproval radiating from Nastasia. The princess never hesitated to remind her of how unreliable Vladimir Von Dread was —how he had caused Nastasia to disobey her father, and how he had leaked the information that caused the death of Mrs. Egg. Additionally, anyone who worked for a scoundrel, such as Gaius, must in the long run prove himself unreliable. Rachel tried to explain to Nastasia her theory as to why she thought that Mrs. Egg's death had not been caused by Von Dread, but Nastasia refused to consider the possibility that the Wisecraft could be at fault.

The only person with whom she felt entirely at ease was Gaius.

When he was near, the buzzing fell silent, and she felt like an ordinary young woman. It was as if the tempest within her became calm and balmy when he approached. She wondered if this was because she had picked him as the center of her world, the one person she trusted above all others, or if that thought had cause and effect reversed, and she had picked him partially because he had this wonderful calming effect on her thoughts.

She loved him all the more for it.

Occasionally, as she stared out the window at the chaos of fall colors, having perhaps just finished a drawing with no new subject in mind, she could keep the fear and sorrow at bay by just thinking about Gaius. She recalled their time together in the fog-shrouded tower, reliving the highlights: hugging him for the first time in the misty herb garden; leaning against him in the bell tower, his arm around her shoulder; and, ah, the kisses.

She dwelt for a time on their private training sessions together, in the hallway and at the Knights meetings. From there, her thoughts slid to the moment when Von Dread winked at her. The memory of it made her feel a little giddy. She knew he must not wink at many girls. He could not maintain his imposing demeanor if he behaved thus toward everyone. She did not know what she had done to cause him to let his guard down slightly, but it delighted her.

But what else did one expect from a young man who managed to look commanding and magnetic even in his sweat pants—a young man who *jumped onto* oncoming jets about to crash? Her imagination drifted to her previous daydream, in which the looming prince had curtly informed her that he had chosen her to be his queen and planned to wed her as soon as she came of age. Previously, she had imagined that he had kissed her. (Her imagination skirted away from recalling the fantasized kiss itself. That would be disloyal.) What might come next?

In her new daydream, she imagined defying him, her eyes flashing as she vowed her eternal loyalty to his lieutenant, Mr. Valiant. She imagined him trying to kiss her again. She imagined stomping on his foot.

By the following week, her fantasies had altered. In her imagination, the tall, looming college boy had already kissed her, and now she daydreamed about how she dealt with the affront. She pictured various reactions. Sometimes, she was cool as an ice sculpture. Other times, she was frantic and panicky and behaved far more emotionally than she would ever act in real life. At first, she decided Gaius knew what Dread had done and would try to protect her—without offending his boss, if he could. This fantasy scenario often led to a second duel, only this time Gaius turned Dread into a sheep!

But Rachel was not the sort of girl who found it pleasant to have men fighting over her. So, by the end of the second week, she had switched to yet a new scenario where, in which, to protect the friendship between Dread and Gaius, she did not tell her boyfriend about the older boy's advances. Thus, Gaius was puzzled as she continued to do increasingly dramatic things to avoid his grim boss. This storyline was filled with angst and heartbreak, and once she found her cheeks covered with tears.

Yet, this imaginary anguish was preferable to reliving the real horrors that threatened to overwhelm her. Overall, Rachel found her fantasy scenarios quite satisfying.

• • •

A week before Halloween, their music teacher, Miss Cyrene, called for a review—a practical, where the students were to demonstrate their command of the enchantments they had learned thus far. Rachel practiced with the other students in class, dutifully preparing to demonstrate her less than stellar control over breezes and will-o-wisps. She hesitated to show off her skill at whistling, partially because it was only useful for hexes. Defensive enchantments, as hexes were officially called, required short, crisp notes. This she found easy to reproduce. But summoning enchantments, such as that used to call domestic will-o-wisps, required more elaborate melodies.

Rachel knew that it was possible to whistle whole symphonies. She occasionally heard her parents whistling Bach or Brahms, as they walked the long hallways of Gryphon Park. However, she herself did not have the sustained breath control necessary to accomplish this. Even if she had, it was one thing to resist the tickling of the magic that rushed through her lips for a few short notes, it was another thing entirely to maintain control of her lips under the tingling onslaught of such magical forces for a sustained length of time.

Luckily, at least half the class was not significantly better than she was. The canticle students from Spencer were not particularly skilled musicians, except for Sebastian Powers—whose father was a Member of the Parliament of the Wise and whose grandfather had been the previous Grand Inquisitor before Cain March. Sebastian had been playing since he was a small child and was a superb musician.

The majority of the Dare students, on the other hand, had played instruments before they arrived at Roanoke. Some of them, like the princess and Sakura Suzuki, played amazingly. Brunhilda Winters had played the French horn in her junior high marching band, and Kitten Fabian had performed at piano recitals since she was a child. Then there were others, like Seth Peregrine and Zoë, who claimed they were good musicians, but Rachel wasn't entirely certain the ruckus they played could properly be called music.

From their dainty tutor's expression, Miss Cyrene agreed.

All over the classroom, her classmates began tuning their instruments, preparing for the practical. Banjo and accordion warred with *shamisen* and *shakuhachi*. Ian MacDannan had bagpipes of a red and black tartan, a cornet, and a lap harp. He kept switching back and forth among the three. Seth and David Jordan had lost interest in the assignment entirely. With their bass guitar and guitar, they broke into a song about a hound dog.

It was because of moments like these that students almost never brought their familiars to music class. Too many ended up either howling or scampering away in fear.

As more students tuned-up and began playing, the will-o-wisps zipped to and fro, responding to competing summonings. Soon, the poor, little, glowing lights seemed to be listing to the side, as if they had become punch drunk. A few students managed to keep their small group of will-o-wisps nearby. Princess Nastasia had coaxed her will-o-wisps into circling her head, like a Swedish candle crown; while Sigfried kept altering the summoning song, trying to get his wisps to dive-bomb one another.

Miss Cyrene finally gently insisted that Ian pick a single instrument for the demonstration. She called some wisps to her, using her voice alone. The sound was so glorious that everyone in the room paused. Listening to the beautiful singing, Rachel titled her head slightly and peered at their bird-like tutor. Tilting her head the other way, Rachel was reminded of a woodcut illustration in an ancient bestiary. It came from the same book as the hidden page with description of an *Angel* that she had recalled only after the Elf gave her the memory-protecting Rune.

"Psst," she whispered to Nastasia and Joy, "doesn't our tutor look a lot like a siren?"

"Very likely," Nastasia replied graciously, from where she sat strumming the red, blue, and transparent strings of her harp. "Members of the Wise are all descended from some kind of supernatural creature or another. That is how we acquire our talents for sorcery."

"It's why everyone here is so beautiful," chirped Joy. Then she blushed and pulled on her mouse brown hair. "Except for me. I'm plain as a pancake."

Rachel felt a moment of sympathy for the other girl. She, too, had noticed that a great deal of the students seemed to be prettier or handsomer than she was. In their class, no one else was as gorgeous as Sigfried and the princess, in face, in the entire school, only Von Dread and Rory Wednesday compared. Still, a great many of the other students were strikingly attractive, and Rachel often found herself feeling plain in comparison.

"Unusually beautiful or unusually ugly," said Wendy Darling, who had been practicing nearby with Brunhilda Winters. She spoke sincerely and without the brashness that many of the other American girls displayed. She placed her trombone on the table beside Joy, her dark hair floating around her face like a lovely thundercloud. Her blue eyes were startling, both intelligent and intense. "Some of us are descended from the beautiful ones. The Plant Danu. Other gods. Noble fey. Others are descended from the Unseelie, or other entities from the less pleasant side of the fey."

Rachel was a bit in awe of Wendy, though she seldom interacted with the other girl. The daughter of Six Musketeers James Darling and Ellyllon MacDannan Darling, Wendy had inherited her famous mother's love of dance. She spent her free time at a ballet studio in the gym and wore dusty rose leg warmers that peeked out beneath her robes.

"Like Lola Spong," Joy shuddered. "She's said to be descended from a troll or an ogre."

Rachel, whose run-in with the toad-like Miss Spong had been less than pleasant, found it easy to believe.

"Is that why?" asked California cheerleader, Brunhilda, who preferred to be called Hildy. Wendy's best friend was a gymnast and an all-round athlete who had grown up among the Unwary. The two girls had joined the fencing team together and had bonded over their shared interest in athletics and the cute boys on the sports teams.

"Why what?" asked Joy.

"Poor, little, glowy buggies." Hildy lowered her French horn and watched her will-o-wisps zip back toward their night hood in the ceiling. "They're pooped. But, back to your point: I've been, like, wondering about that. People say Hollywood is filled with pretty people. So many good-looking kids head out there to try their hand at film and TV that even the waiters and the clerks in the airport are drop-dead gorgeous. I mean, serious hotties! And they're all like, 'Look at this face!'" Hildy stuck her neck out and pointed all her fingers at her cheeks. "Think I'll make it in the movies?' And my friends and I are like, 'Yeah, you and a million others. Now finish bagging my groceries, bag dude.'

"But when it comes to pretty faces, Roanoke takes the cake— and the platter and the table it's sitting on. There are people at school—like that upper school senior, Rory Wednesday or our princess here—who are so beautiful, that it makes you want to, like, gouge out your eyes after you see them. Because you know you will never see anything so exquisite, ever again."

"Did you know that Joshua March once kidnapped her? Rory, I mean." Wendy's startling blue eyes sparkled. "It was back when she was twelve, and he was ten. He climbed in her window, put a pillow case over her head, and tried to fly her out in a kenomanced bag. He would have gotten in big trouble... except his father is the one who gets people in trouble. So, Joshua got off easy. Oddly, he and Rory been friends ever since. And no one's friends with the Marches—No one wants to risk being questioned by their father."

"Where did all this happen?" asked Hildy.

"At the lower school," Wendy explained. "I was nine."

"You went to the lower school?" Zoë's eyebrows rose. "I figured someone must have actually gone there. But you're the first person I've met who admitted to it."

Wendy said, "I was a day student. My brother Michael's there now. He still goes home on weekends."

"Didn't realize the Marches and the Wednesdays went to the Lower School?" said Joy.

Hildy shivered. "Weird to imagine being here since kindergarten."

"Seven," said Wendy. "The lower school starts at age seven."

"Seven." Hildy shrugged. "Close enough. Hey, did you know that Rory Wednesday's hair has blue..." she waved her hand, patting her head. "... what are they called? You know. Those thingies where some top hairs are a different color from the others?"

"Highlights?" Zoë added pale green strands to her dark green hair.

"Yeah, highlights! That's it!" Hildy's head bobbed from the rapidness of her nodding. "Blue! Oh, and whose idea was it to have a high school and a college—both with freshmen, juniors, et cetera—in the same building? No one can ever tell what you mean when you say someone's a senior! Are they an upper school senior? Or a college senior?"

"I have blue highlights, too, though not many." Nastasia peered at her own golden locks and held out a hair. "Usually, they are only visible in the brightest of sunlight."

Rachel leaned close, peering. Sure enough, the lock she held out was a pale blue.

"Could there be a relationship?" Wendy asked. Pointing her toe, she lifted her foot onto the table and stretched over it, bouncing.

Something about her expression made her face resemble that of her older brother. A lump rose in Rachel's throat, as she recalled overhearing John Darling's comments about her. A renewed desire to see Sigfried skunk the louse ignited in her breast.

"What might it be?" asked Joy. "What kind of fey has blue hair? Sea nymphs? Stromkarls? Rhine Maidens? Rory Wednesday is known to be descended from the most famous of the Rhine Maidens. Maybe the princess here is, too."

"My boss, the P.E. teacher Mr. Chanson, has a steely blue tint to his hair," Rachel said thoughtfully. "He's also extremely handsome."

Behind her, Astrid Hollywell lowered her banjo and sighed. Astrid was a painfully shy young woman with caramel skin and tight black curls, who always wore a scarf over her black robes. When Rachel looked at her, she blushed and ducked her head.

Astrid murmured, "Mr. Chanson *is* very handsome."

Rachel threw her a conspiratorial smile and a wink. Astrid kept her head down, but the corners of her eyes crinkled with pleasure.

"Isn't there anyone in the World of the Wise who's just normal?" asked Hildy.

"You mean other than Joy?" quipped Zoë. She held up her Maori war trumpet and gave the pukaea two long toots, producing a fountain of multi-colored sparks. "Nope. Just look at us. The princess is divine. Wendy is like a Pre-Raphaelite dream. You're a California golden girl, Hildy. Griffin's a little China doll. And me?" She spread her arms and shrugged. "I'm like a goddess." She flipped her short green locks. "A goddess of hair."

"Yeah, like, other than Joy." Hildy snickered. "Just kidding, O'Keefe. You're cute enough... at least by the standards of everywhere but Hollywood and here standards. And not everyone in the room is a total hottie. Those Spenser Hall kids are pretty normal-looking. Well, except for Amaranth Kyle, but she always looks like she's had a rat-hair day. And Suki Wong. But Asian girls are, like, double hot. So what can the rest of us do?"

Zoë laughed. Joy pouted. Rachel felt uncomfortable and looked down.

"In central California," Hildy added, "we have all these beautiful people I mentioned, but even we had some ordinary people. People with acne, or on crutches, or something. Here, I don't see anybody with, like, birthmarks, or deformities, or anything—much less people with actual disabilities. Do they not let people with disabilities into Roanoke?"

Zoë shrugged. "Magic heals everything."

"Not everything." Rachel looked up again. "There are two blind upperclassmen, Verthandi Odinson and her brother Hod. They're seers. I think they're descended from Norns."

"Wait...." Hildy leaned forward. Her blonde hair with its streaks of pale gold fell across her face. "Rory Wednesday is descended from Odin, but the Odinsons are descended from Norns?"

The others laughed. Wendy lowered her foot and raised her other leg, stretching over that one. "They're probably descended from Odin, too. To hear Grandma MacDannan talk, Odin got around." Wendy's intense blue eyes danced with amusement. "You'd think she had been personally scorned by the man. Er—god."

"Maybe she has," replied Rachel, who had heard all number of interesting stories about the uber-magical MacDannan family.

"I doubt it," Zoë snorted, "no one has seen a real god in generations."

Wendy put both feet on the floor and made an attempt to reign in her cloud of dark hair. "There's a girl in the Lower School who's in a wheelchair. She'll be here next year, Kora Chandler. Her parents were performing Conjurers. There was an accident."

"I heard about her," Rachel said. "Mrs. Heelis told me when she was lecturing me on why I should never conjure improperly again."

"Why didn't they, like, fix her with magic?" Hildy asked.

Rachel felt herself go pale. "In the dream mist? If you get injured there, magic doesn't work to heal...." Her voice trailed off, as a thought struck her.

Wendy nodded, her face sad. "Her parents died."

"That is truly sad," Nastasia said gravely. "Every child should have a parent. We must do our best to make her comfortable when she comes."

Rachel glanced at Sigfried, who had managed to get his confused wisps to fly in a figure 8, but he had not heard them.

Rachel thought of the scrubby area behind Roanoke Hall—the place where magic did not work well. What if the boys who had caused the explosion that left the place resistant to magic had somehow drenched the place in the same mist that had made it impossible to heal Miss Chandler? She made a mental note to pursue the issue.

At the front of the room, Miss Cyrene watched the brooding Wulfgang Starkadder blast objects across the room with a wind produced by his accordion. Rachel looked at her thoughtfully and then turned to her friends again.

"But back to our tutor," she said, "I didn't mean 'descendent from a siren'. I mean she looks like a real siren. Himerope—that's her name, right?—that's a real siren's name."

"That's silly," scoffed Joy. "Why would a real siren be here, teaching children?"

Rachel shrugged. "What else would a real siren do in our modern age?"

• • •

Rachel passed her practical—barely. She managed to summon only three of the tired, abused will-o-wisps, but apparently three were enough. Or maybe she passed because she was able to produce a reasonable gust of wind. It was not as strong as the gust she could have produced by whistling, but Miss Cyrene announced that it would do.

"Hey, other members of the Die Horribly While Debating Club," Siggy came up between Rachel and Zoë, as the girls walked out of class, "Wheels, here, and I—"

"Wheels?" Joy asked. She and Nastasia were walking to Rachel's right.

"Forrest. Our ride. The one who can get us to and fro," Siggy explained, sticking his thumb out at Zoë. "Wheels."

"Oh.... Got it." Joy nodded.

"You-know-who sent me a dream and asked me to bring Wheels to visit her."

"Wait. Who-know-who?" Joy asked again.

"The fl-Eay." Siggy stopped and cocked his head to the side. "Elf-Hay? F-Elay? Lucky, how *do* you say elf in Pig Latin."

Lucky cocked his head in imitation of his master. "*Fey? Lares? Lemur?* Or is that Human-Latin. Wouldn't the pig version be, 'Soo-ii'?"

Rachel groaned when he said the word *elf* aloud. "Sigfried!"

"Huh? Anyway, the one whose name I have no idea how to hide wants to see Zoë."

"We're not supposed to tell!" Fear jagged at Rachel's chest, as she recalled the Raven's expression when he warned them that if more than three people knew of Illondria, it would lead to her death.

Siggy shrugged, unconcerned. "She asked me to bring Wheels. What am I supposed to do? Tell her, 'No'? It's her life. She must know how dangerous it is. Want to come?"

"We cannot go," Nastasia said firmly, cutting off Rachel's enthusiastic reaction before it got started. "The Roanoke Tree is off school grounds. We may not go there."

"No, it's not," Rachel objected, feeling her face flush. This was the very conversation she had hoped to avoid. "The whole island belongs to the school."

Nastasia frowned, her face severe. "Nonsense. Obviously, they meant the wards of the school. We cannot go, Sigfried. Tell... the person involved that she will have to come here. Or meet us in a dream."

Nastasia walked on with firm purpose, as if the matter had been settled. Joy went with her. Rachel turned her head and met Sigfried's eyes. With the slightest of motions, they nodded at each other.

CHAPTER EIGHTEEN:

BEHIND ENEMY LINES

"WHAT'S THIS ELF-PERSON WANT?" ZOË ASKED, PEERING OUT OVER the zipper of her backpack.

Inside Zoë's backpack was a chamber about thirteen feet in diameter. It was not a neat, house-like space, like within the princess's bag. Rather, it was a messy collection of her belongings. Underwear, lingerie, comic books, jeans, and old soda cups lay scattered every which way. Rachel had sat down on a purple fake-fur coat with black leopard spots. She was a bit embarrassed when the thing poking her knee turned out to be a large, lacy, black bra with cups larger than her fist. She glanced at her own unimpressive chest and sighed glumly.

Outside, Sigfried called. "Um, Griffin... how do I get this to stop dragging to the right?"

"Left lever down... but just a bit!" Rachel stuck her head out of the pack.

Beneath her, by about a man's length, flowed the gray-brown waters of the Hudson. To the right, she could see the shore of Roanoke Island. To her left, the forest north of Storm King. Somewhere in front of her, unseen by either her eyes or her memory, a chameleon-elixired Sigfried was riding her steeplechaser by himself for the first time. Rachel winced as they jerked suddenly to the left.

"Just a bit!" she cried.

"Er... got it. No wait, now, we're... argh!"

The view from the backpack spun wildly, trees and rocks and the far shore flashing by. The sky turned sideways. The river water drew immensely closer.

Splash!

Water rushed into backpack. Cold spray shocked her face. Zoë shouted and lunged to secure the zipper. She had only just begun to slide it, when the deluge stopped. Looking out, Rachel saw the river bobbing beneath them and Lucky's head above them. The gold and red dragon craned his neck and peered at them, one jade eye filling much of the opening of the bag.

"I got 'em, Boss," the dragon raised his head, "but the broom got away."

"Oh, Griffin, that's rough," commiserated Zoë.

"It should turn visible now that I'm not on it," called Sigfried. "Maybe you can hunt it down."

Rachel stuck her arm out of the bag and waved her hand around. "*Varenga*, Vroomie!"

The steeplechaser, just a faint line in the distance, turned obediently and zoomed back to her outstretched hand.

"Wow." Zoë blinked. "That was cool, Griffin."

Rachel shot her a half smile.

"What do we do now?" asked Zoë.

"I'll take care of it," replied Rachel.

Music practicals might not be her strong point, but flying she understood intimately. Rachel jumped onto the seat of her bristleless and ducked her head. She shot out of the backpack and flew down low over the Hudson. She could hear Sigfried's teeth chatter as he shivered in the late October water.

"*Obé!*" She ended the magical effects of the chameleon elixir that was hiding Sigfried from her sight. Then, she cast *tiathelu*.

Sigfried weighed well over a hundred pounds, and the water made him heavier. Rachel strived and grunted, but she was unable to lift him. All she could manage was to pull his upper body out of the river. Sighing, she settled for dragging him through the river toward the shore. Lucky dived down and grabbed his master's robe in his mouth, helping her to pull.

Siggy whooped with delight. "This is great. Bet you could water ski this way."

"Okay, I'm going to let you go as we approach the rocks. I don't want to bang you into something." She released the cantrip and leaned forward, panting from the effort of lugging Sigfried's body through the water.

Siggy sank out of sight. A moment later, he reappeared coughing and sputtering. He stood up and walked to shore. Rachel suddenly felt very grateful that the river was shallow here, for it occurred to her that it was very unlikely that Sigfried knew how to swim.

"We are out of view of the school and the proctors," Rachel called down to him. "Why don't you get in the backpack, and I'll fly."

Siggy climbed, dripping, into Zoë's red and blue backpack. Lucky flew it to Rachel, who put it on over her robes. Then, she darted off around the coast and to the north.

She shivered as she flew above the rippling river. She had a sweater under her robes, but it was not proof against the late October chill. The autumn colors were nearly gone, the upper slopes of Storm King Mountain entirely bare. Lower down, sparse spots of red and orange remained. The waters of the river ran full of floating points of color.

Rachel shot over the north-most part of the island and over Dutchman's Cove, until she crossed one of the stone walls that was part of the wards hiding the Roanoke Tree—apparently, it was a much more powerful obscuration than was ordinarily used, because ordinarily, Rachel was able to see through them, but not this one. The great tree with its seven massive branches—each one sporting a different kind of bark and leaf: oak, beech, birch, ash, elm, hickory, and maple—rose before her like a wall of rough wood. She zipped around, flying low over the great fence-like roots as she searched for the nine-foot tall hollow in its side.

As she approached the tree, Rachel could feel the hush, the exhilaration—that awe-inspiring sense that the folk of the forest were near. She slowed down and raised her head, floating slowly through the forest, listening. Soft sounds teased her ears. Was that laughter? Bells? The wind? Even when she recalled her memory, she could not quite make it out.

Fairy noises were like that.

Rachel smelled the tantalizing herbs of the Elf's garden before she saw the great hollow. Illondria stood waiting for them. She wore an iridescent gown, the color of the sky reflected off autumn leaves. When she moved, it rustled like a wind passing through the forest. She waved to them. They landed. The elfin woman welcomed them warmly, quickly bundling the soaking Sigfried into the tree, when he emerged from Zoë's backpack.

Within the trunk was a wondrous dwelling—cabinets, chairs, tables and more, all carved from the living tree. At the far side of the room, a spiral staircase swept upward and out of sight. The glow of will-o-wisps brought out the warm grain of the polished wood. The air smelled of wintergreen and fresh sap.

Inside the cheery chamber, a fire burned. Rachel halted and gawked at the fireplace. The dancing flames were blue and green with hints of lavender at the bottom and edges. Instead of curls and points, each tongue flickered into shapes—horses, castles, cars, rabbits, clouds, mountain peaks. Heat came from it, or at least Rachel thought it was heat, for the autumn chill vanished, but, she was not sure she felt heat. Perhaps it was radiating cheer and well-being.

The elf woman glided behind the spiral staircase and out of sight. She came back with an earthenware pitcher, the sides of which were the color of running water. The glaze was so cleverly crafted that it looked as if liquid were pouring from the top, running down the vessel. Even after Rachel touched the cool, dry sides, her eyes refused to give up the illusion. Illondria held the pitcher over some rose-colored, fluted, crystal glasses and poured. What she poured, Rachel could not say. It flowed, and yet it did so in a languid manner, as mist might if poured from a teapot. The color was pearly yet tinged with the glow of a sunset.

"Don't worry," the elf woman's voice rang like sweet bells as she set the glasses before them. "This is safe for your kind. It will not make you unfit to eat the food of the mortal world."

Zoë shook her green head, her braid and its feather flying, and stepped back. But Sigfried lifted the drink and quaffed it. His expression went funny, and he blinked rapidly several times. After squeezing her eyes shut and hoping for the best, Rachel took an exploratory sip.

Her mouth remained dry, and yet something entered it. It was sweet and light, like drinking the scent of honeysuckle, and yet it reminded her of mountain tops and a thunderstorm over the moors. A warmth spread through her that had nothing to do with heat or cold.

"That's... brilliant!" crowed Siggy, extending the arm with the glass in it. "May I have another?"

The elf woman shook her head. "That would probably be unwise. Your kind seldom drink such draughts. To drink too much might bring on... unexpected results."

"Really?" Siggy perked up. He was no longer shivering. "What kind of results? Cool ones? Can I grow a second head? Make music come out of my ears? Turn into a dragon? I'd *love* to turn into a dragon. That would be the best. Here, give me another swig!"

With a gentle smile, Illondria whisked the pitcher back behind the spiral staircase.

Rachel took another sip. The sorrows of the last two months tasted salty and sour in her mouth. Then, they faded a bit, with only the tingle of a minty sweetness left.

Disconcerted, Rachel put the glass back on the table.

Zoë made a noise in her throat. She was staring upward, looking this way and that, her mouth slightly open. Rachel was pretty certain that the other girl was looking at something Rachel could not see.

"Oh!" Zoë cried, when the elf woman returned. "So this is why it's so easy to get around Roanoke at any hour of the day or night! I thought it was because Sarpy sleeps so much. Those are your dreams we're walking through! They're... huge!"

Illondria smiled. "I was once a queen of the Lios Alfar. Our dreams encompass worlds."

"I can see... all the way to the moon," Zoë said. "That's something!"

"To the moon! I want to fly to the moon!" Sigfried cried fiercely. "If we made a flying broom the size of a sequoia, do you think it could reach escape velocity? We'd have to have Griffin fly it, though. I wouldn't want to go into a tailspin in low earth orbit and fall off. That could end badly. What do you think, Lucky? Think we could leave tonight?"

Lucky, who had stuck his long flickering tongue into Rachel's abandoned glass, pulled it back quickly. "Oh definitely, Boss." He cocked his head. "Wait, there's gold on the moon, right? Not just cheese?"

"Tons!" Sigfried declared. He had pulled a half-eaten marshmallow out of his pocket, stuck it on the jeweled end of his wand, and was trying to roast it over the blue and green flame. The marshmallow did not catch fire, but it did seem cheerier. "I read in a magazine that satellite pictures have shown that the top foot of regolith —that's moon soil to all you uninitiated—at the south pole of the moon has 100 times the concentration of gold of the richest mines on earth!"

Lucky straightened up on his legs, so he stood as tall as a large dog. His long scarlet whiskers twitched. "Yes! Yes! Tonight! We've got to get to the moon before the evil scientists get there and take our gold!"

Rachel was not certain if Lucky meant to imply that there was a group of evil scientists out there, or if he just meant that the scientists who had discovered the moon gold—and thus might take it from him—were evil.

"Whoa, Nelly. Hold your horses... or brooms... or dragons," Zoë waved her hands back and forth. "No one's going to the moon today. Okay? Hm? Eventually... maybe. But we'd have to find out stuff, like whether there's air on the dream moon."

The elf woman returned and held her hand out to Zoë. "Come, Miss Forrest. I shall give you a gift. It will make it so that your companions shall not need to hold your hand to keep from falling back to the waking realm when you walk in the land of dreams."

"How's this going to work?" Zoë whipped her braid around, suspicious. The feather *thwapped* rhythmically.

"I will put a Rune upon your body—you may pick the place. These are the sacred Runes guarded by the World Tree. There will be pain, but only briefly. This Rune will allow you to make the dream stuff near you more solid."

Zoë rocked back on her heels. "Pain versus not losing my friends, not falling into foreign kingdoms filled with demon worshippers, and not getting expelled. Done!"

Illondria took Zoë up the spiral staircase. There was a blood curdling scream. Rachel clutched the back of a chair. Siggy popped the strangely-cheery marshmallow into his mouth.

While chewing the gooey, sugar-treat, he mumbled, "Y-u scre-med like 'at, too."

"Hey, what about me?" Lucky watched with large, liquidy, puppy eyes as his master chewed.

"Oh, sorry, Luck." Sigfried took out a Snickers bar with a bite taken out of it. He stuck it in the blue-green fairy flame for half a minute and then tossed it to Lucky. The dragon swallowed it in one gulp and then burped with satisfaction.

Footsteps on the staircase. The tall elf woman glided back down, followed by a pale Zoë who was holding the right side of her stomach.

"Miss Elf," Rachel curtsied politely—she felt too shy to call the great woman by her name, "do you know if there is a temple to Saturn anywhere in the world? Or whether the demon who wishes to summon him up will have to consecrate a new one?"

"A temple to Saturn?" Something like fear moved behind the stars that served the tall, graceful being for pupils. "No. Not that are standing. He was overthrown."

"So... if someone wanted one, they'd need to consecrate the ground first, on the dark of the moon, right?"

"You mean defile,"—the Elf drew herself up. She seemed to tower above the rest of them, vast and terrible in her majesty—"not consecrate. They would need to defile the ground with the blood of a loved one, probably a youth or child." She shuddered. "'Tis a vile ceremony. Why do you ask?"

"Some lesser demon wants to call up the demon who was also named Saturn."

"She means Muldoon or Memphis? Something like that," volunteered Sigfried, trying to lick the sticky marshmallow innards off the several-thousand-dollar ruby on the tip of his wand.

"I know of whom she speaks." Illondria's voice was soft like a distant wind. "Please, never say his name. Especially here."

"They are trying to summon him," Rachel said worriedly.

The elf woman lay a comforting hand on Rachel's arm. "Fear not, little one. There's no danger of *his* coming."

"Then he is not dangerous?" Rachel asked hopefully.

"Oh, he's dangerous! He is the most dangerous of them all, save one. But he is..." the elf woman glanced up and to the south, though whether she was looking at the polished wood of the chamber wall, into her dreams, or beyond to some distant land or vision, Rachel could not tell, "... otherwise occupied. He will not come."

"He almost came at Beaumont. He threw Siggy from the tower."

"What?" The elven woman's skin grew several shades less luminescent, as if her blood carried a glow that diminished when it ran from her face. "No. It must not be! You are certain?"

Rachel nodded.   Illondria whispered something under her breath. Recalling several times, Rachel was nearly certain she had said: "Phanuel's sacrifice cannot have been in vain!"

"Who is Phanuel?" Rachel asked curiously.

The elf woman gave her a very kind smile. "Someone you would have liked very much."

"Why is this particular demon so dangerous?" asked Zoë.

"He must be stopped at all costs!" cried Rachel, remembering the moment in the tower. The pain rose again in her chest.

"At all costs!" echoed Sigfried, his eyes like burning coals.

"Do not let his corruption touch you, children." The elf woman looked at them with some concern. She stared off to the south again, as if lost in thought. Turning back to Zoë, she said, "All demons are dangerous, because they bring with them evil and destruction. But many of them are limited in the accomplishment of their evil by their own vices. Their devotion to their besetting sin, be it anger, lust, or sloth, interferes with their ability to carry out their fiendish plans. Sooner or later, their own weaknesses draw them away from their intended path. But there are two to whom this does not apply: the Prince of Darkness and the Prince of the Earth.

"We will not speak of the Prince of Darkness." The Elf shuddered like a willow in a gale. "The one you speak of is known as the Prince of the Earth. He is different from the others. He is clever, supremely intelligent. And his besetting sin is desperation—and his resulting ruthlessness served rather than impeded his cleverness.

"To this end, the Prince of Darkness made this one the governor of the fallen material world. Among his other infernal inventions, the Prince of the Earth invented the Tyranny of Time, the force that makes it so that all things mortal run down and go bad and grow old. From that, he introduced the idea that a bad thing done now might produce a good thing in the future. He called this idea: *sacrifice*.

"In the early days, eons ago, when he truly was the Prince of the Earth, and all the worlds of Sideria bowed to him, he would not even send rain unless the sacrifices had been performed to his satisfaction. He was a tyrannical ruler. He even ate his own children, lest they threaten his reign. Eventually, all the powers—those Below, those Above, and those in the Twilight Lands—joined and overthrew him.

"But even that was not enough to stop what he had put into motion. In the long run, to end the Tyranny of Time called *sacrifice*, the One on High was required to send—" the elf woman's voice suddenly cut off. "But we are not allowed to speak of that here."

"Why not?" Siggy scowled. "Why not speak about things that are true? Who is stopping us?" He pulled out his wand, as if he planned to attack the one doing the stopping.

Rachel considered what they had just learned. Stepping forward, she lay a hand on the elf woman's arm. "Tell me, are we behind some kind of enemy lines? In the territory of the demons, perhaps?"

The elf woman tilted her head thoughtfully and then nodded. "You might put it that way, little one."

CHAPTER NINETEEN:

ONE CLASSY LADY

RACHEL, SIGFRIED, LUCKY, AND ZOË MADE THEIR WAY BACK TO CAMpus through the dreamlands. The Rune worked just as the Elf had predicted. The others were able to let go of Zoë's hand without falling. They arrived back on campus filled of ideas for new experiments, but Nastasia and Valerie both had too much homework to participate. Further dreamland experiments were put off for another day.

A few days later, Rachel had a free period between the end of her classes and when she had to report to the gym to perform her job as Mr. Chanson's assistant. Stopping by the mail room, she found a package waiting for her that was almost as big as she was. It proved to be light, however, so she was able to awkwardly maneuver it onto her steeplechaser and take it up the stairs, outside, and to the roof of Roanoke Hall. There, she opened the window of the secret place she had found the day of the jumbo jet and slipped inside with her prize.

Inside was a hexagonal room containing a cream-and-rose couch, an end table, and a throw rug. Over the last few weeks, she had aired it out and beaten the sofa cushions, so the place was no longer as dusty as it had once been. Now, she eagerly ripped open the brown paper and pulled out a peach damask slipcover, a large cream and peach quilted comforter, and two giant satiny throw pillows, creamy with bright iridescent blue and green peacocks whose tails trailed off the pillows.

Eagerly, she slid on the slipcover, puffed up the throw pillows, placed them in the corners of the sofa, and wrapped herself in the comforter. Then she threw herself onto the cushions of the couch and lay in warmth and comfort.

She lazily opened the letter that had accompanied the items she had requested from home. In it was a breezy note from her mother, telling her that all was well and asking about her classes and her friends. At the bottom was a P.S. that read: *Your Father sends his love.*

Rachel stared at the line, trying very hard to feel grateful. Instead, a hard spot about the size of an almond formed in her throat and would not be dislodged, no matter how many times she swallowed.

He was not coming.

If he had been planning to come, she would have heard from him by now. He would have included a message saying when he would arrive. He was not coming. He did not care about hearing her version of the events. Now there was no one to whom she could tell the truth.

Well, there was Gaius, of course. He might even know about her memory by now, if Topher had told him. And she really wanted to tell Gaius everything as soon as she felt it was the right time, but....

It was not the same.

For one thing, Gaius was not in a position to stop the demon.

Somewhere in the back of her mind, a nasty little voice whispered: *Father would have been here already if it had been Sandra.* Rachel bit her lip and pushed that voice away. But for the first time in her life, she felt a real sympathy for the wild antics of her sister Laurel.

She lay there staring at the ceiling, which was a pale gold marred by several large cracks, feeling glum. But it was too nice a day to waste feeling sad. She wanted to appreciate the new improvements to her hideaway in peace. To cheer herself, she let her thoughts drift. What fun it would be to bring Gaius up here. Would he like her private domain? Would he kiss her? Might they snuggle together, curled up like puppies? Would he try something... untoward... if she curled up with him like that? Or was John Darling correct, that she just was not desirable enough to tempt an older boy?

Closing her eyes, she imagined that she was older—much older, like fifteen or sixteen! By then, she was sure to be shapely like the other women in her family, even though she might not be much taller. She was only a few inches shorter than her mother and gaining on her quickly. She imagined coming back from summer vacation all mature and beautiful and watching Gaius's eyes widen when he saw her.

That would feel very nice.

They would still be together by then, of course. They were going to stay together forever and have six children, five great sorcerers and a librarian. Or maybe it should be four great sorcerers, a librarian, and a farmer, to take over Gaius's family farm. Gaius's father would probably appreciate that. She imagined the eight of them—herself, Gaius, and the flock of children, the littlest one toddling behind on his short legs—walking along the moors, watching cows in a field.

Or, what if they were no longer together? What if that girl from Drake, Tess Dauntless, got him back—if they ever had been dating. No one could tell her for sure. But everyone agreed that Tess wanted to steal Gaius from Rachel. Salome had told her that the kids in Drake were all certain it was just a matter of time.

Rachel tried to imagine how she might feel, coming back to school at fifteen to discover Gaius on the arm of that blonde schemer —the pain of betrayal, the feeling of loneliness, the knowledge that she would never love again.

She imagined explaining that to Von Dread, when he returned to visit the campus—he would have graduated by then—and tried to press his claim again. (This fantasy, of course, being a sequel to her last one.) She imagined placing her hand over her aching heart and turning her head away, unable to so much as look at him.

In her daydream, Von Dread leaned down and kissed her. She was no longer the girlfriend of his lieutenant, after all. There was nothing to stop him from seizing what he desired. He scooped her up and laid her down beside him in a meadow of sweet-smelling herbs. As his mouth crushed hers, her lips parted, and she gasped softly, yielding to his kiss. His fingers moved across her side and stomach, leaving a trail of fire. His hand slid upward, cupping her. . . .

No!

No, no, no, no, no!

Rachel squealed and sat up.

Why did these kinds of thoughts only ever attach themselves to Dread?

Pulling the comforter around her, she sat up on the couch and forced her imagination back to safer territory.

. . .

Flying class went well. The students were making good progress. Sakura was now handling her broom as well as the rest of them, which still caused Rachel's heart to flutter oddly. How strange that Sakura's current improvement was because of the loss of a talent that created order and, thus, interfered with magic, a talent the Raven had been forced to remove from her.

Hildy was flying so well that Mr. Chanson declared her a flier. She immediately joined her team for Track and Broom. At Roanoke, all freshmen were assigned to intramural sports teams. The boys teams were the Marauders, the Spartans, the Druids, and the Guardians. The girls teams were Amazons, the Nymphs, the Maenads, and the Furies. Students remained on their assigned teams for a year. At the beginning of sophomore year, they were assigned to new teams by draft, with the winning team of the previous year getting the first pick of the incoming sophomores. Students then remained a part of their new team for the rest of their lives. Even as adults, alumni were welcome to return and play for their teams —though they seldom did. Hildy was a Fury, and the team cheered when she joined them. Rachel herself had been assigned to the Maenads, but she had never shown up for a game.

As Rachel hung the Flycycles up in the broom closet after class, the P.E. teacher stuck his head in the doorway and flashed her a winning smile. He was an extraordinarily handsome man, his jet black hair shot through with steely blue highlights. Recalling the earlier conversation on the subject, Rachel wondered from which supernatural creature he might be descended.

"You have a visitor, Miss Griffin," he said mildly, adjusting his glasses.

Rachel stepped out into the hallway of the gym. There, looking pretty as a picture as she stared out the window, was her sister Sandra.

Sandra turned and spread her arms. She had shoulder-length, mahogany hair and extremely dark eyes with a mere hint of a tilt, which gave them an exotic look. She was dressed in mundane clothing with a warm parka and slacks. To Rachel, these unfamiliar garments added to her sister's general exoticness.

Rachel ran and hugged her. Her sister laughed and hugged her back, tightly. Rachel stayed there for a moment, engulfed in her sister's familiar warmth, breathing in her sweet scent with its traces of honeysuckle and rosewater.

"Thank you, Mr. Chans—Roland." Stepping back, Sandra gave the handsome P.E. teacher a very sweet smile.

Mr. Chanson beamed at them. "My pleasure, Sandra. And thank you, Rachel, for your good work."

Rachel curtsied, and she and Sandra left the gym, walking hand in hand.

"*Unni!* You're here!" Rachel cried. She jumped up and down, her broom bobbing in her free hand.

Sandra laughed gaily. "I promised to visit when things calmed down."

They talked animatedly, their conversation leaping back and forth between the night they fought Veltdammerung and how Rachel was faring at school. Sandra, of course, did not remember anything that had happened after they left the first chamber. She believed they had all been rescued by Finn MacDannan. She led them along the path that ran by the athletic fields, under the canopy of trees, with their sparse yet brilliant autumn leaves, and to the boardwalk along Roanoke Creek. The creek was lovely with waters rushing over rocks. Red and yellow leaves swirled in the eddies. A leaf landed on Sandra's head. She held her chin up proudly—like a lady of quality in a pretty hat—before plucking it off with a laugh and tossing it into the river.

Then, her eyes grew serious. "Rach, Father's worried about you."

"If he's worried, why doesn't he come and see me?" Rachel asked belligerently.

"He has come, *dongsaeng*," Sandra said soothingly, falling into their familiar habit of using the Korean diminutive for addressing siblings. "Three times. Once after you were attacked by a wraith. Once after you were attacked by an evil tutor who turned into a dragon. And once after he and I spent several days in lock-down at the Wisecraft building in New York, after same said evil tutor temporarily escaped custody. The third time, he was so worried, he came here in the middle of the night and spoke to the dean. He made her send someone up to your room to check on you."

"You mentioned that before," Rachel frowned. None of those visits were after the fight against Veltdammerung, when Rachel had so very much to tell him.

Sandra took after their tall father. Now she knelt down on the boardwalk, so that her face was closer to Rachel's, a little below rather than well above. She lay a hand on Rachel's shoulder, her dark eyes searching her little sister's face. "Rachel, you're being careful, right?"

Rachel shook her head slowly. "No. Not careful. Just brave."

"Don't be brave, *dongsaeng*!" Sandra grabbed her, holding her at arms length, shaking her. "Be careful. Rachel, if something happened to you, I can't even imagine.... And I don't even *want* to imagine how Mother and Father would take it. Promise me you'll avoid every danger you can! Please?"

Rachel's heart ached with sadness, but she bit her lip and shook her head. "I can't do that, *unni*. There are things only I can see. And no one else—well, except Vladimir Von Dread—seems serious about saving the world. Somebody has to do it. Or... it won't matter if any of us are careful, ever again."

"Rachel, you're not saving the world." Sandra made a noise of exasperation and stood up. "You don't need to protect the planet. You *can't* protect the planet. You're thirteen!"

So many things struggled to bubble out of her mouth that Rachel had to press two fingers against her lips to keep it all in. This was what she lived for, the opportunities to share her secrets; for the joy of seeing the awe and wonder on the face of her loved ones—as she revealed the treasures of knowledge she had so painstakingly collected.

And yet, she had to keep quiet.

What cruel god had placed her in this situation, where she continually discovered secrets but was forbidden to share them?

She thought of the Elf, the kindness of her star-lit eyes. She thought of the Raven, his eyes shining as he gazed down at her and spared her. She could not betray them. She swallowed and said nothing.

"Give Father any information you come across," instructed Sandra. "Let him take care of it. If your princess friend has any more visions, report them immediately. Father has people working for him all over the world. He has contacts in the mundane world, too, in many different governments. The Wisecraft knows there are problems. If something is wrong, we'll fix it."

Rachel gazed over the railing of the boardwalk into the rushing water. She did not point out that Father had specifically instructed her to stop sending him reports.

"Sandra, can we talk about this later?" Rachel asked suddenly. "Can't we pretend, for a little while, that this is a perfectly normal year, and the worst thing in my life is that Peter's not talking to me?"

Sandra frowned, annoyed. Then she sighed and brushed hair from her face. "Very well. We can play pretend. But remember what I said. Just because you are away from home, doesn't mean you're an adult. Father and Mother don't want you doing anything dangerous. If you get hurt here, Father will pull you from school and have you tutored at home."

Then I mustn't get hurt, thought Rachel fiercely, *or at least not seriously.*

They walked silently for a time. A flock of geese honked overhead. A few songbirds chirped despite the chill. The boardwalk brought them to a lovely waterfall with a little pool at the bottom. The sound of the rushing water was soothing. Sandra leaned over the railing and closed her eyes, letting out a long sigh.

Then she opened them. "Wait, why wouldn't Peter be talking to you?"

Rachel sighed, too. "He doesn't like my boyfriend."

"Is this the boy you mentioned in your letter? Did you actually kiss him? Were you petrified? *Dongsaeng*, I don't think you should be mixing magic and… kissing."

"The petrifying and kissing were before he became my boy-friend. And I petrified him. Not him petrifying me. He insisted I practice the hex, so I could defend myself... and because of that I was able to petrify people during Mordeau's attack and other times. And I won a duel."

"Is it another freshman? That cute boy who was with you when we fought Egg?"

It took Rachel a moment to realize to whom Sandra referred.

"Sigfried!" Rachel squeaked. "Good gracious, no!"

The very idea seemed *so* wrong.

"No," Rachel continued, "he's not a freshman... my boyfriend, I mean. He's older."

Sandra rolled her eyes. "Stop being evasive. You know if he's older, I will know who he is. I only graduated last spring. I hope he's not too much older, Rachel. Older boys... you shouldn't be dating them."

"He's a senior at the upper school." Rachel said seriously. "He's very nice. Only I didn't know, until after I started dating him, that he's Peter's personal nemesis. So my brother, the dweeb, believes he is only dating me to irk him, which just isn't true!" She stamped her foot. The boards of the walk reverberated with the force of it. "So Peter wanted me to break up with him, and had this whole, 'if you've ever trusted me' thing going that made me feel very bad... but what kind of a girl would I be if I broke up with a boy who fought Vladimir Von Dread for me!"

"Wait, Peter's personal enemy?" asked Sandra. "You can't be talking about Gaius Valiant. Er, right?"

Rachel nodded.

"Good," said Sandra. "Peter would go insane if it were that one. So, who is he?"

Rachel blinked in confusion. The grammar had outwitted her.

"I meant, yes... Gaius Valiant."

"Ohhh," said Sandra, in a rather Zoë-like way. Then she began to look as if she was about to laugh but was trying very hard to not look amused. Rachel had never seen Sandra's dissembling skills utterly fail before.

"So," Sandra coughed twice, "Peter didn't take this too well, I assume?"

"No." Rachel's face was entirely serious, but her eyes had begun to sparkle. "He didn't."

"He'll probably get over it. Maybe." Sandra shrugged. "Young men are very proud, and Peter is no different. I have heard that what happened between them was some over-excitement during a duel. Peter'll probably get over it. Eventually."

Rachel watched the spray from the falls strike the rocks. "I hope so."

Sandra said gravely, "That doesn't mean that Peter may not be right. You are very young to have a serious boyfriend, Rachel. I didn't date until I was in college."

Rachel blinked. *Sandra had dated?* This was the first she had ever heard of it.

"I didn't set out to have a boyfriend," she explained, "it just happened."

Sandra knelt in front of Rachel again and said very seriously, "Only kissing, Rachel. That's it. Do not do anything else. Nothing you wouldn't do if I were also in the room. Boys his age can be... pushy. Don't let him do anything that you.... Don't let him do *anything!*"

"He's very gentlemanly." Rachel gazed at her sister earnestly. A warmth came into her eyes as she spoke of Gaius. "He looks out for me, makes sure I can defend myself, tries to convince me to be careful." She blushed a little. "He's only ever kisses me very lightly. I explained to him that thirteen-year-olds don't... you know...." She turned bright red. "... snog."

"Good!" Sandra whispered back. "No snogging until you're sixteen. Dad'd explode."

The image of their handsome, dashing father exploding made Rachel giggle. Then her face became serious again. "Sandra, having a boyfriend at my age is strange. I know that. At first, I was quite frightened, partially because he's not a tame boy, and I didn't know whether he would be gentlemanly or not. But it has been such a comfort—with all the horrid things going on—to have one person who is entirely on my side. He's fun to be with, and he's very smart.

And he helps me with my magic. I just wish I knew what to do about Peter."

"You can't do anything about Peter, sweetheart," Sandra said. "He's going to have to work it out with Gaius. Who, by the way, I like. He's always been very sweet to me. And rather refined considering his upbringing. Not a bad first love."

A joyful light came into Rachel's face. She lunged forward and hugged her sister, hard. Sandra had seen Gaius in action over the last three years. And she *liked* him. Someone in her family approved of her boyfriend. It was as if something had finally gone right with the world.

Underneath, though, she rankled at the phrase *first love*. This was not a *first love*, she vowed to herself. This was *true love*, and it was going to last forever.

"Thank you, Sandra." With her face buried against her sister, she added, "Peter asked Von Dread to make Gaius stop dating me, and Gaius, who worships Dread, fought him." She pulled back so she could see her sister's face. "He fought Vladimir Von Dread! He did really well, too! For a while. Eventually, he was turned into a shee—ram! I made Vlad put him back."

Sandra's eyes lit up at the mention of Dread. "So, you've met Vlad? He is an impressive young man, isn't he? I wouldn't have thought he and Valiant would ever fight. Vlad's as close with Gaius as he is with Bill. I wouldn't mind speaking to him before I go...."

Rachel stepped back. "It happened only hours after, while under the effects of the *Spell of True Recitation*, Gaius would only talk about how much he respected Von Dread. So he would not have fought him, if he didn't really like me." She lowered her eyes demurely, so pleased.

"I wish I had seen that," murmured Sandra.

Rachel leaned forward and confided. "Zoë and I got to see Vlad dressed down in a shirt and sweat pants. Oddly, he looks even more impressive that way—maybe because most people fail so miserably to be impressive in sweats. We can go look for them—Gaius and Vlad."

Sandra laughed. "Nooo, I came here to see you. So tell me about your classes. Do you even care about them? Has all the non-class excitement drowned them out? I hope not."

Rachel and Sandra chatted for a time, as they walked back to campus. Rachel filled her sister in on her classes and her new friends, including the famous Sigfried the Dragonslayer and the Princess of Magical Australia.

"Oh, speaking of Magical Australia," Rachel's eyes sparkled, "the Crown Prince of Magical Australia expressed an interest in marrying me, but we decided that we would not suit. So I suggested he ask Laurel, which he did... or at least he got her permission to ask his parents to talk to our parents, though I don't know if anything has come of that."

Sandra blinked. "That's... ah... interesting."

As they left the athletic fields behind and walked toward the Commons, they came upon three proctors walking the other way. All three young men straightened up the instant they caught a glimpse of Sandra Griffin. One of them was Rachel's friend Mr. Fuentes, who gave her a big smile. The other two were Matt Scott, Mr. Fuentes's shorter, blond friend, and Coal Moth, who towered over the others like a beanstalk grown from magic beans. He had curly black hair, a smile that showed very white teeth, and a cowboy hat that he wore even while on duty. He immediately tipped his hat to Rachel and her sister.

"Hallo, gentlemen." Sandra gave the three young men a very kind smile and stopped to chat with them. All three of them, particularly Mr. Scott, gazed at her intently as she spoke, as if they did not want to miss a single expression, especially not a smile.

Rachel watched this speculatively. She thought back to the carefree smile Sandra had flashed at the handsome P.E. teacher and to Sandra's comment about not dating until she got to college. Nothing had been said at home about Sandra dating, ever. Rachel suspected that her parents did not know Sandra had dated, either.

Did Sandra have a boyfriend now? Was there an Agent back in London whom she liked? If not, might she end up dating Mr. Chanson or one of these proctors?

Carefully, Rachel pictured her sister with each of the young men and the P.E. teacher. She could imagine them doting on her sister, but none of them seemed right. Sandra needed someone... fiercer?

With more scope? Less mild-mannered? Definitely, it would have to be someone who would not be shaken by the attention other men paid to her lovely sister.

Rachel mulled over the question as her sister and the proctors chatted about the current whereabouts of people Rachel did not know, older students who had already graduated. Instead of listening, she spent the time trying to picture the ideal boyfriend for Sandra.

After all, she had helped Ivan and Laurel get together. Maybe she could help Sandra, too.

It was the least a little sister could do.

CHAPTER TWENTY:

SO SWEARS DREAD!

THE SISTERS RETURNED TO DARE HALL, WHERE SANDRA SENT A STU-
dent to fetch Peter and Laurel. Peter rushed up, very happy to see
their sister. Laurel's approach was more subdued. She and Sandra did not always see eye to eye, but she greeted their older sister
cheerfully enough. The four of them sat down on the purple leather
seats in one of the common rooms. It was a small room with a long
arched window, overlooking the paper birches and ferns behind the
dorm. There was a damp spot on the rug, and a faint odor of spilled
elderflower pressé.

Peter was a slender young man whose striking features were
a perfect blend of their Asian mother and their handsome father.
Until recently, he had been short, but now he was gaining height
quickly. He sat down stiffly, his back ramrod straight. The impression made by his perfect posture, however, was somewhat under-
mined by the fact that he kept sneaking glances at the book that lay
open in his lap.

Wild free-spirit Laurel was tall, though not as tall as Sandra.
She was a curvy young woman, and her subfusc uniform—a white
blouse, a split ribbon like a narrow tie, a black skirt, and a half-
cape falling from her shoulders—covered her figure in an appealing fashion. She plopped down on her back on a couch and kicked
her stockinged legs in the air, sending her shoes flying, much to the
dismay of their older sister, who ducked.

After the four of them chatted amiably for a few minutes, Rachel
turned to her brother. "*Oppa*, did you tell Topher Evans that we're
one-quarter Korean?" She held her breath, afraid he would refuse
to speak to her directly, but the question took him so by surprise
that perhaps he forgot he was angry with her.

"Yes. Of course."

"Why?"

"Because we are." Peter seemed puzzled by her questions.

"No we're not. Grandpa Kim's mother was English."

The puzzled expressions on all three of her siblings resolved into looks of understanding.

"That was Great-Grandpa Kim's second wife, silly," laughed Laurel. "Grandpa Kim's mother was Korean."

"There is a portrait of Grandpa Kim's mother over the fireplace at Aunt Melissa's house. Do you recall it?" Peter asked. Then he bonked himself in the forehead with his fist. "Of course, you recall it. You're Lady Rachel of the Indefatigable Memory. Foolish me."

Rachel thought of the painting that hung on her aunt's wall. The pale woman portrayed was dressed in a traditional, high-wasted, Korean *hanbok*.

"So, Great-Grandmother Kim is not our great-grandmother? Then how come Mum come to look...." Rachel pressed her lips together.

There was no way to express what she wished to say politely in front of her brother. As it was, Peter's cheeks were already gaining rosy spots.

Laurel smirked. "... like a China doll designed for the Playboy Mansion? No idea."

Rachel glanced from her sister Laurel, who — though not as voluptuous as their petite mother—was still shapely enough to require custom-made underclothing, to Sandra who—while she could buy her undergarments off the rack—was still extremely appealing to boys. The Englishwoman, who was apparently Great-Grandpa Kim's second wife, had been well-endowed. If she was not Rachel's mother's grandmother, from where had the Griffin women inherited their male-dazzling figures?

Rachel sighed. With her luck, she might take after their real great-grandmother and end up with no figure at all.

She stared down at the damp spot on the rug. For as long as she could remember, she had believed that Great-Grandpa Kim's second wife was her great-grandmother and that she herself was one-eighth Korean. Now, both of those things had turned out not to be true.

It was not that the truth was better or worse, it was just that the change was disorienting. Compared to discovering that her grandfather had an unknown family who had been murdered by a demon, the discovery that a great-grandmother she had never met was a different woman from the one she had believed her to be was a small thing.

Still, she felt as if her world had been torn apart and stitched back together in a slightly wrong pattern.

"Did you all know," she blurted out, "about Grandfather's other family? The ones who died in the 1890s?"

Her sisters stared at her as if she had begun spouting off in a foreign language.

"What?" Laurel kipped up so that her knees were under her. "Who made that up?"

"Where did you hear this?" Sandra grabbed the arm of her chair.

"I knew," Peter said solemnly. "Their graves are in the family graveyard. I used to help Grandmother put wreaths on the gravestones the night before Beltane and Samhain, to make sure they rested peacefully for the next six months. I know who everyone in the graveyard is."

"I... had no idea," murmured Sandra softly, though which thing she had no idea about—Grandfather's family, or Peter's outings with Grandmother—Rachel could not tell. Her older sister was looking at Peter with new respect.

"Thunderfrost's Boy was his son, our Uncle Myrddin," said Rachel.

"Thunderfrost?" Laurel's forehead furrowed. "You mean the ghost horse who appears when a family member is in need?"

Rachel nodded. "The boy who rides Thunderfrost. Haven't you lot seen him?"

Peter and Laurel just gawked at her.

"Ah." Sandra nodded. "Yes. I... did not realize who he was."

Peter looked down at his hands and mumbled. "Sorry. I only talk to dryads... and Vivian."

"Who's Vivian?" asked Rachel and Laurel simultaneously.

"The ghost who lives in the book chamber. You know, that bedroom filled with bookcases where I sometimes read? That was her bedroom," Peter explained. "She was one of our grandfather's daughters. The eldest one." He paused. "I suppose she's our aunt."

"And you've talked to her?" asked Sandra curiously.

"Not conversed, not as such," answered Peter. "Mainly, we've read together."

"Like Myrddin and I used to go riding together," said Rachel.

"That's not fair." Laurel threw a throw pillow at Peter, who batted it out of the air. "I haven't seen the ghost horse or talked to the ghost girl."

"That's because you're too busy flirting with boys," Sandra observed dryly.

Laurel looked smug, despite that Rachel could tell she was still shaken. "Oh, that's true. I might've missed the *ghost* boy, but I can tell you the name of every *real* boy within miles."

Sandra rolled her eyes and shook her head.

Laurel continued cheerfully, "Not that I mind of course. I am much of not a fan of ghosts." She shivered. "Just knowing that the Dead Men's Ball takes place near here is enough to give me the willies... even though I know it's outside the school, wards, and the ghouls won't get in."

"Not me," Rachel sighed. "I wish I could go."

Laurel stared at her as if she had gone utterly crazy, but Peter nodded solemnly. Rachel smiled at him. He almost smiled back, before he must have remembered that they were not speaking. He jerked his head away and stared at the spill on the rug. Rachel looked down at her lap and sighed.

Just then, Sigfried walked by the open door, with Lucky snaking along overhead. They were both humming the song for dispersing a fog. Eager to introduce her friends to Sandra, Rachel leapt up and called to him.

Sigfried came striding into the common room and endured the torment of being introduced to her siblings. Lucky had a better time of it, because Laurel immediately began squealing over him and petting his soft fur. Sandra, too, gave into temptation and petted the golden dragon. Lucky crooned contentedly.

"So, how are you enjoying school?" Sandra asked Sigfried.

"It's the bomb! Best place I've ever been!" Sigfried lit up, grinning. "No one beats you. You don't have to scrub the floor or lug heavy things around. And you can eat as much as you want, three times, every single day! It's like paradise! The only drawback is that we have not yet learned to concoct explosives."

Sandra tilted her head, as if not quite sure what to make of this. "What about your classes? How are you finding them?"

He shrugged. "They're okay. If you like studying and quizzes and such bother. I do like Make-Cool-Spells-in-Vials class. And Blow-a-Horn class. Also, Pull-a-Skunk-out-of-Nothing Class isn't too bad. The rest I could do without. But I sleep through them, so it's almost like not having to go. The after-class stuff is much more interesting. Rachel and I are in a club where we're learning to duel. I like that! I can't wait to learn how to blow up our opponents. Or disintegrate them. It's not as loud, but you end up with a pile of dust on top of their shoes."

Rachel's siblings listened to Sigfried with identical expressions, which Rachel read to mean that they had no idea how much of what he was saying to take seriously.

"Duel?" Laurel frowned up at Rachel, from where she lay on the floor, her feet curled over her head, rubbing the belly of Lucky, whose back foot jiggled like a dog's. "Rachel, you're not in the YSL. And we really don't do a lot of dueling, anyway."

"Not the YSL," Rachel turned to Sandra. "We're in a club called the Knights."

"Hang on!" Peter half rose from the couch, nearly dropping his book. He fumbled to catch it. "Not the Knights of Walpurgis!"

"Yes," Rachel nodded. "Those Knights."

All her siblings began yelling at once.

"What!"

"*Dongsaeng!* No!"

"Rachel, how could you?"

"Do Mum and Dad know? They'll be livid!"

"Only those practicing black magic join the Knights!"

"What do you mean?" Rachel asked, taken aback. "It's a very nice group. I'm learning a great deal. I'm rather a good duelist, too... for a beginner. I've won several duels."

"How did you possibly come to be in the Knights?" Sandra looked shocked. Then, suddenly, she looked amused. "Oh! Wait, of course. Never mind."

"Gaius asked me," Rachel said, adding defensively, "The night everyone was invited to the Young Sorcerer's League, except for me."

Peter went very stiff and looked terribly disapproving.

"You don't need an invitation to join the YSL, you ninny," Laurel smirked at her, her chin resting on Lucky's stomach.

"Everyone else I knew received one," Rachel countered. "Upperclassmen arrived and escorted them. Except for me."

Sandra shot Laurel and Peter a dark look for forgetting their little sister. They both lowered their heads, chastened.

"It's good to see you all," Sandra rose to her feet. "But I must get back to work. I just came to see Rachel and make sure she was okay."

"She doesn't come to see us." Laurel pulled down on one eye and stuck out her tongue.

"You didn't get kidnapped and nearly killed by Veltdammerung," Sandra replied tartly.

"Rachel was kidnapped? When?" cried Peter, aghast. He had no aptitude for their mother's dissembling technique and could not hide how upset he was, even though he was clearly trying.

"A couple of weeks ago," Rachel said offhandedly, adding hurriedly, "but Sandra has to go, and I have one more question I must ask her. Privately."

Sandra took her leave of the others, and the two sisters stepped out into the hall.

"Yes?" Sandra asked kindly, brushing a finger across her little sister's cheek.

"*Unni*," Rachel gazed steadily up at her sister, "Mortimer Egg, Jr. and Juma O'Malley. Do you know if they're all right?"

"Did you know them? I didn't realize... yes, of course, you would! They're in your class," mused Sandra. She smiled and tapped Rachel's nose. "Yes, sweetie. Your two friends are fine. Young Mortimer is staying with relatives, his uncle on his mother's side, I believe. He's suffered a huge shock, of course. But I am sure he'll recover with time. Juma is staying in a safe house. I can't say more about it than that."

An idea struck Rachel, a very unpleasant idea.

"They need to sacrifice a family member—Veltdammerung, I mean. To bring in this new demon they want as their master."

"Who told you about..." Sandra began, frowning.

Rachel rolled her eyes impatiently. "I'm the one who found it out. If you know about it, the information came, originally, from me and my friends. The point is, Juma could be in danger, and there's a leak at the Wisecraft office in New York."

Sandra patted Rachel's shoulder comfortingly. "You're worried because of the death of Mrs. Egg? That's sweet of you, but that leak's been found. Turns out a student here told someone who should not have known."

Rachel rolled her eyes a second time, her eyes pausing momentarily at the zenith. "Sandra! That student was me. And the person I told was Vladimir. We're not the leak!"

"Oh!" Sandra's eyes grew large. "Oooh! No. Vlad would not...."

Rachel nodded solemnly. Sandra bit her lower lip, thinking.

"I will look into this, Rachel," Sandra said. "If necessary, I will have your friend moved."

"Make sure his tiny elephant stays with him," said Rachel. "That's very important. It makes his evil mother turn back into his good mother, or something like that."

Sandra did not even blink at that.

Rachel asked, "If I write Juma a note, could you give it to him?"

"Of course."

Rachel jotted off a short friendly note to Juma and his tiny elephant, Jellybean, and handed it to Sandra, who tucked it in her purse. Sandra gave Rachel a last hug.

"Remember," Sandra whispered in Rachel's ear, "if things get too overwhelming here at school, I would be delighted for you to come spend a few days with me in London." Then, she set off, murmuring something under her breath that sounded like "... and now for Vladimir."

Rachel raced back to the common room and grabbed Sigfried. Waving goodbye to Laurel and Peter, who had both risen to leave, she pulled Siggy out of the room.

"She's going off to talk to Von Dread," Rachel cried, her eyes gleaming.

"Do you want to spy on her?"

"Yes! Of course!"

"Von Dread is cool! That I am willing to do for free."

The two of them ran pell-mell from the dorms. They found a bench on the Commons and sat down. In Rachel's calling card, Sandra walked across the campus toward Drake Hall. About two thirds of the way, she stepped behind some trees. She pulled a mirror out of her purse and checked her appearance. She frowned and put away the mirror. Then, she walked out of the woods, crossed to Roanoke Hall, and went into the coatroom behind the spiral staircase. There was a small sink there beneath a round mirror with a gilt frame. She washed her face, reapplied a small amount of blush and eye shadow, and put on some lip gloss. Pleased with the results, she headed off towards Drake Hall again.

She had made it as far as the bridge across the moat around the imposing dormitory when she ran into a young man with a scar across his face. Rachel recognized him as Seymour Almeida, a member of the Knights of Walpurgis. He stopped and gawked at her.

"Hi, Seymour." Sandra flashed her dazzling smile at him. He blushed noticeably.

"Hey, Griffin," he said, smirking. "You here for your Dreadsy?"

Sandra grinned. "You know he might turn you into an aardvark, if I tell him you called him that, right?"

Seymour continued to smirk. "But you're good people, so you won't tell him, right?"

"No, probably not. But could you go in and tell him I am here?"

He looked as if he was considering it. Then, he gave her a quirky grin and headed up the stairs and into the dorm. Less than a minute later, Vladimir Von Dread came through the front door flanked by Valiant and Locke. The three young men came down the stairs to meet her.

Sandra smiled at them all, but she gave Dread a breathy, "Hello, Vlad."

Dread gained a slight shade of color in his cheeks. "Hello, Sandra. It is good to see you."

She smiled at Gaius, who gave her a slight bow.

"Gaius," Sandra scolded, wagging her finger, "you didn't even ask me if you could court Rachel. I think I may be offended that my friend didn't speak to me before he started dating my little sister."

He looked a bit sheepish, (*Rammish*, Rachel thought fiercely), "Easier to ask for forgiveness after it's all done than be refused and have to apologize for disobeying, eh?"

"Gaius, I forgive you." Sandra crossed her arms. "But you had better protect her."

He bowed again. "With my life."

Sandra turned to William Locke. Locke inclined his head.

"Sandra, it is a pleasure to see you again. I must say, the school is not nearly as bright without your smile."

"Bill, it's great to see you, too. I hope you're getting what you need from your studies this year. I have to say, I am surprised you haven't switched over to Minnesota Academy for Alchemy and Thaumaturgy."

"I would not be able to work with Vlad as easily."

Sandra nodded. She glanced sideways at Dread. "Gentleman, not to be rude, but I really need to speak to Vlad alone."

Locke and Valiant nodded and returned to their dorm. Von Dread offered Sandra his arm. They strolled into the woods, until they were alone. Releasing her, he crossed his arms and looked at her calmly.

"Have you been well?" Sandra watched his face attentively. "Rumor has it you faced down a rogue jumbo jet a few weeks ago."

"Well enough. I have more tasks to accomplish than hours in the day, as always, but I am managing to keep up with my work —though it was easier when you were here to help me. As to the plane," a shadow of a frown flickered across his otherwise impassive features, "that night, I had an unexpectedly disturbing nightmare that...." Von Dread made a dismissive gesture. "'Tis no matter. Why did you come?"

Sandra stepped very close to him and murmured, "I miss you, Vlad. I am... feeling remorse over my answer."

"I also feel remorse over your answer," replied Dread. "You do yourself a disservice. You would make a fine queen. And you would have plenty of time to readjust to the life of a princess. My father will, most likely, live another century at least, probably two or three. He is the picture of health. If you marry me, we will have a great deal of time to live together and raise a family, before we must take the burden of the entire kingdom upon our shoulders."

Sandra looked at him hopefully, but then she shook her head. "Vlad, I am sorry, I can't. You know I work for the ministry. And my father.... I'm sorry."

Dread reached out and grabbed her, pulling her against him. "Sandra, you need not apologize. I was hoping you had come because you changed your mind. But you came because of your youngest sister, correct?"

Sandra nodded. "Please, will you protect her, Vlad? She told me some things. I hadn't realized—"

"I shall do all within my power to keep her safe. She is a wealth of information, some of which I cannot, yet, ascertain how she collected. But even if she were like your sister Laurel, and did nothing with herself, I would still make sure she was protected. She will be my sister-in-law soon enough."

Sandra tried, half-heartedly, to push him away. "I should go—I have—"

But he interrupted her with a kiss. Her entire body tensed for the first few moments but then she relaxed and melted against him. They kissed for some time, then he released her and pushed her to arm's distance.

"Sandra Griffin, you are the only woman I will ever love. I have vowed this, and I shall do all in my power to erase any objections you have. You will be my wife." He raised his hand. "So swears DREAD!"

She blushed and looked away, but she said, "I love you too, Vlad."

He swelled up even larger than normal when she said this. She stepped closer and kissed him on the cheek.

"Goodbye, Vlad," she whispered in his ear and walked away quickly.

• • •

Rachel spun around and grabbed Sigfried's arm, jumping up and down and squealing with sheer delight. "He wants to *marry* her!

My sister will be a princess! When Laurel marries Ivan, they will both be princesses! And someday, queens!"

This was, however, only her second reaction.

Her first reaction, as she watched Dread and Sandra speak, had been a tiny voice in the back of her mind that wailed: *But he is supposed to marry* me*!*

Rachel sternly ignored this traitorous voice. It was hardly appropriate, considering that she had just vowed to love Gaius forever. Pushing the thought aside, she danced around in a circle, celebrating the good fortune of her sisters with deliberate cheer.

"What kind of nightmare rattles Dread?" Siggy asked, impressed. "That would have to be one super-duper-scary nightmare! Even scarier than the Starkadder nightmare! Dread would never be troubled by a mere gallows dream. He's too cool."

"I have a guess. He was on the plane that day, Siggy. Remember how you and I tried to stop it from outside? Von Dread jumped *inside* the plane to try and stop it."

"Jumped, like magic teleport?"

Rachel nodded.

"Ace!" Siggy shouted, leaping from the bench and punching the sky. "And this time I mean flying ace, like what Dread was when he took over the controls. So, you think he dreamt about smashing into the school and killing everyone?" Siggy suddenly snickered. "Or, maybe he dreamed that a really bright light filled his dream—like a camera flash went off or something."

Rachel laughed. "Could be, though I can't imagine why that would be unnerving."

"Obviously, he thought it was a death ray." Grinning like a gargoyle, Siggy raised his right hand, palm out, as Von Dread had done, and shouted. "So swears Dread! He is so cool! I want to be like that, too. So swears Smith!"

"Me, too!" Rachel leapt to her feet and raised her hand. "So swears Griffin!"

"So swears Smith!"

"So swears Griffin!"

And they continued thus for some time.

CHAPTER TWENTY-ONE:

BLOOD SISTER OF A BLOOD

BROTHER

"THERE HE IS!" RACHEL GRABBED SIGGY'S SHOULDER AND POINTED. "Do you see that boy, the one dribbling the soccer ball? With the spiky hair? He's the one I want you to skunk! He said some very rude things about my boyfriend and me."

She pointed at where John Darling walked across the Commons with Arun Malik, Claus Andrews, and John's cousin, Liam MacDannan. Rachel felt bad about skunking Liam. He was a serious boy, with a delightful Irish accent, and he was always quite nice to her. Upon reflection, she decided that if he were accidentally sprayed, it would be an acceptable civilian casualty. He was the one who chose to be friends with a rude, big-mouthed rotter.

"Finally!" Sigfried exclaimed with glee. "A target I can sink my teeth into. Or rather sink into my flaming skunk spray." He looked around, rubbing his hands. Then he pulled out two vials of chameleon elixir. "Okay, get your broom ready. Here's the plan."

• • •

Hidden among the trees, the two of them downed their chameleon elixir, and both of them jumped onto Rachel's steeplechaser. Siggy conjured the skunk. As he faded from her view—or rather as images of the background trees replaced his face—Rachel could see him partially as he drew the skunk into being with the *muria* cantrip. Lucky lunged forward and set the conjured creature afire. Then, Siggy sent it winging toward John Darling with a *ti* cantrip.

Again, she could not help admire his command of the basic cantrip. If he could do all this with *ti*, what was he going to be able to do when he learned *tiathelu*?

Rachel waited as Siggy launched the skunk through the air, directly at Darling. Then she shot forward, weaving through the trees at high speed. Siggy lost control of the floating, burning, conjured skunk when a tree passed between him and it. When they arrived at their new location, far from where the flaming skunk had first appeared, he took control of it again with a *ti* from his wand, which was surreptitiously hidden under his arm.

The startled-looking conjured creature floated through the air, aflame and spraying wildly. Its tail blazed like a torch. With an elegant spin, Siggy changed its direction, skunk-spew sprayed all over Darling, Andrews, and Malik. MacDannan, who was behind them, threw himself down and covered his head with his arms. Whether that saved him, Rachel could not tell.

John Darling was struck straight across the face. Shouting, he dropped and rolled. The fallen leaves—red and orange and brown —swooshed beneath him.

Sigfried slipped from the broom and called softly, "Now."

"*Obé*," Rachel ended the effects of the elixirs.

Screaming like a banshee, his hands waving above his head, Sigfried burst from the trees and ran toward the offending skunk. A few other students on the Commons were running toward the disturbance as well, though most were running the other way.

Siggy shouted dramatically. "Behold, it is another flaming skunk! Threatening innocents! They're in perilous peril! We cannot let those flaming skunks win! Even if we get sprayed! Even if we die! Even if we go down in flames! We. Will. Not. Let. Evil. Flaming. Skunks. Win!"

In a sinuous blur of red and gold, Lucky arrived in all his glory. Drawing back his head, he breathed out a truly gigantic gout of dragon fire. The flaming skunk vanished with an audible *pop*. The crowd cheered.

Rachel flew up and leapt from her broom, purposefully stumbling slightly, as if she were arriving in a huge hurry.

"Is everyone all right?" she cried, deliberately breathless. "Is there anything I can do?"

Others had arrived, too. Someone was helping Liam to his feet. Rachel moved toward John Darling, as if she intended to help.

Lying on the ground, leaves in his hair, John tried to sit up. He coughed terribly. His eyes were red and watering, and his skin had turned a sickly green. The stench of skunk was so terrible that just approaching him caused Rachel's eyes to smart.

Rachel stood with arms akimbo, regarding him coldly

"I would say you look like a *jackass*," she used the same word he had used for Gaius, "but I've known a few donkeys. They don't deserve the comparison."

The older boy's face grew blotchy with embarrassment. Turning on her toes, Rachel abandoned him to his skunky fate.

• • •

Ten minutes later, Rachel and Sigfried lay on their backs behind Dare Hall, laughing hysterically and rolling back and forth in the lacy ferns. Above them, the late October light filtered through the remaining golden leaves. Glimpses of perfect blue and fluffy white were visible between the branches of the paper birches. A brisk breeze rustled through the trees, shaking free a leaf or two that landed on the students and Lucky. The stems of broken ferns poked into their backs. The smell of crushed fronds fragranced the air.

"Did you see his face?" Rachel launched into another fit of laughter.

Siggy was lying on his back, grinning ear to ear. "The hero. Once again. Lucky and me."

"We've got to be careful though," Rachel said. "If you show up every time there is a flaming skunk, someone will figure it out. Maybe we should launch one sometime, and let someone else get the glory for stopping it."

"Never!" cried Siggy, grinning. "No one is as brave as I!"

"True," Rachel smiled back. "But you don't want them to catch you."

"I'm not afraid of them! I'm a sorcerer. I know magic."

"Er... so do they. And loads more than us."

"Ah." He looked unimpressed. "Besides. What can they do to me?"

"Well... expel you for starters," Rachel mused philosophically.

"So? True, I wouldn't be here with all the free food and my beautiful G.F. I'd hate to go back to my old life, except I know magic!"

"In the World of the Wise, everyone else would know a great deal more."

"But the mundanes don't. I could go back to the real world. A Wary among the Unwary. I know magic! I'd like to see the expression on Bruiser and Squiddly at the orphanage after they've taken a flaming skunk to the face!"

The mirth fled from Rachel's face. "Siggy… if you did that— tried to go back to the Unwary world and use magic—they'd take your memory away. The Obscurers, I mean." She shivered. "Make you forget you knew any magic. And then, you'd just be—"

"A punk." Sigfried scowled viciously. He was quiet for a while, all the humor gone from his face. Finally, he declared with extreme seriousness, "I would die first!" Under his breath, he added, "Or they would."

From the tone of his voice, she believed he actually would go down fighting before he returned to his former life.

She declared stoutly, "You are absurdly brave, Sigfried Smith."

"Or maybe just absurd," replied Siggy, a shadow of a grin beginning to return.

"I like to think of the Boss as cowardice-challenged," contributed Lucky, his serpentine length still rolling back and forth through the ferns.

"Or maybe common-sense challenged," announced Sigfried. "At least that's what Valerie would say. And it's important to give my G.F. her say, even if she's not here to say it herself."

Rachel sat up and made a half-hearted effort at securing her hair, which was currently flying every which way. "Speaking of G.F.s. Or rather, of B.F.s. I've been meaning to ask you. You bought twelve calling cards in all, didn't you? And you have given them so far—to me, you, Valerie, Nastasia, Joy, Zoë and Salome, right? Do you have plans for the other five?"

"Hmm?" he shrugged. "No, not yet. Did you have anyone in mind? Maybe Flops-Over-Dead-Chick. She did save my life. I'd like a chance to return the favor, were she to get into trouble."

"That's a good idea. But that's only one." Rachel pressed her palms together in a beseeching gesture. "Could you give one to Gaius? Please?"

"Who?"

"Gaius."

"Who is this guy?"

"Gaius Valiant."

"Never heard of him."

"My boyfriend!"

Lying on his back in the ferns, watching the clouds, Sigfried shrugged with a supreme lack of interest.

"Siggy! I'm asking you a favor!"

"What's in it for me?"

"What do you want? And no more doing your school work. I'm not doing that again!"

Sigfried sat up, grinning. "I want treasure."

"You want *more* treasure?"

"Sure. You can never be too rich."

Lucky's head bobbed up and down eagerly in agreement. He snaked over and laid his chin on Sigfried's lap. His large, unblinking jade eyes watched Rachel eagerly.

"Um—I'm not sure how—" began Rachel.

Siggy cut her off. "Specifically, I want your help with books and such. Library stuff. You help me find lost treasures. Ships that went down and their general vicinity. That kind of thing. Then, Lucky can dive down there and find the hoard. Or help me find some old barrows that might have kings buried in them. I can look through the earth with my amulet."

Rachel considered. That sounded easy enough and even surprisingly feasible.

"Okay, you have a deal," she said with a nod. "You give Gaius a mirror, I'll help you find another treasure."

"You give it to him yourself." Siggy reached into one voluminous pocket and pulled out a square green calling card, which he handed to her.

Smiling gratefully, Rachel slipped the card into her pocket. She looked at his face. He seemed so intent—so brave and boisterous, and yet so young and vulnerable. All of which made him inexpressibly dear to her. She wished she could put a name to the fierce devotion she felt toward him. It was not the slightest bit romantic. But she still wished that they shared some real bond, something that could be named and respected by others.

Rachel rose to her feet. Siggy lunged at Lucky, and the two of them rolled around, sending up a spray of golden birch leaves. Watching him and Lucky frolic among the autumn leaves, she recalled the look of longing on his face when he saw Joy's dream room and wistfully wished for a sister.

"Sigfried, do you know what a blood brother is?" Rachel asked impetuously. "Would you like to be my blood brother?"

Pushing Lucky aside, Sigfried jumped to his feet, reached under his robe, and drew his knife. In one motion, without pausing or flinching, he made a savage yet shallow cut along his forearm, just to the side of his wrist. He held the wound toward her, staring her in the eyes.

Meeting his gaze, Rachel held out her own arm for Siggy to cut —held sidewise, so that the cut would be in the matching spot, on the outside of her right wrist. He made this stroke with more care. It hurt. Rachel gritted her teeth and refused to cry. Blood ran down her hand.

She touched her cut to his until their blood mingled.

"There. It's done," Rachel announced fiercely. "We're sister and brother now."

"And I shall defend you with my life," Sigfried declared. He held up his hand. "So swears Smith!"

Rachel raised her own blood-covered arm. "So swears Griffin!"

A feeling of nausea assailed over her. She swayed on her feet.

"I... don't feel very well."

"Hm," Siggy peered at her. "Blood cooties? Magic? Faintness at the sight of blood?"

Rachel thought of all the sacrifices that she had been forced to attend for various religious festivals: pigs, doves, horses, dogs, cows, sheep.

"I do not grow faint at the sight of blood," she replied haughtily. "I am a duke's daughter."

"Let us go see Nurse Moth. She's nice. Not like most adults. She actually takes care of a bloke. I haven't seen her yet today. I'll carry you. Maybe we can get sweets. Look more wounded." Siggy scooped Rachel up into his arms and ran around Dare Hall, down the path to the Commons, and across the lawns to the infirmary.

"We could take my broom." Rachel's head bounced up and down on his shoulder.

"No time. My sister could be dying."

"Um... probably not," Rachel murmured, but she did feel strangely light-headed.

Siggy maneuvered his way through the door and into the Infirmary.

"Look in your memory to see if something unseen happened," Siggy said as he placed her on the nearest cot. "Also, see if you can contact Lucky via mind-waves now."

Rachel, who was beginning to feel better, thought back, but there was nothing there she had not seen the first time. Mentally, she called, "*Lucky?*"

Sadly, nothing happened.

The nurse did not seem happy to see them. She glared as she looked Rachel up and down. "You seem to be in one piece, *non?*" She looked rapidly from Sigfried to Rachel, noting the blood. "What have you done to your arms?"

"I was practicing with my trumpet in the hall and accidentally blasted a suit of armor carrying a halberd, so that the weapon dropped. It is my fault; Miss Griffin is merely an innocent bystander," answered Sigfried.

"We fell and landed on something," Rachel answered simultaneously.

Sigfried cleared his throat. "Ah, yes—about that: to be precise, I was practicing with my trumpet in the hall and accidentally blasted a suit of armor carrying a halberd, so that the weapon dropped, and when Miss Griffin and I went to pick up the mess, we fell and landed on something. It is my fault; Miss Griffin is merely an innocent bystander."

Rachel held up her arm and asked hopefully. "Can you make sure it leaves a little scar?"

She was pretty sure the nurse understood what had actually happened. She saw the French woman's eyes dart to Sigfried's arm, where his cut had already begun to heal. Rachel assumed other people did this kind of thing occasionally. Of course, she could be wrong. Maybe she was the only student at Roanoke who had read Rosemary Sutcliff books at a vulnerable age.

Nurse Moth eyed them dubiously. She disappeared into the back, returning with iodine and cotton swabs. She wet a few swabs in the healing waters of the fountain at the center of the room. Returning to where Rachel and Sigfried were, she cleaned both their cuts with burning, stinging iodine.

"Cool. Now I am a *man*," crowed Siggy, holding his arm aloft. "I love the sting of iodine in the morning. Stings like… victory!"

The nurse sighed and cleaned up the mess.

Rachel asked, "Some of his blood splashed on my arm, and I felt kind of ill. Is that normal?"

Siggy gestured at Rachel. "What do you think made her sick? Dirty Orphan Disease? Space-Virus? Is she just allergic to me?"

"*Je ne sais pas.*" Nurse Moth ran her scrutiny sticks, two lengths of wood carved with runes and set with gems of various colors, up and down Rachel, but none of the gems lit up. Her lips formed a moue. Then, adjusting her white wimple, she lifted her silver flute to her lips.

"No!" Rachel cried, "please!"

"*Oui?*" inquired the nurse in her native French.

"If you heal it with enchantment, there won't be a scar. There's supposed to be a scar!"

The nun of Asclepius pressed her lips together into a thin line. Then, she sighed and played a different melody. Rachel's arm tingled. The flesh mended together, leaving a faint scar.

"Thank you!" Rachel exclaimed in delight.

Nurse Moth lowered her flute and hung her head. "Tell no one that I have done such a thing. It is shameful."

"It's worth it," Rachel murmured, as she gazed at the scar, her eyes shining. "I've got the bravest boy in the world for my brother now."

Sigfried grinned a grin so dazzling that it could have blinded moon nymphs.

• • •

Rachel and Sigfried walked across the Commons. Nearby, Lucky rolled through the red and orange leaves, creating a small tornado of fall colors. Watching him, Rachel blanched. It had not occurred to her to consider what was going to happen when the princess found out about this? Would Nastasia be angry that she had not been included? What would Rachel say if the princess asked to be her blood sibling, too?

"Shall we tell everyone that we're siblings now? Or have it as our secret?" Rachel asked. "If we tell them, that's fine. Then everyone knows... but some of the others might want to do it, too... and things like this aren't as special if everyone does them. If we keep it a secret, that's one more secret we have to keep. But it stays more special. Or you could tell Valerie, and I could tell my family. And we could leave it like that—which is what I suggest. Then we don't have to keep it a secret, but we don't have to spread it around either."

Siggy looked puzzled. His brow furrowed as if he was annoyed. Rachel's heart lurched oddly. Did he think she was trying to renege on their new family bond?

She added hurriedly, "I thought of keeping it secret only because, in the books, blood brothers always seemed to be secret... normally, it is revealed decades later, when one brother comes to save the other. At the climax."

"The MacDannans don't hide from the world the fact that they are brothers," said Siggy, "nor does the princess go around saying she is not a Romanov. There is no point in being my blood-sister, if the bad guys aren't aware that to mess with you means a swift, one-way ticket to the screamy, ouchy, Land of Wow-I-Weren't-Expecting-My-Face-to-be-Burned-Off-by-the-Kid-With-a-Dragon."

"Very good, then!" Rachel inclined her head smartly. Silently, she prayed that the princess would be too well-bred to kick up a fuss.

Lucky came and sniffed her, his whispers tickling. "So, uh, we're all family now? Okay, let me know if you need someone burned. Or if you need someone's familiar eaten."

Rachel bowed to Lucky. "If I need any familiars eaten, you'll be the first person I call!" She peered around carefully, as if looking for wayward familiars in need of extermination.

Lucky snaked up to Sigfried. "*Psst.* Boss, she called me a person. I think she might be dragon-blind."

"You and Griffin are both persons because you both fly," Sigfried explained seriously, "whereas I'm a crippled, naked monkey-boy."

"Ah. That makes sense." Lucky's head bobbed up and down rapidly. "Welcome to the family, bizarrely-short-brainy-girl."

"Thank you, Lucky." Rachel curtsied.

• • •

That night, Rachel sat down to write letters. The first one was to Sandra. Before she wrote it, she spent a few minutes contemplating what she had learned that afternoon.

So she had been entirely wrong about Dread. He was not a fortress, aloof and separated from all things. He was the pursuer, besieging her sister's fortress. Rachel could not blame him. Sandra was beautiful and charming and good at everything to which she turned her hand. What more could a young prince desire in a queen?

Sandra would be perfect for Dread!

The big question now was: what could Rachel do to forward Vladimir's suit?

The first thing that came to mind was to suggest to him that he find some excuse to appear in front of Sandra in his sweat pants, preferably while he was sitting on his bed, looking forbidding. Rachel was fairly certain that seeing him this manner would destroy any remaining objections her sister might be entertaining.

But, that did not seem practical.

Second, Sandra might be more interested in marrying Dread if she understood the degree to which he needed her. Sandra was an astute student of human nature. She probably knew everything about Vladimir that Rachel had deduced. But just in case, she felt it might be wise to share her musings with her sister.

With this in mind, she wrote:

Dear Sandra,

It was great to see you! I was so happy you came by.

I must say I'm puzzled by Peter. He originally said my dating Gaius was such a bad thing, but then he hasn't done anything to try to stop me. What kind of protective older brother is he? Not that I want him to stop me, mind you. It's just that I can't help thinking that, deep down, he doesn't care.

On a different subject, I've been thinking about it, and I think you should marry Vladimir Von Dread. It would be great fun to have two kings as brothers-in-law. But, more importantly, I think Vlad is poised on the edge of a very dangerous precipice, and someone has to keep him from going the wrong way. Some of my friends say they can detect evil in him... I can't. Apparently, I don't have the detect-evil power... but he did do something very bad to the princess—the equivalent of pushing her through a door that he had been told might have alligators, spikes, and a volcano on the other side, merely because he wanted to find out where the door led.

He's going to be a king someday, and I don't think there's any question that he will be a just king. He is obviously very concerned with upholding the law. But whether he turns out to be Just and Great, or Just and Cruel, has yet to be determined. I think he needs someone to besiege the fortress of his heart and lead him towards Great and away from the precipice of Cruelty.

I would do it myself, except I have other things to do, so you will have to take up the cause. You should be good at that. You are so gracious and joyful and kind. Just tell him that you want to help save the world, and he's bound to like you. You are very pretty.

Anyway, thank you very much for coming! Sorry you didn't get to meet the princess.

Love,
Rachel

PS: Oh, and we have a new brother. That Sigfried

Smith boy I introduced you to, — the famous Dragon-slayer.

The second letter read:

Dear Mum and Father,

I hope all is well at home with everyone and that Widdershins doesn't miss me too much. Please make sure he is getting plenty of oat treats and that Oliver or one of the other stable boys is exercising him regularly. Maybe one of the tenant farmers, such as the Banks or the Meyers, would like to send one of their children up to the manor to ride him.

I thought I should inform you that we have a new family member. I now have a blood brother: Sigfried Smith, the bravest boy in the universe. He comes with a dragon. So, we now have a family dragon. Lucky is very useful and loyal, but he likes to eat familiars and animals in the sacrificial pens. That's a bit of a problem, but not that often.

Love you!
Rachel

CHAPTER TWENTY-TWO:

SLAYING ELVES AND CHESTNUTS

ALL HALLOWS' EVE DAWNED, COLD AND OVERCAST. THE TREES ON campus were nearly bare, a few last leaves clung to the dark, skeleton-like branches, fluttering in the chilly wind. The sky was filled with dark birds, wheeling and cawing—crows maybe, or starlings. Occasionally, flocks of them landed on roofs or lamp posts, their cries echoing like raucous jeers.

By late afternoon, the campus had been decorated for the holiday. Jack-O'-Lanterns, their leering grins and triangular eyes lit by cheery candlelight, lined the walkways and sat beside doors. Chinese lanterns had been strung across the Commons. Their orangey paper sides glowed brightly against the dreary day. The bonfire was already being built in the fire ring in the Memorial Gardens, near the lily pond.

A second bonfire would be set by the proctors atop Stony Tor.

All across campus, students were already turning their garments inside out and tying sprigs of twig to their familiars' collars to keep wandering spirits at bay. Not that such entities could cross the school wards, of course, but traditions were still traditions. There would be a party that evening, with candy and games led by the Gnosis students from Dee Hall: blind man's bluff, apple and candle, bobbing for apples, three luggies, moon mirror, leap-the-tin-cups, and other games of divination. Curfew had been lifted for the night, and students were free to stay up late. Samhain was a religious holiday, so there would be no classes the next day.

In the library during a free period, Rachel leafed through books about the Dead Men's Ball that the librarian, Mr. Poole, had put out for a display. The gathering of the restless dead would be held that night at Bannerman's mansion, not a mile north of the edge of the school's wards. Rachel also paged through *A History of New-York from the Beginning of the World to the End of the Dutch Dynasty*, by Diedrich Knickerbocker, and *Legends and Lore of Sleepy Hollow and the Hudson Valley* by Jonathan Kruk. Both books were so interesting, filled with curious facts about the Hudson Valley in general and Pollepel Island, as the Unwary called the island where Roanoke was moored, in particular. Rachel read about the storm goblin, the Heer of Dunderberg, who had terrorized the Hudson before his capture and imprisonment in Stony Tor; the ghost of Major Andre, a British soldier who was captured in the uniform of the enemy, but who claimed up until the moment he was hanged that he was not a spy; and the Headless Horseman, a vindictive specter who was said to be the ghost of a Hessian mercenary beheaded at the Battle of White Plains on October 28th, 1776, during the American War of Independence.

It seemed so unfair. All these fascinating entities would be gathering tonight, so close to her current location, and she could not go. How amazing it would be to attend the Dead Men's Ball, to see all the shades and spooks in action, to inquire what kept them tied to the world of the living. As she went to put the books back on the display, a longing swept over her as powerful and as irresistible as a riptide pulling a hapless swimmer out to sea. Changing her mind, she checked out both volumes and surreptitiously continued to read them during her next class—glancing at a page or two, then reading it from her memory, then glancing at the next few pages.

After classes ended, Rachel and her friends trudged over to Roanoke Hall to help the festival committee make corn dolls, and the Cooking Club prepare treats for the domestic fey: the *bwbachs* that cleaned the rooms, the brownies who cooked, the *bean tighe* who did the laundry. Rachel and her friends all sat together at a table, corn silk and string everywhere, and chatted as they worked, except for Siggy and Lucky, who ate so much of the caramel for the apples that Joy's oldest sister, Temperance, the president of the Cooking Club, had to ask them to stop helping. Siggy and Lucky came over and plopped down next to Valerie, who sat at the end of the table dipping apples in a self-heating, cast-iron pot of hot caramel. She moved the pot away from them. They pouted.

"So, I'm excited about going into dreamland and not having to hold hands," said Joy, who was painting a face onto a corn woman. "I will be even more excited, if I am not the 'victim.'"

"It will be more pleasant for all of us," agreed Nastasia, who was trying to decide whether to add corn silk or rust-colored yarn for the hair on her third doll. Beauregard lay beside her chair, gnawing on a rawhide bone.

Rachel looked from the princess's neat roll of husk figures to her own lopsided doll, with one arm longer than the other, and sighed. She kept braiding the husks, though, and tied off the little hand.

"You can say that again!" Zoë ran a hand over her head until her own hair was the same pale yellow as the corn silk. She sat nearby, her feet up on a chair, eating one of the caramel apples that were supposed to go to the fey.

Thunder reverberated through the dining hall. A few students glanced warily at the clear sky, but the disturbance was coming from the north. The tor had been rumbling all day. Perhaps the trapped storm goblin was more impatient with being imprisoned on Halloween.

"Wait." Valerie looked up from her work, hot, sticky candy dripping from the apple in her hand. She surreptitiously dropped a little for her dog to lick up, as soon as it cooled. "We found a way to not fall out of dreamland?" She touched the spot on her forehead where she had struck the table after she tried to shake hands with Dream Gaius. "When did that happen?"

Sigfried and Lucky sat beside her, watching, with identical forlorn expressions, the now-forbidden, hot, tawny bubbling goodness. Siggy pulled at the bandage on his forehead from where he had flown Vroomie into a tree, a few days earlier—when Rachel first began trying to teach him to fly it. She had given him several lessons since then. He had previously mastered a Flycycle during flying class, so it was only a matter of teaching him the complexities of maneuvering the steeplechaser. So far, he was doing well. There were many finer points to the device he had yet to learn, but he had successfully mastered both flying at high speed and turning.

Landing was still a work in progress.

"Well, we took Zoë to see—" Siggy began.

"Stop!" Rachel barked. She ducked her head, embarrassed, as people from other tables turned and stared at her. Lowering her voice, she spoke in a whispered hiss. "We can't talk about this. Remember?"

"But... Wheels knows now," objected Sigfried. "And nothing happened. It isn't fair for all of us to know and Wheels, and not my G.F.! Goldilocks deserves to know!"

"She is a proper member of the Inner Circle," the princess acknowledged thoughtfully.

"It isn't a matter of proper or fairness," Rachel implored, trying to keep her voice low. "It's a matter of life and death." She turned to Valerie. "We were told if more than three people knew... someone would die."

"But, don't..." Valerie's voice trailed off. She frowned and counted aloud, "... one, two, three, four, five people now know? I didn't mind not being in the know when it was an urgent matter, and no one else could find out. But now Zoë knows, too. Why was Zoë told and not me?"

"The Unmentionable One sent me a dream," Sigfried explained. "She asked to see Zoë."

"Yep." Zoë dipped her half-eaten apple back into the black pot of hot caramel.

Valerie let out a strangled yelp and waved her hands at the other girl to chase her away.

"So, this mystery is a 'she?'" asked Valerie. "Is it 'she' who will die, if word gets out?"

Several of them nodded. Nastasia finished gluing on the long silky strands of hair and held her doll up for inspection. Thunder shook the chamber again.

"Oh, princess," Joy gushed, "that is the best corn doll I've ever seen. That may be the best one made on the planet earth. People from other planets are going to be drawn here, as if by a magnet, to view its perfection!"

"Um... thank you," the princess said stiffly, staring carefully at her handiwork. Joy's ebullient praise embarrassed her, but she was too well-mannered to object.

Valerie dipped another apple on its twig stem into the bubbling pot. "Let's not change the subject. I admit to feeling very inquisitive about this mysterious 'she'... from whom Siggy received herbs and Alchemy tips, and now Zoë got to talk to her, too, and, I presume, received the gift of keeping us from falling out of dreams. I was restraining my curiosity, because I thought it was important to keep the matter secret. But if everyone knows but me... that's not acceptable. Having both a detective father and a crusading newshound mother, I was born with a nose for the unusual, the curious. And I *hate* not knowing things. If everyone else knows, I think it is only fair that I know, too."

Rachel looked down at her corn doll. She completely sympathized with that argument. Were it her, she would feel exactly the same way. And yet....

"So, we tell Valerie." Siggy turned his chair around and straddled it. "Here's what...."

"No!" Rachel cried. "You can't kill the... her!"

"Rachel, be reasonable." Nastasia laid her doll on the table and gathered green husks to start a fourth. "The only evidence we have that anyone is in danger is the opinion of that unpleasant raven-person, and he does not strike me as at all trustworthy. I think it is unfair to exclude Valerie based on such flimsy evidence."

"Exactly!" Siggy leaned forward eagerly.

"Besides," continued the princess, "it occurs to me that we could take our... friend home. To her home. We did go to a dream version of her home, she and I, when she was teaching me how to use my gift, but we could not get from the dream to the waking world. With Zoë's help, however, we could do such a thing." She glanced at Zoë, who nodded.

Rachel jumped up. "Let's do it now!"

"We are busy now," replied the princess primly. "Besides, we are not allowed to leave campus. I was thinking that if we waited until the Thanksgiving holiday, we would be able to leave campus without violating any rules. Also, if it took time, or we wanted to stay there a few days, our absence would not frighten anyone."

"Oh, what a good idea!" breathed Rachel, her mind filled with images of the great forest the Elf came from, where trees grew out of the tops of the canopies of other trees.

"I am not waiting until Thanksgiving!" Valerie violently dipped an apple in the caramel. "You've told me this much. Tell me the rest."

"No," Siggy agreed. "That is too much to ask of a curious, fearless reporter girl! It is as inhuman as torture."

"But—" Rachel began.

Joy cut her off. "Princess, you're the leader. What do you say?"

"Yeah!" Siggy looked at Nastasia. "What is your decision, Fearless Leader?"

"Let's put it to a vote," Nastasia said pleasantly.

"No!" Rachel cried, grabbing her head. "You can't put someone's life up to a vote!"

But they voted. Only Rachel objected.

"Great!" Siggy grinned like one of the nearby Jack-O'-Lantern. "I have been waiting and waiting for this! Have I mentioned how much I *hate* secrets?"

Rachel looked around.

Where could she go for help? Gaius? Von Dread? Her friends would not listen to them. Mr. Fuentes lounged against one wall, but if she went to him, what good would it do? She could not tell him why she wanted him to keep her friends from telling a secret, without revealing too much herself. The Elf's friend, Mr. Gideon? She could run to his office. He might not be in on Halloween, however, and the princess had already made it clear several times how disappointed she was in their True Hiss tutor for not having been straight about the purpose of the detention duties upon which he had sent them. Nor could Rachel ask the Raven for his help. Even if he would have come, which was unlikely, she did not know his name to call him.

Rachel pushed back her chair to stand and leave. She wanted no part of this. If they were going to commit homicide—elficide?— they were going to have to do it without her.

She rose and took a step from the table. Then, her steps slowed, for she had just remembered something.

It had been a cold late-November day. The early morning frost had lain across the moors. Rachel, bundled in a thick red wool coat held shut by three toggles, had needed to run to keep up with her grandfather's long strides. She had been five, and he had been the center of her world.

Ten minutes previously, a servant had come from the stable and informed Grandfather that Warlock was failing. The great charger had served Rachel's grandfather as his steed for over a century, accompanying him into many battles. Now, however, the beast had grown so feeble that even magical healing could no longer ease its pain. Grandfather had listened to this news with a stony face, nodded, folded his paper, and told Rachel to fetch her coat.

They had walked down to the back paddock, their breath forming foggy puffs before them. Within, Warlock rolled on the cold ground, unable to regain his feet. His pain-filled whinnies had cut through the cold morning like the blare of a trumpet. His eyes had been wide with fear. It had hurt Rachel to see such the noble beast so reduced. She was used to him towering above her, a wall of sleek black and shining white, his nostrils flared, his ears pricked, his fluffy snow-white mane and feet-feathering floating about him like clouds. His forelocks and tail were black, but they, too, seemed airy as cloud-stuff. He had been a gorgeous animal, swift as the wind. And when he galloped across the moors, only Thunderfrost himself —Warlock's great, great, great grandsire—was more glorious.

At the gate to the paddock, Grandfather had paused and placed his hand on Rachel's shoulder. He had gazed down at her seriously.

"Your mother will fuss, my child. She will say you are too young, and I should not have brought you. But I say, one is never too young to learn the nature of duty. And there is no greater duty than duty toward those who love us."

Rachel had gazed up at him, her eyes dark and steady.

Grandfather had squatted down until they stared eye to eye. "Remember this, Lady Rachel Griffin. If the time should ever come when some charge under your care must die, you do it yourself. With your own hand. You owe them that."

He had risen and walked into the paddock, leaving Rachel at the gate with several of the stable hands. As she had watched, he had paralyzed the pain-crazed horse with a stream of blue sparks from the amethyst on one of his four rings of mastery. Then he had stridden to the barn and came back with a sword and a belt, the buckle of which was made of ivory and shaped like an elephant. He had strapped on the old worn belt, which Rachel knew was enchanted and would give him the strength of many men. Kneeling beside the old horse, he had laid his hand upon the sleek, sweat-soaked coat and leaned over, whispering something into Warlock's ear.

Then, he had risen to his feet.

With a single overhead blow, her grandfather had sliced through the steed's neck, cleaving the head from the shoulders. Blood had spouted out like a fountain. Then, a stable hand had covered Rachel's eyes, and she saw no more.

As they had walked back to the house, his hand again resting on Rachel's shoulder, Grandfather had said gruffly, "Never kill anything you love with magic, child. That is the beginning of the path that ends in the black arts. Never take a single step down that path."

Back in the dining hall at school, Rachel turned around and rested her hands on the top of her chair. She leaned forward and spoke very precisely.

"Very well. If we are going to tell Valerie, let us do it correctly. I will tell her—everything. But not here. We have to find some place more private. And let us pray to whatever deities might listen that Nastasia is right, and I am wrong."

• • •

In the end, they decided on the soundproof studios in the back of the theater in Dare Hall. Beauregard came with them, but Valerie left her dog romping about on the commons. Rachel had not even known such chambers existed. The group of them tromped across campus and along the leaf-strewn gravel path to the dorm, passing where Yolanda Debussy, Agravaine Stormhenge, and some other college students were attaching the sheet to the lavender ribbon-bestrewn horse skull that was to be Dare's *Mari Lwyd* for the Mummers Parade.

Rachel found this a bit strange. She was used to mummers at Yule, but apparently things were done differently in America.

They crossed the black and white marble of the foyer and entered the cavernous, dark theater, blindly fumbling their way to the back, where, with the help of a flicker of dragon fire, Valerie found a light switch. Then, they made their way into one of the sound-proof rooms and shut the door. The studio was bright white and empty except for a few music stands and two chairs. Zoë immediately sprawled across both chairs, sitting on one and resting her feet on the second. Rachel and Nastasia remained standing. The rest sat down on the floor.

"I will tell you everything," Rachel said severely. "But no repeating any of it, to anyone."

She closed her eyes briefly, pressing her fingers against her temples. Then she opened her eyes again. With a finality like the falling of her grandfather's sword, Rachel recalled and recited the events of their meetings at the Roanoke Tree with the Lios Alfar queen, Illondria, daughter of Idunn, the caretaker of the World Tree.

• • •

Dinner consisted of roast pork, collard greens, buttered Hubbard squash, Indian pudding, and pumpkin pie. The Mummers Parade followed. This event did not involve elaborate costumes—those were saved for the Masquerade Ball, which was apparently held later in the year. Students did dress in quaint, inside-out outfits, however, messing up their hair and painting their faces. Rachel's friends did her hair up in three pigtails and painted her face rusty brown and white, like a fox. Joy wore ribbons tied to six different small braids. Her sister Mercy came by and painted her face with green and gold glitter. Zoë turned her hair orange and black, and even Nastasia joined in, wearing a traditional Magical Australian fairy costume.

Led by *Mari Lwyd* from each of the seven Arts—with college students, hidden under the white sheet that represented the white horses' bodies, carrying the festive skulls—the procession wound from dorm to dorm. Students banged on gongs or blew ox horns, with barking dogs and the thunder from the tor occasionally adding to the cacophony. The parade ended at the Memorial Gardens where a warding student from De Vere lit the bonfire—officially starting the ceremony to honor the dead of Roanoke.

The ceremony itself was performed by Nighthawk, the school's Master Warder. As the sky darkened, the fire grew taller. Soon, it was a towering pillar of dancing, crackling flames. Sparks, like fireflies, escaped into the darkness, rising toward the night sky. Rachel stared up at the tiny points of fire until they became lost in the stars above.

After the ceremony, friendship roasters were set-up around the bonfire, and chestnuts were handed out. Two by two, friends moved into the roaring heat and placed their nuts into the roasters. If the nuts emerged nicely warmed, the friendship was destined for good things. If the nuts split or dried out, then there was to be rough times ahead.

Rachel and Sigfried placed their chestnuts in the roaster together. They waited, trying to find the right distance away from the blaze to stand—though no matter where she picked, it seemed to Rachel that the heat from the fire felt blisteringly hot against her face and hands and yet the back of her neck was cold. To her and Siggy's delight, their nuts came back piping hot and smelling of chestnutty goodness. When the shells cooled down, they ate their nuts happily, sharing bits with Lucky. The taste was divine.

Joy put her first nut in with the princess and whined in dismay when her nut cracked. She grumbled that the fire had grown too hot, and the roasters should be moved back. The others ignored her. Nastasia caught Rachel's hand, and the two of them ran, laughing, to get more chestnuts. They placed two more together in a roaster.

A large log caught and flared. The bonfire grew suddenly hotter. With a deafening bang, Rachel and Nastasia's chestnuts exploded, shooting little bits of shell and nut-meat all over the nearby students.

"Oh!" the princess cried.

She looked so dismayed that Rachel felt as if one of the shards of shell had lodged in her heart. She reached over and squeezed her friend's hand.

"It doesn't mean anything—chestnut roasting," Rachel whispered in her friend's ear. "It's not a real divination. It's just a game."

"If you say so." Nastasia's face looked very pale in the firelight. She squeezed Rachel's hand in return and then lifted her chin courageously. "You are right, Miss Griffin. We mustn't let such minor things interfere with our festive joy." With renewed cheer, Nastasia tried again with Zoë.

As the other two girls carried their nuts toward the bonfire, Rachel moved away, into the leaping shadows of the night. The exploding chestnut had upset her much more than she let on. The pain of the imaginary shard still stuck in her heart. That, combined with her willing participation in telling Valerie about the Elf, left her feeling frightened and sad.

Away from the bonfire, all was silver and shadows. The moonlight was very bright, as the moon had been full three days before. The cold blew through her garments. Its bite was all the more shocking because the heat near the great blaze had been so great. Rachel leaned against a shrine to the flower goddess Pomona, as she waited for her eyes to adjust. All around students laughed and shrieked. Girls giggled and peered at their nuts. Boys threw shell bits at each other or chucked leaves and sheets of loose-leaf paper into the fire.

On the far side of the blaze, Rachel could see the silhouettes of tall figures that might have been Von Dread and William Locke. She wondered if Gaius was nearby. Closer, she saw a pretty Middle Eastern student chucking chestnuts at her girlfriends. Nearby, Rachel's roommate Kitten searched through a bag of nuts with her best friend, sophomore Almathea Kern.

To their right, some of the older students were preparing tiny walnut barges topped with little conical candles, which could be launched on the lily pond, or—for the more adventurous—on Roanoke Creek, for another divinatory game. Another group of students cut into a ginger ring cake, a tall girl exclaiming with delight when she discovered the first prize of the evening, a ring, in her slice. Two burly boys shouldered past them, carrying a big barrel of water in which apples bobbed. Behind came a third boy carrying a long stick. An apple hung by a rope from one side. The other end had a candle stuck to it.

Over by the shrine to Hephaestus, older girls poured melted lead through the opening in an old-fashioned door key and into a bucket of water. As soon as it hit the liquid, sizzling, they squatted to stare at the shapes that the hardened lead had formed. Rachel recognized Oonagh MacDannan, Xandra Black and Freka Starkadder among their number. Students studying molybdomancy stood by to help interpret the divinatory outcomes.

Thunder rolled across the campus again. To the north, she could see the orangey brightness of the second bonfire atop Stony Tor. Rachel turned away, sighing. In the shadows, Kitten's tiny familiar sat a bit of a distance behind its mistress, licking its paw with regal dignity. The Comfort Lion turned its head and met Rachel's gaze. The firelight glinted off its golden eyes. Rachel might have been imagining it, but she had the distinct impression that the little familiar did not approve of divinatory games.

Nonetheless, the little Lion glanced to the left, where Rachel's other roommate, Astrid, stood alone in the dark, her ubiquitous scarf trailing behind her. Her head was lowered, forlorn. A lone chestnut rested on her palm. Impulsively, Rachel ran forward and took a nut from the bag. Then she approached Astrid.

"Would you like to roast a nut?" she asked simply.

The shy girl nodded gratefully. Together, Rachel and Astrid made their way to a roaster, a little ways around the fire from where their other two roommates were, and set their chestnuts side by side. They stood quietly, Astrid staring shyly at the ground. She kept wiping her cheek and then having to do something with the grease paint that had now smeared onto her fingers. When the timer popped on the roaster, the two girls cautiously examined their nuts.

Rachel gave a soft cry of delight. Both nuts were perfectly roasted, moist and warm, with the shell peeled back from the tawny meat in just the right way. When they cooled, the two girls happily peeled the perfect chestnuts and popped them in their mouths, smiling at each other.

Maverick Badger's gruff voice rose above the festivities, announcing that those who had lost loved ones were invited to make their way to the Hudson to launch paper lanterns. Students queued up to go. The same longing that had assailed Rachel during the afternoon seized her again. Looking around at her friends, happily playing games, she made a sudden decision.

Taking her leave of Astrid, Rachel ran back to Dare Hall and fetched Vroomie.

Chapter Twenty-Three:

Crashing the Dead Men's Ball

"I've decided to crash the Dead Men's Ball," Rachel murmured, stepping up beside Sigfried, her steeplechaser swinging in her hand. "Do you want to come with?"

"Crash something, you bet!" Siggy grinned as he and Lucky leapt and danced around the bonfire. "I'm all about crashing. What are we crashing into? Is it flammable?"

"The Dead Men's Ball. Where all the spirits of the restless dead gather."

"What... you mean ghosts?" The fearless boy actually looked unnerved. "Oh no! Not me. Ghosts scare me!"

"Oh. Right," Rachel recalled their previous conversation on the topic, the first time they had flown by Bannerman's mansion. She did not want to go with someone who was going to be uncomfortable. That would take the joy out of it. "All right. I'll ask someone else."

She looked around, wondering which of her friends might want to come along. Zoë, maybe? She seemed fearless. As she searched for the other girl, her gaze fell on two tall silhouettes and a shorter one on the far side of the bonfire. She took her leave of Sigfried and headed that way.

"Psst, Gaius," she whispered, tapping him on the shoulder. His hair looked normal, but he did have two streaks of blue war paint across his cheeks. With his garments inside out, the motley squares patching the holes in his robe were even more obvious. "I'm going to sneak off campus and crash the Dead Men's Ball. Would you like to come?"

Gaius jumped, startled by her sudden appearance. For one crazy second, she feared he would try to stop her, or worse, report her to the proctors.

"Let's go check it out, shall we?" He bowed and offered her his arm.

Together, they followed the procession of students heading to the shore of the Hudson.

. . .

Down by the water, students wishing to launch mourning lights lined up in front of a table maintained by the Roanoke Seers Club. Those who had lost loved ones took candles and put them into boat-shaped paper lanterns. Farther down, by the docks, girls knelt to chant and wail, while young men stood by, silent as ghosts. Some of the lanterns were already afloat on the dark waters of the Hudson, glowing a cherry-gold as they sailed under the shadow of Storm King Mountain.

Rachel thought of stopping to launch candles for her grandparents, or maybe for Myrddin, but the line was long. If she waited, the crowd might dwindle, and they might lose their opportunity to slip away unseen.

Rachel and Gaius moved toward the lights flickering in the ruined castle that had once been Grand Inquisitor Bannerman's arsenal. It was traditional throughout the Western world to set plates at dinner on All Hallows' Eve for departed loved ones. On this night, those wronged often returned to wreak vengeance, while grateful shades came back to give blessings to their kin and loved ones. The dead could not come onto campus, but no one wished to dishonor them. So, the Cooking Club had brought tables to the ruined castle. There, places had been set on fancy china, with a little corn doll at each place, for Roanokean students, alumni, and staff who had died recently or whose shades might still be wandering. Rachel felt sorry for the shade that found itself sitting before her lopsided doll. The table for the recently dead had only a few place settings, but a number of tables had been prepared for those killed during the Terrible Years.

With a sudden rush of gratitude toward the Raven, Rachel silently gave thanks that they had not needed to set a place for Enoch Smithwyck.

Rachel and her boyfriend wandered over, as if to investigate the offerings, and then kept going, out the other side of the ruins, into the darkness of the outcropping of rocks beyond. They stopped in the black shadow of the ruined castle. Thunder shook the tor again. The rumble was more muted down here at the far end of the island.

Rachel lifted her broom. "Shall we?"

"Indeed." Gaius sounded amused, though she could not quite see his face. "Though we are going to miss some of the games back at the dining hall after the ceremony. And Fairy Gifts."

Rachel looked back wistfully for an instant, then she shrugged. "I never receive good fairy gifts anyway. Or, rather, I receive wonderful gifts, such as Wealth or Fame… and then I get 'the present' that comes with." She sighed and chanted:

> "Your choice is bad when you entrust
> Your happiness where moth and rust,
In time, turns all your wealth to dust.

"After which, Mother Hubbard poured dust all over me and hung a dust-pan from my neck."

"I've never gotten a Fairy Gift, but Topher received *Honor* last year, and he got a bellows blown in his ear on the theory that honor is nothing but air," chuckled Gaius.

"Who plays Mother Hubbard and gives out the gifts?" asked Rachel.

"It was the dean last year. The year before, it was Dr. Fallon from the Art Department. Though I have heard that Mr. Tuck did it one year, dressed up as an ugly woman. Wish I'd seen that. Mr. Tuck is a riot."

"I love him in language class. He makes everything so clear."

Gaius nodded. Then he tapped his inside out pocket. "Thanks for the calling card. It's nice to know that we can reach each other in case of emergencies."

"You're welcome!" beamed Rachel, but she thought, *Thanks, Sigfried, and I haven't paid him yet.*

They climbed onto the steeplechaser and floated up the coastline. The night wind blowing down the river was cold. The two of them huddled close together. Rachel could feel her boyfriend's warmth through her clothing. The light of the near-full moon reflected like a silvery road before them, leading up the river. To the northeast, she could see the flickers of the second bonfire, the one set atop Stony Tor.

They flew out of the cove by the dock and northward. It would have been quicker to fly north from the commons; however, that would have required flying over the row of trees that marked the wards of the school. Crossing the wards caused magic to fail. Rachel did not dare fly across them, lest her bristleless fail, too, and they tumble from the sky.

They passed the rock outcropping beside the docks and were coming up alongside the walled orchard when Rachel heard a gruff voice in the darkness. She slowed to a near halt.

"The sheets are doing their thing tonight, as usual. Have you got the salt?"

Another voice, this one with an Irish lilt, answered, "Aye. I have a whole package."

A third voice spoke, rather louder, "Um, so, we're really going to jump a bunch of ghosts? Why, exactly, are we doing this?"

The second voice teased, "Ohhh. Look at Mister Loves-the-Undead over here."

The third voice objected, "They're just ghosts. They're not vampires. They're harmless."

A fourth voice growled, 'Oh yeah? What about Headless? Is he harmless?"

The third voice spoke again. "Well, he's a phantom. That's different."

The third speaker was definitely the princess's brother, Alex Romanov and the second was a MacDannan. Rachel was not as certain about the rest, as they were deliberately lowering their voices.

Rachel whispered, "Is that Abraham Van Helsing and his vampire-hunting cronies?"

Gaius whispered back, "Sounds like Alex Romanov, at least. I've hardly ever spoken to Van Helsing. He's... odd."

Rachel and Gaius rounded the high stone wall of the orchard, which was walled on three sides. The fourth side, facing the river, was open. Hidden behind the wall, a pile of boys and two girls huddled together over the light of a few candles. The boys were Abraham

Van Helsing, Conan MacDannan, Alex Romanov, Max Weatherby, Laurence Colt, and the Ferris Twins—generally known as Arrick and Efrick Ferret. The girls were Max's younger sister Sarah and her friend, Winifred Powell.

Arrick stepped from the pack and puffed out his chest. "Stand down, civilians on deck."

The pile of boys tried to look casual. Winifred, who wore glasses over her grease painted face, smiled and waved. Sarah kept peeking out from behind the gnarled trunk of an apple tree.

Rachel waved at them as she flew onward, as if flying a bristle-less off campus at night was a perfectly normal thing to do. This might not have gone over so convincingly, except for two factors. First, she was alone with her boyfriend, so maybe the others thought the two of them were sneaking off for a little time by themselves. And second, it looked like the vampire-hunting club had the same idea she and Gaius did, so they were hardly in a position to tattle.

"We should have brought some salt, too," Rachel mused, as she and Gaius flew onward.

"I have some." The warmth of Gaius's breath on her cheek was a pleasant contrast to the chill of the night. "And an amulet with a twig of broom. We in Vlad's group pride ourselves on being well-prepared. I also have a couple of packets of peony seeds. Here, take one." He slipped one into her hand. She stuck it into her sleeve. "Many of the restless dead feel compelled to stop to count all the seeds, which can give you time to get away. Probably would not work on Old Headless, though."

"I have my clothing inside out," Rachel said, "and the Horseman doesn't come until midnight. We should have plenty of time to go and come back. Besides, I don't think we need to fear the Wild Hunt. Doesn't it just collect wayward ghosts? That's what it does at home, anyhow, when it rides across the moors. Laurel and I rode out to see it once. It was quite spectacular!"

Gaius made a noise that might have indicated amusement under his breath.

"What?"

"It's just that most of the girls I know were afraid to go down to the docks to float lanterns tonight. You're something different,

Rachel Griffin."

"Not so different from Sarah and Winifred," Rachel pointed out.

They passed marshes and then a stretch of forest. In the silvery moonlight, the hemlocks along the shore swayed in the dark like shaggy specters. The shoreline moved east, and Rachel flew over the rocky island with a single lone fir tree, She knew this meant that they were close to the northmost edge of the school's wards. After this, the shoreline moved west again, and more hemlocks swayed.

When the trees changed to marsh again, and she caught sight of cattails, Rachel knew that they were now alongside Bannerman's house. Looking up the hill, she could see the silhouette of the mansion's turrets against the moon-bright sky. Behind it, farther away, was the orangey-red glow of the bonfire atop the tor. As she navigated her steeplechaser eastward and inland, she caught sight of a faint light gliding through the darkness of the marsh—a large phosphorescent white glow accompanied by small phosphorescent green ones.

A tingle ran down Rachel's spine. The shadow-strewn night suddenly seemed spooky and dangerous. The haunting strains of violins, horns, and bells played in her mind in three-four time. Behind her, Gaius began to hum the tune she had been imagining.

Rachel halted and backed up her broom.

"What?" asked Gaius.

"That was eerie. I was just imagining that same waltz."

She felt Gaius shiver. He said, "I can 'hear' it perfectly, but I can't hear any music... with my ears, I mean."

Together, they hummed a few bars of the music they were imagining in perfect unison. Rachel shivered, too, and leaned against him.

"You know, we don't have to keep going," Gaius murmured softly. "You are still astonishingly brave for having made it this far."

"No! I want to go on. It's just...."

"Spooky? Unnerving? 'Terrifying beyond the capacity for rational thought?'"

"I wouldn't go that far." Rachel smiled into the darkness. "Unnerving is a good word."

"Why do you want to go forward?—Not that I am saying you shouldn't—" Gaius amended quickly. "It's just that I am rather curious as to your reasoning. At least eighty-nine percent of the girls at school would pay *not* to see a ghost, and we go to a school of sorcerers."

"Why?" The question caught Rachel off guard. She had to think about it. "I guess it's part of wanting to know things. I've realized recently that I say 'I want to know *everything*,' but what I really want to know is secrets. Forbidden things. Forgotten things. Especially forgotten things. I feel so sorry for the things that no one remembers."

"And that's what ghosts represent, isn't it?" Gaius asked, surprised.

Rachel nodded. "All ghosts have a forgotten thing—some secret no one knows about—that's holding them to the mortal world. If we could find it, we might be able to help them pass on to... wherever it is that the dead are supposed to go. It is as if each ghost is its own mystery."

As Rachel spoke, it occurred to her that now that Azrael was bound up again, Myrddin might feel his business on earth was finished. The idea that she might never see Thunderfrost's Boy again made her feel both hopeful for him and slightly sad.

Gaius nodded. "That makes sense."

"Does it?"

"Yes, I can understand that," Gaius said. "I know that ever since the princess told me about her vision of my past, I've been obsessed with who I might have been and how I came to be here. I can't stop thinking about that space station that blew up. I... think I had something to do with that. I'm seventy-nine and a half percent certain."

Rachel thought of Dream Gaius, staring at the star-faring galleons. "You have no way of knowing that for sure, Gaius."

"Rachel, I have this persistent feeling that I was... not a good person."

"But you are now," Rachel said firmly.

Gaius swallowed and nodded. She waited a moment, but he said no more.

"I want to see what those lights are." Rachel gazed down the shoreline at the floating luminescence coming their way. "Shall we proceed?"

"No time like the present."

Rachel flew her broom over the marshes. She could smell the boggy water. They moved cautiously toward the eerie gliding glow. Once closer, they saw that the iridescent white came from the gowns of a procession of young women with long flowing hair, who glided barefoot over the marshes toward the mansion. The green glow came from wild will-o-wisps—the kind that would lure a mortal to a soggy, boggy doom—hovering above the outstretched palms of the young women. The sight of the dead maidens with their ropey locks, bearing the pale light of fey wisps, sent shivers dancing up and down Rachel's body.

"What are they?" Gaius whispered.

"Wilis."

"Willies?" Gaius's voice took on an odd quality, as if he were making a Herculean effort not to snark.

"Yes, Wilis."

"Which are?"

"The spirits of maidens who died from a broken heart. Like in *Giselle*."

"Which is?"

"Don't you watch classical ballet?"

"Not on a regular basis. No." Gaius's voice sounded tight, as if he was trying to contain his mirth.

"Aren't you an upper school senior?" Rachel turned at the waist and frowned at him. "We're learning about them in Freshman Music. How could you not have studied Wilis?"

"I know. I know. Shameful. But, frankly, if it doesn't give me magical powers when I summon it up, I haven't really paid a whole lot of attention. Unless it's dangerous. Are Wilis deadly?"

"Only to handsome young men, whom they *dance to death*," Rachel replied dryly.

Gaius's mouth formed a silent "O". "I will make a point to avoid those particular beauties. Luckily, I brought my own."

Rachel blushed in the darkness and quickly turned the broom up the slope toward where the mansion stood at the top of the hill.

Bannerman's mansion rose black against the surrounding bare trees, its turrets silhouetted against the starry night. Part of the roof was missing, and the circular far wall had a gaping hole in it. Half-rotten faces and glowing eyes stared out from what struck Rachel as a Spanish-style porch with high arched windows separated from each other by round columns. The strains of a waltz from *Swan Lake* swelled from inside—though Rachel could still hear it more clearly in her head than with her ears. Through the broken or glassless windows issued an eerie blue-violet glow that danced and flickered.

"Almost looks as if they are playing Snap-dragon," murmured Gaius.

"Yes it does," Rachel replied.

The blue-violet glow did look eerily similar to color of burning brandy.

"That's another game we're missing," said Gaius.

"My family plays Snap-dragon at Yule," replied Rachel dryly, "so I will not miss my chance to burn my fingers grabbing flaming raisins."

"Nobody burns their fingers playing Snap-dragon," scoffed Gaius.

As they circled, looking for a good spot to land, he added cheerfully, "Speaking of fire. Did you hear that one of those burning skunks sprayed Darling and Andrews?"

"Yes. I saw that." Rachel was glad he was behind her, because she was having trouble repressing her malicious grin.

"Wish I could have seen that," Gaius mused wistfully.

They landed the broom on the stone veranda and cautiously approached the house. Low moans issued from within. The unearthly blue-violet glow flickered from somewhere inside the run-down mansion. It made her and Gaius's faces nearly as pale as those of the Wilis. Gaius's pale blue skin made an interesting contrast with his two streaks of darker blue war paint. Resting her broom against a corner of the house, Rachel stepped through the broken wall into the mansion and halted.

The shades of the restless dead were everywhere.

Her heart began pounding. Rachel nearly turned tail and ran. Gaius's words, about her being brave to have come this far, echoed in her mind. There would be nothing shameful about leaving now. After all, she had seen the Dead Men's Ball.

How many other students—or mortals of any kind—could say that?

But if she left, she would never know more. She would never know what caused the strange blue-violet glow. She would never know if the shades she had read about in the books she had taken from the library were truly here. She would never know why there was beautiful sweeping waltz music, for she could hear it clearly now, even with her ears, issuing from such a grim and grizzly place.

Besides, if she left now, what would she have to show for her day? Killed an elf? Made a lopsided corn doll? Was cursed by an exploding chestnut? That hardly seemed like the way she wanted to remember her first All Hallows' Eve at Roanoke.

Gathering her courage, Rachel walked forward to face this new adventure.

Chapter Twenty-Four:

The Dead Denizens of the

Hudson Highlands

GHOSTS, GHOULS, WHITE LADIES, AND SPECTERS, ALMOST TOO faint to behold, sat on a circular bench inside the chamber into which the hole in the wall opened. Others milled about the old mansion. Some could almost have been mistaken for living men. Others were ghastly to behold, skeletal faces with bulging eyeballs rolling in their sockets, or bloated drowned faces, half-rotting bodies with bones gleaming white where the skin was missing. Still others were ghouls, hideous dead who had been transformed into ungainly monstrosities. Near these, the odor of rotting flesh nearly made her gag.

The majority of those present were sailors—many with seaweed clinging to their rotting garments. Some had been so long amidst the waves that barnacles grew from their hands and faces. Their garments varied from the black garb of the old Dutchmen to the simple browns of hard-working folks, to sou'westers, to the spiffy sailor suits of navy men. Over by the large gap in the far side of the chamber, looking south down the river towards West Point, five rougher-looking Dutchmen conversed, their heads close together. They had a grizzled, hard quality that made Rachel wonder if they were pirates. A young girl floated beside the Dutch sailors dressed in a strange garment of vests and skirts and boots that Rachel could not place. Unlike the other specters, she did not sit or stand upright, but seemed to be flying, her body stretched out behind her in the air. She hardly looked human with her enormously-large black eyes and her hair that flowed around her like living kelp.

The hairs on the back of Rachel's neck rose. She trusted in her inside-out garments. Yet, she was aware of the unnatural, potentially dangerous nature of their ghostly companions. Gaius gazed around alertly, his wand in his hand. Without being intrusive, he made certain he stayed close to Rachel, where he could protect her. Surreptitiously, he tugged on the chain around his neck that held his amulet containing a twig of broom, slipping it onto the outside of his robes.

Several ghoulish entities backed away from him.

The music had fallen quiet. The band began tuning their instruments, an eerie sound even in the best of times. Rachel shivered and stepped even closer to her boyfriend. He squeezed her hand.

A blood curdling shriek caused the two of them to clutch each other. Again, she considered bolting. Had she not seen enough?

But if she ran, she would never know what had caused that screech, and that might be worse than staying. It was a sound that could haunt a person's nightmares for a lifetime. It was partially to keep at bay the encroaching darkness at the edges of her mind that Rachel did bold things, such as stride into a party full of the shades of the restless dead. She did not need to give the darkness any more fuel.

Refusing to give in to her fear, she looked around. The screeching came from a feminine figure in white, ghostly and pale. The moment the shade was done uttering her horrible wail, she returned to wandering listlessly through the chamber. Rachel breathed a sigh of relief. Beside her, she felt Gaius's tense body relax slightly.

Half a dozen other women stood wringing their hands and weeping. Most wore simple pale shifts. One crying figure, however, wore ancient native garb of leather, feathers, and beads. Another glided along in a homespun wedding gown. Yet another had no form of her own but was merely a collection of mist and dried leaves blowing in the shape of a woman.

Beyond the circular chamber was the main room, which was currently serving as a ballroom, though nobody was dancing at the moment. Eerie blue-violet fire flickered in the hearth, casting all those haunting the old mansion in its indigo glow. Even the white bridal gown of the shade who drifted noiselessly across the chamber appeared a violet-blue.

At the far end of the ballroom, a ghostly dais had been erected upon which played a merry group of musicians. These shades seemed quite different from their moribund companions. They looked like perfectly ordinary Edwardian gentlemen, except that they glowed slightly, and Rachel could see through them. They laughed and chatted as they tuned their instruments, three violins, three cellos, a bass fiddle, and a piano. Rachel wondered idly how difficult it was to move a ghostly piano.

Near the door where Rachel stood was a group of specters who wore manacles or even long chains that they dragged with them. These chains made no noise, and yet Rachel heard them rattling in her head. Beside her, Gaius was singing under his breath: "*We're Marley and Marley. Whooooo. We're Marley and Marley. Whooooo.*"

When he noticed Rachel watching him, he said, "From the *Muppet Yule Carol.*"

"The what?" asked Rachel.

He tapped her on the nose affectionately. "Don't you watch classic Muppets?"

"Not on a regular basis. No," replied Rachel, with almost exactly the same mirth-suppressing tone of voice Gaius had used about *Giselle.*

The young woman in the homespun wedding gown glided toward Rachel. Her face was half-gone, her eyes lonely and sad. Rachel, ignoring the tremblings of trepidation in her limbs, approached the ghostly bride.

"Excuse me," Rachel asked softly, recalling the books she had read that afternoon about the entities that haunted the Hudson Valley, "are you Gertji?"

The young woman looked at her. "Yes! It is I! My beloved? Is that you? Have you come for me?"

"Um... no" Rachel said softly, "but I was...."

Gertji drifted toward Gaius. "My beloved? Is that you? Have you come for me?"

He shook his head, a bit unnerved. The young woman with her wedding gown and her ghoulish face drifted onward, approaching her fellow shades, endlessly repeating her question.

Gaius watched her go. Then he looked back and forth from pirate shades to Dutch ghosts to ghoulish brides. "Wish I had thought to invite William along. This might have been a great place for his people to test out their new project. Of course, having an O.I. rapid response team come rushing in here, testing their latest invention, might have rather spoiled the mood."

A dandy dressed in British garments from the period of the American War of Independence, lace and vest, tight pants and high boots, stood near the door to the ballroom. He had a sorrowful demeanor and a noose around his neck. A terrible cold accompanied him. Rachel and Gaius both began to shiver.

The ghost reached out and attempted to grab Gaius. "Why did they hang me and not Arnold? He was the traitor! I was innocent! Why did they hang me instead of Benedict Arnold?"

"I... c-can't h-help you." Gaius stepped back, his teeth chattering.

The ghost continued to drift closer, imploring. The chattering of Gaius's teeth grew louder, but he stood in front of Rachel, keeping the spirit from moving toward her.

"Wait. That's Major Andre. I know what to do," Rachel cried. "It was in the book."

She stepped around Gaius and looked the handsome yet haggard ghost in the eyes, asking loudly, "What party are you?"

The ghost's pleading fell silent. The cold dissipated. The figure of the forlorn British major vanished, leaving only the scent of peaches.

"Wow! That was... rather good," Gaius had stopped shivering, though he stomped in place, hugging his arms, in his attempt to regain his warmth.

"It was in the book," Rachel repeated. "*Legends and Lore of Sleepy Hollow and the Hudson Valley.* That was the phrase used to catch the major when he was traveling in disguise: '*What party are you?*'. I guess he remembers where things went wrong for him when he hears it. Still, it's very sad. He had been cajoled into going in disguise and had objected because he did not want to stoop to spying. But the British had killed an American spy, so the Americans executed him."

"And this happened almost two hundred and fifty years ago, and he hasn't moved on?" Gaius whistled. "Poor guy."

They approached several other of the less hideous denizens, but the shades either ignored them or, like Major Andre and Gertji, merely repeated the same few phrases continuously.

"I wonder if this is what Bedlam is like," murmured Gaius.

Rachel met his gaze and nodded wordlessly.

The music began playing again, this time with a music hall piece Rachel recognized called "I'm Shy, Mary Ellen, I'm Shy." It was a song her grandfather used to sing occasionally. He had told her it had been a favorite of a band leader friend of his who had died a tragic death. Rachel hummed along with the humorous tune.

With the return of the music, a change came over the spectral crowd. The old seamen lifted their heads; the white ladies raised a hand to their tear-strewn faces and looked about them; the floating girl swayed to the music, a peaceful look on her pale face, which had a blue cast from the flickering flames the color of burning brandy.

One of the sailors, a near-toothless old man with a long tangled beard, actually looked right at Rachel. He even gave her the kind of smile that a fatherly man might give a pretty child.

Rachel crossed to stand before him and curtsied. "Hallo. Who are you?"

"Old Thom," said the old sailor. "Sailed on *The Swallow*, carrying iron ore for the blast furnaces up river. Ship went down at World's End."

"World's End?" Gaius asked, intrigued.

Rachel pointed out the empty window and down the Hudson. "I read about that in the books, too. It's what they used to call that section of the Hudson just north of West Point, where the wind comes down off the Highlands, and the water is over two hundred feet deep. It's where the Heer of Dunderberg used to attack. Many ships were lost there."

The grizzled old sailor nodded. "You can still see a few of the wrecks at low tide. Not the ones that went down in World's End proper, mind you."

"Tide?" asked Gaius. "Isn't this a river?"

"Don't you know about the Hudson, boy?" The grizzly sailor scratched his immaterial beard. "The Hudson has a tide clear up to Albany. The natives that lived in these parts called it *Muhheakan-tuck*, The River That Runs Both Ways. They say if you toss a log on the waters up that way, it will take a year to reach Manhattan. Goes eight miles south each day and then seven-and-a-half miles north again."

"I had no idea." Gaius blinked. "Been here over three years."

"Where you from, boy?"

"Cornwall, England."

A grin split the old sailor's face. "From Cornwall, England, to Cornwall-on-Hudson, eh?"

"Yeah," Gaius nodded. To Rachel's puzzled look, he said, "That's the name of the town to our left, where Storm King Mountain is."

"Cornwall-on-Hudson? Really? So, is that where Roanoke is?"

"Oh, I think Roanoke's at Roanoke," Gaius replied. "We have our own post office."

The music changed again. The band launched into the "Blood Waltz". Ghosts and ghouls floated or shambled into the ballroom beyond.

"Nice band," said Rachel to the old sailor. She wanted to talk to him more, but she was not sure what to say. "Where do those musicians come from?"

The old sailor grinned his near-toothless grin. "They haunt a wreck in the Atlantic."

"Say, Mr. Thom," began Gaius.

"Just Old Thom."

"Old Thom... do you know any of the others here? Can you tell us who they are?"

"Sure I do! Been coming for years. Now, let's see...." He turned and examined his fellow spooks. "Most, as you probably know, are sailors whose ships went down in these here waters. The Hudson takes his toll, especially back when Old Dwerg was free."

"Dwerg?"

"The Storm Goblin." The old man glanced nervously at the tor, but it remained silent.

"That there Indian woman," he continued, pointing at the Lenape maiden. "She's a spirit from Raven Rock. So is the one made of leaves and wind. And the shrieking one is from Spook Rock. They all died lovelorn. Lost their sweeties, one way or another. You scared Major Andre away. Figure you already know who he is."

"And the floating girl?" asked Gaius curiously.

The old seaman shook his grizzled head. "Don't know 'em all."

"If you don't mind my asking," inquired Rachel, "how is it that you are here… and not gone on to wherever the rest of your crewmates went? What holds you here?"

"Well…." The old seaman looked sad. "When *The Swallow* went down, that left my Sally and the little 'uns all alone. So I thought, before I went on, I'd fly by and take a last look at 'em."

The old sailor paused, working his lips back and forth, a habit he might have developed before he lost most of his teeth. "When I got to the farm, there had been a fire. Whole place burned down. No sign of Sally. No sign of the little 'uns. I looked and looked, at Aunt Jane's, at her brother's place." A single pale tear slid down the ghost's face. "I couldn't find 'em."

Rachel crouched down in front of where the old sailor was sitting. "I'm so sorry, Old Thom. Do you…" she took a deep breath, "do you remember where the farm was? Your children's names? Your family name? Anything that might help?"

Tears streaming down his face, the ghostly sailor recounted what little his memory still retained. Rachel listened intently.

"That's all of it," he finished, wiping his face savagely. "Not that you'll remember."

"I will remember." Rachel rose to her feet and spoke seriously. "I remember everything."

The band reached the rousing end of the "Blood Waltz," with the thunder rolling off the tor providing the percussion. Gaius and Rachel stopped for a moment and listened. As the music stopped, the shades around them, including Old Thom, went back to their previous insular behavior from before the music had begun.

No amount of talking would rouse the old seaman.

"That is very kind of the band members to come so far," Rachel murmured. "From a wreck in the Atlantic. That's a long way. Most of the other entities here seem to be local."

Gaius looked back and forth between the ghoulish sailors with their barnacles and seaweed and the cheerful musicians bustling about on the dais in their top hats and bow ties, tuning their instruments and chatted. "Why are they so different from the others?"

Rachel glanced over at them. In the blue-violet light, the musicians hardly looked any different from her or Gaius. Had she not been able to see through them, she would not have known they were ghosts.

"I don't know." She grabbed his hand, pulling on it as she went. "Let's go find out."

CHAPTER TWENTY-FIVE:

THEY DIED AT THEIR POSTS

LIKE MEN

RACHEL AND GAIUS CROSSED THE FLOOR HAND-IN-HAND, DODGING hard-faced Dutchmen and hand-wringing ladies in white. The mansion smelled better inside, musty but not rotten. By the dais, where the band played, a fresh breeze blew with a hint of the sea upon it. Rachel breathed deeply as the two of them approached the nearest musician, a man in an Edwardian suit. He greeted them cheerfully, despite his enormous, evil-villain style mustache. He had a pleasant face, a receding hair-line, and he rested an elbow atop his cello.

"Hallo, what have we here?" He smiled at Rachel. "A wild *kit-sune* visiting from the East?"

Rachel, who had not thought about the fact that her face was still painted to look like a fox, giggled with delight. Gaius, who was standing beside her, looked from the ghost's tux to his patched robes and winced, as if he felt underdressed.

"Miss. Sir." The ghost bowed. "In life, I was Percy Cornelius Taylor. How do you do?"

"Hello, I am Rachel Griffin," Rachel curtsied politely, "and this is my boyfriend, Gaius Valiant. We are honored to hear you play. I hear that you come from a wreck in the Atlantic. Have you haunted a ship for a long time? What is it like?"

"Cold. And dark," replied Percy Cornelius Taylor cheerfully. "But it gives us plenty of opportunity to practice. Looking forward to the last of the passengers disembarking. You know how it is: people fret, worrying they left something behind. Or they're just not sure what awaits them at the new port. It's all bully, though. We'll keep playing till the last of them is comfortable enough to go."

"What kind of a ship is it?" Rachel asked. "Is your wreck in the midst of the barren depths all by yourself? Or are you near other sunken ships?"

"There are quite a number of vessels resting in our part of the Atlantic. Sadly, many of them still have passengers. Sometimes we go and play for the other ships, too. We are not held to a particular place, as they are. So we can travel more freely all year, not just on All Hallows' Eve and Walpurgisnacht. As for our ship, it is the greatest ship beneath the waves," Percy Cornelius Taylor twirled his handlebar mustache, "the *RMS Titanic*."

"The *Titanic*?" Rachel cried in surprise. "The *Titanic* itself?"

"That is quite amazing," murmured Gaius.

"A friend of my grandfather's died on the *Titanic*," Rachel murmured, stunned.

Gaius squeezed her hand. Then he addressed the ghost. "Wait, I've heard of you! You and your band played while the *Titanic* sank. You refused to go on the life boats, unless everyone else was saved first, and you kept playing to keep the crowds calm. There's a memorial to you in Southampton. I've seen it! The inscription reads: '*They died at their posts like men.*'"

"Does it now?" The ghostly gentleman looked humbled yet pleased.

"It does."

"That's quite flattering. And yet, truly, does it not describe most of those here?" Percy Cornelius Taylor spread his arms, indicating the gathering. "Are not the majority of those gathered tonight sailors who went down with their ships?"

"That brings us to the question we came to ask," said Gaius. "How come you and your companions are so different from the other ghosts?"

"I was not afraid of death." The ghost gestured at the other musicians. "Neither were my band mates. Because of this, we are not unwillingly trapped on this side. We can wander the world as we see fit. Most of the time, though, we stay with our ship and play for our fellow passengers who have not been as lucky. Who I was before is not very important. What is important is not to fear death. You don't want to end up like these poor fellows." He waved his hand toward the crowd of white ladies and ghoulish seamen.

"You gave your lives up willingly, sacrificing them for others?" Rachel's eyes shone with admiration. "How wonderfully brave. I hope someday that I can live up to your fine example." She slipped her hand into Gaius's and squeezed it. He squeezed back.

The ghost gazed at her kindly. "I hope that you will live a good full life and never be called upon to do so, Miss Griffin, but I thank you for your kind sentiments."

"You are welcome." Rachel glanced down shyly.

"You are brave young people, to come tonight. It has been many long years since living students have come to dance with us. Probably due to fear of *him*. Let's see, how long has it been?" The ghost tipped back his head. "I'd say not since Marigold Merryweather Moth's wedding, which was not long after our first engagement here."

"Living students used to come?" Rachel asked in surprise.

"That was the purpose of this assembly, originally. Those dead sailors still attend out of memory of the event they visited in life." He gestured toward the hard-looking Dutchmen Rachel had taken for pirates. "Once the living stopped coming, other ghosts and spooks in the area began to gather here as well."

"What was the original purpose of the Dead Men's Ball?" asked Gaius.

"You don't know?" The ghost's semi-transparent face registered surprised. Rachel could see a broken window behind him, and the lights of the distant Newburgh-Beacon Bridge twinkled through his head. "Then you must not know the story of how the once-floating island of Roanoke came to be moored in the Hudson."

Gaius looked chagrined. "We haven't gotten to that in True Hiss."

"You've been to Dutchman's Cove?" Percy Cornelius Taylor asked.

Gaius shook his head.

"Yes," Rachel said. "There's a cave with an ogre and a hulk of a man-o-war in the bay."

"And do you know the name that good ship bore when it sailed the seas, Rachel Griffin?"

Now, it was Rachel's turn to shake her head.

"Ah, child," Percy Cornelius Taylor's eyes sparkled, "that cove is the final resting place of the most famous ship to ever sail the Hudson. Some would call her the most famous ship to ever sail the Seven Seas."

"Even more famous than the *Titanic*?" asked Gaius.

"Even so," the ghost replied.

"The Storm Ship," Rachel breathed.

"The what?" asked Gaius.

Rachel said, "Diedrich Knickerbocker mentions it in *A History of New-York from the Beginning of the World to the End of the Dutch Dynasty*. He said that it finally found a safe port in the Hudson! He even said it was near Pollepel Island!"

Gaius looked her blankly. "Famous? I never heard of it." Then he added, "But I've heard of Diedrich Knickerbocker. His real name was Washington Irving."

"Perhaps you've heard of this ship by her real name, too," said the ghost. "She was called *The Flying Dutchman*."

"*The* Flying Dutchman?" cried Gaius. "The one whose captain is that squid guy?"

"Siggy said the same thing." Rachel gave him an odd look. "There was no squid."

Percy Cornelius Taylor said, "The ship of the cursed Captain Hendrick Vanderdecken."

"What happened?" asked Gaius. "How did it come to be here?"

"Well, as you know, Captain Vanderdecken was cursed that he could never come to port—unless a maiden proved true in love and waited for him for seven years. He was only able to touch dry land for one day out of every seven years. However, the power behind the curse did not consider Roanoke dry land—because it was a floating island."

"Oh!" breathed Rachel.

"Captain Vanderdecken would dock here for supplies. This ball, originally called the Dutchman's Ball, was held every year in his honor, in the hopes that he would meet a young woman and fall in love. So that the curse could be broken, and his crew could go home."

"What happened?" Rachel asked.

"He fell in love with a lovely young lady named Marigold Merryweather Moth. Merry-Merry Moth for short. When she was still waiting faithfully for him, seven years later, the curse broke. He was set free."

"Wow!" Rachel cried in wonder. "I know their granddaughter, Rowan Vanderdecken. She's in my class at school. And it happened right here?"

"Yes, indeed! But when the spell that made Vanderdecken's ship wander ended, by some quirk of fate, the spell that made Roanoke Island wander also ended."

"So that's why we're grounded here?" breathed Rachel.

"It is, indeed."

"And they kept holding the ball, even though the Dutchman himself no longer attended?" Gaius asked.

"The living members of his crew went home, but the dead members continued to return each year. They do not understand that they are free."

"Where do they go normally?" asked Rachel. "Do they haunt the hulk in the cove?"

"Occasionally. Mainly, they travel the seas, as if blown by the trade winds. Going where they went in life. It's a bit more interesting than hanging about an old wreck that no one visits, and it keeps them away from *him*."

"Him?" asked Gaius.

Percy Cornelius Taylor shuddered. "The Horseman."

"You mean the headless Hessian who rides around with a Jack-O'-Lantern?" asked Rachel. "He leads the Wild Hunt, right?"

"He does indeed." The ghost nodded seriously. "Every All Hallows' Eve, he rides up the river from Sleepy Hollow, arriving at midnight exactly. You lot had better be safely back behind the wards of your academy before he gets here."

"Why should we be afraid of the Wild Hunt?" asked Rachel. "Doesn't it just round up ghosts? Back home, the leader of the Hunt is Gwyn ap Nudd. He's a distant relative."

"The Hunt is different here than in back home in Mother England, child," the ghost said. "This Hunt rounds up mortals so foolish as to be out on All Hallows' Eve, and 'tis not kind to them. Oh, no siree!"

"Oh!" Rachel looked around nervously. She leaned toward Gaius. "What time is it?"

"So annoying not to have a cell phone," murmured Gaius. He tipped his head back slightly and spoke aloud. "Vlad, what time is it?" He paused and then gave her a reassuring smile. "It's only quarter after ten. Plenty of time."

Rachel gave her boyfriend an appreciative gaze and then turned back to Percy Cornelius Taylor. Gazing up at the ghostly gentleman, she asked hopefully, "Do you ghosts know anything about the afterworld?" She leaned forward and added almost at a whisper, "Or about angels?"

Percy Cornelius Taylor shook his head gravely. "I cannot speak to you of the other side. Only of those caught in between."

"What about demons? Do you know anything about what they are up to?" asked Rachel.

"About what?" The ghostly cello player cupped his ear and leaned forward. "I'm sorry. I don't know that word."

"I guess not." Rachel bit her lips. Then, she looked up again. "As to those caught in between, is there hope?"

"There is always hope, Miss Griffin."

"I feel so sorry for them." She gestured toward the ghostly entities haunting the mansion. "Is there anything I can do to help?"

"Most of those caught in between—that I know of—are trapped deep beneath the waves. You would not be able to reach them. And, frankly, little can be done for them now. They have been lost for so long, they don't even remember where they were headed. All you can do is hope they will eventually notice where they are and decide the time has come to move on."

Rachel nodded slowly but added, "If there is ever something, please don't hesitate to let me know."

Before he could reply, a mass of boys in robes, and two rather attractive young ladies in long, flowing ball gowns came plowing into the mansion. They threw salt and cast cantrips, shouting a bunch of different things. Many of the ghosts and ghouls scurried backward. Unfazed by the salt and sorcery, the young girl with the enormous black eyes and the long tendrils of hair, which spread out about her like kelp, floated towards them. She opened her mouth, revealing a mouthful of pointy, shark-like teeth.

Efrick Ferret shouted, "They're too powerful! Cheese it!"

They all went piling back out the gaping hole in the porch wall. A moment later, Winifred Powell popped back in. "Sorry about the disturbance. Have a nice Dead Men's Ball." She curtsied quickly, turned, and left.

Rachel blinked. "I hope they had fun doing that."

Then, she began to giggle. The difference between her world—worrying about the demon Morax summoning his master Moloch, or saying the wrong thing and killing her Elf—and their world—jumping a few innocent ghosts for excitement and finding them too terrifying—suddenly seemed terrifically funny.

"Third year in a row," mused Percy Cornelius Taylor. "I guess it's become a tradition."

"You think, after three years, they'd be better prepared," Gaius drawled, amused.

As she watched the vampire-hunting club flee down the hill toward the river, an idea struck Rachel, a splendid idea.

"Mr. Taylor," she asked shyly, "may I ask you a question that might be a bit... er... indelicate? I hope you will forgive me. I don't know much about ghostly etiquette."

"You may ask. We are not like these others."

"I have a friend who is very dear. He's my blood brother." She held up her arm and showed him her scar. Gaius looked on with interest. "He has done such kind and wonderful things for me, and I have done very little for him. He has his heart set on finding sunken treasure. Is there a ship somewhere you know of that has treasure on it? A ship where he could send his pet dragon to collect the treasure without troubling any ghosts?"

Percy Cornelius Taylor thought for a bit, absently strumming his cello. Gaius said nothing, but he listened intently.

"I know of a wreck that might suit," said the ghost. "It has a great deal of treasure, and the pirates who plundered it had no fear of death, so none remain. Access to those waters is blocked by ice at the moment. But the way will thaw in the spring. I could come find you when it's passable again."

"Sounds perfect!" Rachel clapped her hands.

"If I lead this... er... dragon to this ship, I shall require services in return. Five tasks which, honestly, should not be too much of a burden. Especially for one with the resources of the ship of which I speak. Do you agree?"

"I agree," Rachel replied, without hesitation. "Though I can only agree for myself. I suspect that Sigfried will agree with me, though. So, you will have the resources of both of us at your disposal."

She put out her hand to shake. The ghost accepted, and the two of them shook hands, though Rachel could not feel the insubstantial ghost. A pleasant tingle ran through her body.

"Oh...." Rachel moistened her lips. "I should mention... um... I'm not a person who is good at hurting people. If these favors involve harming someone, I don't know if I can do them. Otherwise, we're good."

Percy Cornelius Taylor replied gravely, "I would not ask you to harm anyone, young woman. I need two items returned to the families from which they came. I believe it will help two of my brethren to pass on. One is an engagement ring, and one is a necklace. They rest at the bottom of the sea. I will lead the—ahem, dragon—to them. I shall tell you the names of the people they should be delivered to. I know you will remember." He smiled at her and gave her two names with exact addresses, which he declared to be current residence of the ghosts' descendants. Rachel nodded, though she wondered how he knew about her perfect memory. Maybe he had heard her speaking to Old Thom.

"The second two favors require that money, from the treasure I will direct your friend to, to be given to two additional families." He gave her the addresses of these two families, one in Ireland, one in California.

"The last favor is: a violin was stolen from the London Philharmonic Orchestra. It once belonged to one of us, and we hate the idea that it isn't with its proper owner. We know who stole it, and his address. Could you please pass this information on to the authorities? The, um, Unwary authorities that is. The thief is not of the World of the Wise."

Rachel memorized the addresses and faithfully promised that the objects and the money would be delivered when the time came. She also promised to immediately write a letter to the Unwary authorities.

The other band members gathered around them now and bowed to Rachel. Their leader, a young man with brown hair and a pleasant smile spoke up.

"Lady Rachel, in life, I was Wallace Hartley," said the youthful ghost. "I knew your grandfather. I see his good character has been passed down to his children and his children's children. You do him proud."

"Thank you!" Rachel beamed. "He was a great man. I miss him very much."

Wallace Hartley smiled. "When the day comes that I see him again, I shall tell him."

"Wait? You knew Grandfather! Are you his friend who used to play 'I'm Shy, Mary Ellen, I'm Shy'? The one who died tragically!"

The band leader gave a bright smile. "That I am."

"He spoke of you," said Rachel. "I never realized you were the same friend who went down with the *Titanic*."

"We had some good times, Blaise and I, hunting phooka and brollachan on the moors, betting on horses at Ascot. Some mighty fine bangtails out of Gryphon Park! We went to sea together once and managed, between us, to defeat a kraken that had been terrorizing the shipping lines. Quite a big blighter it was, too!"

"Did you...." Rachel's voice faltered. "Did you know Myrddin and Vivian and his other children. The ones who were... lost?"

The band leader shook his head gravely. "I did not meet the general until a decade after that sad event. When I knew him, he was a grim man carrying a heavy burden. Though he labored to keep his personal sorrows from interfering with his performance of his duties. However, I have heard that, soon after I perished, a woman he had loved in his youth brought the sunshine of happiness back into his life."

Rachel blinked. It was hard to imagine her stern grandmother as the source of anyone's "sunshine of happiness." She turned to the whole band, curtsying.

"It is an honor to be able to help you," she said.

"On the contrary," Hartley spoke on their behalf. "Thank you for your help with our work. It has been a long time, and, sadly, shall be longer still. With the help of people such as yourself, I am confident we shall accomplish our goal."

The musicians clapped and bowed to her again, and then all but Percy Cornelius Taylor returned to their instruments.

"You and your band mates are extraordinary, Mr. Taylor. I'm very honored to be here," Rachel said as properly as she was able.

"Thank you for coming." He beamed. "We get very few visitors, besides that rowdy gaggle of youngsters. And now, my band mates are striking up. I must return to my cello." Percy Cornelius Taylor bowed.

With that, he rejoined the others. The band began playing again, launching into the Victorian era song, "Asleep in the Deep."

As Rachel turned around, she came face to face with a body she recognized from her trek into dreamland. As when she had seen it hanging from a noose, it was dressed in Transylvanian traditional garments: black pants, black embroidered vest, and the enormous, stiff pleated sleeves—as if the wearer had stuck his arms into starched, white accordions. Only this time, there was no black velvet bag covering the head.

Rachel looked up and gasped, shocked. She recognized the face of the transparent, shaggy-blond, Adonis who leered down at her.

Remus Starkadder.

All her trepidation, which had lifted while she was speaking with the musicians from the *Titanic*, came back with a vengeance. She took three panicky steps backwards.

"Gaius!" Rachel fairly shrieked.

Gaius spun around and then froze, going pale. The two young men regarded each other.

"Starkadder."

"Valiant."

What was he doing here? Had he come to seek revenge for her paralyzing him during the battle against Dr. Mordeau?

"What happened to you?" she cried. Frissons of terror traveled along her limbs. For the first time that evening, she felt truly frightened. "A-are you... dead?"

Rachel felt strangely disoriented. She clung to Gaius's arm.

The ghost grew even paler. "I was found guilty of treason for conspiring against my older brother. My father the King hanged my brother Fenris and me in Corvinus Square for all to see."

"And he made your brothers and sisters go home and watch?" Rachel whispered. She pressed her fingers against her mouth, hardly able to breathe from the horror of it. "Poor Freka!"

No wonder Freka had burst into tears, when Rachel had suggested that any sibling of the Transylvanian princess's must be a fine person. Rachel flushed with chagrin at the memory. And to think that she and Siggy and the princess had mocked Remus, when they had heard he was to be sent home to his father. They had assumed that any punishment assigned by a boy's own parent would be light.

How cruel the memory of that mockery now seemed.

"Yes... Freka. That is why I am here," Remus spoke urgently. He tried to grab Gaius's arm, but his hands bounced off the other young man's inside-out garments. Gaius shivered. "I must reach Freka, but I cannot pass the wards of the school. Please! Ask her to come to the docks to speak to me! I waited tonight, hoping, but she did not come."

When Gaius did not answer, Remus cried, "Please. It is urgent! I beg you."

"Urgent why?" Gaius asked. "Don't you have all the time in the world now?"

Remus shook his head. He looked terrified. "Fenris and I—we have been given a brief reprieve. But if Romulus does not forgive us, we will be tortured for all time! We will be dragged down to...."

Caw!

Remus looked around nervously. "I... can't say too much. But you must tell Freka. She must come to speak with me. Tell her that she must convince Romulus to forgive us!"

"I will," Rachel said solemnly, her initial terror fading.

She stared up at the dead young man. She recalled how she had felt when he had used black magic to torture the princes, how she had hated him with a cold, icy hatred. As she regarded him now, a frightened shade, the frozen lump inside her thawed.

A warmth flooded through her, a feeling of sorrow and pity.

Remus looked down at her. "You're the girl who defeated me. In the Summoning Vault."

Rachel gave a shake of her head. "Gaius defeated you. That was his spell. I just stood in the right place at the right time."

Gaius put his arm around her shoulder and pulled her close. He gave Remus a smile that looked suspiciously like bared teeth. "This is Rachel Griffin. My girlfriend."

The shade of the Transylvanian prince looked her up and down. Rachel found herself awkwardly aware of her inside-out clothing, her painted face, and her three, off-kilter pigtails. He shrugged. "Puny thing, but I suppose she's pretty enough."

"Where's Fenris?" Gaius looked around, but there was no sign of the chestnut-haired young man he had dueled the day Dr. Mordeau attacked. Rachel counted backward from the eldest Starkadder brother and realized that Fenris would have to have been Gaius's classmate, possibly in his core group, since they were both Thaumaturgy students living in Drake Hall. Gaius must have known the dead boy very well. They might even have been roommates.

Remus shook his head sadly. "He has reverted."

"Reverted?" asked Gaius.

"To our old form." Remus paused. "We Starkadders are not lycanthropes, you know. We are anthrolyks."

Rachel took a moment to parse this out. "You mean you are wolves who turn into men?"

"Exactly." Remus glanced around nervously. "I must go. I dare not leave Fenris alone for too long."

"Wait, before you go!" Rachel cried. "I have a question."

"Yes?"

Remus had grown fainter. Rachel could now clearly see the Willies and specters standing near the wall behind him.

"What does this mean?" Pulling a piece of paper and a pen from her inside out pockets, not an easy feat, she wrote: *Darius Northwest átment a hold tükrön, eltûnve mindörökre.*

He looked at her strangely. Rachel wondered if he was going to object to her having violated his castle. Or worse, blame her for Beaumont's demise.

"A rough translation might read: *Darius Northwest passed through this moon glass, never to return,*" he said. "And now I must go. Please. Remember. You promised! Tell Freka to come see me. Before it is too late!"

CHAPTER TWENTY-SIX:

THE SWAN WHO WOULD BE KING

STANDING ON THE RUINED PORCH AS THEY PREPARED TO CLIMB onto her steeplechaser to depart, Rachel smiled at Gaius, "That was rather amazing, wasn't it?"

"Rachel, I suddenly feel like, even with what I am doing, I am not doing enough," Gaius shook his head. "Those men have been dead for over a century, and they are still trying to help other people. I feel... humbled. Not that I was swelling with pride to begin with."

Rachel gazed at him adoringly. His reaction seemed much deeper than what she would have expected from a young man his age. She could not imagine Siggy or even her brother Peter responding in such a fashion. "I'm sure there's more you can do. We have a lot of resources between our groups. Maybe the first step should be to decide what help is most needed."

"If there is anything I can do to help you complete the five tasks, I would like to do it. As a matter of fact...." Gaius turned on his heel and walked back into the haunted mansion.

Watching him, Rachel made a decision. When the time came that Lucky retrieved the treasure from the ship, she was going give a small part of it to Gaius. Sigfried could have the lion's share, but Gaius would get a portion. She would not to mention it now, she decided.

She would keep it as a surprise.

Rachel ran after Gaius, catching up as he reached the dais where the musicians played. He stopped next to Percy Cornelius Taylor and looked up earnestly, his serious expression at odds with his blue war paint. "Sir, I would like to help you with what you are doing. I do not require treasure or payment. Please let me know what else you need."

Mr. Taylor said, "The five tasks I asked of Miss Griffin and her friend are the ones I have thought of for now. But given time, I can, I am certain, think of others. I will need to investigate and ponder. May I come and speak with you again?"

Gaius nodded. Rachel gazed at him, her eyes a glitter with admiration.

"Thank you, Mister Valiant," Percy Cornelius Taylor inclined his head in respect toward Gaius and then toward Rachel. "You and your young lady are both a credit to the living."

Picking up his bow, he returned to playing his cello.

The musicians struck the opening chords of a waltz. Ghostly couples gathered, taking their places on the floor. Rachel saw sailor ghosts pairing up with Wilis. The ghost of Major Andre had returned. He bowed before Gertji, in her homespun wedding gown. The two of them took their place, waiting for the dance to start.

Rachel slid her hand into Gaius's. "That was very noble of you. You can definitely help me with the five favors. I don't know how to write to Unwary authorities. Or how to turn treasure into money. And then there's searching for Old Thom's descendants. I could definitely use your help."

"I would be both happy and honored," replied Gaius. "Though for the last one, I recommend you ask Valerie's father. Didn't you save him from a fiery dragon-related death when he was a goose? I bet he'd be happy to help."

Suddenly, he pulled away and bowed before her. Rachel took a step backward, confused.

"May I have this dance, Miss Griffin?"

"Most certainly, Mr. Valiant." Rachel curtsied in delight.

She stepped forward and placed one hand in his and the other upon his shoulder. The two of them waltzed around the room to the glorious strains of "The Skater's Waltz." Twirling across the dance floor, Rachel felt a rush of gratitude to her grandparents for insisting she learn to waltz. She was by no means a great dancer, but she moved with a graceful swirl and did not embarrass herself by stepping on her partner's feet.

Gaius was not an accomplished dancer, but he was neither was he awkward. Ordinarily, it would have been the man's responsibility

to make sure that they did not bump into other couples, as it was the woman's to avoid treading on her partner's toes, but that was not much of a challenge here, since they were incapable of bumping into the ghostly dancers. Still, Gaius did see that they did not dance through any other couples, which might have been considered rude.

Rachel, her heart overflowing with love, gazed up at his face with its slightly-smeared stripes of blue war paint. What an amazing evening. She was certain she would not have felt nearly so confident had she come with someone else. Gaius was so supportive, so witty, so clever, and so compassionate, not to mention that there was a certain comfort, when surrounded by specters and ghouls, to being in the company of one of the Roanoke Academy's best duelists.

They circled the floor, swept away by the lilting music. The moment hung like a jewel amidst the traumas of Rachel's trouble-filled life. Doubly so due to the piece the musicians had chosen. "The Skater's Waltz" had long been Rachel's favorite. She could not hear its lively strains without recalling her mother sweetly humming it, as she taught Rachel to skate on the lake at Gryphon Park. The weather seldom grew cold enough to freeze lake water in Devon, but her mother had stood on the shore near the boat house and played her flute. Silver sparks had drifted across the lake, until the whole surface had frozen solid, and the gazebo on the small island had been coated with patterns of jagged frost. Hearing that melody still brought with it a promise of hope and cheer and hot chocolate.

As the piece came to its triumphant finale, punctuated by a peal of thunder from the tor, Gaius spun Rachel to a stop and dipped her over his arm. Rachel had practiced such dips many times with her dancing instructor, but that had not prepared her for the exhilaration of the real experience. She gasped as she arched backwards, suddenly off balance, and laughed giddily.

When at last he drew her upright, Gaius pulled her to him. She rested there, her cheek pressed against his chest.

"Gah! That's cold!" Gaius jumped. "Hey, who are you? What are you doing?"

Rachel glanced up. A young man dressed in dark, elegant clothing was tapping Gaius's shoulder, as if requesting to cut in and dance off with his partner. His fingers bounced off Gaius's clothing, but

Gaius shivered. The ghost drew his hand back in dismay, as if touching the inside-out garments had caused him pain.

It was a young man whom Rachel recognized.

"Myrddin!" Rachel cried in joy. Turning to Gaius, she declared, "This is my uncle. The one I told you about."

Gaius bowed graciously, making a sweeping gesture from the ghost to Rachel. "I would be a cad were I jealous of my girl's deceased uncle. Please. Be my guest."

The elegant opening strains of "The Blue Danube" spilled through the room. Rachel took her place across from the ghostly boy, waiting for the long introduction to end so that the dancing could begin. One hand hovered over Myrddin's immaterial shoulder. The other, she held near his hand. A faint scent of lavender accompanied the ghost, which was only proper for the shade of a young man who had been heir to immense lavender farms, the main crop grown at Gryphon Park propre.

The waltz began in earnest, and the partners began to dance. With slow, solemn grace, Rachel and Myrddin swept around the room. She stared up at him, smiling slightly. The ghostly boy gazed back at her, his face serious, but his pale eyes ablaze with gratitude.

They sailed about the floor together, in time with the other ghostly dancers. Myrddin could not touch her inside-out robes, so his hand hovered just behind her back. His other hand appeared to clasp hers, though all Rachel could feel was a coolness that soon made her fingers tingle uncomfortably. Still, she did not remove her hand. When the climatic finale arrived, the ghost could not dip her, but they spun rapidly together, ending with a bow on his part and a curtsey on hers.

Then, Thunderfrost's Boy was gone, and Rachel stood alone on the floor, her fingers tingling from the cold.

Looking around, Rachel's heart leapt into her throat. Over by the violet-blue hearth, Gaius stood surrounded by Wilis. The pale women with their flowing tresses leaned toward him, trying to touch his face and hair with their long insubstantial fingers. Rachel ran toward them, her heart hammering. The other side of the ballroom seemed unexpectedly far away. She felt as if she were trapped in one of those nightmares where she ran as fast as she could but never traveled anywhere. Terrified, she ran faster, but someone else arrived first.

The floating young girl in the strange garments, with the long flowing kelp-like hair descended upon the Wilis. They hissed at her like snakes, but they slowly backed away from Gaius. When they had departed, the young girl turned and ran a long blue-white finger along Gaius's cheek. He jerked back, clapping his hand to his face.

"C-cold!" he gasped.

Rachel arrived out of breath and leaned over, panting.

"Fear not, Gaius Valiant." The floating young girl-entity spoke with a high sweet voice, and yet there was something eerie, almost disturbing about it. "I shall not hurt you. Nor you, Rachel Griffin." She turned her head and fixed her all-black eyes on Rachel. "The two of you helped my mistress, when she was in distress. I am grateful and in your debt."

"W-who are you?" Gaius asked, startled. "And, more importantly, what are you? You're not a ghost. Your finger was solid. I could feel it."

"I am a fetch," replied the young girl. She gazed at them with her enormous eyes.

Rachel's mind raced backward, searching her memory for a time when she and Gaius rescued anyone who owned a fetch.

"Oh!" she cried suddenly. "You are the China doll, aren't you? The talking doll that belongs to Magdalene Chase!"

The fetch-maiden nodded.

Rachel thought of the pale little girl who was the only student at Roanoke smaller than she. She remembered coming upon the little porcelain doll attempting to drag her mistress to the infirmary, after Magdalene refused to yield to the geas that attempted to force her to hurt her classmates. Rachel and Gaius had found the two of them— the unconscious girl and her doll—and brought Magdalene to the Infirmary.

During the first week of school, Magdalene had come to meals sporting huge bruises. Her sister, who was actually her cousin, had been beating her. Dread had put a stop to that, at Rachel's request, but Rachel did not know if the doll knew that this, too, had been Rachel's doing.

"You were kind to my mistress," the fetch-maiden said to them both. Turning to Gaius, she added, "and you are trusted by the Swan King. I will look out for you. No Wili shall dance you into your grave."

"Swan King!" Rachel leaned forward. "You mean Vladimir Von Dread!"

"Wait. What's that?" Gaius looked back and forth between them intently.

"That's what the gypsies called Vlad in the princess's vision of his past. They called him the Swan King, and one of the knights called him the Beggar King."

"Vlad is rather interested in hearing about that vision. If you could convince your princess to speak with him, he would be very grateful," said Gaius. Turning to the floating fetch-maiden, he said, "Do you know something of Vlad's previous life? Or did you just call him that because the swan is the national symbol of the kingdom of Bavaria?"

"My mistress and I hail from Lohengrin, where the Swan King ruled. We were under his protection." She turned her overly- huge eyes to Rachel's face. "That is why his detractors called him the Beggar King. Because while he was ruthless to his enemies, he protected the weak and the downtrodden. No one molested widows or orphans in a territory ruled by the Dread King."

"He had three names?" Gaius looked confused.

The fetch-maiden nodded. "To his people, he was the Swan King. To his enemies, he was the Dread King. Only those who dared to mock him called him the Beggar King, though I believe it was a moniker that he wore with pride."

Gaius blinked.

The fetch-maiden shrugged. "He had many more enemies than friends. History remembers him as the Dread King."

"That does fit him," murmured Gaius.

"Why did he have so many enemies?" asked Rachel.

"He was a conqueror and a slayer of all who opposed him. Once he had conquered a land, he set up great statues. Using the same secret art that allows me to look through the eyes of the porcelain doll, he watched his subjects from those statues. If he spied any mistreating a widow, or a child, or a poor man, or a gypsy, they died a screaming, horrendous death."

"That... sounds like Vlad, too," Gaius said. "Well, except for the screaming, horrendous death part. He's very insistent about us protecting those less able than ourselves."

"How many lands did he conquer?" asked Rachel.

"By the time the Four Horsemen rode abroad, he was the master of sixty-five worlds."

"Sixty-five *worlds*?" choked Gaius.

"There are sixty-five worlds!" cried Rachel.

A look of sorrow came over the fetch-maiden's pale bluish features. "Not anymore. Once there were millions of worlds, billions. As many as there are stars in the night sky. But most of them were lost. Only fifty remain."

"Oh my," whispered Rachel.

"That's... really upsetting," muttered Gaius. "So. Beggar King. Dread King. Swan King, eh. Does it say something about my boss that, of those three, Swan King is the hardest to swallow?"

"He does have a cloak of black swan feathers," said Rachel.

"How'd you know that?" asked Gaius, surprised.

"He had it in the past, too," said Rachel, not adding that she had seen it in Von Dread's closet the time she visited his bedroom. "It was in the princess's vision."

"He wore it in the old days," said the fetch-girl, "before his death."

"He... died?" asked Gaius.

"Died. Or was spirited away moments before his demise, as happened to many—including my mistress."

"How?" Gaius asked.

"After the World Tree fell, the Arcana could not agree on how to defeat the Four Horsemen..." the fetch-maiden began.

"The *World Tree* fell?" Gaius gasped.

"I saw that," whispered Rachel, recalling the great white wolf and the corpse of the deer beside the huge, broken trunk in the dreamland of Transylvania, "... or a dream version of it."

The fetch-maiden said, "I do not know what dire enemy felled the World Tree. Perhaps, it was the Svartalfar, who had been gnawing on it since the dawn of the sidereal universe. Perhaps their dread mother took revenge for the death of her son, Delling. Perhaps, it was some more dire and yet unknown enemy, I know not.

"But as I said, the Arcana were divided. The Dread King and six others chose to act, without waiting for the proper concord. Their act shattered Saturn's Table. All seven died—or were thought dead —but their efforts succeeded. The Horsemen were vanquished. The few worlds that remained did not perish."

"I wonder if I was involved with that," muttered Gaius.

"Oh! You are that Gaius Valiant!" The fetch-maiden began to giggle like a little girl. "The Destroyer of Star Yard. The Doom of the Galactic Confederacy!"

"You've heard of me," he said darkly.

"You are famous. Or infamous."

"Was I..." his voice wobbled between hope and dread, "... an evil conqueror, too?"

She threw back her head and laughed, a shrill girlish laughter, giving them a glimpse of her shark-like teeth. "No, you were an over-confident fool who made a single deadly mistake."

"Great." Gaius grumbled morosely. "Not an evil super villain. Just a galactic-empire-destroying buffoon."

Rachel lay her hand on Gaius's upper arm, hoping to comfort him. He ran his hand across his face, smearing his war paint, and tried to smile at her.

"Were the Starkadders from your world, too?" Rachel asked curiously, hoping that a change of subject would give Gaius an opportunity to recover.

"No," the fetch-maiden looked disdainful. "The get of Geri hail from Toverwald."

Rachel's brow furrowed. "Geri, as in 'Freki and Geri'? Odin's wolves?"

"The same." The fetch-maiden turned to Gaius, who was still looking troubled. "Fear not. Perhaps, you are like my mistress. She is far different now than once she was."

"Was she a gypsy?" asked Rachel.

"No, a lamia."

Rachel made a noise in her throat, aghast. "There are *good* lamia?"

"No. None. My mistress was evil, far more evil than young Master Valiant, here. More evil than the Dread King, for he had noble goals to excuse his butchery. My mistress lived in the swamps with the other lamia and preyed on children. She ate babes and sucked the marrow from their bones. I was her fetch."

"Is she evil now and hiding it?" asked Gaius sharply.

"No." The little fetch-maiden's face was suffused with joy. "Now, she is good! Her heart has grown large. And I can be good, too. I have been promised... but I may not speak of that."

"What changed her?" asked Gaius.

"It was the m—"

Caw!

"I dare not say." The fetch-maiden ducked her head. "Or the One Who Comes on Wings of Darkness will steal away my recollection of things that once were."

"You mean the Raven?" Rachel gazed out the window into the night, but the eerie dancing blue-violet flames did not illuminate any black birds, not even when she thought back.

"Of *that one*, I shall not speak." The fetch-maiden shivered.

Gaius asked, "Will you answer questions for Vlad, if he comes to speak to you?"

But the fetch-maiden was staring out the window toward the place from which had come the raven's cry. Winds were rising, moaning as they blew through the broken house. Peal after peal of thunder rolled down from the tor, shaking the few remaining panes of glass.

"I have stayed too long. I must away," and she fled.

"Well, that was...." Gaius cocked his head, as if listening. "What's that, William? ... Yes, I'm still out. Oh!" He turned to Rachel, his eyes wide with alarm. "It's 11:52!"

Grabbing each other's hands, Rachel and Gaius raced for the door and her broom.

Chapter Twenty-Seven:

Wild Hunted

Rachel and Gaius raced southward, flying along the shore of Roanoke Island toward the docks. It would have been faster to fly directly to Roanoke Hall, but Rachel dared not fly over the school's wards, lest her steeplechaser fail.

Storm winds blew violently up from the south. Trees swayed back and forth like frenzied temple dancers. The remaining autumn leaves were ripped from their branches and sent swirling up in great spirals. There was no rain yet, but powerful gusts buffeted the broom, knocking the riders this way and that.

Twice, they were tossed into a loop, flipping end over end. Each time, Rachel rapidly maneuvered the levers to bring them upright again. She had flown through blustery winds, but nothing like this. The air was swirling, gusts coming from unexpected directions. If she hit the airflow incorrectly, it struck the blades of the tail fan sideways, collapsing them or altering their arrangement. This set the entire device spinning, something Rachel had never experienced before. These conditions would have been much easier to negotiate had she been on her stomach, with her feet directly controlling the tail fan. With Gaius behind her, that was impossible.

These were the most difficult flying conditions Rachel had ever encountered. She loved it. She ploughed into the gusting winds, shrieking with sheer exhilaration.

It was not until she began to have trouble breathing that she realized that her boyfriend was clinging to her with all his strength. Glancing over her shoulder, she saw that his face was as pale as the shifts of the white ladies they had left behind at the mansion. His expression was stoic, but his body, pressed against hers, was trembling.

Oh.

Oops.

Rachel reached over and jiggled the levers. The air around the steeplechaser became calm and quiet. She righted the device and flew slowly and evenly.

"What just happened?" Gaius croaked hoarsely.

"I turned on the becalming enchantments."

"What? Magical air stabilizers?"

"Enchantments to make the air still around us. All high-quality bristlelesses have them."

"Why did they take so long to come on?"

Rachel bit her lip. "I... only just turned them on."

"You forgot you had them?"

"Not at all."

"Then why...."

"You seemed a bit discomforted by the flying conditions."

"You turned them on... for me?"

"Yes," she finally admitted.

"But you were screaming in fear."

"What?" Rachel's voice rose, sounding very English. "Certainly not! That was joy."

"Oh." Gaius cleared his throat. "That's embarrassing. I'd hate for my girlfriend to come to the conclusion that I'm a big coward."

"Not to worry," Rachel replied primly. "I understand that someone who does not fly might have a hard time distinguishing between what's dangerous and what's... oh, my!"

Ahead, a storm front rushed upriver on a collision course with the two students. Lightning arced beneath the enormous thunderheads, illuminating torrents of driving rain. In the glow of the electric brightness, Rachel thought she could make out grimacing, howling faces in the dark gray clouds.

"Um," Gaius swallowed, "I gather that's dangerous."

Rachel was too busy gauging speeds and calculating distances to answer right away. Finally, she said abstractedly, "I think I can make it to the docks."

Leaning forward, she coaxed the broom to greater speed. To her dismay, its response was sluggish, not at all what she was expecting.

Terror gripped her chest, choking her. Was something wrong with her beloved Vroomie? It had never....

Ooohhh.

"Gaius," she called, "the becalming enchantments are producing drag. I have to turn them off."

"Do what you must," he replied gamely. "I promise not to embarrass you."

With a brisk nod, Rachel released the becalming enchantments. The violent gale winds struck them, flipping them end over end. Driving rain hit them in bursts. Rachel could feel it washing make-up from her face. She gripped the handlebars with extreme determination, fighting to steady the device.

"Hold on!" she shouted.

Gaius's arms held her firmly around her waist, but not so tightly as to interfere with her breathing. He had his wand in his hand, the back sticking up his sleeve, so as to be certain that he did not lose it. In the brief glimpse she had of him as they flipped head over heels, he was keeping watch intently, his face determined, if a bit green.

Rachel righted Vroomie and zoomed forward, driving against the winds. She urged the steeplechaser to greater and greater speeds, but it was like pushing through rushing water. Half of the time she went backward more than forward. She felt like one of those logs Old Thom had mentioned, the ones that tried to make it from Albany to New York by floating down the River That Runs Both Ways.

"I don't think we can make it before the storm reaches us!" she yelled over the winds.

"We'll have to land!" Gaius shouted back. "What about the walled orchard? Where we saw Romanov and his friends?"

Rachel gauged the distance, adjusting for the winds. "I think we can make it!"

She pressed forward. The wind resistance grew stronger. She pushed the broom, bringing it to even higher speeds. Never before had she reached the steeplechaser's top speed, but perhaps she was nearing it now because the bristleless began to tremble. Rachel pressed hard.

The steeplechaser stalled.

Down plummeted Rachel, Gaius, and all. Rachel screamed.

"Should I panic now?" her boyfriend called calmly in her ear, his wand in his hand.

"Yes. Definitely panic," she shouted back, but his calmness stiffened her resolve. She had deliberately stalled her broom out many times and then engaged it again. Unless she had actually damaged it somehow, this time should be no different. She urged the broom forward.

Nothing happened.

Refusing to squander her time on fear, Rachel stayed focused. From the library of her mind, she withdrew all at once every reference to "broom" and "stall" she had previously encountered, searching for something that might help. Immediately, a possible cause leapt out: *jammed tail fan*. She glanced back but could not see around her boyfriend.

"Gaius," she shouted, "kick the tail blades for me."

"What?" he yelled back over the roaring winds.

"The tail blades."

"What?"

"Tail fan! Move the blades toward each other." She tried to pantomime what she meant with one hand.

"Like this." He pointed his wand behind him.

The steeplechaser caught and shot upward. They cheered. Then their voices died in their throats.

The Horseman bore down on them. He galloped in the midst of the thunderhead, gale-force winds whipping the night around him. He rode on a black charger, a headless man in a Hessian uniform and a billowing mantle. Under his arm, he carried a Jack-O'-Lantern. Light flickered from the sharply triangular eyes and leering, angry mouth. It was not a cheery candle flame, however, but the blue-violet glow that had illuminated the ballroom of the dead. In its light, the storm clouds seemed to be filled with phantoms and specters, all circling the Horseman like hurricane winds around the eye of the storm.

The spooks were not the only things accompanying the headless rider. A pack of blind, eyeless hounds, as pale as corpses except for their blood red ears, loped through the night air. Their baying cries echoed up and down the Hudson Valley.

The Wild Hunt approached.

"Go down!" Gaius screamed.

Rachel tried to dive, but the winds buffeted them backwards, spinning them first left and then right. Without direct control over the fan blades, she had to gauge how far their spin would take them and compensate with the levers, which often led to overcompensation and sent them spinning in the opposite direction.

The Horseman and his Hunt grew ever closer. The hoof beats of his horse smote the air like thunderclaps. The headless body raised its false head on high. The eyes of his Jack-O'-Lantern flamed with malice.

They were not going to make it.

"I love you, Gaius," Rachel shouted out as her last words, but the wind tore the syllables from her lips before they reached his ears.

Caw!

Silence fell.

The winds grew still.

The spinning steeplechaser slowed, coming to a stop in mid-air with Vroomie facing the other way, northward up the river. Enormous feathered wings of black stretched out before them. To either side of the wings, the winds raged and whirled. Between the thirty-foot wingspan, however, all was calm and motionless. At the center of the two arching wings, a eight-foot-tall man stood in mid-air. He was shirtless with black pants and bare feet. His face was as calm and solemn, as an ageless mountain range. His eyes were red as blood. In his hand, he held a hoop of gold.

Behind them, the Horseman thundered closer. The eyes in the Jack-O'-Lantern glared with wrath. The winged figure gazed back, his wings curved ever so slightly around the little oasis of calm.

Then the hounds parted, and the Hunt thundered to either side, leaving the tiny island of tranquility untouched. The Horseman veered to the left. He passed so close to them that Rachel swore she could feel the breath of his enormous coal-black steed. The Wild Hunt raced onward, upriver toward Bannerman's mansion, with the Horseman cantering behind them.

Rachel watched them go. Then she looked back at the winged figure. His eyes were gray now. Steady and serene, they rested upon her face. He nodded once.

Rachel nodded back, smiling very slightly.

His eyes returned to scarlet. He cupped his great wings with their huge black pinions. As if pulled by a string, he suddenly moved upward and away, dwindling and transforming as he sped backwards, until he was but a black speck of a bird that flew untroubled by the raging storm.

The driving rain and sleet struck Rachel and Gaius, soaking their hair and garments. Rachel ducked her head, to protect her eyes, and pressed forward. Two tendrils of icy-cold wetness slipped around her collar and ran down the back of her neck, causing her whole body to twitch. Shivering in the October cold, she dived.

"What, in the name of everything that is sacred, was that?" Gaius's voice sounded uncharacteristically high.

Rachel called back, "That was the Raven."

"You mean *that* was the thing I promised to protect you against? Good grief!" There was a pause, then, grimly, "I'll do my best."

Warmed by his devotion, Rachel seized control of the broom once more and dived down, until they reached the safety of the walled orchard. Dismounting on shaky legs, they huddled together on the leeward side of the wall. Gaius wrapped his arms around her and stood over her, doing his best to protect her from the brunt of the icy storm.

"I must say," Gaius said, when they had stopped trembling quite so violently, "I'm not sure I am going to have to. Protect you, that is. I had the distinct impression that this Raven likes you. He did just save our lives."

"I like him, too," whispered Rachel, whose heart was too full to yet speak of it.

"Wait. What happened to evil Doom of Worlds and all that?"

"Remember the thing I can only tell one person?"

"Yes! I've been thinking about that! Just haven't had a chance to ask you about it."

"It's too long to tell now." Her teeth were chattering violently.

"Tomorrow, then." He pulled her more tightly against him, trying futilely to protect her from the elements. She leaned on him and took comfort in the warmth of his strong arms.

"Definitely!" she replied firmly.

They huddled together in the cold and wet until the winds died down. Then, they hopped aboard the steeplechaser and quickly flew back to campus.

Rachel forced her near-frozen jaws to move. "I'll drop you off at Drake."

"You certainly will not!"

"I beg your pardon?"

"No girlfriend of mine is going to have to go home alone on All Hallows' Eve. Even an amazing, super-brave girlfriend. You fly to Dare. I'll walk from there."

Despite the bitter cold and wetness of the night, a warm, buoyant feeling rose inside Rachel. She flew to her dorm and landed. Climbing from the steeplechaser again, Gaius gave her another hug. Then, he took a step back.

"Thank you, Miss Griffin," he stated, "for a most entertaining night."

Leaning forward, he gave her the sweetest of goodnight kisses.

• • •

When she reached her room, she took a long hot shower, to drive away the bone-deep chill, and then curled up under her quilts. Outside, the storm winds raged and howled. The chimes that hung from the eaves and nearby trees shook violently. Bell-like notes rang out like fairy horns amidst the cacophony.

Lying in bed, Rachel reviewed the entire evening. To her chagrin, she discovered that there were nearly twice as many denizens of Bannerman's mansion in her memory as she had seen with her eye. She felt like kicking herself for not having taken the time to examine her memory while she was there.

She thought about all the things that had happened in one evening: her decision to be the one who told Valerie about the Elf; the exploding chestnut; the trip with Gaius to the Dead Men's Ball; meeting Gertji, Major Andre, Old Thom, Percy Cornelius Taylor and his band mates, including her grandfather's friend Wallace Hartley; and dancing with Myrddin. She felt especially clever about having found a potential treasure for Sigfried. Oh, and she finally had a translation of the Beaumont plaque from Remus Starkadder!—she made a mental note to speak with Freka the next day. She contemplated the strange things they had learned about Gaius and Von Dread from the fetch-maiden. How brave and dear Gaius had been! Finally, she recalled their wild race home.

She lay for a time half-asleep. In her head, the shades from the Dead Men's Ball danced among the great trees of the Elf's homeland. As she drifted off to sleep, she wondered idly if the fetch-maiden could leave the porcelain doll any time, or whether the girl was bound into it, and could only depart on a night when the dead were free to wander the earth. And if the fetch-maiden was bound, was it by a spell similar to the one that had restrained Azrael? Was her possession of the doll similar to Azrael's possession of the hapless Mortimer Egg and Morax's of the purple-robed man whom the demon had entered? And if similar, could all such entities possess bodies in a similar fashion?

Even the Raven?

That night, she dreamed she stood upon a roof with Sigfried and some others. She did not have her broom. Across the commons, an enemy dropped one of her friends from a great height. Terrified for the falling one, Rachel leapt from the roof, shouting:

"Jariel!"

Caw!

In the dream, the Raven dived out of the sky and into her body. Black wings sprouted from her shoulders, and her eyes turned red as blood. The two of them, acting as one, swooped forward, rescued the falling friend, and defeated the enemy.

It was the most wonderful dream she had ever dreamt.

Chapter Twenty-Eight:

Though the World May Burn

"Eeevil! I told you he was evil!" Salome arched her back into a bridge atop a table in the Storm King Café and raised one leg, pointing her toe toward the ceiling. Her skirt slipped down revealing her black-tights-clad thigh. She pursed her deep red lips. "Vladimir Von Dread is sooo evil! Not that I object to him anymore, mind you. He's actually kind of cool, not to mention brain-stunningly gorgeous, but... conqueror of sixty-five worlds! Totally eeeeevil!"

Siggy's eyes grew huge, fixed on the shapeliness of her inner thigh. A happy dreamy look came over his face. Then, yanking his gaze away, he grabbed a fork off the table and stuck it into his own thigh until he grunted with discomfort.

"Um, Miss Iscariot," Siggy raised his palm to form blinders, blocking his view of the young lady. "I don't mean to sound critical, but this may not be the best place for a display of modern dance. Right, Lucky?"

"I don't know," Lucky cocked his head to one side and then the other, "maybe it's a mating dance. You should bite her on the back of her neck and drag her off to the harem cave. Do you have the hot volcanic sands ready for the eggs?"

"Lucky," Sigfried replied sternly, "I have explained to you about no harems." He leaned over and put his arm around Valerie, who rolled her eyes. "Miss Iscariot may be eye-burningly attractive, but I am a one-woman man."

"I am with Mr. Smith, Miss Iscariot. Perhaps this is not the best venue to appear so unclad," murmured the princess, who sat at the same table as Siggy, sipping her tea. Her Tasmanian tiger sat regally beside her.

"Oh you people. You're such prudes." Salome flipped her legs over her head and landed lightly on her feet on the floor. She spread her arms. "Ta-da!"

She adjusted her skirt with lackadaisical slowness. The older boys at the far table were not as chivalrous as Sigfried and watched the whole thing with prurient interest. She turned and gave them a languid, smoky glance over her shoulder.

"Does your boyfriend mind you doing that?" Rachel asked, thinking with pleasure of the moment, during the Knight's dueling period, when she had bested the handsome and arrogant Ethan Warhol.

Rachel was sitting beside the princess drinking an egg cream. Sigfried was next to her, eating three separate banana splits at once. He had needed to buy three in order to be able to taste every flavor the café carried. Lucky stood next to him. His four legs, the bottoms of which were scaled, were fully extended. He was loyally helping his master eat the ice cream feast. Beside Lucky sat Valerie and Joy. Zoë sat at another table, her feet stretched across two chairs, reading the latest issue of the comic book, *James Darling, Agent*.

On the table in front of Valerie lay the information Old Thom had given Rachel. Valerie had agreed to send it to her father to see if he could find any surviving members of the old sailor's family. Rachel had given the information about the stolen violin to Gaius, since he had so clearly wanted a chance to help. He figured between Vlad and William, he would be able to take care of contacting the Unwary authorities.

"What can he do about it?" Salome shrugged her shoulders in a fashion pleasing to the upperclassman boys. "If he wants the gorgeous lusciousness that is me," she made a cute, cheerful gesture, ending with both her hands—and her now flaming pink and fire-truck red nails—pointing at her face, "my entourage of lust-maddened boy-toys is part of the package."

"Miss Griffin, please do not encourage her." Nastasia sat primly, her napkin tucked into her collar. "As to your trip last night to the Dead Men's Ball, it was ill done to leave campus, after we promised the assistant dean that we would not. I must admit, however, that the information you gathered is quite interesting."

"I didn't leave school grounds," Rachel replied, resisting the urge to smirk. "Bannerman's mansion belongs to the school."

Nastasia started to object, but, thankfully, Joy talked over her.

"I can't believe you went to where ghosts were *on purpose!*" Joy squealed. "My sister Hope sees ghosts occasionally. The rest of us are terrified. We don't even want to stay in the same room with her on All Hallows' Eve and Walpurgisnacht. She went to light candles last night for our deceased great, great aunt. Faith went with her." Joy pointed at the spirited dark-haired girl with a mischievous smile working behind the café counter. The young woman was dressed in a smart, blue sailor dress and a white paper hat with blue trim. Faith, who was polishing the bar, waved back at her little sister.

"Faith went with her," Joy continued, "but the rest of us stayed far, far away."

"Ha, O'Keefe!" Sigfried declared. "You can no longer make me feel inadequate because you have sixteen hundred sisters, and I have none. Now I have a sister, too! See!"

He drew back his sleeve and pointed at the faintest of scars on his wrist. Rachel pulled back her sleeve, too, and pointed at her slight but more substantial scar.

"Blood brothers!" Rachel declared with delight.

"Blood sister and brother," Sigfried corrected.

"Ew!" Valerie shivered. "That is sooo unsanitary. I feel ill just thinking about it." But that did not keep her from grabbing her camera and snapping a picture of their displayed wrists.

"This from a girl who lets her dog lick her face," murmured Zoë.

Valerie ignored her. "If you like, I can announce your new family relations in the *Roanoke Glass.*"

"Do that!" Sigfried commanded. "Say: Sigfried Smith and his brother Lucky acquire a new sister-accomplice!"

That made Rachel giggle. She smiled at everyone and then glanced at her drink, using the moment to recall her friends' expressions as Sigfried announced their new relationship. If the princess was upset about not having been included in the blood brother ceremony, it did not show on her face.

Rachel breathed a sigh of relief. That was one concern out of the way.

Time to confront another one.

"Um, Nastasia," she said casually, "now that Von Dread knows as much as he does, from the fetch-maiden, would it be okay if I told my boyfriend about your vision about Dread?"

Nastasia sipped her tea and considered the question. Finally, she nodded. "It would be unbecoming of me to object at this juncture. I did not wish that reprobate to profit by his offense against me. But under the circumstances, further objections on my part would seem churlish. You have my permission."

"Thank you." Rachel smiled lightly, as if the matter were of little consequence. Inside, her heart was singing. She could not wait to tell Gaius and Vladimir about the princess's vision.

"About the vision, Rachel, there is one other thing..." Nastasia said. "When the Horseman of Death read my mind, he was very surprised that Von Dread was still alive. He thought that he and the other Horsemen had killed Dread. It was not a happy surprise to him."

Rachel nodded. She glanced down at the letter that had arrived for her that morning. Salome and Nastasia's opinions of Dread were in stark contrast to Sandra's. Unfolding the letter from Sandra, she read it a second time.

Dear Rachel,

First, I passed on to Father your concerns about your little friend. Father has had Juma and his elephant moved to a safer location.

Now, to your questions: Vladimir is not an evil man. Nor will he ever be. He is driven and will do whatever is necessary to protect the world and those he cares about. If he pushed your friend through a door, I am sure he knew what he was doing. He would never endanger someone recklessly.

As to marrying him... I am not sure Father would approve. The kingdom of Bavaria is a dictatorship. Father does not believe in that sort of government. He also thinks that Bavaria is conducting certain... operations...

which are highly unethical. I am not sure if it is true or not. If it is, I am sure Vlad has nothing to do with it.

Anyway, my little sister does not need to play match-maker for me. I spoke with Gaius, and he has apologized for not asking my permission to court you. I accepted his apology on the condition that he protect you. I think he will. You have done well for yourself catching his eye.

As to Peter, I think he is trying to give you your space right now. He's not used to the new Rachel. He still thinks of you as a seven-year-old. He will adjust. Eventually. If you need anything, just ask him. He will be there for you.

If you want me let me know. I am but a travel mirror away. I can come see you within the hour. Or, if things become too overwhelming, you can come stay here with me for a few days.

All my love,

Sandra

Rachel folded the letter thoughtfully. She was glad that Sandra approved of Gaius and that Father had moved Juma, but her sister's comments about Vladimir worried her slightly. Rachel liked the prince a great deal, but she had no illusions that he had touched Nastasia for some altruistic reason. Or that it had not been dangerous. Nor was she so convinced that Vlad would avoid participating in projects undertaken by his father sheerly due to ethical concerns.

The difference between her and Sandra was that it did not bother Rachel that Vlad was not entirely scrupulous. She did not approve, but she also understood why he might act as he did. Grandfather had been like that, too.

Across from her, Joy leaned forward conspiratorially. "I can't believe my sister Faith is dating Drew Colt—you know, the older brother of that boy who's in the vampire-hunting club? If she's even dating him! Charity said she caught them kissing at the bonfire—though Faith says that they were just talking. That would be her seventh boyfriend since she came to school. Seventh! Well... according to Charity and Mercy. Faith says it's only been two."

Joy chatted on, and the talk turned to events from the night before that Rachel had missed. She listened for a time, but the longer the others talked, the more difficult she found it to pay attention. Part of it was that she was still tired from the lateness of the previous night. Another part, however, was that after the things she had seen the night before, her friends' interests seemed frivolous and unimportant.

She had slept quite late this morning. There were no classes on Samhain, and attendance at the religious ceremonies down in the Memorial Gardens was not required, so there had not been anything for which she had to rise. Having missed breakfast, she had gathered with the others at the charming soda fountain in the basement of Roanoke Hall to get something to eat. But now, as the others droned on, laughing and teasing one another, she began to wish she had stayed in bed longer.

She had tried to convince Nastasia that since today was a holiday, it would be an ideal day to bring the Elf home. Now that they had spoken of her secrets, Rachel was beginning to feel uneasy on the elf woman's behalf. But the princess had insisted that even though there were no classes on Samhain, they were still not allowed to leave school grounds. So she refused.

Rachel's eyes traveled to the mural on the wall. The storm goblin, the Heer of Dunderberg, stood with arms akimbo atop Storm King Mountain. He was an odd sight in his Dutch garments: orange and green doublet and hose and his pure white sugar-loaf hat. To either side of him, lightning imps leapt with their javelin-bolts sizzling, and mist sprites eagerly reached down with their long foggy fingers. Below in the river were famous wrecks, sunk by the Heer's fury, their crews crying out as they drowned. Only the *Flying Dutchman* remained untouched as it flew above the river's waters.

Rachel had seen this mural before, but it meant much more to her now. She had seen many of these drowned sailors with her own eyes. She felt so sorry for the ghosts who were trapped in this world, unable to go on to their proper resting places. Even worse was the plight of Remus Starkadder, who was in danger of being dragged to somewhere horrible—possibly a place of punishment, considering the bad things he had done during his brief life.

Rachel had been looking forward to finding Freka this morning and apologizing for having upset the other young woman during
their talk at the Knights, but she had been woken by Gaius calling
her on her card to let her know that he had run into Freka and had
passed on Remus's message. So, to her dismay, she had been relieved of that duty. She hoped that Freka would be able to help her
brother. His crimes were bad, true, but Rachel was not certain that
they were bad enough to warrant being punished for all eternity.

Was anything bad enough to warrant eternal punishment?

As she gazed at the painted faces of the drowning sailors and
wondered if there might be anything she could do for the poor
souls she had met the previous night, the candle display next to
the candy case caught Rachel's eye. She glanced at the placards beneath the pretty colored candles: almond-scented for hope, fennel
for strength, olive for peace, frankincense for honoring the dead.

Rising, Rachel bought four frankincense candles. Taking leave
of her friends, she walked across campus toward the Memorial
Gardens, shivering in the early November cold. The fallen leaves
swooshed and crunched beneath her feet. Above, the sky was filled
with billowing clouds, some white, some gray, with tiny glimpses of
blue peeking through.

The morning ceremony was over, and the afternoon ceremony
would not begin for several hours. Currently, the gardens seemed to
be empty. Rachel walked past the fire ring where last night's bonfire
had been held. The scent of burnt wood still lingered in the air,
but everything looked quite different by day. The large trees had all
lost their leaves in the previous night's storm, but smaller fruit trees
still held theirs. Some had turned a candleglow gold and resembled
brilliant flames. Others had become a dark burgundy, so deep as to
be almost purple. Amidst this riot of color, the chestnut omens of
the previous night no longer seemed the least bit ominous.

Beyond the fire ring were the many shrines of the Memorial
Gardens. They were laid out in a circular pattern around the memorial temple, a domed edifice held up by columns, with a cast iron
spiral staircase surrounding the central, innermost column. Above
the dome was a statue of Taliesin the Brave. The shrines themselves
were large rectangles of stone, eight feet tall but seldom wider than

four feet. Some were flat along the top. Others were curved or rose to an arch. Some had bas-reliefs etched into their surfaces. Others had niches carved in them which held a statue. A wire basket into which offerings could be placed sat at the bottom of each shrine.

Rachel walked by the shrines for Hermes and Hecate, both of which were overflowing with offerings today. She passed a pale white shrine, set with a disk of beaten gold, to Amaterasu and a black one to the goddess Hela. Beyond that was the place where she had stood the night before and, beyond that, the spot where Kitten's familiar had been when it turned and looked at Astrid.

The tiny Lion was still there.

Rachel stopped and blinked at it. For just an instant, she wondered if her mind were playing tricks on her, superimposing on her eyesight a memory from the night before. But no, it was really there, crouched beside the granite shrine to the Unknown God, batting at a curling brown leaf.

When Rachel's footsteps stopped, the little tawny beast glanced up, and their eyes met. A strange feeling overcame Rachel. She was reminded of reading a book, of being curled up in her favorite chair in her grandfather's tower library with some great old tome that smelled of leather and brought comfort. Then, the Lion turned its head, and she was back in the present. It glanced toward the shrine to Persephone, where candles were traditionally burned for the dead. Following its gaze, Rachel saw someone already knelt before the gray and black shrine. She glanced back at the Lion.

It was gone.

She looked around, even circling the granite shrine, but there was no sign of the little familiar anywhere. Shrugging, Rachel continued on her way. Ordinarily, had there been another person there, Rachel would have left them to their mourning and come back later. However, the presence of the Comfort Lion made her feel that she should continue.

At her approach, the figure kneeling at the shrine stood. He rose until he was considerably taller than Rachel had expected. Startled, she took a step backward out of trepidation. Then, she recognized the towering figure.

"Vladimir!" Rachel exclaimed, not entirely able to hide the relief in her voice.

"Miss Griffin." The prince of Bavaria inclined his head toward her. "I trust you are well after your nocturnal adventures."

"I am, thank you. Did Gaius... has he had a chance to tell you everything?"

"I would not go so far as to assume that he has told me everything. But he has shared a great deal that was of interest. Have you come to light a candle for your Uncle Emrys?"

A wave of chagrin assailed Rachel. She had not even thought about Emrys when she passed the tables set for the Roanoke dead the previous night. Her father's younger brother had been killed here at Roanoke, fighting the Terrible Five. Perhaps Myrddin would not mind sharing the candle she has brought for him with his half-brother.

Rachel lifted her four candles and murmured, "Among others."

Vladimir Von Dread patiently waited as Rachel knelt solemnly and placed the four candles she had purchased onto the short spikes set there for that purpose. There was a box of matches for those who did not yet know the secret name of fire. She struck one, lighting one candle for her two uncles, one for Old Thom and the other sailors, one for Remus and his wolf-brother, and one for Percy Cornelius Taylor and his band mates.

When she finally rose, Von Dread gave her an approving nod. "They deserve our respect and our remembrance of them, your uncle, my mother, and all the noble dead."

His mother? Rachel glanced at the candle burning brightly beside hers. So, that was for whom his candle was meant. It was strange to think of the tall, impressive young man as a motherless boy.

Touched by the thought, Rachel looked up at Von Dread. She had told Nastasia that she was going to share the vision of his previous life with Gaius, but the unspoken assumption had been that Gaius would then share it with his boss. Was it a violation of Nastasia's trust if Rachel shared it directly with Dread himself? She felt not.

"Would you like to hear about the vision the princess had of you?" asked Rachel. "She has given her permission for me to tell you."

"I admit to being curious," Von Dread replied impassively, his hands clasped behind his back. "Come. Let us walk together, and you can speak to me of what you know."

He turned and led her back by the fire ring, around the lily pond, and into the Oriental gardens on the far side. Rachel walked beside him, trying to match her pace to his. She had to take two steps for each one of his.

They walked through the red gate that led to the oriental gardens, passing the stepped waterfalls with their picturesque arching bridges and the bamboo forest. The *shishi odoshi* made a rhythmic *tock* noise, as pooling water caused its bamboo arm to swing to the down position. Japanese bells chimed softly.

Ahead, a gazebo overlooked a pond. Von Dread led her over the dark-wood bridge leading to the gazebo, stopping beside a fish-food dispenser. He turned the lever, gathered the pellets that it dispensed into his hand, and poured some of them onto Rachel's palm. Cautiously, she sprinkled a few over the edge and then gasped with wonder.

A school of two-foot long koi swarmed around the food, moving so gracefully through the water that they hardly seemed to be natural creatures. Some were dappled like gold-fish, white and gold, red and gold, red and white, others were black with long whiskers that reminded her of Lucky. Watching them, Rachel recalled a tale her Korean grandfather had once told her about a gate hidden on one of the great Asian rivers that would turn a koi into a dragon, if the fish was able to fight its way upstream and leapt through it.

Staring down at the hypnotic motion of the graceful fish, Rachel recited what she had seen in the princess's mirror. She described the medieval armor of the knights, the white, red, and black enchantresses, the Gypsies with their flag, the gigantic green ogre, all of these gathered together on a hill facing the entities that the fetch-maiden had called the Four Horsemen. She described how Von Dread had appeared in his black swan-feathered cloak and had raised an army of automatons out of the earth. She described the marvelous building down the hill that was like nothing she had ever seen, with its windows of pictures made of colored glass and its strange spires and carvings. She also made a point of mentioning that her boss, Mr. Chanson, and Wanda Zukov had both been in the vision.

"Ah, yes… the P.E. tutor." Vladimir's tone was dry and ironic, as if there were some quarrel between him and Mr. Chanson.

As he said this, Rachel suddenly became aware of something she had not noticed previously. When the princess had shared her experience in the thinking glass, Rachel had only paid attention to specific parts of the scene. She had not, for instance, thought to examine the faces of the others who were present throughout the events. Rachel's memory, however, had recorded the whole thing.

Now, as she thought of her boss in his sapphire armor and his golden helmet, she recalled his face as he watched the Dread King, decked out in his winged helm and his robe of black feathers, congeal out of the shadows. Mr. Chanson had looked fiercely disapproving yet firmly resolved. It was exactly the kind of expression that came over her father's face when he was preparing to fight the Morthbrood or to capture members of Veltdammerung—as if, in their previous lives, Roland Chanson had been devoted to the undoing of Vladimir Von Dread.

Vladimir asked her several follow-up questions. Rachel felt obscurely pleased when he looked surprised at the level of detail in her answer. But, of course, she could recall the scene the princess had shown them in the thinking glass as clearly today as if he had asked her these questions at the time.

"That is interesting," he concluded finally. "I do not know what it means, but perhaps I will find out in time. Thank you, Miss Griffin. Your powers of recollection rival Mr. Evans.'"

"You are welcome." Rachel curtsied graciously. "I am happy to be of use. I wish our two groups could work together more often. Unfortunately, any serious collaboration would run into… problems." Rachel rested her elbows on the railing, staring down at the swift motions of the brightly-colored fish. "I am certain I could overcome these objections, however, were it not for the matter of you having acted with extreme disregard for the person and safety of the princess."

"Ah, yes. That."

Rachel gazed at him, her eyes dark and steady. "Nastasia says she told you about the dangers. The first time she disobeyed instructions not to touch someone, she suffered. She suffered personally in the form of injuries. She suffered fear, because the being she met hunted her. She suffered emotionally, because the being attacked her father. Also, someone else was put into tremendous danger by her action."

"She did not tell me in... quite those terms."

"She says that she told you that harm had come to her, but you touched her anyway. In her mind, this act showed tremendous disregard for her person, her safety, et cetera—the same as if you deliberately shoved her through a door that you had been told led to danger."

He nodded but did not comment.

"Here is one thing I have not yet told you," Rachel continued. "One of the Horsemen, Death, looked at her entire memory—possibly compromising secrets of hers, her father's, or ours... including the fact that you are alive, here. Also, when he realized that you and others in the scene were actually here, at Roanoke, he destroyed that version of the scene—perhaps a dream diorama?

"Both of these things suggest that the person harmed by that vision—the person whom the power that told her not to touch you may have been trying to protect—may not have been the princess at all." Rachel reached up and touched his arm, gazing up with concern in her eyes. "It might have been you."

He turned and looked off into the distance for some time. She let her hand fall back to her side and threw more pellets in for the fish.

"That is all right," he said finally. "I hope I did not compromise the secrets of the Nation-state of Magical Australia. If I have harmed myself by my actions, it is not undeserved. I had feared that I might be an agent of the enemy. I think her vision and your conversation with the fetch-maiden who inhabits Miss Chase's China doll has shown that there is a great probability that I have nothing to 'return' to. That is as I wish. I have sworn to protect this place. I will not break my oath for forgotten dreams and past lives."

He sighed. He looked rather sad for a moment. Then his features became calm again. Gesturing with his head toward the bridge, he turned to leave the gazebo. Rachel tossed the last of the fish food into the water, and the two of them continued walking.

As she strove to keep up with him, the image of Salome exclaiming over Dread's evilness came to mind, nearly making her laugh. Rachel glanced curiously at the tall young man beside her. Was he truly evil? Or was he as good as Sandra thought him to be?

Emboldened by Salome's antics, she asked bluntly, "May I ask you a frank question?"

"You may ask me anything, Miss Griffin. I may or may not answer."

"Several of my friends have some kind of evil-detecting powers. Or they say they do. They insist you're evil." Rachel was rather proud of herself for pronouncing this with an absolutely straight face. She peered at him, her eyes narrowing as if attempting to detect evil. "I can't see it myself. To me you merely look effective and competent."

"Am I evil?" Von Dread stopped and gazed directly at Rachel. "Yes, I am. I am most likely the most evil man at this school. Even with my oaths to uphold the laws and protect the world, I would throw that all aside to protect one person.

"Given the choice between the woman I love and this entire world, I would choose her, without hesitation. Such selfishness is the ultimate evil. And, worse yet, I will not even apologize for it. She is worth more than anything else to me. So, when you speak of working closer with me and my people, take that into consideration. If it were the only way to save her, I would watch the world burn."

Rachel stood very quietly, listening as he spoke. She wanted to object, to tell him that his notions of justice and love were wrong. She knew from her experience with her beloved grandfather, however, that if she showed any sign of what Von Dread considered weakness, if she expressed any objection to his vision of life that struck him as 'the mewlings of a bleeding-heart,' she would be, in his mind, forever lumped in with the weak and the foolish. Once that had happened, it would not matter what she said, for he would not pay her word any heed.

If she wanted someday to have a chance to talk him out of believing that burning the world to save one person, even a person as wonderful and dear as Sandra, was acceptable, Rachel could not afford to appear weak. It was like talking to her grandfather or, for that matter, Sigfried. One had to look beyond the violent way that they spoke and figure out what they were truly saying. So, what was Vlad truly saying?

He was saying that he loved her sister very much.

That was a notion she could entirely support.

"Yes. I think we are in agreement. I approve." Rachel gave him a brisk nod.

Vladimir Von Dread blinked. She had apparently stunned him, as if he had been expecting her to run off screaming "monster".

"I… am not sure we are speaking of the same person. Unless she has mentioned me to you. I did not expect she would."

"She did not have to," Rachel replied, "her face shines at the mention of your name."

Rachel thought this was high praise indeed, but he waved his hand dismissively.

"It does not matter. It is up to her to decide when to accept what fate has ordained. I, in the meantime, must work to save this world and, when I have time, figure out something to do to prove to your father that I am not a young tyrant in the making. I am sure she would not be happy were your father to say 'No', when the time comes for me to ask his permission."

"I'll work on my father," Rachel promised. "Subtly, of course. But in the meantime, let's return to the matter of saving the world."

He nodded once. Then, he looked at her for a time without speaking. Rachel gazed back at him, undaunted.

After a bit, she cocked her head. "Why is it, Vladimir, that, of everyone, only you and I are serious about saving the world?"

"I believe, Miss Griffin, this is because we both see…."

KABOOOOOMMMM!

With the noise of ten thousand thunderclaps, the peak of Stony Tor exploded, broken rocks erupting high into the air.

CHAPTER TWENTY-NINE:

COLD AS A TIGER

VLADIMIR VON DREAD LUNGED FORWARD AND DREW RACHEL against him. He leaned over her, protecting her, the bulk of his body between her and the explosion. Everything shook around her, but that one spot felt safe and guarded.

For that brief instance, all responsibility was lifted from her shoulders; everything was fine. Someone else would stop the bad guy and save the world.

Alas, it was a luxury she could not afford. There were those who needed her. She pulled the world back onto her shoulders and drew away from him.

"I am unharmed, Vladimir," Rachel stated calmly. Her voice sounded oddly faint in her ears, which were still ringing from the explosion.

"Good." He straightened and looked her over. Rachel received the distinct impression that he was pleased, or at least relieved, by her composure. Turning, he looked toward the tor. She followed his gaze.

The distant rocky peak of Stony Tor had caved in. Half of it still curved above the tor, like a giant, stone, crescent or a capital C. The rest was gone, leaving a gaping hole. With a noise like a stampede of thunderbolts, lightning imps dashed from their former prison, filling the cloudy sky with dancing electricity. Ribbons of fog, presumably newly-freed mist sprites, twisted and darted among the flashes. In the midst of this, a figure in orange and green stood in mid-air, arms akimbo, shouting into a speaking-horn.

"I must take my leave," said Von Dread. "I am needed else-where."

He did not wait for her reply.

Drawing his fulgurator's wand, he spoke words she had heard him speak once before and dissolved into a pillar of light that reached into the sky. The light vanished, appearing a moment later above the tor. As it faded, a figure she was sure was Von Dread became visible in mid-air, falling. White fire leapt from this new figure, nearly striking the Heer, who darted rapidly to the side. The storm goblin shouted into his speaking-horn, and lightning imps threw their electric javelins at the steadily-falling figure. Before the javelins arrived and before he hit the slopes of Stony Tor, the figure of Dread dissolved into another pillar of light. He reappeared behind the storm goblin, still in mid-air, still falling, still shooting.

Rachel's jaw dropped.

Von Dread was fighting in mid-air.

Or rather, fighting while plummeting toward the ground; that took an extraordinary amount of courage and confidence! She wondered if she would be brave enough to do such a thing.

Rachel's thoughts returned to the moment when Vlad had pulled her to him, stepping between her and the danger. A quote her grandfather had admired, from the American Founding Father John Adams, came to her thoughts: *There are only two creatures of value on the face of the earth: those with the commitment, and those who require the commitment of others.* Underneath the shadow of Von Dread, his robes billowing around her, his body shielding her from harm, Rachel had felt as if she had been granted entry into the second category—for that single instant, she had no longer been a soldier battling dire forces on the front line. Instead, she had been a child requiring the commitment of another.

It had felt glorious.

The distant figure of the Heer of Dunderberg gestured. The lightning imps dived, turning into dazzling blue-white bolts. But they were not diving at Von Dread. Instead, they fell away to the northwest, striking a point in mid-air on the northern part of the island.

"Noooooooo!" screamed Rachel.

Blue-white electricity outlined a gigantic tree, as tall as a skyscraper, that had not been visible moments before. Lightning bolts

danced around it. They were attacking the Roanoke Tree. They were after her Elf.

Her Elf was about to die.

Or dying.

Or dead.

Who had done this terrible thing? Who had let the storm goblin out of his rocky prison?

Fear gripped Rachel, beclouding her thoughts. She knew that she had to calm down, but her mind was a jumble. She tried to think clearly, but she could not hear over the thundering of her heart. Or was that the thunder of the lightning imps?

Cold as a tiger, fierce as bread?

No, that was not right.

As crisp as the moment he had first spoken the words, the memory of her grandfather, glowering down at her from beneath his famous bushy eyebrows, came back to her: *"Fierce as a tiger. Calm as a lake in August. And cool as ice—when you are not as fiery as a furnace."*

Fierce as a tiger, right.

Much saner than bread.

Rachel reached upwards. *"Varenga,* Vroomie!"

She ran toward Dare Hall, not certain whether she might be too far away for the cantrip to work. As she pelted along the leaf-covered pathways, trying not to slip, a familiar red and gold figure zipped toward her.

Falling in beside her, Lucky called out, "Found the blood-kid-sister, boss! She's running. Maybe her tail is on fire, 'cept not sure she has a tail. Poor tailless cripple."

"Hallo, Lucky," Rachel cried breathlessly as she ran. "We've got to get to the Elf! She's in danger!"

"Right! The boss says he has your broom, and he's coming this way."

Ahead of her, tutors and proctors converged on the commons at a run. Students scurried out of their way, except for one tall redhead, who gazed at the tor with her head thrown back, laughing. The dean and the head of security both snapped out orders. Some of the proctors raced toward the gym and the broom closet. But they did not get very far. In a blur of motion so fast that her eye could not follow it, Mr. Chanson arrived with an armful of racing brooms. Proctors and tutors grabbed them and flew northward, following Maverick Badger, who was leading the way. Mr. Gideon took a racing broom from the P.E. tutor and lay it on the ground. Then, her True History tutor casually stepped onto the shaft and gestured. The broom rose up into the air and zipped forward after the others with Mr. Gideon standing on it.

Rachel gawked in astonishment, nearly tripping.

He was *standing* on a broom.

Standing on it.

And flying.

I absolutely must learn to do that, Rachel vowed as she ran.

"That's cool." The dragon watched him go. Spinning, he looked at a spot near the path coming from Dare Hall. "There he is."

Rachel looked, but she saw no sign of Sigfried.

"He's chameleoned out," confided the dragon. "Most people can't see him."

"Including me," Rachel murmured wryly. The words came out in a breathy pant.

Siggy's voice sounded somewhere nearby. "Got your broom, Griffin! Unfortunately, I only had one vial of chameleon elixir left."

"Oh, too bad!" Rachel cried. "I guess I'll just have to risk being seen. Let's go."

"Go which way?" Siggy asked. "The teachers are all going north... not south to the docks. I've been listening in. They're heading for something called the ward-lock. What's that?"

Rachel stopped and leaned over, panting. "A place w-where the wards... can be o-opened... and shut."

Having flown near them, Rachel assumed they meant one of the places where the wall of trees stopped, and there were large rectangular granite stones set into the ground.

"Look, Siggy," she continued when she could speak, "it will be much quicker to get there by following them, but they'll see me if I go. You're going to have to go yourself."

"On... your broom?"

"Unless you can snag another in record time. Think you can manage it?"

"Yeah, sure. As long as I don't hit the wrong lever."

"Do your best!" Rachel told him.

"I'm on it" From the sounds, Sigfried was mounting the steeple-chaser. Lucky moved toward him, fading from her view as he went. "You can watch over the mirror."

With a familiar whoosh, he and Lucky were off.

• • •

Despite his promise, nothing appeared on her calling card until after Sigfried had passed the school wards and was zooming over the tree-tops toward the Roanoke Tree. He was not as fast as many of the experienced riders on their racing brooms, but the majority of the school staff were heading for the tor. Only Mr. Gideon was going the same way as Sigfried, and the steeplechaser outdistanced him, because he stopped to speak to the others before he left them.

While she waited impatiently, wishing she was with Sigfried, the campus buzzed with hectic activity. Students rushed out of buildings to gape at the tor, while the remaining proctors—those who did not go off to fight the Heer—attempted to usher them back inside. Rachel slipped away, returning to the Oriental gardens. She walked among the bamboo and Japanese maples, whose leaves had only just begun to take on the pure, brilliant red they turned before they dropped. She eventually found her way back to the gazebo, where she sprinkled another handful of fish food into the pool and watched the Lucky-like koi swirl and dive for it.

Siggy's voice came from the calling card. "Hey, Griffin-Sister, look at this!"

In the mirror, Von Dread and the storm goblin continued their mid-air battle. In the mural in the café, the storm goblin was por-trayed as a withered and hunched goblin creature. But, now that she could see him more clearly, this Heer looked like a charming, six-year-old Dutch boy, with a round face and hair the color of straw. He wore an old-fashioned doublet and hose of Dutch orange and green and a soft sugar-loaf cap of pure white.

The Heer was a little boy?

Vladimir looked blackened and burnt, but determined. Each time he neared the ground, he vanished and appeared in the air again, thus keeping the storm goblin from darting behind the tor and out of his range. The Heer was bound by two Glepnir bonds. His speaking-horn was missing, and one of his feet was caked in ice. But still, his imps and sprites attacked, throwing lightning at Von Dread and attempting to wreathe him in thick fog. One mist sprite was floating the missing speaking-horn back to the Heer.

More pillars of light flashed over the tor. Agents appeared in their tricorne hats, with their Inverness capes billowing about them. Rachel recognized Darling and Standish among their number. Standish called to Von Dread, assuring him that the Wisecraft could handle the Heer. Vladimir gave a single shake of his head and kept firing.

Below, Maverick Badger flew up to the slope. Rachel recalled that the head of security had been instrumental in catching the storm goblin the first time. He, too, called out to Von Dread. Seeing him, Vladimir nodded once and vanished yet again.

He appeared on the far side of the tor — out of sight of the Agents and proctors, but not out of Siggy's amulet's range — one foot kneeling, one knee bent, one black-gloved fist resting on the ground. He knelt thus for some time, his head lowered, panting.

"Boy, Dread's so cool!" Siggy's voice came over the mirror, overflowing with admiration. "I wish I could be like that! Huh? What's that?"

Behind Von Dread and above him on the slope stood a bull. At its feet lay the crumbled remains of what had once been the wall of rune-marked stones that had kept the Heer of Dunderberg locked into his cave prison. As they watched, the bull pushed the last of the ensorcelled boulders with its horns, sending it plummeting over a cliff.

Von Dread turned and looked up. The bull gazed down the slope. Where the creature's eyes and snout should have been was a human face. The nose of the demon-face widened as it sniffed the air. Its beady eyes narrowed. Its hoof pawed the earth.

Caw!

A giant black raven with blood red eyes dived at the bull.

The demon-face scowled. Then the entire bull dissolved into dark shadow and fled away.

"Oh no!" came Sigfried's voice.

The viewpoint abruptly shifted to the foot of the Roanoke Tree. Flames billowed from the opening of the Elf's hollow. On the ground in front of the doorway lay a charred supine form.

"No!" Rachel pressed her hands against her mouth. "No, no, no, no!"

The view in the mirror showed the dead, crisped body, but she recognized the shape of the head, the cut of the burnt dress, the bits of fern green hair that remained uncharred.

Noooooooooo!

Rachel touched the spot on her head where her memory-protecting rune was hidden beneath her hair. She had been older than language, this dear friend, exiled from her homeland, who had given Rachel such a royal gift.

Tears welled up in her eyes.

Lady Rachel Jade Griffin straightened her shoulders and thrust her sorrow back behind her mask. There would be time for mourning later. The garden was burning, all Illondria's hard work. It would honor her dead friend more to act than to mourn.

The viewpoint of the mirror was still focused on the burnt body. Rachel did not know if Sigfried was staring at it in fascination or if he had gone into shock.

"Sigfried!" Pushing her dissembling skill to a new level, Rachel forced her voice to remain as calm as a lake in August. "Her garden is burning. Pick as many herbs as you can. Quickly. And move away from the door. Mr. Gideon will be coming."

"Er... boss. Snap out of it. Did you hear her?" came Lucky's voice.

"Huh." Siggy sounded disoriented. Then his voice cleared, though there was a note of admiration in it. "Ooo. Did you hear that Lucky? Griffin's as cold as ice! Our friend the Elf is only freshly dead, and she wants us to loot her."

From the sounds, Sigfried was following her instructions.

His words cut Rachel's heart. She tried to explain. "I'm not cold. I just don't want her life's work to go to waste."

"Even colder! Not even waiting for the body to be buried."

Lucky asked, "Can we cremate it?"

Siggy said, "No, Rachel probably wants us to check her pockets for loose change and magic rings."

"Don't waste time on nonsense!" Rachel ordered sharply. Her thoughts moved swiftly, keeping the keening agony at bay with calm, practical thoughts. "The tutors will be coming. Get the herbs! You know how useful they are to your Alchemy. This may be your last chance to gather any. See if you can dig some up with their roots attached, so we can replant them."

"See, Lucky?" The point of view changed to the garden where the dragon was gathering huge swaths of herbs with his mouth. Rachel saw Siggy's hands digging. "Icy as a cucumber!"

"Good grief," Rachel sighed and rubbed her forehead. "Just hurry."

Chapter Thirty:

A Conspiracy of Angels

Dear Sandra,

Yesterday, my Elf died. She was killed by the demon Morax. (Don't say the name aloud.) I haven't cried yet because I've been very busy, but I'm sure I will soon. She was an unearthly elf. She was very tall and very beautiful, and she died because of us. I am very sad.

Here is a picture I sketched of my Elf. I'll call you, if I need you.

Love,
Rachel

The next day, Rachel received a reply:

Dear Rachel,

I am very sad to hear of the death of your friend. I would like to know more about her, if possible. I am not sure I understand what you mean by an unearthly elf. It's okay to be sad when you lose someone you care about. It will take time to get better.

Please, let Father, Mother or me know if you need time off from school. You can come and stay with me in London. I live in a flat in a warehouse conversion. There are Unwary here. They are rather loud, but for the most part, they ignore me. I wouldn't mind having my little sister come stay with me.

Love,
Sandra

• • •

"Rachel, can you meet me in the library?" Gaius's voice came over the calling card as Rachel was crossing the Commons. "I found something I'd like to show you. Well... actually, I'd rather not show it to you, but I think you might rather want to see it."

"Coming!"

It was Friday afternoon, a little more than a week after Samhain. Of what had occurred during the intervening days, Rachel was not quite sure. Her memory had recorded the events, classes, conversations, etc., but unless she called them up and reviewed them, she hardly knew what had happened. Only two things stood out. The first was that the proctor Mr. Fuentes had noticed her distress and tried to comfort her, but since he did not understand that she had lost a friend, his well-meaning attempts to cheer her had gone astray. The second was that she and Nastasia had shared a quiet cup of tea in memory of the Elf, but they had both been too well-brought up to indulge in something as undignified as tears.

Her other friends had spent the last week talking non-stop about the burning of the Roanoke Tree and the slaying of the Elf. Rachel wished they would stop. True, there was no longer a need for secrecy; however, their words seemed like a constant reminder that she was now a murderess. She accepted this difficult truth, but she did not enjoy having it constantly brought to her attention.

What made it doubly hard was that Illondria had been killed after Nastasia announced the plan to bring her home. Wanderlust dug its spurs into Rachel even on good days. Now, in addition to the sorrow of her friend's passing, she had to face the disappointment of knowing that she would not be traveling to see the great forests of Hoddmimir's Wood. Somehow her grief made her longing and disappointment stronger.

She managed to do her schoolwork, but it was hard to concentrate beyond that. The buzzing in her mind that came with a sense of falling was growing stronger and stronger. There was an accompanying darkness, too, that encroached on her senses. Any time she stopped focusing on the task before her, these sensations became worse.

At first, she had thought it might be her imagination, that sorrow and fatigue were taking their toll on her. But when she thought back, she could remember the buzzing very clearly, and she could see the darkness around the edges of her memory. When she remembered back to just after her grandfather died, the buzzing was in her memory there, too.

If she had not been so grief-stricken, she would have been terrified.

After a few days, she had to admit to herself what was occurring. Her mother had warned her that overusing the dissembling technique could have bad consequences. Hiding one's expression did no harm, but Rachel had been using the technique to hide her fear, her anger, her pain, her sorrow—to hide it from herself, so she could continue to function.

This was exactly the kind of thing her mother had warned her never to do.

Rachel thought several times of calling home and asking her mother for help; however, she knew from previous conversations that there was no easy cure. Every time she thought of asking for help, Rachel's mind played out what would happen next: visits to nuns of Asclepius or Hypnos, examinations in halls of healing, being dragged all over the place, and endless, endless questions—questions she probably would not want to answer.

And all this, most likely to no avail. There were many magical cures for colds and broken bones, but very few for madness. Once people believed someone was mad, that was the end of that person's credibility. No one trusted those who went mad. No one hired them. No one wanted to marry them. Admitting that one was mentally unstable was the ultimate confession of weakness.

Grimly, she determined to fight it. So long as she kept concentrating on something, she could keep the buzzing at bay. Maybe once she recovered from this terrible sense of guilt and grief, it would fade again.

The only bright spot in her darkened world was Gaius. When he was around, her thoughts became calm and sane again. She laughed and talked, free of the otherwise constant pain and grief. No buzzing. No falling. No darkness. Even when he was not there, the thought of him buoyed her up. It was as if he was the pillar holding up her otherwise-shaking world. Mentally, she clung to him with all her strength.

Thus, when the young man who had become the most important thing in the universe to her called, rousing her from her gloom, she was delighted and relieved.

She ran all the way.

After the chill of the mid-November day, the heat in the library seemed almost stifling. Gaius sat at a table surrounded by books. He waved her over, gesturing at a chair.

"Hey, cutie," he drawled lazily, looking her up and down in a manner that sent tingles up and down Rachel's body. She blushed prettily and ducked her head shyly. He grinned. "Hey, what was that you asked Ghost-Remus about—with Darius Northwest?"

"Oh!" The recent grief had driven the matter from her thoughts. "I found a plaque in Transylvania, next to a glass that shone with moonlight. It had Northwest's name on it, and I knew Beaumont Castle was the last place he was ever seen."

"So... he stepped through the glass and was never seen again? Where did it go? Timbuktu?"

"He was a great traveler. If he had come out anywhere on the earth, and had not been killed, he would have made his way back home."

"So... you're saying, that glass leads somewhere that's... not on earth? It leads to Metaplutonian lands?"

Rachel's pupils grew wide. "Maybe."

"Can I tell Vlad about this?"

"Yes, you can." She paused. "Was that what you wanted to see me about?"

"No!" he leaned forward, "Look, this is from Plutarch's *On Superstition*—which is a book even we Unwary have. This is what it has to say about the demon you and I were investigating—the boss demon. The one who is also Saturn. Or, in this case, Kronos: '... *with full awareness, they offered up their own children. Those who had no children bought little ones from the poor. They cut their victim's throats, as if they were so many lambs or young birds. Meanwhile, the poor child's mother stood by, without weeping. If she uttered a single moan or cried a single tear, she had to forfeit the money, but her child was sacrificed nonetheless. The area around the statue was filled with the noise of flutes and drums, so that the wailing of the victims did not reach the ears of the populace.'*"

"Oh my!" Rachel sat down, hard.

"It's truly terrible," Gaius said hoarsely. "If there's anything worse than mothers getting paid for letting their children be sacrificed... but only if they don't cry—I don't know what it is."

"Me, neither," she whispered.

"I also found this. It's from Diodorus Siculus, a Greek historian who lived in Sicily in the first century. He is describing a time when the Carthaginians were losing a war. He writes *'They believed Kronos had turned against them. In former times, they had sacrificed to the god the noblest of their sons. More recently, they had been secretly buying and raising children that they sent to be sacrificed.... When they saw their enemies camped before their walls, they were filled with superstitious dread, for they believed they had failed to honor the god in the manner established by their fathers. In their eagerness to make amends, they chose two hundred of the noblest children and sacrificed them publicly...'*"

"Two hundred?" Rachel cried out. "Two hundred of their own children?"

"That's what it says," Gaius's voice sounded hoarse.

"Gaius, we've got to stop that horrid bull-demon from summoning up the other one!" Rachel stated forcefully. "We absolutely must!"

Gaius nodded. "Preferably by this next dark of the moon. We don't want anyone to be sacrificed." He shook his head, sighing. "Only, I have no idea how. The next dark of the moon is only three days away. I've been trying to figure out where the bull-demon's 'place of power' is, but I'm not having any luck."

"I had been so hoping the Wisecraft had captured the bull one. But... obviously not."

"I wish we had a better idea of what demons are capable of. Then, we would at least have a chance of preparing. Besides talking people into casting bad spells, like Egg did, what can they do? I mean demons and all these creatures, including that Raven guy?"

"Other than knocking over castles with a gesture? And stopping time?"

"Stopping time?" exclaimed Gaius.

"Rather like what happened to the storm winds near us when the Raven came on our way home on All Hallows' Eve. Other people stop moving, but they're still moving."

"Scary!" Gaius shivered, as if a cold wind were blowing on his neck. "Anything else?"

Rachel tipped her head back slightly, thinking. For the first time in over a week, happiness stirred inside her. *It was time to tell him everything.* But how to go about it?

"Come with me." She jumped to her feet. "There's something I would like to show you."

· · ·

They flew north on Vroomie, over the tops of hemlocks. The school was being extra careful due to the Heer of Dunderberg still being on the loose—the Agents having failed to capture the storm goblin. So, Rachel had been forced to evade the proctors. She flew south until she reached the creek and then doubled back to the north once under the cover of trees.

They followed the creek, soaring over a series of waterfalls, and then headed westward. Ahead of them, across the river, a great thunderhead hovered over the peak of Storm King. Bolts of brilliant blue-white illuminated the dark storm cloud as the lightning imps celebrated their newfound freedom. Perhaps the Heer was with them, or perhaps he had retreated to his seat of power at Dunderberg Mountain, some twenty miles downriver.

Rachel flew over the hemlocks to the large outcropping of rock, and beyond it to where the woods became particularly thick. There, she hesitated. The naked branches of occasional deciduous trees changed the look of the landscape. Comparing the tops of the hemlocks with those in her memory, however, she soon regained her bearings.

She dived down into the darkness of the forest and negotiated around the shaggy gray trunks. Here and there, a single sunbeam broke through, forming bright shafts of light. A large beam fell upon a statue of a woman with her head bowed. Stone robes draped her body.

"Nice statue," Gaius commented, as they slid from the steeple-chaser.

"Look at her back," Rachel gestured casually. "Do you see any place where something might once have been attached?"

Gaius walked around the statue, examining it. He touched the face where the paler and darker moss seemed to form tear stains. Then, he moved to the back. "No. Not unless it was a long time ago... long enough for lichen to grow."

"You're sure?"

Gaius frowned and looked at the statue's back again, running his hands over the stone shoulders and spine. "Yes. I'm sure."

Rachel drew her mirror out of her robes and spoke into it. "Hey, Zoë? I need a favor."

• • •

The new clubhouse of the Die Horribly Debate Club was Room 321 on the third floor of the north leg of Roanoke Hall. Currently, it looked like an empty classroom with a small side desk, a large central table, a few chairs, and the name of the club written in chalk on the blackboard. A great deal had been said over the last week about how they might decorate the room, but it had mainly consisted of Sigfried making outrageous suggestions, while the girls had squealed in dismay and shouted about why his latest idea was unacceptable.

Now that she had finally made the decision to tell Gaius about her memory, Rachel was so filled with anticipation that even the brief delay of flying back to find Zoë seemed unbearable. This was the kind of moment which for she lived—a chance to reveal something wondrous to someone for whom she cared deeply. She could not wait to see the expression on his face. He was going to be so impressed with her. She just knew it.

"Are you sure I'm allowed in here?" Gaius stuck his head into the club room, where Zoë and Joy were waiting for them. He squinted at the chalkboard. "What a name!"

"Sure. No secrets here yet." Zoë gestured lazily.

Her hair was turquoise today. She sat in an armchair with her feet on the table. Joy stood at the board drawing little flowers and hearts around the H in Horribly. As Gaius walked around the table, Rachel rested her broom against the wall.

"Okay, Gaius, I need you to bedazzle me," she announced. "Then, Joy will watch my body, while Zoë walks you into my dreams."

"We're going into dreamland?" Gaius asked, extremely interested.

"Rather!" Rachel smiled. "My dream space had Dream Gaius in it, and some space-going sailing ships he was worried about, which apparently look nothing like real star ships, and a unicorn. It was a very nice unicorn."

"Uh, Dream Gaius, eh?" He quirked an eyebrow.

Behind him, Joy snickered.

"Dream You made me a little nervous because...." Rachel felt the heat rising in her cheeks. "Well, never mind why. Basically, because he wasn't the real you. I mean a dream version of one's boyfriend isn't one's boyfriend, right? And besides," she muttered under her breath, "he wasn't gentlemanly."

"Definitely," agreed Gaius, frowning slightly. "Though I must say, I am sorry to hear that dream me is not a proper gentleman. Wait, does Dream Gaius hang around with a unicorn? Or was that in some other dream?"

"I think they are friends." Rachel leaned forward, her eyes sparkling. "Dream You and me got to ride him. If you come check it out, I can tell you about my secret power."

His eyebrows shot up. "You have a secret power?"

"I do."

Gaius leaned closer. For a moment, Rachel thought he was going to kiss her, right in front of the other girls. But he leaned farther and whispered in her ear. "Is this the Big Secret?"

"No," Rachel whispered back, "but I need to explain the secret power before I can explain the Big Secret. That's what I've been waiting for."

"Ah! Smashing." He stepped back again.

"As to my secret: Topher already knows it, but, still, please don't tell anyone."

Gaius raised his right hand solemnly, "I will keep your secret. Er... with Vlad's standard clause of: 'if you are planning to blow up a significant portion of the world, the deal is off.'"

Zoë chuckled. "Some parts of the world may need exploding."

"I remember that clause." Rachel gave Gaius a little cheerful nod. She jumped up on the table and lay down. "Bedazzle away! Only paralyze me first, otherwise, it can get... messy."

"Wait, bedazzle?" He frowned. "You want me to cast a *Spell of Bedazzlement* on *you*?"

Rachel, Zoë, and Joy all nodded.

"Is it okay to be repeatedly bedazzled?" asked Gaius. "Maybe we should test it out on Mark Williams...."

"Isn't he the boy I paralyzed?" Rachel asked. She shrugged. "The spell seems harmless."

"It's forcing a chaotic state of mind on you while you are awake. I can't imagine it's a good thing. Even if it's not 'that harmful,' I'd prefer if we tested it out on someone I don't care about. And Mark Williams's star seems to be in rapid decline. Best to use him before he gets turned into a lamp post or something. He really seems to be unlucky."

Rachel pressed her lips together to keep herself from smiling. "If we used someone else, you couldn't meet Dream Gaius or the unicorn... and I could not show off my secret power."

"Oh," Gaius shrugged. "Okay, I'm sure casting it on you once will be all right. We've used the spell quite a number of times during the Knights' practice sessions. No one has turned into a babbling idiot yet. Turned into, at least...."

Rachel and the other girls chuckled.

Gaius drew his fulgurator's wand and pointed it at her. "Here goes!"

• • •

Rachel dreamed she was walking on the moors, singing. Zoë tapped her on the shoulder as she was beginning a new chorus. At least, they had not come upon her naked. As soon as she was lucid, she shifted the dream to her star-studded meadow.

To her disappointment, neither Dream Gaius nor the unicorn were present.

"This is rather impressive," Gaius looked around. "There's so much detail. I thought dreams were fuzzy, you know, at least around the edges."

"You asked what demons and the Raven can do. Look at this." Rachel recalled standing in the forest by the statue.

"Nice statue," murmured Zoë. A silvery light surrounded Zoë's body when she was in the dreamlands nowadays, illuminating the meadow up to about twenty feet in all directions.

"Wow!" Gaius circled the statue. "It looks exactly the same. Impressive, Griffin!"

"Don't go outside the silver light," Zoë murmured. "You'll fall out of dream land."

"Good safety tip." Gaius raised his eyebrows. "Fall out to... where."

Zoë peered downward. "The classroom we just left."

"O-kay," murmured Gaius, his eyes a bit wide.

"Now, look at this." Rachel recalled a different memory. Everything remained the same, except the statue of the woman now had large, stone, bird wings.

"Whoa!" murmured Zoë.

Gaius blinked. "What's that?"

"That's the same statue, as I saw it on the first day of school, in September."

"But...." Gaius walked around the statue again. "Sure this isn't a different statue?"

"Note the tear-streaks on the face. Note the split pine over there and that rounded boulder. This is the same spot."

Gaius frowned. "I... don't understand."

"This is what it looked like the first time, and this..." Rachel called up the recent memory, "... is what it looked like when I went back, a few days later." She switched back and forth a few times, the wings appearing and vanishing. Everything else stayed the same.

"W-why?" asked Gaius.

"I don't know," said Rachel. "But there's more."

She recalled the page from the ancient bestiary, the page that had been hidden from her memory before the Elf's Rune revealed to her. On it was an image of a winged man. The word *Angel* was written across the top in large curly letters. The image was oddly broken into squares and triangles that together made up the whole. Looking closer, she realized that this peculiar drawing style looked very much like the colored-glass pictures in the windows of the beautiful building with all the spires that she had glimpsed in the background of the princess's vision of Von Dread's past.

"'*Angel*,'" read Gaius, glancing from the picture to the statue.

"This page had been hidden from my memory," explained Rachel.

"Wait!" Zoë flipped her braid in a circle with some annoyance. The feather went *thwip, thwip*. "You mean… some power is deliberately hiding references to winged creatures called angels—both from your memory and from the world itself?"

"Yes," said Rachel.

"That's rather disturbing." Gaius gritted his teeth. "Especially since in the princess's vision of my past I had wings… no, sorry, my reflection in the Mirror Nebula had them. What's the point of being a scientist, if someone's changing the evidence?"

Rachel nodded and gestured. Gryphon Tor appeared around them. The ruined castle was behind them. Her family estate, the town of Gryphon-on-Dart, and Dartmoor National Park were before them. The view looked westward toward Cornwall. The lay of the land was as Rachel recalled it from the previous summer.

"And—this," she said.

The view changed, but the changes were subtle. A few of the landmarks in the distance moved to the right or left.

"Creepy!" murmured Zoë.

"You mean, something changed an entire landscape?" Gaius asked. He took a stumbling step forward, pointing. "Hey! Wait! I know this place. Right there, where things changed! That's where my father's farm is! That's where *I* live!"

"Even creepier," sang Zoë in a sing-song voice.

"Really? You live so close to me?" burst from Rachel's mouth.

Embarrassed to be caught paying attention to such trivial personal matters at such a time, she added quickly, "That change happened when I was three and a half. I wonder if that was when the Raven brought you here."

"Maybe…." He swallowed with some effort but then gave her a kind smile. "Sorry. It's one thing to be told you come from another world. It is another thing to see evidence of it."

"What could do such a thing?" Zoë asked. "Add a whole farm to Cornwall, I mean?"

"Could you do that with kenomancy?" asked Gaius.

Rachel's brow furrowed. "Technically, yes... but I have never heard of sorcerers adding such a massive space before."

"So you are saying that demons... or angels—do we know the difference?" asked Gaius.

"The page in the bestiary says angels are heavenly messengers," replied Rachel. "Demons seem to be chthonic."

"So, demons, and creatures like them, can knock over towers, stop time, change statues, change memories, and change landscapes?" asked Gaius. "But why? Why change the statue?"

"I keep thinking about that. I wonder if this statue is like the orphaned words," Rachel said slowly. "The words that no one knows what they mean, like *steeple, friar,* and *saint.*"

"You mean," Gaius said, "you think the statue's left from some previous state of the world—one we've been forced to forget? But that whoever enforces the amnesia—your friend the Raven, perhaps?—accidentally left in this evidence of the former state?"

"Yes," said Rachel.

"But... for what reason?" Gaius pushed. "Is he evil, this Raven? Or is he on our side?"

Rachel did not answer. She wanted to blurt out that the Raven was not evil, but who was she to know, really?

She was the girl who could not tell a familiar from a house cat.

"The whole thing is crazy." Gaius shook his head. "Is any of this related to why there's a Lion who looks tiny but is actually gigantic?"

"You mean the Comfort Lion?" Rachel gestured again, recalling another memory.

The scene played out around them. The three of them stood in Rachel's bedroom. *The tall, arched window was open. On the windowsill sat an enormous raven, jet black with blood red eyes. It addressed a tiny Lion on the bunk of the sleeping Kitten Fabian.*

The raven croaked harshly, "You are not supposed to be here."

The Lion sat regally. "I was called. Where I am called, I come."

"None of my people called you."

"You called one of my daughters. I am always in her heart."

"You need to depart."

The Lion yawned. It turned in a circle three times and settled down to sleep.

"That happened the first night I slept at school," explained Rachel.

"Okay, that's triply creepy!" Zoë shivered. "Does stuff like that happen in my room?" Rachel turned and looked out the window of her dream dorm room, until they were surrounded by paper birches and ferns. It was the only way to keep herself from remembering the Raven standing in Zoë's room, over the pile of frozen, sleeping girls.

"So, these demons, or angels," Gaius drawled slowly, "have a conspiracy to hide something from us, and we have no idea why? Or what is being hidden? And we can't do anything about it?"

"Yes," Rachel nodded. "Exactly."

Chapter Thirty-One:

Plunged Into Darkness

"Rachel," Gaius gestured airily at the moonlit bedroom around them, "how are you doing all this? Making these images appear around us? They're so clear and crisp. I couldn't do this... recall exactly what the land around my farm looked like, for instance. Much less recall what it looked like when I was three!"

This was the moment for which Rachel had been waiting. She grinned with joy. "*That*'s my secret power."

"You have dream control? No, wait. You mentioned Topher knew your secret. You have a perfect memory, like Evans?" guessed Gaius.

Rachel bounced with excitement. "Yes! Exactly! Let me show you."

She cast around for something that Gaius might enjoy seeing and lighted upon a memory that fit the bill perfectly. She recalled the night Gaius had spent as a sheep. She and Zoë had snuck through dreams into Von Dread's room, so that Rachel could use the boon Vlad had promised her, in return for her efforts to save him from Dr. Mordeau, to get him to restore Gaius's proper shape and buy Gaius a new wand. She recalled the events exactly as they had occurred. Gaius stood in the midst of the diorama and watched with great interest the confrontation between his girlfriend and his boss. He saw her insist that Von Dread take Gaius back into his good graces, quoting what Gaius had told the Agents while he was under the influence of the *Spell of True Recitation* as proof of her boyfriend's loyalty to the prince.

"There!" Rachel smiled at him when she came to the end, anticipating his pleasure at seeing how bravely she had stood up for him. "Exactly as it happened."

Gaius turned on her, his face bright red. "H-how do you know what happened when the Agents interviewed me? That's word for word what I said."

"Can't tell, sorry." She shook her head sadly. "Promised my source."

"Your source was spying on *me*?" he practically shouted. "Tell it to stop. Please. Did your source see all the interviews with the Agents? Including Dread's?"

Rachel bit her lip. She wished desperately that she had left out the part where she told Dread about Gaius's interview with the Wisecraft, but it had not occurred to her to consider effect it might have on him. In retrospect, she felt a tremendous wave of sympathy for him. She had not meant to embarrass him.

"Yes. Vlad was so impressive!" Rachel cried, hoping give Gaius a chance to regain his composure. She recalled Von Dread's interview with the Wisecraft Agents, where he conducted himself admirably despite being under the influence of the *Spell of True Recitation*.

"Sweet as!" Zoë exclaimed in admiration, "Dread really is way cool."

Gaius, on the other hand, looked shell shocked. If anything, he looked more upset than before. "You know, I have to tell Vlad about this, right? Not about your memory, but this information.... Either one of the Agents is the source of your information, which is extremely disappointing, or you have methods none of us have even guessed at. Either way, this is quite alarming."

Rachel felt the blood desert her face. Her stomach flipped upside down.

He was going to betray *her.*

Worse, he was going to betray Sigfried and his amulet to Von Dread. "You're... you're going to tell somebody? B-but... you promised! Nobody is being killed, and many people have been saved! You can't tell!"

"You said not to tell anyone about your memory," snapped Gaius. "When did you say I couldn't talk to anyone about anything said here?"

No!

The single pillar holding her mental world together snapped.

Inside her head, her mind seemed to come unmoored. She tried to resist, to pull herself together, but it was not working. Here in her dream space, she could not hide the disintegration of her inner well-being. There was a loud rushing noise. Darkness began encroaching around the edges of the landscape.

Zoë looked around nervously. "What's going on?"

"Please, Zoë," Rachel managed to speak, but she felt so nauseous she feared she might become ill. What happened if someone became ill in dreamland? Would her body vomit back in the waking world? "Can you take Gaius back down and wake me up. I-I don't want to talk about this here."

Gaius scowled, looking tremendously annoyed. He had never been angry with her before. Now she felt both ill and frightened. The color drained out of the scene. The details remained sharp, but the landscape started to appear inked instead of real.

"Fine." Gaius stomped away from Zoë, until he was outside the circle of silver light. He fell back into the waking world.

"It's okay. Joy and I can talk to him." Zoë's silvery light went dim, and she disappeared.

Odd things occurred. Rachel started losing her lucidity. Her thoughts drifted like a ship without a rudder. The weight of all the terrible things she had suffered these last two and a half months crashed in upon her. She could feel her sanity coming apart like an unraveling sweater, falling into shreds. The dream spun rapidly toward nightmares.

It was a dark and terrifying feeling, knowing that she had tried her best, but her mind just could not bear the pain and sorrow that had been piled upon it. It reminded her of the way her arm had snapped, the time she flew into the grandfather clock and the force of the blow broke the bone. Only this was a thousand times worse. Bones could be mended, but Rachel knew of no magic that could mend madness.

Suddenly, the world snapped back to normal. Rachel stood in dreamland beside the winged statue. Looming over her, singing softly, her eyes wise and kind, stood her Elf.

Her dead Elf.

Rachel threw herself at the lady elf, wailing. Illondria knelt and held her, stroking her back. Her body felt warmer than a normal person's, but not uncomfortably so. Rachel sank into her embrace.

"Little one," Illondria whispered in Rachel's ear, "you have been given so many burdens and over such a short time. Even I would balk, and I am eons older than you. It is a testament to your race that you can adapt so quickly."

"My elf!" Rachel cried out in joy. "I didn't kill you! You're alive!"

"No." Illondria shook her head sadly. "I am dead. I just haven't passed over yet. But you are not the one who killed me, child. Never think that."

"But I told Valerie...." Rachel's voice faltered.

"No, child. The mistake that revealed me had already been made by that time, and you took care not to be overheard. Mr. Smith and Miss Forrest spoke about me in a public place. They unwittingly pronounced the demon's name during the same conversation."

"Oh." Rachel wet her lips. "But.... I still...."

Illondria's eyes shone like stars of kindness. "No, my dear one. Never."

"So... you're a ghost?"

"You could say that. Yes." She held Rachel at arm's length, brushing the hair from Rachel's eyes. "Oh, little one, I am so sorry. I thought I would be with you a bit longer. I left things undone. In addition to everything else weighing upon you, you must stop the summoning of the Archfiend. Great sorrow will befall you and those you love should he wake."

Rachel bit her lip and nodded.

The Elf looked down at her kindly. "Let me show you something I often liked to see, when I was feeling the weight of the world."

The dream rippled. They stood at the foot of a truly gigantic tree rising up from a vast forest. Rachel knew it was enormous because there were great cities nestled around its base, and a tiny hollow, near one root, contained a magnificent metropolis. She and the Elf seemed to be standing on a silver pathway, the color of moonbeams, in the midst of a vast darkness. Ahead of them rose the floral giant. Above, smaller trees, still as large as sequoias, grew on the titanic branches, and a second group of trees grew out of the canopy of these giants.

"This is the great tree Yggdrasil, the World Tree. My people guard it—or did, before it fell. The many worlds hang like fruit from its branches. My lord Duneyr once told me that all worlds have a great tree grown from saplings of this one greatest tree. Yggdrassil is as large as the entire continent upon which your body currently lies."

Filled with awe, Rachel forgot her sorrow. This was exactly the kind of vista that she longed to see when she wished to travel to other worlds.

Suddenly, Rachel began laughing. "Oh no! I've been arguing with my boyfriend over whether he can tell Vladimir Von Dread information that he got from seeing a memory of—*me talking to Vladimir Von Dread.* For heaven sakes, Vlad already knows all that! *I* told him!"

The Elf smiled at her, though Rachel had the feeling that the tall woman did not entirely follow what she was saying. Still, Illondria did seem pleased when Rachel laughed.

They stood together watching the World Tree and its surrounding forest. The darkness felt thick around them. The silver path shone beneath their feet, ringing softly like the sound of distant bells. Rachel was aware that time was passing, quite a bit of time. Her sorrow began to ease, as if the cause of it had occurred long ago. The terrible grief she had felt at the Elf's death also lessened. A sense of calm settled upon her.

"Illondria, you are holding time still," came a familiar harsh caw. "Is there a reason?"

Rachel spun around. An enormous Raven flew over the silver pathway. As it came closer, the otherworldly vision faded, and the three of them stood by the dream of the winged statue again. The Raven cocked its head and gave the statue a look. The wings vanished. The bird landed, pecked the ground three times, and then turned into an unbearably handsome, shirtless, eight-foot-tall winged man.

"I merely wished to comfort this little one before her friends wake her," said the Elf.

"Ah," the Raven gazed down at her, "it is you."

"Yes." Rachel curtsied. "Thank you for saving me from the Headless Horseman."

"Did you?" asked Illondria. If she did not know better, Rachel would have thought the Elf was smirking. "How quaint and out-of-character of you, Guardian."

The Raven regarded her calmly. In a burst of courage, Rachel ran forward and hugged his leg. Her head came up to his hip. He sighed but did not cast her away.

"Oh, that looks like fun," murmured Illondria.

She glided forward and hugged him as well. She was only a foot shorter than him. The Raven closed his eyes, as if seeking to endure such indignities without complaint.

"Guardian, lean down," asked the elf woman. "Please?"

He frowned but obliged, leaning over with a wary look in his scarlet eyes. With a gesture and a wink, the taller woman communicated her meaning to Rachel. Moving as one, the two of them leaned in and kissed him, one on either cheek.

The Raven's eyes widened. A frisson traveled over his body. It reminded Rachel of a cat's fur puffing up. She was still laughing when she awoke.

• • •

Opening her eyes, Rachel found herself lying on the table in Room 321. Joy was off to one side, looking both embarrassed and extremely amused. Zoë stood, arms crossed, glaring at Gaius, looking anything but amused. Gaius looked sheepish. (*Rammish*, thought Rachel.).

When her eyes opened, Gaius rushed to her side. "Listen, I won't tell anyone. I trust you. I apologize for my doubts."

Zoë, who was standing very tall and glaring, relaxed a bit.

Rachel sat up. "Gaius, were we arguing about whether you could tell Vlad the contents of... my conversation with Vlad?"

Gaius blinked. "Um...."

"Well, this was great, but I have to be leaving," said Zoë, "and so does Joy."

"I don't have to go anyw—ack!" cried Joy.

Zoë dragged her from the room.

Rachel slipped from the table, a tiny seedling of joy battling through the crusted, half-melted ice that had recently encased her heart. At last, Gaius knew her secret. Now they were alone. She could finally tell somebody about the Elf and the Raven. She could barely speak from the anticipation.

Gaius stood looking at her thoughtfully. "I would prefer if you didn't spy on me. I understand some of the information you have gained has been extremely helpful. But I think I do have some right to privacy, don't I?"

The happiness inside Rachel wilted.

Was he still talking about this? She stood there for an uncomfortably long time, feeling totally baffled and uncertain of what to say.

"I-I don't know how to do that.... I don't really have any control over what I find out."

It was not that she did not feel sympathy for him. She did, very much so. If she were in his position, she would probably be upset, too. If only she had just picked the scene to show him more wisely

"I'm sorry, I may have jumped to a conclusion," he said. "If you have no control over the avenue that this information is delivered through, then of course I can't ask you to stop it."

"Do you want me to protect you and try to hide your secrets? ... I-I can do that." Rachel stared at some really interesting floor tiles. "Do you want me not to tell you when I find out things about you.... I could do that, too."

"If you can honestly say 'Gaius, you have no right to privacy' then, fine," he continued, as if he had not heard her. Perhaps, he had not. "I will shut up about it. I do think, though, that I have some right. Dread would say none of us do. That the world is more important than privacy. But I am pretty sure you've learned nothing that could save the world from spying on me."

Rachel swayed, as if someone had slapped her. She had waited so long to share her innermost secret with him. She had so hoped that he would be pleased with her cleverness and her unique gift. How sad that, after all that waiting, his only reaction was to browbeat her over something for which she had already apologized.

She wanted to tell him that, of course, she would never betray him. He was the most important thing in her life! But the darkness and the buzzing had returned. She feared she might lose consciousness. Her face remained calm, but she failed to control the expression in her eyes. She gazed at him like an injured animal who was trying to crawl back to the master that had beaten it.

"I'll try to protect you, Gaius. I-if I can keep someone from spying on you, I will," she struggled to speak clearly. Holding up her hand, she promised softly. "So swears Griffin."

Despite her distress, she was struck by the irony of her promise. Considering how boring Sigfried would find the idea of using his amulet to watch Rachel's boyfriend, it was unlikely that she could have talked Siggy into spying on Gaius, even had she wished to.

"Thank you. I appreciate that." He rubbed his eyes. Then, he glanced at Rachel. "Um. Are you all right? You're looking very pale."

Suddenly, he was beside her, pulling her into his arms. Rachel swayed against him like a puppet whose strings had been cut. Placing her palm on his chest, she closed her eyes. Within the circle of his embrace, the buzzing and the darkness slowly died away. Tension seeped from her body. The knots in her stomach untied themselves. She rested, letting him rock her back and forth as he kissed her forehead repeatedly, whispering over and over, "It's okay. It's okay."

Opening her eyes again, she lifted her head, her lashes half-closed and her lips slightly parted, to see if he would kiss her. He did, a very light and soft kiss.

Relief came, but with it a wave of nausea, the kind that occasionally followed moments of high adrenaline. "I... I don't feel too good. Could... we sit down?"

Gaius helped her to a chair and ran into the hall, coming back with a cup of water from a water dispenser in another club room. Rachel sipped the water and gave him a thankful smile.

"I didn't mean to embarrass you, Gaius. I'm really sorry."

"I didn't mean to upset you, either. It was just a lot to take in all at once." He leaned against the table beside her. "That whole situation with the *Spell of True Recitation* was awkward. I didn't like feeling like I couldn't control my responses. It was... unnerving. And then finding out someone else saw it...."

"I was so impressed with you," Rachel blushed slightly, "and relieved that you didn't say: 'I work for Professor Mordeau, and I've been sent to seduce Rachel Griffin to try and influence her Agent father.' It never occurred to me you might be embarrassed.

"I told Vlad what you had said about him because I couldn't think of any other way to get you back into his good graces. I figured if he knew how you supported him, even when you couldn't lie, he would realize what a good fellow you were. I was trying to help."

"I know," Gaius nodded, "and I rather appreciate not being a sheep. Really. I just wish I could have avoided it all together, you know, by beating him instead of losing. Or I would have settled for a tie...." He chuckled, adding, "That fight ruined my record. I had been undefeated."

"Aw! Oh no!" Rachel cried, crushed on his behalf. Then she looked down shyly, biting at her lip. "So... did you like my secret? Or were you so embarrassed that all your blood rushed to your face, and none was left for your brain?"

"Impressed? Yes! A hundred times yes! I was impressed by all of it. I wish we could have stayed. I'd like to see more."

"I wouldn't mind having you come back into my dreams again... but not today." She was quiet a moment, savoring his admiration, even if it was belated. "You can even tell Vlad my secret. Topher figured it out."

"How in the world did Evans figure out your secret? Wait, was it during that first Knights meeting? You gave a report, and, forgive my weak memory, but I thought it was very... in depth. An unusual attention to detail, though most people probably thought you were showing off for Dread or Starkadder. But even I had no idea about what you could really do."

"Dread or Starkadder!" Rachel snorted. "The only person I wanted to impress was you."

"I've never been unimpressed with you."

Rachel rose and picked up her broom. She reached for his hand. "Come on. It's time for me to tell you the Big Secret."

• • •

They flew up to the belfry where they had spoken the day she came back from Beaumont. Sitting on the marble steps, the twilight sky growing darker by the minute outside the windows, Rachel told him everything: about the Elf; about her gift of the Rune from the World Tree that protected her memory; about how she was now immune to the *Spell of True Recitation* and to geases; about the Raven; how he had been forced to change Sakura and to erase her friend's memories—emphasizing that this was the part that he absolutely must keep secret; how doing this to her would have harmed her; how she volunteered to let him change her for the sake of the world; and how he had been so impressed by her devotion that he had spared her.

It was such a relief to finally tell someone all the things she had been bundling inside, but as she recalled recent events, sorrow mixed with her joy.

"So, just to make sure I understand exactly what I can and can't say, the secret is: that this Raven can come and knock us out and change our... souls? What were those glowing balls he pulled from their bodies?" Gaius knocked on his chest. "Do we all have one of those? I've never even heard a story about such a thing?

"Anyway," he concluded, "We're not supposed to mention that we have such things or that he can change them, right?"

Rachel nodded, "Right."

"And that's why he had not wanted your Elf friend to give you the Memory-Protecting Rune, right? Because then, he couldn't just change your memory... without taking that away, which probably would have been a major operation—changing who you were."

"Right," Rachel nodded again.

"I'd love to meet this woman. The Elf."

She had not told him.

Oh, Gaius," her voice broke—only for an instant. Then she had her mask back in place. "The bull-demon. He killed my Elf."

"He... what?" Gaius blinked.

That all came spilling out, too, how she and her friends had caused the Elf's death by talking too much. The only thing she did not say was that she had just seen Illondria again. The recent events in dreamland seemed too raw to share.

"Rachel, I am so sorry for the loss of your Elf," Gaius spoke sincerely. "I had no clue she even existed. The loss of that avenue of information is painful for me to consider. The method of her loss even more so. But that was not your fault. You know that, right?"

Rachel nodded, but she bit her lip.

"Listen, I know this may sound wrong," Gaius said earnestly, "but you need to keep as quiet as possible about the Elf and what happened to her. Don't let a guilty conscience hamstring your future efforts. You do not want our enemies whispering about how trusting you with information can lead to someone's painful, fiery demise. I do not mean to be harsh, but I do need to be blunt. That woman should have been protected, but, instead, she was murdered. Best to let that whole affair disappear from history. We will avenge her death. I promise."

"The worst part is that she knew," Rachel whispered. "She knew if she talked to more than three of us that she would die. Yet she still spoke to Joy and called Zoë to her. She was so brave."

To her horror, her eyes brimmed with tears. She quickly brushed them away.

Gaius pulled her into his arms again and hugged her tight. Rachel leaned against him, her face stolid and set, trying not to cry. But it was no good. The tears she had been resisting for over a week began flowing over her lashes.

She lowered her head and hid her face against his chest, weeping.

He whispered, "It is okay to be upset about this loss, but you should also be happy that she thought you all worthy of sacrificing herself for. I... honestly do not know how someone can place so much trust in strangers. I know that it was well placed, though."

Rachel started to straighten up, but Gaius's brave words made her wail again. She cried against his shoulder, her body shaking.

Yet, she was also terrified. If she showed emotional weakness, her boyfriend would lose interest in her. The moment she could regain control of herself, she straightened and gave him a curt nod to show she was okay.

Gaius did not say anything. He just held her and kissed her on the cheek, close to her ear. A sweet tingly sensation spread through her body. That made her smile.

"She was older than language," Rachel marveled when she felt she could speak again. She sniffled slightly. "And she gave up that life to help us. The Raven tried to warn her. He wanted to protect her. She didn't listen."

Rachel stopped talking because it suddenly struck her how much she and her Elf were alike—not listening to those who told them to be careful, doing what they thought was right. It made her love Illondria all the more.

"If it is too painful, you do not need to consider it," said Gaius, "but I was hoping you would show me the times you met her. The way you showed me the Raven and the statue?"

"I would love to!" Rachel said. "Oh, do you know what she told me!"

Rachel told Gaius about the Library of All Worlds, repeating the words that Illondria had said to her: *I see you, years from now, in a place of great knowledge. A library such as no other that has ever existed. And happy, with these things far behind you. Do not falter, I think your victory is assured. Though achieving it will be great work.*

Then she held very still waiting for his reaction.

Gaius gazed at her, utterly fascinated. He began asking questions about libraries and information retrieval systems. He wanted to know if, when she created her library, she could make some areas that allowed for magical properties of texts and others that used mundane technology. He seemed very, *very* excited, explaining that he finally saw some hope that his desires to be both a scientist and to be a sorcerer might not be mutually exclusive after all.

They talked about the Library of All Worlds for over an hour. The world outside grew dark with only a few faint stars twinkling in the otherwise overcast sky.

"So this Rune of yours," Gaius asked when their conversation had come to a pause, "it lets you remember changes made to the world, right? Kind of like being able to see through obscurations—if you were an Unwary. Only you can't be tricked by the Metaplutonian equivalent of an obscuration, right."

Rachel blinked at the thought. "It rather is like that. Yes."

"Great!" He looked relieved. "Then all scientific pursuit is not futile. If they can't make you forget, then we still have at least a seventeen percent chance of figuring things out after all."

Rachel lowered her lashes demurely, pleased. "I am glad to be of use."

"You bet! Now if we could only figure out where this demon's.... Hey!" Gaius straightened. "These visions the princess has, can they be induced? Can she ask for one? Ask where this mysterious 'place of power' is?"

"I don't know." Rachel pulled out her calling card. "Let's find out."

CHAPTER THIRTY-TWO:

BANISHED KNIGHT

"SO, YOU SHOWED ALL THIS TO THE DEAN ALREADY?" ZOË ASKED Nastasia, gesturing at the dreamland around them. Her tiger-spotted quoll sat on her shoulder, looking around curiously with its black, bead-like eyes. "But she didn't recognize it, eh?"

Zoë, Nastasia, Rachel, Gaius, Joy, Valerie, Sigfried, and Lucky stood in the midst of what looked like fuzzy Grecian ruins, with eroding columns over a marble staircase and piles of sand-colored rubble all around them. Pillars reached skyward. In the distance, Rachel could see ocean and mountains beyond. She turned slowly in a circle, hoping that she would recognize some angle as a photo she had seen once in an encyclopedia, but nothing matched her memory. Of course, it did not help that Nastasia's dream image of her vision kept blurring and wavering.

Nastasia nodded. "When Gaius asked me if I could request a vision, I did so—" the princess glanced warily at Gaius, who was standing to one side leaning against a pillar "—and one came. I then shared it with Dean Moth. She is informing the proper officials."

Rachel winced, hoping that the Wisecraft had discovered their leak and stopped it. She could tell her friend would have preferred not to have brought Gaius with them, but Nastasia could hardly insist that he be excluded, when the whole project had been his idea. This left Rachel in the uncomfortable position of not knowing where to stand.

She wanted to be close to Gaius, especially since they had just recovered from their first row, but Nastasia seemed so fragile after her vision that Rachel did not wish to leave her alone, either. So, she was standing next to the princess, who shot her a grateful look that went a long way toward making Rachel feel she had chosen the right spot. She squeezed her friend's hand, and Nastasia smiled faintly and nodded. If only the princess and Gaius could get along. Then, she would be able to stand near both of them.

Joy was also nearby, looking on with concern. Every few seconds, she asked the princess if everything was all right, if Nastasia wanted to wake up again, if she needed a glass of water—where Joy would have fetched water from in dreamland, Rachel had no clue— but Joy's attention seemed to make Nastasia more ill-at-ease rather than less.

When Joy stepped away to look at something Zoë was pointing at, Rachel pressed her friend's hand again.

"Are you okay?" she whispered.

"Yes." The princess gave her a very brave smile. "I'm just a bit... disturbed at having people inside my dream. I keep fearing I'll get distracted and change the dream around us, accidentally portraying some private thought or memory not meant for others."

Suddenly, Rachel felt much more sympathy for Nastasia's position. It had taken some effort, when the others were in her dream, to make sure her mind did not wander. She was not sure that she would have wanted a friend's boyfriend, whom she did not know well tramping through her dreams, and she had more control over her memory than most.

"So, this is the demon's 'place of power'?" asked Gaius, looking around with interest.

"I do not know," said the princess. "What I asked for was the location where a sacrifice might take place. So we could stop it."

"Looks like Greece or the Middle East." Zoë kicked a piece of rubble. It puffed into mist. "I haven't spent much time there. We should have asked one of the March kids to come in here with us. They live in Greece part of the year."

Gaius came over and squatted down, examining the piece of rubble she had kicked, which had appeared again. Standing, he kicked one of the stones. It dissolved into a puff of mist and then reformed. He tried this several times, kicking a large boulder and then a column—the latter of which did not seem affected—and examining the outcomes.

Rachel glanced at Nastasia, but she was not paying attention to him. Apparently, dissolving pieces of the dream landscape caused her no mental distress.

"I know how to find out where this place is," grinned Sigfried.

"How?" asked Rachel.

"Walk away from Zoë."

"What?" Valerie punched him in the arm. "You're making no sense, boyfriend."

"Actually, he is." Gaius straightened up from where he had been watching mist reform into a crumbled brick. "If we walked away and fell into the waking world, we would be there. In the place these—" he gestured around them, "—columns and ruins represent, right?"

"Yes!" Rachel clapped her hands with delight at the simplicity of it.

"And then we could go ask a bunch of Greek or Arabic speaking people where we were. And they wouldn't have an owl's hoot of a clue what we were saying. Great plan." Zoë rolled her eyes. "And how do we get back? Not a lot of people in the Middle East dreaming about Roanoke... unless we just so happen to run into Mrs. March again... which is not that likely. Who's for violating our promise not to leave school grounds and getting expelled! Hmm? Raise your hand? Anyone?" She looked back and forth.

Rachel sighed. Siggy scowled.

"We could invite Mrs. March here," said Joy. "She's the princess's family friend."

"Is she?" asked Gaius. "She's the conjured woman, right? The Grand Inquisitor's wife? Why don't we try to reach her on a talking glass? Maybe she'd know where this place is."

Nastasia replied primly, "Dean Moth had a photo taken of the image that appeared in the thinking glass when I showed her this vision. I have no doubt that the Wisecraft will find it."

"Wish I could get a photo back home." Valerie snapped a picture. Everyone else covered their eyes from the glare of the flash. "My friend Wally could do an image search and see what came up."

"That would only work if it is a mundane place," Gaius replied. "If it is a place of the Wise, a place obscured from mundane men, it won't show up on the Internet."

"I will make the dean aware of Sigfried's idea. Perhaps the Agents will ask for Zoë's help. She could bring them here and let them drop out into the real landscape," promised Nastasia. "I don't believe there is more we can do."

"There must be more we can do," said Gaius. "This demon must be stopped."

"At all costs," murmured Rachel and Sigfried, simultaneously.

"Not all costs," Nastasia replied graciously. "The ends never justify the means. But, since this demon is a bad thing, we should be willing to do anything within our means that is moral to stop it. Even if it is difficult or requires great sacrifice."

"You don't hesitate when fighting evil," Sigfried said, an angry grimness in his voice. "That thing nearly killed me! Besides, it was evil. Really evil. I could feel it. Doesn't matter what you have to do to stop a thing like that!"

"It always matters," admonished the princess. "We can fight bravely, of course, but not in a fashion that is immoral or unlawful. Rules are rules."

"At *any* costs," repeated Sigfried fiercely.

Rachel felt in her heart that he was right. And yet, her thoughts returned to her conversation with Vladimir about letting the world burn to save her sister. Hard as it was for her to say this, especially while recalling the horrible feeling she had experienced when the demon started to appear in Beaumont, she offered cautiously. "I guess not at *any* cost. I mean… we would not want to sacrifice the very things we wish to protect."

"In other words, we do not want any Pyrrhic victories," said Gaius, "which is appropriate, considering that we are discussing a deity worshipped by the Carthaginians. Oh… wait. Wrong Roman war. That would be a Punic victory, wouldn't it?"

Rachel giggled.

There was something really cute about a boy who knew his Roman wars.

"Against pure evil, there are no rules," Sigfried insisted, an angry light burning in his eyes. "Right, Lucky?"

"Course, boss," said Lucky, in his gruff, dragon voice. "He killed the nice-smelling elf who let us roast marshmallows in her cheer-fire."

"At the orphanage," continued Sigfried, "you could always tell which of the new kids would end up as hamburger, and which would end up on top. The ones on top were those who were willing to do whatever it takes to win. Gouge eyes, bite ears, burn faces, whatever. You do what it takes, or you lose."

"And we don't want to lose," added Lucky. "Losing is bad. We might lose important stuff, like our gold!"

"We have to be willing to do anything to stop this guy," Siggy continued, "mow him down, blow him up, char him, fillet him, explode him, burn him, incinerate him. Whatever it takes."

"No, Mr. Smith," insisted the princess sternly, "only what is moral, legal, and proper."

Nastasia spoke calmly, but Rachel could tell that her friend was extremely agitated. The subject was of extreme importance to her, yet Siggy was oblivious to the princess's distress.

On the other hand, Rachel could tell that the issue mattered to Sigfried in a completely different way. There was a strange sort of emotion, almost panic, in Siggy's eyes. Rachel wondered if he were seeing again the charred body of the Elf, or perhaps something from earlier in his life, some humiliation or beating he had seen or had done to him.

"That's ridiculous!" Sigfried raged. "Proper? These guys did not throw down a gauntlet or issue a challenge or anything! We cannot tie our own hands! If the world is destroyed, what does it matter that we fought according to proper rules? If they are all ganging up on you, you fight dirty. You hurt them! Hurt them until they stop! You fight to win, or you are a nothing!"

"But if you do not behave morally, then you yourself become evil," replied the princess. "Then you are also nothing."

"If that's what it takes, then that's what it takes!" Siggy declared fiercely. "He must be stopped! *At all costs!*"

The scene around them wavered and faded away. They were standing in a blurry haze.

"You are no longer my knight!" snapped Nastasia.

Sigfried's eyes grew round with horror. "You... you can't do that! Liege-lords can't fire their vassals!"

"I may do as I like. You are dismissed."

Sigfried looked utterly devastated. His expression wrenched Rachel's heart.

Nastasia, however, had turned away. "Miss Forrest, I would appreciate if you would take these people out of my dream. I would like to wake up now."

• • •

Back in Room 321, the group split up, heading in different directions. Siggy stomped from the room followed by Lucky, who faithfully tried to stomp in imitation of his master, but who really was not built for it, his claws scrabbling against the floorboards, and Valerie, who looked resigned. Nastasia, her face stony, set off in the opposite direction, followed by Zoë and a fawning Joy. As Rachel turned to go, Gaius caught up with her, touching her elbow.

"I nearly forgot." He smiled at her. "I have something for you."

"For me?" she asked.

"It's yours. I wanted to return it." Out of his pocket he pulled a familiar, thin, cedar box.

"Oh, my wand!" Rachel cried with delight. She took the box and slipped it into her pocket. "What did you find out?"

"Sorry it took so long to get back to you. I had to wait for William to get back. He was at O.I. helping put the final touches on that secret project I told you about. The one based on Blackie's work. Looks like I might be able to tell you about it very soon. Which is good, because if we can find out where the demon is, their new invention might prove useful.

"Anyway, now that he's back, I had William take a look at your wand. He discovered that vestal wands have the unique property that they are very good at catching incoming spells. If you can do an *oré* in time, or if you have some stored in the wand, you can catch spells being flung at you about fifty-five percent of the time. Which might not sound like a lot, but with a fulgurator's wand, the percentage is closer to twenty-two. Apparently, this has been tested extensively."

"Really!" Then, she sighed. "Unfortunately, I'm horrid at the *oré* cantrip."

"I happen to be excellent at it, Miss Griffin." Gaius gave her a cocky grin. "Maybe we could work something out."

"Maybe," Rachel replied, throwing him a coy, sideways glance.

He grinned, adding, "Also, William was able to determine what spells are currently stored inside the gem... beyond those you've added. There is an enchantment that will dispel a storm. A number of *bey-athe* shields. Seven, I think he said. Also, when I ran back to get this while you were talking to Nastasia earlier, I put a few bedazzlements in there for you—in case you guys need to get to dreamland quickly."

"Thank you! That's very thoughtful."

"There was one more thing." He grinned. "William says the wand also contains three charges of the Eternal Flame. That white and gold stuff that burns the innocent and doesn't hurt the guilty." He paused and then chuckled. "Oops... I meant the other way around."

"Excellent!" cried Rachel.

"Let me emphasize," said Gaius, "how rare and valuable that is! Vlad has some charges... because he's a *crown prince*. But the Vestal Virgins don't give the stuff to just anyone. Even Agents sometimes have trouble getting charges of it."

"In other words, once I've used these three charges, I may never be able to get more," said Rachel, adding, "The dean can *conjure* Eternal flames."

"Yeah, I saw that." Gaius sounded awed. "Being able to do that is a very, very rare gift."

Rachel held up her wand. "I wonder if these flames would be effective against demons?"

"Let's hope you never have to find out." He smiled at her. "And now, unfortunately, I need to actually study. How are you feeling? May I walk you home?"

"Of course."

Gaius offered his arm, which she took. He led her down the stairs and across the campus to the porch of Dare Hall. Once there, he leaned down and gave her a kiss, quick and sweet.

Ah. Perfect, thought Rachel, drifting off into girl heaven.

• • •

That night, in bed, Rachel recalled her day. It had been two parts joyful to four parts disturbing, and some of the more disturbing aspects had not really hit yet. She had been aware for some time of the diverging paths of the proper and rule-bound Nastasia and the rebel-who-lives-by-his-own-rules Sigfried, but she had not expected them to diverge quite so dramatically. Feeling as fragile as she did, Rachel did not know if she would survive being asked to take sides in their disagreement. If only she could go away until they were done sorting themselves out. Maybe she should take her sister Sandra up on her invitation to visit.

There was another reason to go to Sandra's, as well. Today, it had been Sigfried who butted horns with the princess, but it could just as easily have been her. She was more eager to placate Nastasia than was her blood brother, but their philosophies were still at odds, especially when it came to rushing into danger versus obeying the adults.

But one reason Rachel constantly ran towards danger, flew at planes, and crashed the waltzes of the dead was because if she stood still, she would have to face the darkness that threatened to engulf her—darkness born of all the emotions she had thrust aside in order to stay calm. She needed a chance to confront the horrors she had encountered, to mourn, to weep, to be weak. And she needed a place to do this where her boyfriend could not see her.

No boy wanted a girlfriend prone to madness.

This would be doubly true for a boy who worked for Vladimir Von Dread—because losing one's mind was just another way of saying one was too weak for the task at hand.

Her thoughts drifted back to the day's few joyful parts. Seeing Illondria had been joyful. Rachel realized that she had forgotten to tell the others about her encounter with the elf woman. She made a mental note to do so the following morning. Were all ghosts solid in the dreamlands? Or was their Elf special because she had been a mistress of dreams in life?

She was relieved to have discovered that she was not a murderess after all; however, the fact that she had been willing to take responsibility for Sigfried's decision to tell Valerie stayed with her. She suspected that however long she lived, she would bear the weight of it. Of all the things that had happened to her since the start of the school year, that one decision had changed her the most. In that one act, she had become a little less like the young girl who arrived at Roanoke and a little more like her grandfather.

Or, she thought, recalling their conversation by the koi pond, a little more like Dread.

The other joyful part had been the excitement with which Gaius greeted her news about the Library of All Worlds. His avid interest in her future plans delighted her. She continued to be impressed with how in sync she and her boyfriend were on, oh, so many things.

She had already decided not to hold his outburst this afternoon against him. Looking back through her memory, watching his face and his reactions, she realized that—in the same way that he had been too absorbed in the matter of his having been spied on to notice her distress, she had been too caught up in her excitement over sharing her secret to properly notice how upsetting he found much of what she had told him. The idea that scientific evidence might not be reliable and that his farm had not always been there had been very disturbing to him. Then, on top of that, he suffered the embarrassment of finding out he had been spied on when he felt so vulnerable.

She lay for a time, staring at the bunk above her and dreaming of their future life together. She imagined a library that somehow spanned worlds. The Elf had said that the worlds hung from the World Tree like fruit. Could a library be built inside the Tree, spanning its branches? Or maybe it should be built in Bavaria, some handsome edifice surrounded by forest. She could then work as a librarian, while he worked for the prince—most likely Von Dread would be happy to support such a venture.

Each idea formed a picture in her head, pretty and perfect like the photos on Yule cards. Some even showed their six children running hither and yon. Rachel pictured the littlest one, the future librarian, who in this particular fantasy was towheaded and dressed in beige lederhosen, nestled in her lap as she read.

And yet, despite all her thoughts of literary and domestic bliss, the scars of the agony she had felt, when Gaius announced that he was going to repeat things that she had told him in confidence, still ached. What would have become of her had the Elf not appeared? If she were not careful, next time it would be the keel, and not merely the rudder, of the ship of her soul that snapped.

Much as she was willing to forgive him, Rachel finally had to face the painful truth that a sixteen-year-old boy, however worthy, did not make a very good center of her universe.

She needed to pick someone else, someone wise to trust above all others.

Caw!

A very large Raven, with eyes that shone scarlet as blood in the darkness, flew through her window without bothering to open the glass. By the time he had entered the room, he looked like a man. Standing eight-feet-tall, he was incomparably handsome, with hair that fell about his face and shoulders like dark feathers. His chest and his feet were bare. Between them, he wore baggy black trousers that reminded Rachel of pirate's garb. From his back spread a pair of truly enormous black wings.

A circle of gold hovered above him, glowing a warm buttery yellow. Its light filled Rachel with a diligent zeal. The emotional radiance ceased the moment he removed the circlet from over his head, but a soft golden light continued to issue from it. In its glow, Rachel saw that her sleeping roommates were completely motionless; not even their chests were moving. Near the bottom of her bed, Mistletoe had been caught by the time freeze in mid-stretch, which looked rather uncomfortable. The only thing that moved was the Comfort Lion, who opened one golden eye and then closed it again.

Rachel scampered from her bed and ran to stand before him, smiling up at him in her white, flannel, Victorian nightgown.

He gazed down at her. "I have come to make a request, Rachel Griffin."

"Certainly!" cried Rachel. "Anything!"

"Would you ask the Romanov princess if she will return Illon-dria to her home in Hoddmimir's Wood? It would be a kindness to allow the greatest of all Lios Alfar queens to speak with her husband one last time, before she must travel on to brighter shores."

"Yes, of course. I will ask her," promised Rachel.

Her heart beat with such excitement that Rachel could hardly hear herself thing. They would be accompanying the Elf to her homeland, perhaps see the broken World Tree with their own eyes? Rachel could not wait. It was all she could do to keep from running over and waking Nastasia right then and there. But she knew if she turned her back on the Raven, he would be gone, and there were things she wished to know.

As Rachel looked up at him, a question burst forth from her. "Please! Can't you do for our Elf what you did for Enoch Smithwyck? Bring her back from the dead?"

The tall being shook his head sadly. "I foresaw Enoch's fate and acted to shield him. I kept his spirit safe." He paused. "You might understand better if you thought of it as if he had not been entirely dead. I had no such opportunity with Illondria. She was attacked by the machinations of my nephew and slain in a manner I had no means to subtly counter."

"Oh." Rachel looked down sadly. Then her head came up again. "What about Xandra? She helped Siggy. Could she...." Her voice faltered at the severity of his expression.

"Would you bring more woes down upon your helpless people? Another demon, perhaps? Or a worse one? Would you have Belphegor or Beelzebub or Amon himself walking your world? Do you think that is a price Illondria would willing pay for her restoration?" The Raven shook his head. "No. Xandra's gift is one that, if used on this world, will always do more harm than good."

Rachel gathered the skirts of her nightgown and curtsied. "Sir, may I ask one more question?"

"I cannot answer questions about matters within my world or pertaining to those living here. Such things must be discovered from within."

"You mean, you won't tell me where the demon's place of power is? Things like that?"

The Raven nodded.

"Oh," Rachel said, disappointed. She puffed up her cheeks and blew disconsolately, sending a stray lock of hair flying. Then she straightened and gazed up at him, her eyes wide and sincere. "What can I do to help?"

"To help whom?"

"You. What do you need?"

"Me? I need nothing. If you will carry this one message, that is all I need presently."

"But… there must be something else I can do for you," Rachel asked hopefully. "A task? A job you need done? Are you hungry?"

"I require nothing."

"Not even to eat?" asked Rachel, visions of gathering treats from the dining hall to feed the Raven dancing in her head.

He shook his head solemnly. "I do not eat."

"Oh." She sighed, deflated. Then, a thought struck her. "You said I could not ask about your world. What about the Keybearers? Do they count as part of your world?"

"No. The Keybearers are part of a greater working. They are ones who have a high and weighty destiny before them—to undo a great harm."

"Am I…" she swallowed, "… a Keybearer?"

"No, child. Your part is to provide the Keybearers with inspiration and support."

"Oh." Rachel lowered her head, uncertain what to make of this.

She felt both disappointed and relieved. If her future the Library of All Worlds, might that be better than what awaited her friends? Certainly, it sounded more to her liking.

"'*They also serve who only stand and wait.*'" The Raven gazed off, as if looking into the distance. Turning back to her, he added, "Though you may find your part to be more active. And more pleasant."

"Is this Keybearer destiny the same destiny that Joy and Nastasia are part of?"

"Not precisely. That destiny has to do with stopping Azrael."

"But… we caught him."

"True, but he has merely been imprisoned, not undone. Were he to be let go, or to escape, my brother would still be a danger."

"Azrael is your brother?"

A great sadness came over the face of the Raven. "They are *all* my brothers."

"Even the angels?"

He smiled ever so slightly and inclined his head.

"Are you an angel?"

The Raven paused for a very long time. "I am."

Rachel gazed up at him, her eyes wide and dark. "Please, may I know your name?"

"No."

"Oh." She lowered her head. Recalling the name she had called in the dream she had after escaping the Headless Horseman, she asked, "May I call you Jariel?"

Something she could not quite identify crossed the Raven's face. Surprise? Amusement? He glanced downward, turning the shining golden hoop in his hand this way and that, sending shadows dancing across the ceiling.

"That is not my true name," he said presently, "but you may call me Jariel, if you wish. I will know that you address me."

Rachel nodded and swallowed. She had hoped she had somehow discerned his real name.

"And now I must depart."

"Goodbye... Jariel."

"Good night, Rachel Griffin."

Then, he was gone.

Standing in her nightgown, the floor cold beneath her bare feet, Rachel glanced from her cat, as he leapt from her bed, to her three sleeping roommates. She looked up at Nastasia's bunk where a single pale hand was all that was visible of her roommate. She thought of Siggy asleep downstairs on his bed of gold.

Sighing, Rachel decided she really would go to visit her sister for the weekend. In fact, she would go right now. Grabbing her coat, she set off at a run for the glass room in the cellar of Roanoke Hall.

Chapter Thirty-Three:

Interlude at Sandra's

"So, what would you like to do first? Eat? Go shopping? Sit and talk? Watch a movie?" Sandra Griffin asked forty-five minutes later, as she unlocked the door to 13 Wharf Place, flat 13B, and shepherded an exhausted and shivering Rachel inside.

"M-maybe just sit and get w-warm." Rachel's teeth were chattering. She wanted to pull her red wool coat tighter around her, but her arms were full of a wriggling Mistletoe. "Do you have a fire?"

"Not a real one, but I have a gas burner that looks like a fireplace. It's an Unwary thing. Come. Sit over here. I'll turn it up, and we can eat popcorn and have a good chat." Sandra smiled at her very sweetly.

Rachel came in and let go of her cat, who immediately leapt up onto a wide sill and gazed regally out the window. Starshine, Sandra's familiar, a slender black cat speckled with such a swirl of white spots that she reminded Rachel of the Milky Way, came stalking daintily across the sill to greet Mistletoe. The two cats touched noses and then ignored each other.

Rachel sat on her sister's couch, blinking. Sandra had arrived within minutes after receiving her little sister's call by talking glass. It had taken some time, however, for the sisters to obtain permission for Sandra to take Rachel off school grounds. Now it was well after midnight back in New York. Rachel was so weary, she could hardly keep her eyes open.

Making an effort to keep them at least half-way open, Rachel glanced around. The flat was an intriguing mix of elegant and utilitarian, decorated with a charming blend of antiques and stylish modern furniture. The outer walls were the unvarnished brick of the original warehouse, but hand-woven Persian rugs decorated the floor. The ceiling was made of rough wood, like the ceiling of an old pub, but a crystal chandelier hung in the center of the dining area. Sandra also kept will-o-wisps, which sparkled and twinkled among the rafters, giving the place an enchanted look.

"You have movies?" Rachel mumbled as coherently as she was able. "Gaius loves movies. He talks about them a great deal."

Sandra looked at her. "Wait! It's the middle of the night in New York, isn't it? Off to bed with you, *dongsaeng*. We'll talk when you wake up!"

• • •

Many, many hours later, Rachel opened her eyes. It was morning again. With only two trips to the loo and one brief break, during which her sister had insisted she eat a bowl of chicken and rice soup, she had slept through the entirety of Saturday.

Sunday morning dawned bright and clear. Rachel rose feeling much better. The buzzing and darkness that had been looming at the edges of her consciousness for weeks had receded into the distance. Her only concern was that tomorrow was the dark of the moon, and she did not know if the Agents had found the bull-demon's place of power. As she slipped out of her sister's large bed, where they both had been sleeping, and padded into the main room, where she could hear her sister in the kitchen busily making breakfast, she wondered how to convince Sandra to share what she knew of the Wisecraft's progress.

No opportunity to question her arose that morning. Sandra cooked her a wonderful-smelling Unwary breakfast with eggs, toast, fried tomato slices, and baked beans. Rachel ate it without complaining, but she decided she liked the old fashioned breakfasts that the Wise ate, or even American ones, better than what the mundane English ate in the morning.

At least, there was plenty of kimchi.

The meal was served on plates of red and gold that Sandra conjured for the occasion. Afterwards, she tossed the conjured china into the rubbish bin. Within twenty-four hours, it would vanish, and any food left behind would remain with the trash. Rachel noticed that her sister kept no permanent plates at all. She and Starshine conjured them anew for every meal. Sandra did, however have their great-grandmother's silver tea service. It rested on her mantel between two of Great- Grandpa Kim's long bamboo *minhwa* wall hangings, one portraying a tiger and the other cranes in flight.

"So I hear you went and added to the family without so much as a by-your-leave?" Sandra pushed back her chair, her lips pressed together with amusement. Her star-spotted black cat leapt into her laps and turned in a circle, kneading her thighs. Sandra winced.

"You mean my new blood brother!" Rachel hid the last of her beans under her napkin. "Well, I figured we live in a massive mansion, with two hundred and fifty-seven bedrooms, of which we—both family and staff—use precisely fourteen, and that includes the extra bedroom Peter uses just to read in. So it wouldn't be the hugest bother to put up another person."

"Two hundred and fifty-seven? Why, it can't be that many! Did you count?"

"Yes, indeed," Rachel replied primly. "I have been in each and every one and can describe it in detail."

Sandra blinked at this announcement. "But does he need a place to be put up? What about his family?"

"He's an orphan."

"Oh! It's Sigfried the Dragonslayer? The boy you introduced me to? The handsome one?" Sandra leaned forward, disturbing the cat, and smiled mischievously at her little sister. "Wouldn't you rather keep that one as a possible boyfriend?"

"Date Sigfried?" Rachel cried, outraged at the very thought. "Never! He's my brother! Besides, Gaius makes a much better boyfriend that Siggy ever would, I tell you!"

"If you say so." Sandra shrugged, shooed away Starshine, and picked up her plates.

"I do!" Rachel replied firmly, gathering her own.

"Shall I show you the neighborhood then?" her sister asked, as they finished dumping the dishes into the bin. "Broadway Market is just over the bridge across the canal. Then we can have lunch at the Cat and Mutton."

They crossed the Regent's canal and spent a charming morning peering at merchandise displayed on carts covered by green and white awnings and eating home-made fudge. The market was a riot of colors and sounds. The smell of fresh bread and warm cinnamon filled the air. Rachel felt shy among the Unwary and wished people would stop staring at her, but her sister's presence, close beside her, was a great comfort.

It was impossible not to feel safe when holding Sandra's hand.

The sisters had lunch at the pub Sandra had suggested and bought a meat pie to take home from a shop called F.Cooke, the sign of which included the quaint claim: *Live Eel Importer*. The window promised *Hot Jellied Eels* as well, but the sisters decided to stick to beef mince pie. Alas, amidst the hustle and bustle, there was no good opportunity to ask Sandra about the Wisecraft. Rachel also wanted to talk to her sister about Dread, but she could not gather the courage to introduce the subject.

They walked along the long row of carts whose owners were hawking their wares. Sandra kept offering to buy things for her little sister, but Rachel insisted that she did not need anything. Only at the end of their expedition, as they were about to depart, did Rachel suddenly grab her sister's arm and point at a display in the window of a store that had been painted a pretty light blue.

"That! *Unni*, I want that!"

"Are you sure, sweetie? Isn't that a bit young for you?"

"That's what I want," Rachel insisted firmly.

Sandra made the purchase, and Rachel happily walked back to the flat, one hand holding her sister's, the other clutching a plushy, stuffed lion with a bright red bow tied around its neck. It would make a wonderful addition to the secret room with the couch.

That night over dinner, she did try to subtly ask her sister questions about the matter of the bull-demon, but all Sandra would say was, "Now, you worry about resting and feeling better and leave that matter in Father's capable hands."

As they finished, however, Sandra added, "I will tell you one thing, Miss Inquisitive. You were right to worry about your friend Juma. Just after Father had him moved, the first family he had been put with reported that a red-haired woman showed up looking for him."

"Serena O'Malley," exclaimed Rachel.

"Exactly," replied Sandra. Then she smiled. "Oh, and there's a letter for you."

Rachel took the letter and examined it. It was from Nastasia. Before leaving Roanoke Friday night, Rachel had written the princess a note letting her know about the request to bring the Elf home, asking very nicely if Nastasia might wait until Rachel returned before doing this. She also urged her friend to patch things up with Sigfried.

Nastasia's reply read.

> *Dear Rachel,*
> *Thank you for your thoughtful note. I will wait for you to return before taking action on the matter of our mutual friend.*
> *As to Mr. Smith, I feel no animosity toward him. He is still a treasured friend. But he expressed values that I felt were not appropriate for a knight in my employ.*
> *I trust you will soon be feeling better.*
> *Sincerely,*
> *Your friend,*
> *Nastasia.*

Rachel was pleased that Nastasia was not angry at Sigfried, but remembering Siggy's face, she was not so certain that he was going to get over the incident quite so easily. He took this knight business very seriously. It could not feel good to the young orphan boy to have his solemn oath of fealty rejected.

Borrowing her sister's stationery, she wrote cheery notes to Nastasia, Sigfried, and Gaius, about what a nice time she was having in London and how she hoped to be back in a few days.

The next morning was Monday, November 13th. Rachel did not yet feel ready to return to school. Sandra made her a big breakfast and then set off to work, giving her little sister the run of the flat. This was the moment for which she had been waiting. Stretching out on her sister's bed, Rachel closed her eyes and mourned.

She reviewed her memory, pausing on each disturbing event since the beginning of the school year, both major ones, such as the death of the Elf, or the moment when her father told her to be an ordinary girl, and trivial issues, such as discovering she had been deceived her whole life as to the identity of her great grandmother, or having mistaken a house cat for a familiar. Each memory came to her as crisp and painful as when it had first occurred, entirely undimmed by the passage of time. As she experienced it again, she let herself be torn by the grief and horror she had dodged the first time, especially the emotions she had shunted aside with her mother's dissembling technique.

Then, she wept, cried, wailed, trembled, and did all the other things that she had so carefully resisted during the last two and a half months.

The day passed slowly; she cried for hours. Sometimes, she threw herself around on the bed, screaming and punching the mattress. Other times, she lay still, weeping and hugging her plushy lion. At one point, Mistletoe leapt up onto the bed, and Rachel cried with her face buried in the black and white cat's soft fur, but he was soon gone again, bored with being used as a pillow. Or maybe he did not like getting wet. Occasionally, she rose and went to the loo or drank a glass of water but even as she did these things, the tears kept flowing.

One realization became quite clear as the process of mourning helped bring the last few weeks into focus. She could not go on forever pretending she was something she was not. Gaius deserved to know who she really was, even if it meant that he would break up with her and go off with some more mature girl, like Colleen MacDannan or Tess Dauntless. During one of her breaks, she wrote him a letter, which unfortunately came out a bit tear stained. It read:

> *Dear Gaius,*
>
> *I want to tell you the truth. I am very sick, and Sandra is taking care of me. Something has broken in my mind, and I can't seem to stop crying.*
>
> *Vlad would say that I am weak, and I fear it is true.*
>
> *I know you like me because I seem so strong and clever and competent. But this isn't so. I have been hiding how bad things are for me. All my friends seemed to be able to deal with what has happened during the last two and a half months, but I can't. I don't know why this is.*

So now you know. I realize that boys don't like girls who are weepy and broken. I'm sorry for trying to deceive you into thinking I was okay.

I understand if you don't want to be my boyfriend. But I hope we can still be friends. You are the sole bright spot in my rather dark life.

With all my heart,
Rachel

She slipped it through the post glass. Then, she lay down on the bed again and wept some more. She couldn't stop. Her eyes ached. Her whole body hurt.

She continued examining her memories. Hours went by. Eventually, she came to the day that the Elf was murdered. She was not looking forward to re-experiencing these memories. As she was recalling walking into the Memorial Gardens to light candles for ghosts, however, something strange happened.

The little Lion in her memory turned and spoke to her. *"Come unto me and I will give you rest. For my yoke is easy, and my burden light."*

Her surprise was so great that she stopped crying. A gentle sense of comfort spread through her, much like the feeling that came when petting the little familiar.

She replayed the scene three times, but it remained the same. She could not tell if this event had just occurred, or if it had happened two weeks ago but had been obscured until she actively remembered it. Each time she recalled it, however, her feeling of peace and well-being grew.

Rachel rose and padded into the kitchen. Outside, the sky was already growing dark. An almanac she had once glanced at reported that the sun would set at this time of year in London by quarter past four. Sandra had left her a lunch in the fridge, a strange silver box filled with coldness that she had read about in books but never actually seen before this trip. Rachel opened it cautiously and took out the sandwich. Her sister's cat rubbed hopefully against her ankle, hoping for a bit of fish or cream. Rachel obliged, putting a bit of food down for both cats. There was also a bag of crisps on the counter. Taking the crisps and the sandwich, she sat down on the shiny black leather couch, eating her food and flipping through a coffee table book on *Temples of the World*.

The sandwich and crisps tasted surprisingly good. The pictures in the book were charming, showing the bright white temples of Hera and Zeus, the rugged wooden shrines to Frey and Freya. Some pictures had people in them — Unwary folk carrying flowers and honey cakes to a temple of Lucina, the Roman goddess of childbirth, or folk of the Wise lighting candles in the temple of Persephone at Eleusis. There was even a photograph of a deacon of Dionysus sacrificing a goat. Rachel turned that page quickly.

The next page showed a photograph of a picturesque ruin of an old temple, tall marble columns and sand-colored rubble. Rachel paused and cocked her head this way and that. If she turned it a bit, it looked rather like the princess's vision. She leaned over and read the inscription.

Oh. Of course!

Rachel grabbed her calling card. Did they have a range? Talking glasses worked across the ocean. She tapped it and called experimentally. "Nastasia, Siggy, Zoë, Gaius!"

There was no answer. Sighing, she rose and paced. Where was Sandra's talking glass? She found a mundane telephone but not the familiar green glass. She had to tell someone! She....

"Rachel?" Zoë's voice came from her card.

"Yes!" Rachel cried.

Other voices came from the green card.

"Hi, there!" cried Joy

"Hello," the princess said politely.

"Loud and clear," came Valerie's response.

"Rachel, is that you?" The last one was Gaius.

"Nastasia? That vision of yours. Did it look like this place?" Rachel cried excitedly. She held the calling card in front of the book.

"Perhaps," came Nastasia's voice. "I am not entirely sure. Many ruins look alike."

"That looks rather like the place we saw in dreams!" said Gaius. "Where is that?"

Rachel said, "It's the Temple of Saturn. In Carthage."

There was a moment of absolute silence.

Then Gaius called excitedly, "Okay. I think I might be able to do something to help. Um. I'll call you later!"

"Bye!" she called, delighted that he still sounded like his old self.

With a pang, she realized that her letter would not arrive where he was until tomorrow. He did not know the truth yet.

Siggy's voice came over the card. "Hallo, Griffin? Did you call? Sorry, I was in the loo trying to convince Lucky that toilet bowls are not drinking fountains for dragons. I gather the card I hid in the off-campus-talkie-room downstairs worked! It's tied both to your card and to ours, so we can all speak to each other. Clever, wasn't it? Actually, it was Goldilocks's idea. What's up?"

"We found the place," she said. She held up the picture.

In the card, she could see the calculating look on Siggy's face. He slid his hands into his pockets. "I'm not sure that's it. Nastasia, can we see it one more time?"

"Yeah!" Valerie was standing beside him. "We should compare the two images."

"I don't remember it as well as I did, but... I don't see why not," Nastasia replied. "Give me ten minutes to go inform the dean of this latest development."

Zoë's voice joined in. "Griffin, come meet us."

"Um... how?" asked Rachel. "I'm in London."

"Just go to sleep and dream of Roanoke."

"Right. I'll do that." Rachel had intended the reply as sarcasm, but an idea came to her. Running back into the bedroom, she grabbed her wand from her bag. Then, she lay down on the bed and took a deep breath.

"All right. Here goes!"

Pointing the wand at her face, she fired off one of Gaius's bedazzlement spells and tried very hard to keep thinking about Roanoke.

• • •

They cantered across the star-studded ocean, moonbeams flying about them like lances. The waves rose and fell beneath them like mountains. His arms held her waist firmly. Leaning down, he whispered in her ear.

"Weren't you heading for Roanoke?"

Rachel blinked.

She was riding her dream unicorn across a dark ocean filled with stars that moved beneath the surface like fish. Behind her rode Dream Gaius. He gave her his too-cheerful grin that didn't quite look like real Gaius. Apparently, her girlish subconscious was not able to entirely capture Gaius's spirit, though Dream Gaius then followed the grin up with a very Gaius-like quirk of his eyebrow. "Roanoke?"

"Oh! Right!"

Rachel recalled standing on the commons. Ribbons of mist curled about the lamp posts. From behind her came a shout. Zoë, Siggy, Joy, Valerie and Nastasia pelted across the dream-grass toward her.

"This is... very convenient," Rachel laughed. She turned to thank Dream Gaius, but he and the unicorn were gone.

"So... what do we do now?" asked Joy. "Stand back while the princess shines her princessy splendor?"

"Something like that," drawled Zoë. "Nastasia?"

Nastasia concentrated, a furrow between her brows. The landscape around her and the others started to change. Rachel kept her eyes on them, so that her dream did not separate from theirs. Soon they were standing among blurry ruins.

She walked around examining different angles. It was difficult, because Nastasia did not fill in anything she had not seen, so if Rachel stepped away from the princess, things became merely fuzzy and gray.

"Here, I think." She recalled the photo from her sister's book.

A vivid, crisp landscape sprang up overlapping part of the princess's blurry one. Nastasia frowned petulantly, looking annoyed. Rachel's initial excitement grew dull and the pain that had been quieted by the memory of the Comfort Lion came rushing back. She pushed it aside and concentrated on the task at hand.

"Definitely the same landscape," drawled Zoë.

"What do we do now?" asked Valerie. "I could go out and try to contact my dad. But it would take time for me to reach him on this phone-forsaken island. I'd have to get my cell and run to the docks.

And he hardly has a lot of contacts in... where is Carthage these days?"

Rachel consulted a map from her mental library. "Tunisia."

"Really?" Valerie looked surprised. "Weird. How did Aeneas end up in Northern Africa when he was sailing from Troy to Rome? Wasn't Troy in Greece?"

"Not Greece, Asia Minor. What we now call Turkey." Rachel tilted her head, thinking. "Speaking of Greece. I just thought of a possible way to get a message to the Wisecraft safely. I'll be right back."

CHAPTER THIRTY-FOUR:

A UNICORN TO THE RESCUE

RACHEL REMEMBERED.

A grassy hillside appeared around her. Nearby, a spring burbled from an opening in the hillside. The waters danced with a melodious rhythm. In the distance, islands sparkled on a blue, blue sea. Nearby, ten women lounged on the steps of an amphitheater, nine draped in white, and one clad in black. Seeing this last figure, who rose to her feet with panther-like grace, Rachel began to run.

"Mrs. March! Mrs. March!" Rachel tried just dreaming that she stood next to the black-clad woman. However, the dreamstuff of the amphitheater and the hippocrene were not affected by her attempts to control what was around her.

Rachel ran.

"Rachel, how nice to see you again." Cassandra March had covered the distance much more quickly than Rachel could have. Now, she gazed down with very dark eyes that reminded Rachel of Sandra's. "That was good work you and your friend did in Transylvania. The Wisecraft caught Rupert Lawson and his colleagues, thanks to your information and the breath-theft talisman you turned in."

"We found the demon's place of power," Rachel blurted out, but she could not help but feel very pleased at the other woman's news.

Mrs. March's pupils grew wide, exactly the way Rachel knew hers did when she accessed her memory, matching clues. If it meant the same thing, Mrs. March was thinking very fast.

"Tonight is the dark of the moon," said Mrs. March. "They're going to kill somebody."

"Right."

Mrs. March wet her lips. "We must stop them. Where is it? I'll wake up and tell Cain."

"The Temple of Saturn in Carthage." Rachel recalled the photo.

The ruined temple appeared beside them, on the side that was away from the hippocrene and the Muse. Only, this time, a temple was rising out of the rubble, bricks and stones coming together to reform the ancient building. In front of it stood the bronze structure Rachel had seen in one of the books in the library, a bull-headed furnace with arms outstretched to accept its victims. Under it, a fire roared.

Cassandra March grabbed Rachel by the shoulder and yanked her sharply, pulling her behind a pillar.

In front of the furnace-statue and the reforming temple stood the bull-headed demon and a number of purple-robed Veltdammerung cultists, some of whom were playing drums and woodwinds. One of the cultists had her hood back; a riot of red curls spilled down her shoulders. Beside her, gazing blindly ahead, as if he were asleep and not lucid, stood Juma O'Malley.

"No!" Mrs. March gasped, whispering. "They found him! It never occurred to my husband that they might not bother looking for his physical body and would just grab his dream self." She looked around frantically. "Rachel, I must go tell Cain. Get yourself back to safety."

With that, Cassandra March vanished.

Rachel peeked around the pillar to take one last look, to make sure she had not missed seeing anything.

"Have you spoken to my sister?" said a familiar voice.

Rachel spun around. The ghost of Remus Starkadder stood behind her, still dressed in his native finery with his huge white accordion sleeves and his black vest.

"Oh, it's you!" She put her back to the column, so the Veltdammerung followers would not see her. She figured that with all the drums and music, they would not hear her, so long as she kept her voice down. "Um... no. Gaius spoke to her. But that was two weeks ago. Didn't she come to see you?"

"She did, once," he said, pacing back and forth. He seemed more solid than when she had met him at the Dead Men's Ball, but not nearly as solid as her Elf had been. "But she has not come back. I have not heard anything regarding Romulus."

"How long do you have?" Rachel asked politely.

"The time has passed. I have been granted... an extension." The ghost fidgeted nervously.

"Oh. Well. That's good."

"Maybe." He stared off into the distance beyond the hippocrene.

Suddenly, he started and turned around, gazing back and forth between the Greek mountain side and the Tunisian ruins.

"Where... are we?"

"In dreamland," Rachel replied. Without moving from behind the pillar, she indicated the ruins behind her with a motion of her eyes. "There's a demon over there."

The already pale ghost grew paler. "What are you doing in such a place? Hardly seems a safe location for a young girl."

"I'm not really here," Rachel whispered back. "I'm in London, at my sister's flat. I'm just dreaming I'm here."

"Seems like a strange dream for the daughter of the Duke of Devon," he muttered back.

From behind them came a heartrending wail.

"Mama! Mama, no! Don't hurt me! You promised you wouldn't hurt me. Mama! No!"

Rachel spun and peered around the pillar. Two of the purple-robed figures held Juma stretched out in the air by his arms and legs. Serena O'Malley stood between them, holding him under his back, or trying to, as he writhed and struggled. She seemed to be attempting to move him up the stairs of the temple toward the outstretched arms of the bronze statue.

Gaius's words came back to her: *If there's anything worse than mothers getting paid for letting their children be killed... but only if they don't cry—I don't know what it is.*

Swallowing, her mouth dry, Rachel thought: *Maybe this.*

Kneeling down, she peered around the pillar for a better view. Was could she do to help him? She had not yet mastered the Glepnir cantrip. Perhaps she could paralyze someone, but there were many people there. Had she had her wand, she might be able to freeze a number of them very quickly, but her wand was back in England, lying on the bed with her sleeping body.

Listening to Juma's piercing shrieks, as he begged his mother to remember her promise not to hurt him, was too painful for her to bear. Rachel could not stand it. She could not stay here and watch. She would....

She had turned away from the temple. The ghost of the Transylvanian prince had vanished, but her unicorn was back. The beautiful white beast with its shining spiral horn munched grass next to the burbling hippocrene.

Rachel's lips parted in excitement.

"Unicorn!" Rachel raced to the beast and hugged it. Pressing her cheek against its sleek neck, she whispered. "You're a figment of my dreaming imagination, right? Can you change shape... if I want you to? Like other dream things?"

The unicorn nickered in agreement.

"Okay." She thought of an image very, very clearly. "I need you to look like this."

The unicorn shimmered and assumed the new form.

"You need to go over there." She pointed toward the temple and furnace-statue. "Run!"

Over by the temple, Serena and her two helpers had carried the struggling Juma up the marble stairs and through the columns. The statue was a mere three feet away. Juma was crying and cringing away from the extreme heat radiating from the open furnace. The desperate, struggling boy caught sight of the former unicorn.

"Mama," he shouted with joy. "Look!"

Serena turned her head. Her gaze fell upon a tiny elephant with big floppy ears advancing on her in a charge that would have done Hannibal proud.

"No!" she screeched, her face a mask of hatred and ugliness.

Then, everything about her changed. Her expression became gentle; her manner startled and timid; her hair less fiery and more auburn. Shock and dismay crossed her features.

Screaming like a banshee, she grabbed her son with all her strength and yanked him away from the startled cultists.

"Juma! This is a dream!" she shouted. "Wake up. Sweetie, you must wake up!"

"Jellybean!" Juma called to the tiny elephant, who was actually a unicorn. "I love you!"

Then the young man was gone.

Rachel slumped against the pillar, taking large gulps of air in sheer relief. She had not even realized that she had been holding her breath. It was all right. Juma had woken up. The real Jellybean would be there to greet him.

To her delight, the moment she stopped concentrating on the false Jellybean, the unicorn reappeared beside her, glorious and un-stained. It nuzzled her face. She put her arms about its head. Pressing her forehead against its soft nose, she let out a single sob of relief.

Behind her, at the temple, she heard the angry screech of Serena O'Malley reverting to her evil version. It was time to be away from here.

Rachel recalled standing next to her friends in Nastasia's fuzzy version of the ruins. The others were still there, waiting for her.

"That was hardly what I would call coming right back—" Zoë's voice cut off when she saw Rachel's face. "What happened?"

Rapidly, Rachel told them.

"So, they tried to sacrifice that kid with the stupidly-named ele-phant?" asked Sigfried. "He should have called an elephant Peanut."

"I think that elephant suffered from stunted growth, boss," of-fered Lucky. "Wasn't it kind of small? Or did they grow it that way to make it snack-sized? I mean he named it after candy, he must have expected somebody to eat it, right?" Lucky looked hopeful.

Valerie gave both of them a dark look. "This is serious, boys. What are they going to do next? Go get Juma in person? Grab a kid from a nearby town? Do you think...."

But Rachel never got to hear Valerie's question, because at pre-cisely that moment, she woke up.

· · ·

Someone was banging on Sandra's door.

Rachel jumped off the bed, catching her wand before it clat-tered to the floor. From her bags, she grabbed one of her school robes. It must have been the one she had worn on All Hallows' Eve, because there were still traces of grease paint on the collar that the laundry *bean tighes* had failed to remove. Throwing it over her nightgown, she stuck her wand next to some packet in the pocket and ran to the door, skidding to a stop on the polished wood of the floor.

They had not discussed visitors. Did Sandra want her to let people in?

"Sandra? I know you're in there. It's your neighbor, Marie. I thought I heard something. Open the door."

Rachel stood still, torn by indecision.

The voice grew louder and more angry. "Open the door!"

Rachel took a quiet step backward and then another. She recognized that voice.

It was Serena O'Malley.

Turning, she ran, looking left and right for a place to hide. Not finding an obvious one, she settled for a trick she had used often in hide-and-seek games. She raced into the bedroom, bunched up the covers, climbed under them, and curled up into a ball beneath one of the mounds, in the hope that the blankets would merely look rumbled and discarded. She held her hand over her mouth and tried to breathe very quietly.

There was more banging, and then much more banging, followed by a loud crack. Then came the sounds of a woman's footsteps moving through the apartment. Laying in the stifling heat under the covers, Rachel began to tremble. Her blood roared in her ears. Her whole body was shaking. Her heart hammered so loudly against her ribs that she was surprised she was not receiving complaints from the barges on the canal outside her bedroom window, much less the next room. She felt more frightened than she had at any previous point in her life.

She was alone with the violent, crazy woman who killed Mortimer Egg Jr.'s mother, and there was no one she could call for help. No one who would come save her. Her wand was in her pocket, but she was too frightened to reach for it, lest that motion be the one that betrayed her. She wished she had brought the plushy lion under the covers. At least she would have had something to hug.

The footsteps paused at the bedroom door and then move past. Rachel's heart missed several beats. Dare she hope?

"Out of my way, cat!"   Serena O'Malley's angry voice carried through the apartment. Over the connection she received from the familiar bonding ceremony, Rachel could feel Mistletoe hissing at the newcomer. *Good for him!* "This is taking too long! Where's the little pest? That ghost had better not have been lying to us!"

A tiny gasp escaped Rachel's lips. She covered her mouth more tightly. Remus Starkadder had told Veltdammerung where she was. Why would he do such a thing?

Oh.

Recollecting her conversation with the dead prince, Rachel realized that she should have known something was wrong. The shade had turned pale when she mentioned the demon, yet the ghosts at the Dead Men's Ball had not known what demons were. She should have realized that Remus, who had made a deal with Egg in life, might still be under the sway of Veltdammerung, even in death.

Footsteps grew suddenly louder. Before Rachel could pull out her wand, the blankets were ripped from the bed, exposing her body to cold air.

"There you are, you little minx!"   Serena O'Malley bent and lifted Rachel by her throat.

Chapter Thirty-Five:

Saturn's Army

"Rachel, I'm home! I have a surprise!" Sandra's voice sang out, followed by, "Good gracious! What happened to the front door? Rachel? Rachel!"

Relief flooded through Rachel. Sandra was home!

Everything would be okay.

Serena O'Malley jabbed her in the ribs with the tip of her fulgurator's wand. Blue sparkles danced across Rachel's body. Her limbs froze, unable to move.

Then, light was everywhere.

· · ·

Warm air and the sound of drums was the first thing Rachel noticed. Then the light faded, and she stood under the night sky, surrounded by men in purple robes carrying torches. In front of her, flames leapt out of an open door in the bottom of a huge furnace with outstretched arms and the head of a bull. The firelight illuminated marble steps, columns, and a bit of the brass of the furnace-statue.

Beyond and above, Rachel could see the bulk of the temple, a rectangular building with an octagonal tower that rose from the top of it—each story of the tower smaller than the story below it, like eight-sided nest-&-stack blocks. The whole temple was plated in gold, or perhaps, gold-tinted glass, upon which the reflections of the furnace flames flickered and danced. At the edge of her field of vision, was the glint of city lights. Beyond that was a deep blackness. Rachel could smell the ocean.

In the distance, there was a flash, like heat lightning, across the sky.

"Master," Serena knelt before a robed figure with glowing coals for eyes and bull-horns protruding from his temples. Rachel recognized him, the man from Beaumont, whom the demon Morax had possessed, "I have brought you a sacrifice."

The glowing coals swiveled to Rachel. *"What good is that one. No one here loves it."*

Serena bowed her head. "I have a plan, your viciousness. We can do it the other way."

The red-haired woman rose and returned to where she had left Rachel, some twenty-five feet away. "You two, watch her. You six, come with me."

Serena and her minions departed. In the distance, another flash of heat lightning.

The temple was still forming, Rachel realized. Parts of it were merely ghostly shadows. As she watched, rocks and rubble rose into the air, making the ghostly form solid. The stones rumbled and grated, as they jostled for their ancient positions. Rock dust mingled with the scent of the sea.

More flashes in the distance. There was something odd about the lightning. Rachel recalled it one fraction of a second at a time. Slowed down, she saw white pillars bright against the dark of the night.

Someone was jumping.

The horned man raised his arms. *"Ancient servants of my master, arise and serve me! Mine elite, my master's followers, rise. Stir!"*

The ground trembled. The robed cultists with the torches turned and looked outward. Time went by. Nothing seemed to happen, except that Rachel counted more pillars of light, flashing in and out in the distance.

"Why does nothing come forth?" bellowed Morax, through the mouth of his horned human servant.

One of the robed figures stepped forward and bowed to one knee. "Your viciousness, the Romans salted the earth. The dead cannot rise here."

A noise like the wrathful bellow of a bull rose from Morax. The horned man raised his head and sniffed the air.

"Ah! I call the ones given to my master!" Morax's voice was beast-like and grating. *"Arise! Come forth!"*

More flashes in the distance. Suddenly, Rachel realized what she was seeing. The Agents were looking for this place. Mrs. March had alerted her husband, and he had sent his people to Tunis through the nearest glass. Now they were trying to find this temple, but none of them had ever been here or knew what it looked like. They were using an advanced trick to make their jumps look like lightning, so as not to draw the attention of the Unwary.

She wished she could do something to help them, but she could do nothing at all.

It was frustrating not to be able to move, but a strange calm settled over her. Her previous terror fled. She did not even feel frightened. It was as if her lack of ability to act had relieved her of all responsibility, and now she could calmly await the unfolding of events.

In her heart, however, she made one solemn vow. She was tired of being paralyzed during battles. If she lived through this, she was going to insist her parents buy her an anti-paralysis talisman. Once she had it, she would to wear it at all times, even in the bath.

"Morax, I did as you asked. You promised my brother and me a kingdom." Remus Starkadder's voice came faintly from the darkness.

The horned man gestured. The ghost jerked into view as if pulled by a chain.

"*And so I did. A kingdom of pain!*" grunted Morax. "*You are of no more use to me. To Hell with you, where you belong.*"

The shade of the handsome, blond Transylvanian prince let out a bloodcurdling, horrible scream. Pale, colorless flames lapped at his legs. They began to consume his insubstantial form. He looked so vulnerable, so young, as his face contorted in unspeakable torment.

Paralyzed, Rachel could not avert her eyes or close them. She was forced to watch as the terrified prince was simultaneously devoured by the flames and dragged down into the ground.

It was horrible to behold.

She could not scream or even twitch. The horror remained locked inside her, searing her with an excruciating spiritual agony. The image of his tormented face would be with her for as long as she lived. She did not care what he had done, even betraying her. No one should have to suffer so terribly—not for so much as a moment, much less forever.

Everything within her cried out against such evil as this.

Another flash, this one close at hand. Serena O'Malley reappeared with a paralyzed Sandra and a second person.

Mother!

Three burly, robed cultists hustled Rachel's diminutive mother up the stairs and to the right of the temple porch. They turned her toward the statue, holding her arms. In the light of the flames, Rachel could see her mother, as gentle as a fawn, with eyes as dark as any doe, staring pale-faced at her paralyzed daughters. Her lovely face was completely calm, but Rachel could see her hands. Her pinky fingers were rigid as stone.

"My, my. The Duchess of Devon," smirked Serena O'Malley, stalking back and forth at the bottom of the marble steps. "Isn't it ironic? All that power, and no way to use it. No instrument to play enchantments. No cantrips... since you can't move your arms. And I have your rings of mastery." She held up her hand. Objects glittered on her palm. "You're helpless."

Serena's sarcastic banter turned to a snarl. "So here's the deal, duchess. I am going to kill your youngest daughter. If you do not react, if you don't weep, or cry, or say word, I will spare your older daughter." Serena turned to the horned man. "Is that acceptable?"

"*Yes. If it proves to be of stern stuff, the older daughter shall go free.*" Morax spoke from the man's mouth. "*If not, kill them both before the mother's eyes and consecrate both the temple and the priest —since our first efforts, last month, were interrupted by the Wisecraft.*"

"She'll crack, master," said one of the robed thugs. "She's a frail little thing."

"But a tempting morsel," crowed another. "May we have use of her when this is done?"

"*Only if it breaks,*" rumbled the demon. "*Otherwise, it may go free.*"

Ellen Griffin's face was a mask of perfect calm. Her voice was sweet and gentle, and yet it rang out clearly for all to hear. "Touch one hair on the head of a single child of mine, and it shall be the last thing you shall ever do. My husband will find you, and he will destroy you, utterly. And nothing shall keep you safe: neither walls, nor wards, nor sacred weapons."

Serena O'Malley snorted derisively.

Around her, however, the Veltdammerung followers shifted nervously, as if, perhaps, they did not think being threatened with the wrath of Agent Griffin, The Duke of Devon, was a laughing matter.

Watching her mother, so calm and collected, her eyes ablaze with faith in her husband, Rachel could not help but think that, if they could have seen her now, her imperious Victorian grandparents would finally have applauded their son's choice of wife.

"*Now we begin,*" bellowed the horned man. "*When this is done, we go to my master.*"

Serena's voice faltered slightly. "Go to him?"

"*When first I spied it, I did not recognize his prison,*" replied the demon. "*Now that I know where he is, it will be a simple matter to rouse him during Saturnalia.*"

"Excellent." Serena O'Malley's eyes gleamed red in the furnace-light as she rubbed her hands together.

"*The hour soon dawns of my master's return. First, he shall waken. Then, he shall retake his ancient throne. Once again, agony shall be the law of the land, and all the universe shall tremble. And with each sacrifice in my master's honor, the Enemy shall weep blood —for He shall be forced to admit the slaughter of His Lamb ended in failure. The great sacrifice-to-end-all-sacrifices has come and gone; yet nothing has been accomplished. Mortals still pay my master's toll of pain.*"

The two men watching Rachel lifted her up, tipping her sideways. The star-studded night sky shone above her. For a time, that was all she could see. The constellation of Orion shone above her, the three stars of the hunter's belt twinkling brightly. Below, she could see the higher portions of the eight-sided tower atop the temple, gleaming like golden glass in the firelight.

The tower moved closer. The heat of the furnace kissed her cheek. Then, it grew uncomfortably warm. Then stifling. She could not even squirm away as Juma had done.

As she stared at the stars, her right cheek feeling as if she had stuck it in an oven, Rachel wondered whether the Raven would have come to rescue her, had she been able to call him. No, she decided. He would not. A supernatural force, like the Horseman, was one thing. Veltdammerung, a group of human beings who had called up dangerous magic, was quite another. It was like the difference between questions about the world Outside and questions about the dealings of men here within.

The heat grew hotter still. Rachel composed herself to die.

She was not happy to be going so young. She had wanted to grow up, to learn magic, to see the Elf's home, maybe even to marry, have a family, and become the librarian of the Library of All Worlds. True, she had given up all that when she gave her life to the Raven, but he had returned it, and she had hoped to make something of it —to justify his faith in her.

But it was not to be.

She wondered if, once she was gone, Gaius might carry on with that plan in her memory. The thought made her happy.

Around her was drumming and chanting. She thought by the jerks of motion that she was now two stairs from the top. She wondered how those carrying her could stand the heat. Maybe they wore protective talismans or had cast cantrips to shield themselves ahead of time. Though she told herself that she was still fearless, her heart felt odd in her chest.

It was very sad to be about to die and not even able to cry.

Seeking comfort, she thought back, one last time, to her last meeting with Kitten's familiar in the Memorial Garden. In her memory, the Comfort Lion turned and spoke to her again: "*Ye shall know the truth, and the truth shall make you free.*"

Wait... what? This time was different.

How could that even happen?

The idea he had voiced so astonished Rachel that it entirely derailed her fear. Knowing everything was all very well. But was that what she truly wanted? Or did she want to know *the truth*? What a shame that she would not live long enough to discover the answer.

"GERONIMO!"

Sigfried Smith plummeted out of mid-air and landed, feet first, on the cultists carrying Rachel toward the statue's arms. At precisely the same moment, Rachel's mother whistled. Blue sparks flew from her mouth and struck the nearest of the cultists carrying Rachel. The result was that the five of them, Rachel, the three cultists, and Siggy, tumbled pell-mell down the steps.

Lucky, who had been wrapped around Sigfried, flew free and barreled into the bull-horned man, knocking him backward, toward the furnace.

"Pick on someone of your own supernatural magnitude, your stupid bullish-bully!" growled the dragon.

"Oh, gee!" Sigfried exclaimed in the least convincing voice ever. He stood with one foot on the back of the head of one of the cultists, pinning him down. "I just accidentally fell out of dreamland! I must have wandered too far from Zoë Forrest. Purely by mistake."

From behind her mother, whom Rachel could see from her current angle, laying head down across the fallen cultists, there came a bloodcurdling shriek.

Rachel knew that sound!

"Siggy, did you fall out again?" came Zoë Forrest's sing-song voice, as she swung her greenstone *patu* into the head of one of the brutes holding Rachel's mother. "You silly boy. I'm sure that happened entirely by accident!"

Freed of the thugs Zoë had just decked, the Duchess of Devon's voice cried out, "*Obé!*"

Rachel's limbs moved.

Without even getting up, Rachel whistled, freezing the man beneath her and then the one struggling under Siggy's foot. Grabbing her wand from her pocket, she cast one of the shield cantrips stored by her grandmother on herself and another on Sigfried. Then, she rolled to her feet and turned toward where she had last seen Sandra. Spells from angry cultists out in the dark somewhere bounced off the shields. Behind them, the enormous furnace-statue rocked dangerously as Lucky and the horned man wrestled.

"Rachel, are you all right?" came her mother's sweet voice.

"Yes. Mummy!"

"Stay where you are!"

A flash of light, and Serena O'Malley appeared next to the diminutive duchess, up on the temple porch. The red-headed woman pointed her wand at Rachel's mother, but the tiny, doll-like duchess threw up a *bey-athe* shield, deflecting the attack. The Duchess of Devon retreated, moving out of sight, but, Rachel could hear her mother's whistle and see the pretty glints of tiny blue sparkles dancing in the night. Whether they reached their target, Rachel could not tell.

"We must free Sandra!" Rachel cried. "She's over there!"

"She's okay at the moment." Siggy still stood, one foot still resting on the paralyzed cultist's head, watching Lucky and the man with the bull horns wrestle back and forth. His arm pointed off to the left, firing bursts of silver or blue sparkles, without even turning his head—apparently he was sighting with his amulet. "I just paralyzed the jokers who were guarding her."

"Still," Rachel said, "we should...."

A flash in the sky, closer than before. Its gleam illuminated something strange. A parade stretched away to the southwest. The foremost members had nearly reached the courtyard of large slabs in front of the temple. Hundreds marched toward them, perhaps thousands. A shiver ran down Rachel's spine. The light of the jump had bleached their faces and bodies bone white.

Click-clack.

Beside her, Zoë shivered. "What's that?"

"There are people approaching," Rachel whispered back. "Lots of them."

Click-clack. Click-clack. Click-clack.

"Why are they making *that* noise?" Zoë sounded spooked. The three students moved closer together, though Siggy still faced the other way, watching Lucky.

The vanguard of the parade came into the torch-light. They marched with a jerky motion, like marionettes. Yet there was something wrong with this army. Beside her, she heard the hiss of Zoë's indrawn breath.

Skeletons marched toward them, with bones that were cracked and black with soot. Or rather, some were skeletons. Others had flesh, but it was a dried, shriveled flesh, like a mummy, and what there was of it was blackened and charred.

"Are they ghosts?" asked Siggy, finally turning around. He was trying to make himself look, but his arm was up in front of his face, shielding his eyes.

"Just skeletons." Zoë's voice shook.

"Oh, that's all right." Siggy lowered his arm and looked at the new arrivals, twirling his trumpet between his fingers. "Um… why are they so short?" His voice caught oddly. "Oh, no. That is… so gross! Why does evil always have to be so gross?"

Rachel looked again, a cold sweat forming on the back of her neck, despite the heat from the furnace up the stairs behind her. Sigfried was correct. The figures were all too short, ranging from four feet tall to tiny ones that crawled slavishly along the ground. Most of them were around three feet. With them walked the bones of some animals, lambs, perhaps, or dogs?

Rachel felt her blood turn to ice.

The ones given to my master. The demon had summoned the remains of sacrificed children out of the Tophet of Carthage.

"Baby zombies?" Siggy's asked. "That is so wrong! This demon must go down!"

"Skeletons, not zombies," Zoë corrected, coming up beside him. Her face was grim, but she took a battle stance, greenstone club in hand. "I hate the idea of having to smash the corpses of children. Unfair psychological advantage for the baddies!"

A pillar of light lit the scene. Cain March appeared momentarily about a hundred yards away, his Inverness cape billowing around him. He was a lithely-built man, handsome and bearded, who reminded Rachel of a youthful Agamemnon. (Perhaps one whom, upon arriving at Troy, had forgotten about Helen and grabbed Cassandra instead.) He surveyed the scene for an instant, his eyes narrowed, and he vanished again.

Half a dozen pillars of light flashed around the temple grounds. Cain March had returned with some of his Agents. Rachel saw her father appear, along with his best friend and second-in-command, the implacable Templeton Bridges. They stood together illuminated by torchlight, a pale figure and a dark one in billowing cloaks and tricorne hats, with their tall staffs in their hands. Spell-fire flew back and forth between the Agents and the cultists.

Rachel cheered at the arrival of the Agents, but there were only six of them to fight five times as many cultists and an army of un-dead. True, they were baby undead, but that idea was so disturbing that Rachel did not even like thinking it.

The cultists ran forward toward the Agents, firing off spells. The army of little skeletons surged like a bone-white glacier, com-ing slowly but inexorably toward the stairs where Rachel and her friends stood. Across the temple courtyard, they swept over where one of the Agents stood. He was knocked from his feet and carried forward by the undead wave. All around him the little skeletons—some dead nearly three thousand years—attacked him with what-ever they could grab. Some hit him with rubble or bricks. Some bit him. Other wielded their own arm bones as knives. Rachel saw one of the taller skeletons, perhaps of a boy of nine, stop and put on the Agent's tricorne hat.

It seemed so much like something a living boy would do that Rachel suddenly found herself unable to swallow.

"Okay... um... suggestions?" murmured Zoë. "I mean, I can play whack-the-kiddy-skeleton as well as the next gal with her own Maori war club. But, even on my best day, I think I can only whack three or so at a time."

Siggy glanced warily over his shoulder. "Normally, I would sic Lucky on them, lighting 'em up like birthday candles, but he's a little busy. When do we learn to throw fireballs?"

The clinking-clanking army of skeletal children drew closer. The odor of charred bones reached Rachel's nostrils. The soot-blackened skulls of the foremost members glistened in the torch-light. Whooping, Zoë ran forward, whacking the taller of the young forms, sending heads flying like balls off a tee. Sigfried played a blast of wind. Silvery sparks that smelled of fresh spring rain swept a swath of them aside, their bones tinkling like ivory xylophones as they collapsed. Rachel tried a blast of wind, too, but hers was not strong enough to do more than rattle bones. Paralysis turned out to be ineffective against skeletons. She attempted a Glepnir bond, but nothing happened.

"How did you two find me?" Rachel called to her friends, as she tried to think of something else helpful to do.

"Mrs. March came to see if you had made it back safely." Zoë smacked three skeletons. They collapsed like dominoes. The *patu*'s keening shriek rent the air. "She helped us find the real dream version of the temple."

"How did you get by the cultists up in dreamland—to get down here?" asked Rachel.

"Goldilocks blinded them with her camera flash!" Siggy shot her a huge grin. "Some of the purple jokers even ended up in another scene, some sunny place. My G.F.'s so smart."

From their left came a bellow. A flaming something flew by overhead, as if thrown by a catapult. Siggy let out a shout. Whatever it was sailed all the way across the horizon and out of sight.

"Lucky!" Siggy shouted, followed by, "It's okay. He's okay. But he's kind of far away. I think he's out to sea."

Another bellow. The horned man now stood in the courtyard. He gestured. Over to the left, Cain March and Templeton Bridges were thrown a good ten yards. Both of them flipped in mid-air and landed lightly on their feet. A flash of light, and Rachel's father jumped, appearing next to the paralyzed Sandra. He grabbed her from where she stood in the midst of motionless cultists and vanished again.

Rachel breathed a sigh of relief.

Had her father only just caught sight of her sister, she wondered. If so, did he even know that she and her mother were here? Of course, Sandra would tell him.

The flood of undead children was beginning to close in around them. Rachel stepped on the skeleton of a crawling toddler and fell down. The skeletons turned toward her, looming over her. Bones clacked, and jaws snapped. Empty eye sockets stared down at her. One face was black and mummified with withered, raisin-like eyes.

"*Obé!*" she shouted, gesturing with one hand as she used her other hand and her legs to scuttle backwards and leap back to her feet. The Word of Ending had the desired effect. A few of the closest skeletons clattered to the ground, but there were many, many more coming.

Rachel ran to stand closer to Zoë and Siggy. They tried to retreat up the stairs and around the temple, but four-foot flames shot now leapt from the open furnace door. After only three stairs, the heat was unbearable. They returned to the bottom.

The skeletons were closing in from all directions. The heat of the furnace blew hot on the backs of their necks. Rachel's leg brushed against the bottom step. There was precious little room left.

"*Obé*," she cried again.

Three more fell—three out of thousands.

"If only we could get them to come at us a few at a time," Zoë said nervously. She glanced from the surging horde to the furnace ablaze behind them. "This is not the greatest spot. We have got to come up with something better. I am so not going to die, killed by skinless pre-schoolers. Should we retreat into dreamland?"

"And let the demon get away?" Siggy blew another blast, scattering another ten children and lambs. "Lucky! Get back here! Hurry!"

Zoë snorted, "I'm having trouble just keeping the baby skellies here at bay. I haven't the foggiest what to do against the demon."

"We can't leave," Rachel cried shrilly. "My mother is still here."

She looked up to the porch where her mother had been but saw no sign of her. "Siggy! Can you see her?"

"Sure," Siggy did not bother turning his head. "She's fighting the crazy red-headed woman. She's doing pretty well, considering that she doesn't have anything but her mouth. Looks like she can do magic by whistling, like you do. She's really good."

"I learned to do that from her," Rachel smiled slightly, her heart beating with concern for her mother, alone against the crazy Serena O'Malley. "We should go help her!"

"Can't go up the stairs," Siggy replied. "Too hot. We'd have to get through the bone-kiddies and around to the back of the temple."

Click-clack. Click-clack. The child skeletons grew ever closer, their bones gleaming golden in the light of the furnace.

"Well, we have to do something," muttered Zoë.

"I'm not sure what..." Rachel began, searching her memory for anything that might help against hordes of undead—baby or otherwise.

Oh, wait.

Reaching into her pocket, she yanked out the packet she had felt there earlier. Gaius had given it to her on All Hallows' Eve. The paper was a bit warped from having gone through the wash, but when she ripped it open, hard round peony seeds fell into her hand.

"Here goes!" She threw the seeds, scattering them upon the ground in a semi-circle between them and the approaching army of undead kids.

The skeletons moved forward, as inexorably as ants. But the moment they came near the peony seeds, even though the hard, raisin-sized seeds were barely visible in the poor lighting, each child-like form bent or knelt and began to count. As Rachel watched them, she hummed a soft lilting melody with a simple beat.

Beside her, Zoë and Siggy were humming the same song.

"The children...." Rachel clutched Zoë's arm. Her mouth felt dry. "I think... they're singing."

The eyes of her friends grew round in the furnace light.

"Do you mean that ditty in my head is a three-thousand-year-old, Carthaginian children's counting song?" murmured Zoë.

"Wait!" Siggy took a step backward, ending up on the first stair. Sweat gleamed on his skin from the heat. "You mean that there *are* ghosts here? I thought they were just macabre marionettes! I can't attack the ghosts of little kids! What would King Arthur say?"

"I can see them," Zoë said hoarsely. "In dreamland."

The three of them stood, unwilling to attack, as the undead remains of dozens of two and three-thousand-year-old sacrificed children bent over counting peony seeds in the dark. The little skeletons surrounded them on all sides, except behind them where the heat of the furnace had grown unbearably hot.

"If we go back into dreams... will there be ghosts there?" Siggy sounded nervous.

"Yes," said Zoë. "They're everywhere."

"And in dreamland," said Rachel, recalling the Prince of Transylvania, "ghosts are semi-solid. We'd be entirely surrounded."

Two more flashes, then four, then a dozen. Teams of men dressed in black suits, moving in sync, each knelt and pulled from kenomanced bags some kind of strange device mounted on a tri-pod. Five teams in all, they circled the demon, each setting up their tripods with the muzzle of their device pointing inward.

"Who are they?" Zoë shouted. "More Agents?"

"No," Rachel called back. "They're dressed wrong. They're...."

In the light of another jump, she spotted a white symbol on the breast of one jump suit.

"Siggy, what is that mark?"

"An infinity symbol," he replied without turning his head. "Or maybe it's a snake forming a figure eight and biting its own tail."

"They're from Ouroboros Industries!" Rachel cheered. "They must be the O.I. rapid response team, and their new secret weapon. Gaius sent them!"

"Valiant sent us the cavalry?" Zoë drawled. "Good for him!"

Another flash. Her father appeared next to Serena O'Malley, who was standing stock still on the far corner of the temple porch, as far away from the furnace as possible. Rachel's mother stood on her tiptoes in front of her, prying her rings of mastery, with their decades of stored spells and conjurations, out of the frozen woman's fist. Rachel's father picked up both women. As they jumped away, Rachel heard her mother's voice calling out her name and saw the startled look on her father's face. Apparently, he had not known she was here.

Crash!

Two O.I. men were thrown across the temple courtyard and into a column, which toppled on top of them. Under the rubble, one man still moved, but the other lay motionless. Two more men in black suits appeared in a flash of light to take their place. There was a whining noise and a narrow beam of umber-colored light traveled from the first tripod to the second.

The demon gestured. Another team was thrown backwards. As they fell, however, they seemed to become weightless and wafted safely to the ground. Rachel suspected they were wearing floating harnesses. Again, more men appeared to take their place. The beam of umber light continued to the third tripod. The glowing line now formed three parts of a pentagon. There were more Agents, too.

Some of them flung spells at the horned man, but he shrugged them off.

The umber beam reached the forth tripod. The mechanical whine grew louder. Rachel smelt a strange burnt air smell. One more, and the fiend would be entirely surrounded.

The demon saw this, too. Bellowing, it gestured. A brave man jumped forward, shielding the device. He was thrown headlong into the temple, which trembled, its stone grating.

The umber beam reached the last tripod, closing the five-sided figure. More beams of umber light sprang up, forming a pentacle inside the pentagon. The whole area within the pentagon began to fill with a thick, burnt orange substance, like glowing caramel.

With a bellow of rage, darkness issued from the mouth and nose of the horned man. The umber substance was filling the intervening space, but not quickly enough. Rachel saw that Morax would escape before O.I.'s secret weapon trapped him.

"Lucky!" Siggy wailed. "Hurry. He's getting away."

More shadows billowed from the bull-horned man's mouth and nose.

"Wait. I have this!" Rachel lifted her wand and shot the demon with one of her grandmother's three precious remaining charges of Eternal Flame.

White fire tinged with gold enveloped the growing shadow. An earsplitting bellow of pain and outrage rent the air. Then, the glowing umber substance filled the entire area. When the white flame died away, the original cultist, no longer sprouting horns, stood next to a large bull with the head of a man. Both were motionless, like flies trapped in amber.

With a loud clatter, all the little skeletons fell to the ground and lay still.

"Phew," murmured Zoë. "The ghosts are gone."

A cheer went up from the O.I. crowd. Rachel and her friends joined in. Siggy blew a flourish on the trumpet. Rachel noted that he was beginning to play rather well. Lucky came streaking out of the sky and crooned along with his master.

"Rachel!" her father appeared in another flash of light, his staff in his hand, his cloak billowing, his stars and lantern medallion gleaming on his chest, his tricorne hat at a rakish angle. He paused momentarily when he saw the other two students, murmuring something like, "Where did these two come from?"

"Um. I think this is our cue to leave, Smith." Zoë threw her arm out and grabbed Sigfried's hand. Lucky wrapped around his master. "See ya, Griffin." With a flip of her braid, she glared over her shoulder at Rachel's father. "You didn't see us."

A puff of mist, and they were gone.

Agent Griffin leaned down and lifted Rachel into his arms, and everything became light.

. . .

The next morning the three Griffin women sat in Sandra's dining room sipping hot chocolate, while Agent Griffin and Agent Vicky Armel, her father's prime Enochian, moved about the flat, laying wards and protections. Hammer blows rang out from where a craftsman from Gryphon Park busily replaced the door.

"Wisecraft Agent Kidnapped in Her Own Flat. I'm going to have a hard time living this one down at work." Sandra looked both embarrassed and amused. "But at least Mum and Daddy captured that O'Malley woman. She's a nasty piece of work."

"So, Mummy had come by to visit me?" Rachel asked, naturally reverting to the more child-like form of parental address when talking to her big sister. She sat petting Mistletoe, who had curled up on a chair beside her, being too large for her lap. "Was that the surprise you said you had?"

"You heard that?" Sandra exclaimed. "You were still here?"

"I heard your voice, right before she took me."

"Oh, what a relief! I'm glad you were not on your own for very long." Sandra leaned back in her chair, visibly relaxing. "I was so worried that you'd be frightened there all by yourself. My heart felt like it leapt right through the top of my head when that boy landed on you, and you fell down the stairs. I'm glad you had the sense to keep your head down and stay out of the fire-fight!

"And yes," Sandra continued before Rachel could get a word in edgewise. "Mum came to see you, as a surprise. Only when we arrived, the door was broken, and you were gone."

"Then Veltdammerung jumped us." Ellen Griffin gave her daughter a chagrined and yet impishly-sweet smile. "What ninnies we were, running around like headless chickens, looking for you, instead of taking precautions for ourselves. Your father gave me quite a lecture."

"What happened to the demon?" Sandra put down her empty cup. "Who caught it?"

"The O.I. rapid response team and their new secret weapon based on the research of our second cousin, Blackie Moth," said Rachel, wiping away her chocolate mustache.

Sandra gawked at her. "And my little sister knows this... how?"

Rachel raised an eyebrow and gave her sister her best arch and mysterious look. "I cannot reveal my sources."

"Oh, you're so funny, Rachel!" Sandra turned to their mother, laughing. Look at Rachel! Imitating Daddy and I. Isn't she just adorable? Do you remember the time she was four, and she put on Father's boots and cloak and hat and took his staff and insisted she was an Agent? She wanted to go to work with him?"

"Oh, yes." Their mother's dark eyes danced with amusement. "She was so tiny! She couldn't see from underneath the hat. It came to her nose!"

"And the b-boots!" Sandra could hardly speak for laughter. "They came up above her knees. She could hardly walk!"

They both laughed and laughed until there were tears in their eyes. Sandra reached over and mussed the top of Rachel's head. "Little sis, you don't need to pretend you have sources you need to protect, just because Daddy and I can't tell you things." She leaned closer and whispered with a happy conspiratorial smile, "It's all right. I won't tell anyone Gaius told you."

Rachel smiled, but underneath, she felt disappointed.

She had been looking forward to telling her family about how she had stopped the demon from escaping. If she spoke up now, it would sound like bragging. Also, it would frighten them, to hear that she had engaged in the battle, rather than keeping her head down.

She gazed down at her cocoa, watching the whipped cream melt.

She hated being treated like a child. One reason she liked Gaius and Vlad so much was that they both always spoke to her as if she were an equal. She felt another pang of sadness. She did know this information, thanks to her wonderful boyfriend who, by now, would have received her letter and who may have decided he would prefer the title: former boyfriend.

Their mother took Sandra's empty cup and went to the kitchen for more hot chocolate. As Rachel sipped her sweet concoction, she finally found the courage to bring up a subject about which she had been longing to speak to Sandra.

"By the way, I'd been meaning to write you about your previous letter." Rachel leaned closer to her sister. "If Father doesn't approve of Bavaria, wouldn't he favor sending one of his daughters to work her will upon the Bavarian heir? To warp him to the ways of good? I mean, couldn't Vlad change the government once he became king? So it wasn't a dictatorship? Father would have to be in favor of that. Really! It's important to think these things out."

Sandra sighed and did not answer. Rising, she crossed to the windows and leaned against the glass, staring out at the brightly-colored barges on the canal below.

"Don't you want to be Queen of Bavaria?" asked Rachel, from her seat.

Apparently, she had spoken too loudly, because from across the room, their mother turned and gazed at Sandra.

Their mother asked softly, "Do you *want* to be Queen of Bavaria?"

Sandra glanced at their mother and then looked away. She did not reply. Their mother blew on her hot cup of cocoa and sighed.

"I'll talk to your father, dear," she said, adding. "Oh, and Rachel, there's a letter for you."

Rachel took the letter and brought it over to one of the windows. Inside was a sheet of lined paper. It read:

> *My feelings for you have not changed. I hope you*
> *come back soon, because I can't wait to see you again.*
> *Gaius*

EPILOGUE

BACK AT ROANOKE, THE NEXT DAY, RACHEL LANDED HER STEEPLE-chaser and sat on the rounded boulder next to the wingless statue. The cold bit through her robes and her wool coat, and the rock was hard beneath her, but she did not care. With fingers nearly numb from the cold, she opened the envelope that had come for her from Detective Hunt and read what was inside.

"Oh!" she whispered with joy. "Old Thom would be so pleased!"

Across the river, lightning lit the thundercloud that still hung over Storm King Mountain. Thunder rolled across the Hudson Valley. The Heer was still on the loose.

"Pleased about what?" asked the old ghost, barely visible in the darkness of the forest.

"You're here!" Rachel cried. "My friend's father found your family! There are photos."

Rachel pulled out the photographs and laid them side by side on the pine needles. "Your family escaped the fire by running to the neighbor's farm. They stayed there for a time, but when news came that your ship went down, they went to live with a cousin in Saratoga."

"Cousin Olivia!" swore the sailor. "Never thought of going there!"

"Your wife never remarried, but she took good care of your children. Your eldest son died fighting in World War I."

The old ghost's face fell. "Poor Thom, Jr. He was such a bright little tot."

"Your second son joined the navy. Made it all the way to captain. Commander of his own ship."

The old sailor grinned a toothy grin. "Good for Freddie! A captain! Me own son!"

"And your daughter married a..." Rachel turned the page, "... a shipwright from Maine and had three children of her own."

"Good old Sue. Knew she'd make good. Pretty as a posey, my girl."

"Oh my!" Rachel gasped, gazing up at the ghost in great excitement. "Her granddaughter grew up to marry, of all people, the son of Captain Vanderdecken and Merry-Merry Moth! Rowan Vanderdecken, one of my classmates here at school, is your great-granddaughter." Searching the line of photos, she found one of the smiling, fiery-haired Rowan and held it up for the ghost to see.

"My great-granddaughter." The old ghost's eyes filled with tears. "A Roanokean."

As he stood, transfixed with joy, the clouds shifted, and a single beam of light pierced the gloom of the forest, striking the exact place where Old Thom stood. It was so bright that, for a moment, Rachel was blinded by the light.

She raised her hand to shade her eyes, but the old sailor was nowhere to be seen. With a flutter of wings, a very large Raven lifted off a nearby bough, where it had apparently been watching, cawed once, and flew away.

It could have been her imagination, but Rachel would have sworn it sounded like a caw of approval.

Here ends *Rachel and the Many-Splendored Dreamland*.

Our heroine's adventures continue in
the Fourth *Book of Unexpected Enlightenment*:

THE AWFUL TRUTH ABOUT FORGETTING

Subscribe to the *Roanoke Glass*, a feature of
the *Wrights' Writing Report*: http://eepurl.com/cg-4oH
to be kept up-to-date on all things *Unexpected*
and the further adventures of Rachel Griffin.

*For more information about the
Roanoke Academy for the Sorcerous Arts, see the school's website:*
http://lampwright.wixsite.com/roanoke-academy

GLOSSARY

Agents—Magical law enforcement. Agents fight magical foes, both human and supernatural.

Alchemy—One of the Seven Sorcerous Arts. It is the Art of putting magic into objects.

Bavaria—A country that exists in the world of the book but not in our world. It is known to both the World of the Wise and the Unwary. It is ruled by the Von Dread family.

Canticle—One of the Seven Sorcerous Arts. It is the Art of commanding the natural and supernatural world with the words and gestures of the Original Language.

Cantrip—One word in the Original Language, *i.e.* a canticle spell.

Cathay—The Democratic Republic of Cathay, a country that exists in the world of the book but not in our world. It is known to both the World of the Wise and the Unwary. It is ruled by an elected council.

Conjuring—One of the Seven Sorcerous Arts. It is the Art of drawing objects out of the dreamlands.

Core Group—A group of students, usually from the same dorm, who attend all their classes together.

Dare Hall—The dormitory at Roanoke Academy that is favored by enchanters.

De Vere Hall—The dormitory at Roanoke Academy that is favored by warders and obscurers.

Dee Hall—The dormitory at Roanoke Academy that is favored by scholars.

Drake Hall—The dormitory at Roanoke Academy that is favored by thaumaturges.

Enchantment—One of the Seven Sorcerous Arts. It is based on music and includes a number of sub-arts.

Fulgurator's wand—A wand with a spell-grade gem on the tip that is used by Soldiers of the Wise to throw lighting and to hold other kinds of spells.

Gnosis—One of the Seven Sorcerous Arts. It is the Art of knowledge and augury.

Heer of Dunderberg—Storm Goblin locked up with his Lightning Imps in a cave in Stony Tor on Roanoke Island.

Jumping—A cantrip that allows the practitioner to teleport.

Magical Australia—A country that is only known to the Wise. It is ruled by the Romanov family.

Marlowe Hall—The dormitory at Roanoke Academy that is favored by conjurers.

Morthbrood—An ancient organization of practitioners of black magic. During the Terrible Years, the Morthbrood served the Terrible Five.

Mundane—Without magic. Refers both to the modern technological world and to those who cannot use magic. It is possible to be mundane and Wise, if one has no magic but is aware of the magical world.

Obscuration—A subset of Warding. It allows for the casting of illusions that hide things and trick the Unwary.

Original Language—The original language in which all objects were named.

Parliament of the Wise—The ruling body of the World of the Wise.

Pollepel Island—The name the Unwary call the island they see in place of Roanoke Island. It is also called Bannerman Island.

Roanoke Academy for the Sorcerous Arts—A school of magic on a floating island that is currently moored in the Hudson near Storm King Mountain.

Scholars—Practitioners of the Art of Gnosis.

Sorcery—The study of magic.

Spenser Hall—The dormitory at Roanoke Academy that is favored by canticlers.

Terrible Five—The leaders of the Veltdammerung, who terrorized the World of the Wise during the Terrible Years. They consisted of: Simon Magus, Morgana le Fay, Koschei the Deathless, Baba Yaga, and Aleister Crowley.

Thaumaturgy—One of the Seven Sorcerous Arts. It is the Art of storing charges of magic in a gem.

Thule—A country that is known only to the World of the Wise. It occupies the section of Greenland that is, in our world, occupied by the world's largest national park (larger than all but 32 countries).

Transylvania—A country that exists in the world of the book but not in our world. It is known to both the World of the Wise and the Unwary. It is ruled by the Starkadder family.

Tutor—The term used for professors at Roanoke Academy.

Unwary—One who does not know about the magical world.

Veltdammerung—Twilight of the World. The organization that served the Terrible Five during the Terrible Years. It consisted of the Morthbrood and of supernatural servants.

Warding—One of the Seven Sorcerous Arts. It is the Art of protecting one's self from magical influences.

Wise—Those in the know about the magical world (as in the root of the word 'wizard').

Wisecraft—The law enforcement agency of the Wise. The Agents work for the Wisecraft.

World of the Wise—The community of those who know about the magical world.

ACKNOWLEDGEMENTS

Thank you to Mark Whipple, John C. Wright, and William E. Burns, III, who breathed the life into the original story.

To Virginia Johnson, Erin Furby, Brian Furlough, Bill Burns, and Jeff Zitomer, who helped iron out the bumps, and to my sons, Orville and Justinian for playing along and particularly to Juss, for wearing a lightning imp under his cat.

To Erin Furby, Katherine Petersen, Laura Taylor, Theresa Murphy, Mark Thompson, and April Freeman for slogging through the early drafts.

To Anna "Firtree" Macdonald and Don Schank, for making it readable.

To Jim Frenkel for the gift of editing, for which Rachel will be forever grateful.

To C J Armstrong, Casey Hand, Lucas Huguet, Josh Huguet, Charlie Jackson, Darren McCormick, Jimmy McGuigan, Tanay Pandey, Junior (JR) Strickland, and Orville, Roland, and Justinian Wright for a performance beyond the call of duty. Troop Two! Second to none!

To my mother, Jane Lamplighter, for listening and making dinner on Wednesdays, so I could write.

About the Authors

L. Jagi Lamplighter is also the author of the *Prospero's Daughter* series: *Prospero Lost, Prospero In Hell,* and *Prospero Regained.* She is an assistant editor with the *Bad-Ass Faeries Anthologies.* She is also a founding member of the Superversive Literary Movement and maintains a weekly blog on the subject. When not writing, she switches to her secret identity as wife and stay-home mom in Centreville, VA, where she lives with her dashing husband, author John C. Wright, and their four darling children, Orville, Ping-Ping, Roland Wilbur, and Justinian Oberon.

To learn more, visit http://ljagilamplighter.com
On Twitter: @lampwright4

Mark A. Whipple grew up in Croton-on-Hudson, which is not far from Roanoke Island. He then attended St. John's College in Annapolis, the mundane sister school to Roanoke Academy. Until recently, he has spent his free time, when not busy torturing Rachel Griffin, protecting the world from video game threats. Now, however, he volunteers with Stillbrave, a charity devoted to helping the families of children with cancer.

UNEXPECTED CHARITY: 30% of the authors' proceeds from the *Unexpected Enlightenment* series goes to charity. Current charities of choice:

Mark's choice: Stillbrave Childhood Cancer Foundation – helping families of children with cancer.

Stillbrave Childhood Cancer Foundation
6731A Edsall Road
Springfield, VA 22151
https://stillbrave.org

Jagi's choice: All Girls Allowed – fighting for the rights and dignity of girls in China, and St. John's College – which, as the Wise all know, was started by two students from Dee Hall.

All Girls Allowed
101 Huntington Avenue, Suite 2205
Boston, MA 02199
http://allgirlsallowed.org

St. John's College
60 College Avenue
Annapolis, MD 21401
http://www.sjc.edu

CPSIA information can be obtained
at www.ICGtesting.com
Printed in the USA
LVOW11s1411131217
559590LV00003B/194/P